David M. Golden grew up in The Black County, the birthplace of the UK's Industrial Revolution. For many years he has lived in Stratford upon Avon, birthplace of the poet William Shakespeare.

He is regarded as one of the UK's top serious fraud and complex crime lawyers. Leading a relatively secluded social life, his is a face more familiar in the residential quarters of Venice, a city that is referred to, almost as a trademark, in his written work.

THE CASE IS OPEN

David M Golden

THE CASE IS OPEN

Vanguard Press

VANGUARD PAPERBACK

© Copyright 2011
David M Golden

The right of David M Golden to be identified as author of
this work has been asserted by him in accordance with the
Copyright, Designs and Patents Act 1988.

All Rights Reserved

No reproduction, copy or transmission of this publication
may be made without written permission.
No paragraph of this publication may be reproduced,
copied or transmitted save with the written permission of the publisher,
or in accordance with the provisions
of the Copyright Act 1956 (as amended).

Any person who commits any unauthorised act in relation to
this publication may be liable to criminal
prosecution and civil claims for damages.

A CIP catalogue record for this title is
available from the British Library.

ISBN 978 1 84386 911 5

*Vanguard Press is an imprint of
Pegasus Elliot MacKenzie Publishers Ltd.*
www.pegasuspublishers.com

First Published in 2011

**Vanguard Press
Sheraton HouseCastle Park
CambridgeEngland**

Printed & Bound in Great Britain

DUDLEY PUBLIC LIBRARIES	
000000504571	
Bertrams	01/12/2011
	£8.99
	SED

CHAPTER ONE

No one in similar circumstances would have been called to the Bar of England and Wales intending to practise as a barrister-at-law.

You see, I readily concede that the name of a barrister might frequently feature in due process. The tradition is for the name to appear at the foot of the page and the name generally belongs to the barrister who drafted the said due process.

However, as I lay in my hospital bed, I perused and considered the due process before me. I noted from the case number that it was only the twelfth injunction that had emanated from the local County Court in the year 1981 *anno domini*. I also noted that the barrister's name did not feature at the foot of the page. Neither was the barrister's name in the middle of the page. On the set of proceedings before me, the barrister's name appeared at the top of the page. Indeed, it was slap-bang where the name of the defendant appears. And the name of the defendant belonged to me, Izaak Gatehouse, who had escaped his home town of Dudsall in the industrial heartlands of the UK and had been qualified as a barrister-at-law for just four weeks, no more, no less.

By my reckoning, I ought to have been in Venice with the love of my life, to wit, one Janie Jetty, businessperson of the parish of Prestwick on Avon in the County of Warwick. By the same reckoning, I ought to have been sat with her in a little out of the way restaurant (the one by the fish market would have been just fine) and I ought to have been feeling proper chuffed on account of the pair of us having entered into an oral contract to become man and wife. During slurps of the rough red stuff that has a propensity to be poured out of a bottle shoved in a straw basket, and, betwixt glances at the incomprehensible menu that had been slapped in my hand the minute I walked in, Janie and I ought to have been planning when and where to start trying for a little Gatehouse if, indeed, Little Gatehouse had not already ventured forth on his journey, for, on the way to the restaurant, I'd intended to take Janie on a detour, down an alley, just at the side of the Rialto, if you get my drift. The only intrusion ought to have been the waiter hot footing it over with a view to taking me to task over the fact that the pasta had not been drenched in engine oil as scurrilously alleged and that it was cooked in cuttlefish ink (an apparent delicacy around those parts). He might cheekily have added that I would have seen that for myself, had I bothered to ask for the menu in English in lieu of jumping the gun and proposing the coming of a second little Gatehouse in the full glare of tables packed with day-trippers from the mainland.

Well, so much for the succinct summary of the oughts. I suppose that, purely for the record, I had best summarise the actual actuals.

I was actually slurping some fizzy glucose drink, and I was actually doing the slurping, not from a wicker-wrapped receptacle via a hand blown Murano glass, but from a plastic bottle via a chipped mug marked *return after use to contagious diseases department*. Further and additionally, the person who had actually hotfooted it over, was actually a sneering, smug lawyer from the City. And, he had actually pointed out that, was I to stop threatening to remove the silken cravat from around his scrawny neck and clog up his windpipe with the same, I would actually comprehend the incomprehensible document that he'd slapped in my hand and see that it was an order prohibiting me from going within fifty paces of Janie Jetty for twenty eight days, unless or until I appeared before the judge to show cause.

"Should you ever again threaten to inflict injury on my person," said William Anker, the said smug lawyer, with a sneer, "I too shall obtain an injunction," and, he exited the hospital ward, and, he did so to the sound of leather on wood as my shoe bounced off the door.

CHAPTER TWO

It was one week later and Mr Walter Tweed, barrister-at-law, head of Globe Chambers, Birmingham, was seated behind his private desk in his private office that overlooked the offices of The Regal Knight Insurance Company. He was pouring through the papers in the case of Janie Jetty versus me, Izaak Gatehouse.

Walter happened to be my learned pupil master and I was his, not so learned, pupil. It was the pupil's duty to assist his (or her) master and, at the same time, learn the ways of barristerhood. All newly qualified barristers had to go through the same process.

"Is this correct, Gatehouse?" As ever, Walter spoke perfect Queen's English. "Have you harassed Miss Janie Jetty?" As ever, he spoke his perfect Queen's English with a drawl. He had probably picked up the drawl as a consequence of numerous flights to the West Indies, such archipelagos having been the home of his parents, whose parents had parents who had first arrived at the said archipelagos under sail and in shackles. The conditions were filthy, stinking, and generally inhumane. But, Walter had only himself to blame for insisting on going by Laker Airways.

"Walter," I protested. "It weren't entirely my fault. Dropping a cat that went and savaged the rabbits in a competition she was judging could have happened to anyone."

"Yes, but it appears to have happened to you." There followed an uneasy silence as Walter proceeded to read the last page. "Gatehouse?" He said it in a surprised manner, with a surprised look on his face. "Is it correct that you confronted the woman in a railway carriage and stated that, unless or until she gave an indication to the contrary, you intended to get to know her in the biblical sense?"

"Aye?"

"Gatehouse!" Now Walter sounded rattled. "Did you or did you not inform the woman that it was your intention to shag her until she begged you to stop?"

"Ah! Well, yes, and no."

"Izaak, my friend?"

"Yes, Walter?"

"Yes or no?"

It was no wonder that Walter had a reputation for never letting a witness off the hook. "Walter," I pleaded. "She was giving me all sorts of mixed messages, like."

"Be seated," drawled my pupil master. I duly obeyed. I sat in the client's chair, to be exact. It was situated in the out reaches of the desk and afforded excellent views of The Regal Knight. "I note with interest," said Walter, "that you were actually invited to accompany Miss Jetty, together with her party, on this ill-fated train journey."

"That's quite correct," I said, and I crossed my legs. However, with a sharp intake of breath, I uncrossed them pretty quickly because the unmentionable place about my person where I'd had an operation was still hurting like hell.

I informed my pupil master that whenever I had been in the company of Janie Jetty she had blushed profusely.

"I tend to agree," said Walter, casually, "that a physical manifestation such as that generally indicates that there is passion within."

"The only problem," I laughed nervously, "is that it turns out that she has an acute allergy to cat hair. Furthermore," I added, with a sigh. "By a cruel twist of fate, I'm the one who unleashed the cats on her in the first place."

"Izaak, my friend."

"Yes, Walter?"

"You will dispose of the injunction nonsense by providing an undertaking to the Court not to harass or annoy this female."

"But, Walter!" I protested.

"But, nothing!" Walter protested in response. "As you know, the provision of an undertaking is a suitable way of disposing of these matters without admitting liability."

"Yes, Walter," I said, meekly.

"And remember," said Walter. "The breach of an undertaking to the Court is a serious matter for which you will be held in contempt." Walter placed to one side the papers relating to the case of Janie Jetty versus me, Izaak Gatehouse. He swizzled his chair ninety degrees and I thereby found myself facing the rear of a clean-shaven head. Next, the head disappeared because Walter bent forwards and he appeared to scoop something from the floor. He once again swizzled the chair and, having gone a further ninety degrees, he plonked a voluminous brief on the desk and grinned. "Enough of this injunction nonsense. I have before me the papers in the case of The Crown versus Jerome Horatio Barclay. Our client, my friend, is charged with a public disorder offence. He was, in short, caught up in one of the recent race riots."

A not insignificant amount of the work sent to my black pupil master related to representing the interests of members of ethnic minority groups. Consequently, there were some who regarded Walter as a bit of a radical. However, true to his calling, Walter never discriminated on the grounds of religion, colour, or race. He was totally and utterly neutral in such matters, as evidenced by the fact that he had taken on a white pupil in his thirty-something year who hailed from, of all places, Dudsall, where the accent was as thick as the grime pouring out of the foundry chimney and where the only black faces were those of the coalminers who had neglected to go via the wash house on their journey from pithead to pub.

It was the early 1980's and in the early 1980's there was a lot of racial tension. Indeed, the tension had turned to violence and there had been rioting in the streets. And Walter's client, Mr Barclay, stood accused of rioting in a Birmingham street.

"What am I to do?" I asked eagerly of Walter.

My pupil master arose and, with a sharp jerk from the back of the knees, he nudged his chair backwards. Having thereby made sufficient space between the desk of the one part and the chair of the other part, Walter edged his way round to my side where we could both enjoy a free and uninterrupted view of the case papers.

Walter hovered overhead, from which position he began thumbing through a bundle of witness statements. "The issue, my friend, is one of identification. This witness," said Walter, pointing at a written statement made by one, Mr Brian Monk, "maintains that a black youth who assaulted him, before throwing a brick through his plate glass window, wore a dark blue shirt." I noted that Mr Monk described himself as proprietor of The Jolly Friar, a fried fish and chip shop. Walter thumbed his way further through the bundle. He stopped about three quarters of the way through. "This," he drawled, "is the statement of the arresting police officer. You will note that, according to him, Mr Barclay wore a bright yellow shirt, whereas..." Walter paused but, only for two seconds, mind. A couple of seconds, however, is all that it took him to locate another of the statements from within the bundle. "Do you see, my friend?" He jabbed a forefinger. "The police station custody sergeant also refers to a yellow shirt."

"And, and," I said, eagerly, and, I jabbed a forefinger of my very own at a loose exhibits page. "Mr. Barclay was momentarily out of view of the witness, Brian Monk, because he walked behind a street lamppost." I navigated my jabbing finger in the vicinity of the relevant page. "Do you see? There is a lamppost indicated on this here plan and our client must have walked behind it."

"You are correct, my friend." I knew not if Walter was being polite or whether I had fitted together a hitherto missing piece of the jigsaw puzzle. Then, I had grounds to suspect Walter of being just plain polite. "The lamppost, Izaak, in common with most of the other lampposts in the City of Birmingham is approximately one foot wide."

"Meaning, Walter?"

"Meaning, my friend, that it will be difficult to convince a jury, even a Birmingham jury, that there was a transmutation of our client into someone else when he momentarily passed behind a lamppost."

"Why is that then, Walter?"

"Because, Izaak. I am not Siegfried. You are not Roy. Also, our esteemed client is not a white tiger."

"I'll make a note of any discrepancy that I can find," I said eagerly, and I began my retreat, intending to find a quiet spot in the general office.

"Before you depart," said Walter, rather sternly. "Is it correct that, during the ill-fated train journey, a large quantity of condoms cascaded from your suitcase?"

"Yes, Walter. I had them for medical reasons."

It was true. I had embarked on the train journey with my suitcase positively bursting with packets of condoms. It was the idea of Ian Prospect, barrister-at-law, in whose country cottage I lodged. He was aided and abetted by Jacob, the local pharmacist. At first instance, the idea seemed rational enough because I needed to protect the unmentionable place about my person that was in urgent need of surgery. However, I hadn't reckoned on the case busting open and, in the process, showering Janie with dozens of the little fellows; and kinky fellows at that.

"Gatehouse! Let it be a lesson to you! No good comes from placing latex between manhood and life!"

I cringed as I exited Walter's office. As I closed the door behind me, I could have sworn that he grinned, just a little.

Anyway, I ventured forth to the general office where I laid forth the case papers on the floor. The desktop, you see, was full of newspapers, empty drink cans, and, I swear, two cradles both containing a baby, one dressed in pink, the other in blue. Now then, I was no paediatrician but anyone could have seen that the pair were nowt but sucklings and they had no place being away from their birth mother.

"The missus has popped in town to go to the shops, Mista Gatehouse, and she has only gone and left we to look after the babbies." Damian Barker, Clerk of Globe Chambers, looked his usual frazzled self. As ever, the tails of his grimy white shirt were popping out of the top of his bulging trousers. As ever, his complexion was as bright red as a London bus and he looked as if he was about to succumb to a seizure. "Oil remove the babbies from the work surface just as soon as the tea am made for Mista Tweed." You will appreciate that the complexion was not on account of stress induced by overwork for it was common knowledge that, of the nine barristers who were tenants of, and practised from, Globe Chambers, only Walter Tweed was in Court every day and therefore required the services of a clerk. Damian, you must understand, was a native of Birmingham. In other words, he was a Brummie. Moreover, most, if not all, Brummies wore faces that were as long as Livery Street and their imminent seizures, as evidenced by the red complexions, were generally the cause of smoking and drinking too much, and devouring almost as much saturated fat as the average Glaswegian.

"Damian," I said. "It's no problem, mate. In fact, if it'll help, I shall make the tea."

"What? Yow, a barrister, will do that for we? No barrister has ever offered to do that for we." The blustering clerk reached deep inside his trouser pocket and he produced a white handkerchief that was as grimy as his shirt and almost as grimy as the smoke regurgitating from the chimney atop the Dudsall foundry on the day after an August bank holiday. "Oi am filling up with tears." In common with most, if not all, Brummies, he was prone to undignified outbursts of emotion. "Sorry, sorry!" Damian proceeded to blubber. "Oi have been under financial pressure since the two babbies arrived and the missus has stopped having intimate relations with we." In common with most, if not all, Brummies, he had uncontrollable urges to blart to the outside world every detail of his life, both financial and sexual. "It's making we ill," he added. I'd forgotten that every headache, muscle spasm, was intended for public consumption, and all. "Will yow look after the babbies while oi go to the lavvy? Only oi have a dreadful pain and oi feel bloated and have a bit of the runs." Reporting on tummy ache and consequential irregular bowel movement was, in my opinion, a Brummie's particular favourite topic of conversation. "Will yow let we go?" Requesting permission to attend the lavatory was a characteristic bred into Brummies as a consequence of coming from a long line of machine tool workers who were obliged to request the foreman for permission to breathe, let alone answer the call of nature.

"I don't mind at all, Damian."

Damian made a dash for the exit and hence the corridor. At journey's end, he would find the conveniences. "Oi hopes that trio won't play yow up," said Damian, as he left and I was reminded that another Brummie characteristic was a tendency that, in all things pertaining to life, there was a propensity to add one and one and come up with the number three. As the blustering clerk bounced down the corridor, I heard a clunk, then a strange swishing sort of a sound, that was quickly followed by an, "Ouch! That ruddy obstacle, again," sort of a Brummie sound.

After Damian had departed, I attempted to concentrate on the case papers that were stretched before me. Now, I had no sooner arrived at a document entitled *Prosecution Case Summary* when one of the sucklings started squawking. I think it was the one that was swaddled in blue who was the guilty party. But, it didn't much matter which one started up first because the other one (be it the pink one or the blue one) was quick to weigh in as an aider and abettor. I'll tell you something for nothing. Had those sucklings not been below the age for criminal responsibility, I fancy that they too would have been hauled before the Crown Court for miscellaneous public order offences or, worse still, found themselves with a noise abatement notice strung around their respective mobiles by the anorak clad jerk from the council who went about town with his decibel reader.

"There, there," I said, jostling one cradle at a time whilst simultaneously making a mental note that (never mind whether the shirt of our client was bright yellow or dark blue) according to a third witness, the person who put a brick through the plate glass window was naked from the waist up. Further and additionally, I observed, the colour of the chest (in common with the colour of the face) was said to be white and not black. Oh, yes, and another thing. The perpetrator was stated to be of the female persuasion meaning that, according to the third witness's account, were Jerome Horatio Barclay to be convicted of rioting in the streets of Birmingham, by week's end there'd be some very shocked faces in the showers at Her Majesty's Prison and at least one incumbent's petition to the Home Office complaining of overcrowding in cells would find itself consigned to the drawer marked *discontinued, inmate has weirdly withdrawn his complaint.*

"Gatehouse, old chap!" It was Ian Prospect who had snuck up on me unnoticed. As ever, he spoke in his quasi-rustic tone. "What on earth are you doing with case papers strewn about the floor? And pray tell me why you have children on the work surface? I sincerely hope that you do not envisage turning up at my abode, The Fly in the Ointment, with a brace of squealing porkers under your arms."

"Ian!" I said it loudly so that I could be heard above the blarting coming from the cradles. "You can't go around calling Damian's pair of sucklings a brace of squealing porkers!"

Ian winced, shrugged, and chuckled. He invariably did that. It was a sort of nervous affliction but he made out that it was simply a characteristic that stood him out from the crowd. Ian scooted towards the desk. He did it in short, quick steps, all the while leaning slightly backwards. It was another of Ian's nervous afflictions but, in common with all things pertaining to life, he had everyone believing that it was they who were out of kilter. And as far as walking went, Ian was convinced that only he had compensated for the fact that the planet Earth swung on its axis at an angle as dodgy as that tower in Italy where, thankfully, the pizza makers are not as incompetent as the architects.

Ian peered into the cradle. It was the one that contained the suckling swathed in blue. "They are too far from the tit, Gatehouse, old chap!" He proceeded to produce from a trouser pocket of his crumpled dark suit, a long clay pipe. Ian diverted his attentions to the suckling swathed in pink and, at the same time, he elevated the stem of the pipe to mouth level and clamped the same firmly between his teeth.

"Ian!" I said it even louder than the time before because the sucklings were now sounding like the struggling monkey at the Dudsall pithead. "You know absolutely nothing about child rearing…"

"Gatehouse! You forget that, in addition to my skills as a trial advocate, I am a breeder of prize winning pigs!" Ian reached into the cradle that contained the suckling swathed in blue and he copped hold of a plastic rattle. He proceeded to use the rattle as a rattle, and he rattled it at both cradles.

"Ian, to my knowledge you've conducted just the one trial!"

"One more trial than you, Gatehouse, old dear!" He spoke through gritted teeth.

I arose from my position on the floor. "Ian!"

"There's absolutely no need for you to shout, Gatehouse."

Ian had a point, for all of the monkey's struggling had succeeded in bringing the cage to the top of the lift shaft and the miners had gone on their way. In short, the racket coming from the cradles had wound down.

"Ian," I said, only quieter than before, "I understand that halfway through the trial, the judge felt obliged to ask his clerk to telephone the Bar Council for confirmation that you are, as you purport, a real barrister."

Ian tossed the rattle onto the work surface and he reached for the inside pocket of his jacket and produced a matchbox. It was no ordinary matchbox because it was made of brass. A petrol sodden lighter had previously completed his set of smoking accoutrements, but it had finally given up the ghost by incinerating itself. It had come as a welcome relief to all, not least the volunteers at the fire depot in Shipsford-upon-Avon. "Sometimes, Gatehouse, old dear, you can say the cruellest of…"

"And another thing," I said. "Your blasted pig, The General, is a champion only because there were no other cloven hoofed entrants in the Prestwick village show."

Ian plucked a match from out of the box and I could see that its pink head was sweating profusely. He plainly had no inkling that brass, and especially brass that had been nestling in a pocket, tended to generate a bit of heat. "Gatehouse," said Ian, and, as he raised the match to the level of his pipe, it spontaneously combusted. Between puffing and sucking, Ian declared, "I must remind you, old chap, that at least the sole entrant in the best pig competition survived to receive her red rosette." Ian had alluded to the fact that I had accidently unleashed Colin, his cat, upon the creatures who were participating in the cuddliest bunny competition. I had simply stopped to compose myself on the way up the marquee where I'd intended to parley with Janie Jetty, the English Rose, who I loved and adored. She was, you see, judging the competition. And Colin, you see, had leapt from his box as I stumbled. And Colin, you see, had a particular penchant for wild rabbit. And Colin, you simply must understand, could not differentiate between coffered Dutch Dwarfs and the mangy flea ridden creatures that burrowed beneath the lavatory block at the end of the garden of The Fly in the Ointment.

"Would you mind looking after the sucklings for a few minutes? It's just that I've told Damian I'll make the tea." I didn't want reminding that, by his wanton acts of violence, Colin had not only disqualified himself from the fluffy pussycat competition but he had simultaneously ruined a potentially special moment for me and Janie. You see, in lieu of going down on one knee, I'd considered it altogether conducive to my wellbeing to go down on both knees and beg the father of young Timmy Jones not to shove the mangled remains of Mr Bobtail where the sun don't shine.

I made my way to the door. My intent was to fill the electric kettle from the red fire bucket that lived beneath the health and safety notice, next to the electricity meter. "Sum bugger has been relieving himself and then leaving his cigarette butts in that ruddy obstacle, Mista Gatehouse." I had quite forgotten just how nippy Brummies can be when going about their toilet and Damian's sudden re-emergence made me jump out of my skin. "Oi think yow will have to fill the kettle from the tap in the lavvy." Damian blustered his way past. "Why, how do, Mista Prospect, sir? Oi day see yow standing there."

"Damian, old boy!" Ian swung around. He removed the clay pipe from between his lips, and he wafted smoke that was billowing faster than from the ancient steam engine in the Dudsall shunting yard. "The family resemblance is there for all to see," said Ian, as the one swathed in blue broke wind.

"Why, thank you very much," said Damian, his jowls flushing pink with pride, as the suckling swathed in pink proceeded to project vomit in the exact direction of the hat stand. "Oi hope them squealing porkers ain't been annoying yow, Mista Prospect."

Ian winced and shrugged as a dark brown fedora copped the lot. It was the pride of Igor Patterson, one of the struggling tenants of Globe Chambers. I don't mind telling you that Patterson could thank his lucky stars that the suckling was just that, a suckling, and not yet on solids. "The fruits of your loin have been no trouble at all," said Ian, with a wince, as I, meanwhile, swiftly darted into the corridor and gave Patterson's crowning glory a good dunking in the fire bucket.

Having ignored, in the fashion above-mentioned, the dry clean only label affixed to the lining, I returned the item of apparel to the stand and draped it limply across the top. "With a bit of starch, it will be as good as new," Damian assured me.

"Nonsense, I'll have it as an engine rag," said Ian, excitedly, with a wince.

"This is a barrister's set of chambers and not a nursery." The utterance came with a drawl and he who had done the uttering was Walter.

"Oh, blimey Ol' Riley," said Damian. "Oi am so sorry, Mista Tweed. The missus has left we to look after the babbies."

Walter approached the cradles. The sucklings were contentedly sleeping, again. I reckoned it was probably Ian's tobacco smoke that had sent them off. Walter reached into a cradle. It was the one that contained the suckling swathed in pink. Next, Walter inexplicably twanged the piece of elastic on a dangling mobile. The causative effect was to send a toy duck spinning, not to mention two silver bells, a miniature of the League Division One Champions Cup that amazingly played *Pop Goes The Weasel* and, more amazingly, was lifted by Aston Villa FC (with some highly controversial goals and dubious offside decisions along the way, I am compelled to add) and a fairy-like figure that was enough to give an adult sleepless nights, let alone a mere suckling. Well, you might know that, with an ensemble like that whizzing overhead, the suckling awoke and went into a frenzy.

"Damian!" barked Walter.

"Yes, Mista Tweed?"

"You are as incompetent a father as you are a barrister's clerk!"

"But, I must protest, Mista Tweed!"

"You are also impertinent," said Walter, and he diverted his attentions towards the cradle containing the suckling who was swathed in blue. Walter twanged that one's mobile and all and, at the sight of miscellaneous knickknacks whirling overhead, the occupant joined his sibling and started hollering. "Any fool," said Walter, above the din, "can see that these children urgently require their mother's breast!" He stared accusingly at Damian. "Were it not for the fact that I have an appointment, I would telephone the Social Services Department of Birmingham City Council and have both children taken into care!"

"Yes, Mista Tweed. Sorry, Mista Tweed."

Ian scooted across and, with a wince, shrug, and a chuckle, he retook the rattle and he rattled it about and the blubbering and screaming immediately wound down.

"You appear to have a natural gift," said Walter. "Unfortunately, the child minding duties must fall upon my learned pupil whilst my incompetent clerk embarks on an expedition to The Bull Ring Shopping Centre in search of Mrs Barker." Walter opened wide the door that led into his office. "Come, Prospect, you are already late for your interview."

"Interview?" My eyes opened wide. "What interview? No one mentioned anything to me about an interview."

Ian winced. "I'm applying for a tenancy, old chap." He shrugged and chuckled. "The Head of Chambers at my set appears to be convinced that trouble and I go hand in hand."

I ignored Ian and, ignoring also the papers in the case of Regina versus Jerome Horatio Barclay beneath my feet, I strode towards Walter. "At the end of pupillage I wanted to become the tenth tenant." As I spoke, I simultaneously rubbed the left toe of my scuffed brogue against the right brogue. The written indictment in the said case, you see, had somehow become entangled in the footwear.

"Izaak," said Walter. "At the end of twelve months, you may make an application as would anybody else. In the meantime, Chambers is in urgent need of a new injection of business and, as you presumably know, Prospect has potentially valuable contacts from the South Warwickshire business community and from Prestwick, in particular."

"But, Walter, this surely has ramifications..." I stopped while I considered the ramifications. The only business contact of Ian's from Prestwick was Janie Jetty. You see, she owned the local food processing plant.

"You were saying?" said Walter.

"It's slipped my mind," I lied, casually, with all the skills of a lawyer. "Also, I must draw to everyone's attention that I am a pupil barrister and not a child minder."

"Then, as the pupil barrister, you had better hurry along with tea." Walter naturally drawled as he spoke his words most cutting and he grinned, just a little. "Just two lumps for me, if you would be so kind, Gatehouse."

"If the talking in your sleep is anything to go by," said Ian, "you need child minding practice for when all those little Gatehouses enter this life." Ian shrugged and winced after he had spoken his own cutting words and he chuckled, just a little. He put the clay pipe to his mouth. "Just the one lump, if you would be so kind." It was said through gritted teeth.

After Walters's door closed, Damian sallied forth in search of Mrs Barker in the Birmingham Bull Ring Shopping Centre. It was even odds that he would never be seen again. As for me, Yours Usurped, I firstly ensured that the sucklings were still safely and soundly snoozing. Next, I took hold of the kettle and made my way into the corridor. I stopped on reaching the health and safety notice. *Now then*, I thought, as I dredged the kettle through the fire bucket, *was that two cigarette butts or just the one?*

CHAPTER THREE

Walter and I found Jerome Horatio Barclay pacing up and down outside Court Number One. We were late because Ian's interview had taken far longer than Walter had anticipated. There had not even been the time for Walter to stop betwixt Chambers and the Crown Court building for the purposes of issuing assurances to various passers-by (the newspaper vendor, the road sweeper, even the odd judge) that he was feeling okay, hunky-dory, indeed, that he was generally in fine fettle. In fact, it seems right and proper to record right here and now that there was never a barrister-at-law who looked such a picture of health. It therefore remained a mystery as to why so many were concerned for the health of just the one. I'd have said it was a mystery up there with how come all those eels can find their way to the Sargasso Sea and back without so much as a compass, and just what the hell is it swishing around in the waters of Loch Ness, not to mention why, contrast sleep deprivation and the use of thumb screws, the infliction of the nerve shattering Birmingham accent on the innocent has never been declared cruel and unusual punishment?

"Mr Tweed!" Jerome Horatio Barclay, spoke with a drawl not dissimilar to that of my pupil master. "I thought you'd forgotten all about me, man!" Walter had pointed him out as we crossed the hallway of gothic arches and stone benches. Our client was kitted out in casual attire. However, don't you go asking me to describe the ensemble because my mind was focused solely on his headgear which consisted of a woollen hat that was very troublesome in my mind's eye. You see, it was huge, stripy, and multi-coloured. However, troublesome though the hat that he wore was, it was nothing in comparison to the troubled look on our client's face. "Man! Oh, man! Oh, man!" He sounded troubled, and all. "I thought I was going to have to do the trial all by myself."

"I'm sorry, my friend," said Walter, in his own drawl that was simultaneously both soothing and reassuring.

"I hope you're feeling fit and well," said our client. Troubled though he was, our client obviously felt a compulsion to add further evidence to the mystery above mentioned.

"Permit me to introduce my learned pupil," said Walter, ignoring our client's enquiry as to the state of his health.

"Hello, Jerome," I said, offering my right hand. "I'm Izaak Gatehouse."

"Damned funny name," said our client, scornfully, and, my right arm was left all by itself, suspended in mid-air. "You can call me plain Jezz," he added, no doubt by way of intention to retain street credibility in the eyes of his peers and not, I fancy, as an act of reconciliation, come act of chumminess, on his part.

I looked at Walter and he tutted. I tutted back and, at the same time, I returned my unshook hand to the side of my trousers.

"Have you seen the instructing solicitor?" Walter enquired of our client.

"Daryl don't appear to have bothered to turn up," said our client, referring to Daryl Bodkins of Bodkins and Company which said firm, according to the letter heading that accompanied the brief, specialised in family matters, tax disputes, accident claims, housing disputes, as well as criminal defence work. *Well,* I thought to myself. *I ain't surprised he's not here considering that Bodkins and Company is comprised of just Daryl Bodkins and an answering machine.* "According to the guy outside his office who sells newspapers," explained Jezz, "Daryl has had a visit from The Law Society and they want to go through his books of account." I took a sharp intake of breath at that revelation and, *Crikey,* my thought processes went, *we can write off seeing Daryl for the duration of the trial*, for it was common knowledge that having unleashed the bean counters, the professional institution would not leave without justifying their presence, even if it meant resorting to the discovery of a paper clip living in file A when file B had, in fact, been stated to be the little chap's residence.

"Very well," said Walter, "my learned pupil, Mr. Gatehouse, will go through the written statement with you whilst I have words with prosecuting counsel."

So, while Walter was away, I went through the facts with Jerome Horatio.

"Well, it's like this," began our client, "I was simply returning home and I decided to stop off to buy some fish-n-chips, like. Then, all of a sudden…"

"Hang on, mate. Slow down, like. I have to write this lot down for Mr. Tweed."

"Okay, sorry, man. Anyway, as I approached the shop, about two dozen brothers and sisters came running past and they were being chased by pigs with batons."

"What?" I ensured that I sounded suitably hoity-toity. You see, that's how barristers are supposed to be.

"Yeh, man. The pigs, You know? Police. They had batons, they did."

"No, no," I said. "Two dozen brothers and sisters?"

"You what, man?"

"Okay, okay," I said. "Let's make this simple. How many brothers do you have?"

"Er, just the one, man, but…"

"Blimey!" I said. "Twenty three sisters! How the hell do you manage to get in the bathroom each morning?"

"You what, man?" Our client anxiously turned towards the Court entrance where Walter was engaged in conversation with another barrister. Indeed, Jerome's head turned so quick that the enormous multi-coloured hat wobbled and the top bit began to list at a most precarious angle. "Mr. Tweed!"

I found myself relegated to fetching tea from the public cafe while Walter finished off writing down our client's account of the part that he played, or did not play, in the public disorder.

Come eleven o'clock, however, a female usher strolled, or rather, marched over. Now, most Crown Court ushers are of a nervous disposition. This one was not. "The judge is about to come into Court," she said, in a manner that was almost as bold as the bright red suit that she wore beneath her usher's gown which, for its part, was black and faded. "This judge doesn't like to hang about," she continued, and, as she continued, her eyes rolled about in her chubby face with its complexion that was as faded as the gown. The three of us, that is Walter, the client and me, I, Izaak Gatehouse, stood to attention. "Oh," added the usher, as we hurriedly made our way towards the swing doors. "I am quite forgetting my manners, Mr. Tweed. I trust that you're feeling okay, today?"

"I am very well, thank you, Madam Usher." Walter paused, only for a second, mind, and he smiled. "Oh, Madam Usher?"

"Yes, Mr. Tweed?"

"I should very much like you to ensure that all prosecution witnesses are instructed to leave the courtroom before the jury is sworn."

"Yes, Mr. Tweed."

"That includes police officer witnesses."

"Yes, Mr. Tweed."

"Is it correct, Tweed?" The enquiry came from a stick insect sort of a barrister who was seated at the far end of the bench on which Walter and I proposed to take up our positions.

"Is what correct?" drawled Walter, disdainfully.

The stick insect shuffled or, rather, slithered over to our side. Indeed, he slithered right up to Walter so that he towered right over him. In the manner of a praying mantis sort of a stick insect thingy, he wobbled his skeletal head this way and that. At last he spoke. It came as a relief because, though praying mantis weren't exactly common up Dudsall way, I knew from the nature magazines in WH Smith and Sons, the booksellers in the High Street, that when they stood wobbling their heads so, it was the surest sign they were about to gobble up something or other. "Is it correct?" he said. "Is it correct, Tweed?" he said again, only adding my pupil master's name, presumably lest Walter did not know that it was he who was being addressed, despite the stick insect being but the distance of a lick from Walter's cheek.

"Spit it out, my good fellow."

"Am I correct in believing that you have instructed the police officers to be removed from Court?"

"You are not mistaken, my good man."

"What? Even the exhibits officer?"

"Yes, even him."

"It is not cricket." The stick insect wobbled his head. "It is simply not cricket, Tweed, and I shall address the judge accordingly."

Walter stepped back apace and, in the process, he very nearly backed into me. "Then, do your addressing now," drawled Walter, "because the judge is about to enter."

"All rise!" bellowed the usher. It was she who had carried out the miscellaneous evictions from Court.

Everyone in Court rose. That was with the exception of Walter, the stick insect and me, because we were arisen already, you see. Alright?

Now, it transpired that the judge was not a judge at all. He was a recorder. That's the name for a part time Circuit Judge, you see. Also, because the judge was not a proper judge, he did not wear the fancy coloured clothes associated with a judge. In lieu thereof, he was kitted out in the black stuff gown of an ordinary barrister. Barrister, you see, being his usual occupation.

"How splendid to see you, Mr. Tweed," beamed the Recorder as he bounded in. He bowed and we members of the Bar bowed straight back. "I have to say," the Recorder went on, after he was seated, "that you are looking extremely well," which was more than could be said of him, for this part time judge was the very colour of the devil's nutting bag. In short, his complexion was pale and dingy. The Recorder was possibly in only his fifty-something year but, to my mind, it didn't look as if he had many more miles to go on the clock. Indeed, I had heard that the estimated length of the trial was five days. *You'd best hurry along, mate*, I thought to myself, *'cause if this trial spills over into next week, you won't be here for the verdict.*

The stick insect coughed. "May it please, Your Honour." He spoke both bold and loud. "I hesitate to make waves but my learned friend, Mr. Tweed, is insisting that those prosecution witnesses who are serving police officers must be removed from Court."

"Quite right," said the Recorder, snappily. "What on earth is the issue in that?"

"Even the exhibits officer, Your Honour?"

The Recorder turned his head in Walter's direction. "Mr. Tweed?" he began.

Walter half rose. "Yes, Your Honour?"

"I presume that you have good reason?"

"I do," said Walter, now fully arisen.

"Well then," beamed the Recorder. "That's all right then. Let the jury panel be brought into Court."

At the exact same time that Walter sat himself down, the stick insect popped up. It was as if he had been sitting on the far end of a seesaw. "But, but, Your Honour…" So spluttered the fellow.

"But, nothing," said the Recorder. "Did you not hear Mr. Tweed? He has his reasons, no doubt. And no doubt," continued the Recorder, whilst simultaneously winking his right eye in Walter's direction, "the reason is that the exhibits officer is also a witness as to fact."

The stick insect returned to his seated position, crossed his arms, and sulked.

Next, the usher brought into Court a chattering gaggle of about twenty or so. A female court clerk (she was sat immediately in front of the Recorder, at a far lower level, of course) told the gaggle that she wanted a bit of hush about the place. When all was quiet, the clerk began to shuffle a pack of cards. They were not playing cards, of course, because each one had the name of a juror in waiting written on the same. Besides, the average pack of playing cards does not contain twelve jokers. The clerk told the gaggle, "I shall read a name from the card and, if your name is called, please come forward." She shuffled the pack and, by a remarkable phenomenon, it was twelve jokers who were obliged to come forward. As they did so, the clerk directed the jokers (well, alright, in three instances, the jokeresses) into the jury box and each one of them proceeded to tumble up a little step that was craftily hiding behind a little door hanging from shiny brass hinges.

Each jury person in turn was told to hold the Good Book in their right hand and, upon giving assurances to Almighty God that they would try the defendant according to the evidence, the trial began. It kicked off with the Recorder telling the jury that a point of law had occurred to him and that he was anxious to share his bit of knowledge with learned counsel and not them. "Whoops!" said the Recorder, as the first juror to depart tumbled down the step that, only five minutes before, he had tumbled up. "Mind the craftily hidden step," he smiled, "because we don't want any of you lot suing the Court."

"Now then," said the Recorder, addressing the stick insect. The stick insect shot to his feet. "I dare say that you are assuming that the outcome of this trial will turn on identification evidence?"

"Your Honour is most perceptive."

"Mr. Tweed?" Crown Counsel returned to his seat and up went Walter. I was reminded of the seesaw effect, all over again. "Mr. Tweed. You will no doubt submit during the course of the trial that a Turnbull direction is required?"

Walter spoke with precision. "In view of numerous miscarriages of justice in cases turning on a person's identity, I most certainly will, Your Honour."

The Recorder casually leaned back. "Warnings about fleeting glances, I suppose?"

"Why, yes, Your Honour."

"Poor light?"

"Naturally."

"Absence of continuous sighting?"

"I beg your pardon, Your Honour?"

"The defendant disappearing from view when he stepped behind a lamppost?"

"Well, I suppose so, Your Honour."

The Recorder leant forward and he clasped his hands. "Well, that is all nonsense!"

"I beg your pardon, Your Honour?"

The Recorder addressed Crown Counsel. The stick insect relished Walter's discomfort and he had a grin from one side of his skeletal face to the other. "The defendant is effectively charged with rioting, contrary to common law."

"Yes, Your Honour."

"Actively participating in a riotous assembly?"

"Yes, Your Honour?"

The Recorder once again adopted his leaning-back pose. In addition, he unclasped the hands, copped hold of a ballpoint pen, and he started rat-a-tat- tatting the thing on a piece of blotting paper.

"With whom?"

"I'm, er, sorry, Your Honour?"

"With whom did he assemble? With whom did he riot? With whom is he charged?"

"Well, er, I..."

The Recorder stopped punishing the ballpoint. He stood up so, naturally, we copied him. "The charge is misconceived and the defendant is hereby discharged."

The stick insect went purple in the face. "I apply to amend the charge, Your Honour."

"Your application is denied."

"Well, what about the jury?"

"They have departed the building," said the Recorder.

The stick insect looked firstly at Walter. Then, he looked at the Recorder. "What? Gone home?"

The Recorder shrugged. "These days, they are permitted one cup of tea and no biscuits. Government cuts, you see? Had they been kept any longer, we would have had a proper riot on our hands. You see, a jury consists of twelve, no more, no less, and..."

"Yes, Your Honour?"

"The dock contains just the one, no more, no less." The Recorder bounded towards his side door. He turned, just the once, before departing. "It is good to see you looking so well, Mr. Tweed."

After the door closed, I grinned, just a little. "Blimey, Walter. Good result, bet you didn't see that one coming, did you?"

Never had I seen Walter look as angry as he did at that moment. "Have you nothing better to do, Gatehouse? I suggest that you make your way to the County Court and deal with that injunction before I am forced to report your conduct to the tenants in Chambers."

I left the dimly lit corridors of the court building and stepped out into the sunlight. I blinked as I negotiated the stone stairs that took me down to street level; such was the strength of the sun that day. It was almost rush- hour and I knew that if I was to make it across the street in one piece I must not hang about. However, before I could step off the curb, I heard a familiar cry. "Gatehouse, old chap! There you are at last!" It was Ian, of course, and he was stood at the front end of his wreck of a motor car that, for its part, was parked in a no waiting zone right in the spot which was generally reserved for the High Court Judges.

"Ian," I said, "it's the first time this year that the sun has been shining for two successive days and you've got yourself a convertible top." I told the truth, for Ian's old MGB had acquired a black hood that matched perfectly the body over which it perched. It was tatty and, in parts, was strangely stained green with moss, but, in the nature of canvas, at least it weren't as rusty as the motor car itself. You see, it was as corroded as an old coal boat.

"Gatehouse, old dear. Unless you have some masochistic desire to roast alive on the drive home to Prestwick, you had better lend a hand getting this blasted top down." So, I leapt to the far side of the wreck and began tugging at the mouldy canvas. "Damnation, Gatehouse, old chap. Put some effort into it." Our exertions proved fruitless and, after many hopeless tugs during which, I swear, I heard a bit of ripping, Ian stood back a pace and he proceeded to wince, shrug, and chuckle. "Gatehouse, old boy. I appear to have acquired a convertible top that will not convert. You will simply have to drive with the thing unconverted."

"Ian?" I spoke with suspicion. "What do you mean, **I'll**, have to drive?"

I was right to sound suspicious because Ian only went and imparted that he proposed to stay in town and he would catch a train later (hitchhike if he had to) while I returned all alone to his cottage, The Fly in the Ointment. "Gatehouse, old chap, I have a pressing engagement that simply will not wait." He proceeded to shrug and wince, before adding, with a chuckle, "Julia is more pressing than most, if you get my drift, old boy? And," he added, "the sun will be set before I am finished and I fear that the headlights are on the blink. And," he added some more, "someone has to entertain the voluptuous Nurse Stringer until my return."

"Nurse Stringer?" I was aghast, I was. "I ain't letting her nowhere near me." Too right, I wouldn't let her within a gnat's whisker because it was Nurse Stringer, the policeman's wife, who had been responsible for near maiming me. It was her, you see, who had incited a junior house doctor to go at my aching appendage with tubes of various circumferences starting with the middle one when the smallest should have been perfectly satisfactory, not to mention less painful. It was all on account of her having a grievance with Ian. A grievance, by the sounds of it, that had been put to bed, being a place (I fancied) where Ian proposed to finish his pressing engagement.

"Julia," said Ian, "happens to be a town and country planning expert. I intend to seek her advice on a matter that is of benefit to the entire parish. Our damnable landlord, you see, is threatening to have the walnut tree chopped down to make way for a new dwelling."

"What? Surely not the beautiful tree in the paddock opposite?"

"The very fellow," answered Ian, with sincerity and (naturally) with a shrug and a wince.

I was tempted that, in the cause of preservation of the environment, I must cooperate. Then, I was brought back to my senses in the cause of preservation of my driver's license. You see, against all the odds, there were no infringements endorsed thereon. "I can't drive this old wreck, Ian! I'll be pulled over by the law, or somutt!"

Ian ignored my protestation that I had alluded to the possibility of being stopped by the police and arrested for offences under various construction and use regulations. He tossed the keys, instinct took hold, and I reached out and copped hold of the same. "I say, well caught, old chap. The Prestwick cricket team require a sound fielder. I shall put your name forward." Ian turned on his heels and, chuckling (with a wince), he announced, "The old girl is very nearly empty, old chap. You had best fill her up at the nearest garage."

"But, I've only got money for fish-n-chips and a few beers!" I served notice of my plight by shouting because, with his legs going like pistons, Ian reached the corner of the street in next to no time. Indeed, Ian had skedaddled sufficiently far away to ensure that even an Olympian shot putter couldn't wing the keys straight back at him. "I'd rather hitchhike back to Prestwick, I would!"

Ian fetched out his ridiculous clay pipe. "You will simply have to go without supper, old chap!" He reached into another pocket and he produced the metallic matchbox. "As for the beer, old boy, just chalk it up to the two yuppies who have moved into Rosemary Cottage!" Ian opened the box and he plucked out a match. The thing combusted before he had chance to give it a strike. "Ouch, Gatehouse, that's hot!" He casually discarded the match and casually crossed the street. It was a brave thing to do in Birmingham for it was common knowledge that a Brummie driver would preferably knock over a babby in a pram than lose a second in getting from A to B, where A can be said to represent the workplace and B can be said to represent any one of a thousand curry houses. Above the nerve shattering screeches of, "Yow need to get a pair of eyes, mate!" emanating from the car nearest, I could hear the screeches of the driver of the car farthest, "Oh, my God, yow maniac! Call the fire brigade! Call an ambulance! Call anyone! Yow 'ave tossed that fireball right into me aged mom's newly lacquered hair!"

I swear that, by the time I had reached the green fields of South Warwickshire, the carburettors were sucking on fresh air.

In fact, it was as well that there had been a quarter mile slope down which I could free wheel, for it had afforded me adequate momentum to climb the one hundred yards or so up the other side and sidle right up to fuel pump number one.

I had no sooner come to a halt than a face appeared at the passenger side window.

"Gosh, Ian! Thank heavens! I am in urgent need of assistance!"

The voice was feminine. The voice had no discernable accent. The voice came from the lips of a true English Rose. It was her whom I loved and adored. It was she who had gone and had me enjoined. It was Janie Jetty. I swear it was!

"Janie! Whatever's up?"

"Izaak!" Janie gasped, and, as she did so, I couldn't help but notice that her teeth seemed almost too big for her face. However, the imperfection, combined with the imperfection of her huge eyes, was simply wonderful. "Izaak! You are driving Ian's car!" She was quick on the uptake, was Janie.

I scrambled out of the driver's side and a conversation ensued thus.

"Janie! I'm fetching Ian's car back from Brummagem, I mean Birmingham!"

"Izaak!" Her huge and wonderful eyes were now sparkling. "My vehicle has a double puncture and I am late for an important business meeting." Janie ran a slender hand through her mousey hair that wasn't too long and it weren't too short, either. In fact, it was just right. I noticed a bead of sweat running down her forehead. "My family… (*not them, again*, I thought, because it was common knowledge that they thought diddlysquat of me, and *My God, Janie, you look stunning in that low cut cream linen suit*, I also thought). I said, my family," said Janie, again, for I fear she had suspected me of being distracted, "will be most concerned." She began to waft a wad of papers. The wafting was driven by her right arm, the hand of which was adorned by a mysterious glittery ring. There was a story to tell there, all right, and I wouldn't rest till all was revealed. "It is I who am to present our portfolio to clients," explained Janie, virtually shoving the papers into my face. "It is what I call a bullet-point presentation."

"Janie," I said. "Just put our differences aside for a moment and hop in. I'll get you to the presentation."

"Izaak," said she. Then, Janie hesitated a moment. She gulped and I noted, with heart-pounding joy, that her chest and swan-like neck had turned the very reddest of reds. "Izaak," said Janie, again, only after a brief interlude. "Why have you gone down on bended knees and begun poking and prodding beneath the vehicle?"

"Just making sure that there are no cats lurking, Janie." I weren't about to be caught out by that one again, I can tell you.

"Cats?" Janie sounded astonished. Her beautiful eyes opened as wide as eyes could possibly go. Simultaneously, the red blushing spread from her neck to the whole of her porcelain face. It was a wonderful sight to behold, it was. "Cats?" said Janie, again. "In the name of Heaven, Izaak, remove yourself from the floor. Cats," she said for the third time of asking and, at the same time, she tutted all to herself.

Having detected no cat, or indeed any form of mammal that might have accounted, by way of allergy, for all of Janie's blushes, I delightedly scrambled to my feet. "Sorry, Janie," and I set about brushing dust from the front of my trousers. "I could have sworn that I saw a cat running under the car and I already bear the scars of having witnessed the demise of a cat beneath the wheels of a motor."

"Do you mean poor Tuppence, Izaak?" Janie alluded to the songbird mangling moggie of my former landlady who'd found herself (*Felix catus*, that is) squished on the very eve of my Bar final examinations. By the by, Janie eyed me with sympathy as she spoke and it came as a welcome change to the wholly unsympathetic manner in which she'd hitherto eyed me as a suitable defendant in her none molestation suit.

"Poor Izaak," said Janie, sweetly and, no word of a lie, she sashayed over, placed a loving arm about my waist and gave me a gentle squeeze.

"Yes, Janie," I said, pitiably. "Even to this day, the death of Sixpence..."

"Sixpence? Do you mean Tuppence?"

"Well, whatever, Janie. But, either way, I still get nightmares, I do, Janie."

"Come, my brave knight in shining armour. I cannot be late." Her words were spoken softly; indeed, they were said in a manner that conveyed intimacy in a manner I thought was nigh on impossible considering that just days previously I too had communicated intimacy, except that mine had been in the form of a public declaration that I was desirous of knowing her biblically unless or until she instructed me to slow down or stop altogether.

"Hop in!" I spoke with child-like enthusiasm. "I'll shove some petrol in this thing, and, tell you what?"

"What?"

"I'll even put it through the posh American carwash. I won't have you turning up at this shindig of yours in anything other than a carriage in pristine condition!"

"Oh, Izaak!" Janie's eyes danced as well as sparkled. "You truly are my white knight," and she duly hopped aboard and placed the portfolio, her bullet point thingamajig, on her luxurious lap. *Lucky ol' bullet point*, I thought.

"This will take just a minute!" So said I, as I manoeuvred the vehicle to the front of the carwash. I proceeded to wind-down the window and immediately took note of a little silver box with an arrow, drawn by use of a felt tip pen. The said arrow was pointing at a plastic token sized slot. At the blunt end of the arrow, I saw writing and I adjudged that the author and the artist who had drawn the arrow was one and the same for the writing was also in felt tip and, moreover, the felt tip was of the same consistency and colour. Further and additionally, there was correlation between the writing and the arrow because the former told its reader, *Please place the plastic token in this slot.* Satisfied that here was evidence that the identity of the author was a little man in a blue uniform and bobble hat who'd enquired, "You're surely not thinking of driving that thing in, are you?" I shoved the token in the slot and, immediately, two ruddy great brushes shot out from a crevice and, as would a pair of whirligigs, one on either side, they came straight at us.

"Goodness gracious, Izaak!" Janie's eyes were ablaze as the front wing mirror flew past, narrowly missed the windshield, but regrettably embedded itself in a sign. It was a sign written with felt tip and it said, *Ensure that there are no loose parts and that aerials are fully retracted.* "Oh, my God, Izaak! I do believe that the car aerial has become detached!" Janie's observational evidence would have been obvious even to the likes of a High Court Judge. You see, a javelin-like object came through the canvas top at the exact same time that *The Archers,* an everyday radio tale of country folk, went on the blink. "Heavens, Izaak! I believe that I have been stabbed!"

Anyway, the whirligigs went about their respective business and, on their way down the entire length of the vehicle, one of them discovered that a side window had been left wide open. So, presumably being a matey sort of a fellow, the thing popped in just to say, "Howdy do," and then it popped back out again, though not before giving Janie's left cheek a damned good exfoliating. At the rear-end of the motor car, the whirligigs met in some sort of fatal embrace and, Turnbull or no Turnbull (for the brushes were indistinguishable from one another in my book) they jointly and severally took it on themselves to rip off the back bumper and send it clattering out of the car wash and straight onto the bonnet of a Ford Corsair whose turn it was next to come on down.

"Sorry, Janie!" I was obliged to holler my apology. It was all the fault of the noisy brushes, you see. I also had to contend with the dripping of the water where the aerial had come through the roof and jabbed her. "I didn't see the sign telling me to retract the aerial!" I hadn't the heart to tell her I'd also failed to take note of the sign telling me that on no account must cars with convertible tops enter the carwash. Mind you, Janie was a bright girl and she figured that one out for herself as the pair of whirligigs made their return journey, promptly adjudged that a landau was a stylish sort of a conveyance, unhooked the canvas top and sent it down to where the back bumper was at.

"Oh, help me, Izaak!" pleaded the love of my life, as warm, waxy water came cascading down. "My hair and makeup are ruined!" Janie made her observation while swiftly glancing in the car's interior mirror only to discover that someone who greatly resembled the rock star *Alice Cooper* was staring straight back out. However, as far as I was concerned, the teardrops of mascara streaming down Janie's cheeks was endearing and made her look naughty, sort of thing. "Are you listening to a bloody thing that I am saying?" *Wow*, I thought, *now she's sounding proper naughty, and all*. However, I must impart that, next, a big horizontal brush came rotating downwards and it did to Janie's hair the sort of disastrous coffering that one would rationally associate with the finished product of an average Brummie cosmetologist.

"Don't worry, Janie." I didn't want the love of my life to be alarmed or anything so I ensured that I addressed her in cheery manner. However, between you and me, the cheerfulness was nothing but a cover for a sense of impending doom. "The hot air blower's just started up! Your hair will be as good as new!"

Janie began to mouth something or other but, what with the blower sounding like a Dudsall Corporation bus, it was impossible to comprehend precisely what it was that she was attempting to impart. It may have been an admission that she had negligently failed to pin together the miscellaneous papers that comprised her client's portfolio. You see, fifty or so sheets of A4 promptly took to the air, fluttered around a bit and then, on tiring of their aeronautical display, they disappeared from view presumably with the intention of seeing what the canvas top, the back bumper, and the Ford Corsair were up to.

Before I had a chance to negotiate the motor through to the exit, Janie ignored a felt tip sign, *do not exit your vehicle until the washing cycle is completed*, and she attacked the passenger side door. Before disembarking, Janie waited for a quantity of soapy water to flow out. You see, six inches, maybe as many as nine, tell a lie, possibly ten inches of the stuff was swishing about her slender legs. Janie wrestled a way through a whirligig (it was fortuitous that the rotating was anti-clockwise since her patented stiletto shoe might otherwise have come winging its way towards me) and she disappeared around the back. I assumed that Janie had gone to collect her portfolio from the bonnet of the Corsair because I heard the muffled cries of a child from behind glass go, "Oh, Mummy! There is a slimy wet monster coming straight towards us!"

My reasoning proved spot-on because, moments later, Janie re-appeared and she was clutching a sodden clump.

"Let's make a Roman pot or sommut," I said, smiling like a probate solicitor who's passed muster in the probate office, with a will forged in his own true hand. "I used to be bostin' good at paper mache in art classes, I did." And, be fair, any one knows that a bit of light-hearted humour relieves the tension. Regrettably, Janie displayed a fiery side to her nature which only went to prove that it was a good man that she needed to see her through life's little ups and downs. You see, she only went and threw the soggy remains of the bullet point presentation, bullet-like, straight at me. "Ouch! That hurt, Janie, that did! You could have someone's eye out with that!" I told the truth, I can tell you, because a couple of pints of water that's been sucked into a fifty page portfolio and then chucked into a chap's right eye, doesn't half sting a bit.

"Oh, Izaak!"And Janie promptly limped away, one shoe on, the other shoe off (having at least had its ballistic trajectory terminated by the windshield of the Ford Corsair).

"Oh, Janie," I said, while simultaneously paddling my feet in the foot well.

CHAPTER FOUR

Later that day, I was contentedly snoozing in the more comfortable of the leather armchairs. Colin was on my lap. Within the huge inglenook, a loveseat that Ian had found in next-door's orchard was roaring away nicely, thank you very much. A wonderful smell of baking apples was wafting about and teasing my nostrils something rotten. Indeed, I was contemplating the removal of my personage with the object of tootling through to where the gas oven was at, intending to baste the little beauties in honey. However, I did no such thing because there came an almighty rattling at the door.

"Yoo-hoo!" went a voice that was both feminine and horribly familiar. "Are you about, Ian, only my husband...?" The voice trailed off as Nurse Stringer opened the door and she strolled straight in. "Oh, it's you," said the nurse disdainfully. Colin took one look, leapt from my lap, and clambered up the curtains. Nurse Stringer helped herself to the other, slightly less comfortable, armchair. Her stripy nurse-type dress rode high above the knees as she settled in. I observed that the nurse held in her hand a tiny doll, no more than six inches from head to toe. She, the little dolly that is, was dressed in traditional national costume. Scottish, I would have said, judging from the abysmal taste. It was very strange, it was. I was about to raise an enquiry as to why it was that a grown woman was going about the parish with a miniature member of the Mac something or other family in the palm of her hand when, with a swish of long red hair, Nurse Stringer diverted my attention. "I see that you have been in the wars, again," she said.

"What?"

"Those."

"Oh! These!" I raised my right arm. "They're just a few insect bites, they are."

"Insect bites? Honey bee stings, I would say. You should have them dressed."

"Anyway," I said, dismissively, "Ian's not here."

"He's not here?" Her emerald eyes flashed and I instinctively sat bolt upright, ready to leap up and hop it, should the need arise. As hereinbefore stated, I had already suffered at Buddug's hands. "He's not here?" said the nurse, once again.

"He's attending to parish business, or something or other," I said, and I duly rose and I nipped smartly to the back of the chair.

"Do you mean he's attending to **someone** or other?" Nurse Stringer sounded miffed, all right, and I was glad that the chair behind which I cowered formed a barrier, a line of natural defence between her and Yours Truly, sort of a thing.

"It's all about saving a tree." I ensured that I sounded suitably officious. "And, while I'm about it..." I was interrupted by the opening of the door and, without as much as a by your leave, Janie marched in. I swear she did. "Janie!" I said, and, after I'd said it, my mouth remained gaping as would a roach in Dudsall cut.

"Izaak! I want a word with you!" The love of my life had not as yet dried herself off. I noted that mascara stains were still about her wonderful cheeks. Janie looked stunning, nonetheless. "Izaak! We simply have to...!" On noticing Nurse Stringer and, more importantly, on noticing that the auburn-haired harbinger was sprawled before me displaying (by accident or otherwise) an indecent proportion of black stocking tops, Janie stopped and she thereby deprived me of an opportunity of knowing whatever it was that we simply had to do or not do (as the case may be). "Oh, Izaak!" said Janie.

"Oh, Janie!" I said. "This is circumstantial evidence, this is!" Janie was having none of it. She turned on her heels (delightfully slender for one so tall), and she slammed shut the big oak door straight in my face.

Nurse Stringer hauled herself up. She had a smirk on her face like that of a tatter holding a pair of snippers on a church roof made of lead at gone midnight. "Evidence of your circumcising or not," she said. "I shall go upstairs and await Ian's return." With that, the flame-haired one strode toward the staircase and she began the long and narrow assent. But, no more than three steps up Nurse Stringer stopped and placed the dolly onto a little shelf. "This will teach the beast not to take me for granted," mumbled the nurse.

How very strange, I thought, after she had gone. *How very strange, indeed.*

I tootled over to the little shelf where the doll was seated with a Toby jug to her left, and a royal wedding commemorative cup to her right. Her little arms were folded and her little legs were tightly crossed.

"Leave that alone!" I hadn't seen the nurse spying from behind the balustrade. She was a sly and naughty one, all right. "Maud, which is the name of my dolly, represents a means of communication by which Ian knows of my mood."

"You what?"

"You know? Can you not see that Maud's legs are tightly crossed?"

"Meaning?"

"Meaning," said the nurse, "that I have a headache. It's very artistic and clever, isn't it, Izaak?"

"Oh, very artistic and clever," I said. *Pervert*, I thought.

After Nurse Stringer had truly and honestly gone, I cocked my forefinger in the thumb of my right hand and I spitefully flicked Maud and sent her reeling. I did it with force so sufficient that I reckon Maud would have gone clean through the window had the Toby jug not been in the way. In the event, the dolly merely bounced off the jug and she came to rest on top of Princess Diana. My wrath in the manner described having been duly vented, I sallied forth to the kitchen, firstly for the purpose of checking on the baked apples, and secondly to find pen and parchment with which to compose an appropriate note. Somehow or other, I simply had to convey to Janie my love and devotion and, on the basis that all attempts at doing so verbally had failed, communication by writing was the obvious answer. I would have to think of a means by which to deliver the note to

the changeling without anyone finding out. *But,* I reasoned, as I scribbled away, *I'll worry about that when I've got somutt down on paper.*
My dearest Janie.
So far so good. I stopped and pondered awhile. Be fair, it was the most important letter that I had ever written and my, not to mention Janie's happiness depended on my literary skills.

If you wish to join with me in suing the owners of that American-type carwash, then why not arrange to meet somewhere discrete. I am told that the key to the parish church is kept beneath a fallen gravestone and we could let ourselves in at, say, around about midnight on any day of your choosing except Thursday because Thursday is little Friday and suspicions will be aroused if I am not participating in the jollities at the public house on little Friday. Not, you understand that jollities come before any goings on that may (or may not) develop between us. Should your chest and neck redden, I now know that it will be by reason of your passion and not as a result of an allergy to animal fur. But, lest I be mistaken, take heart that there are no rabbits up at the church and, even if there are, I shall ensure that Colin, the cat, is kept under lock and key so there can be no chance of him tearing them to bits before your beautiful eyes...

I was just putting the finishing touches to the fifteenth page of the work of art abovementioned, when the door flew open and in flew Ian. He had an angry look about him.

"Gatehouse!" He had an angry sound about him, and all. "I have been past the garage and I cannot believe what you have done to Rosemary!" Ian was alluding, of course, to his wreck of a motor car.

"Now then, don't go blaming me." I uttered the protest in my very best Dudsall manner. At the same time, I hurriedly secreted the epistle of love into a pocket. "It's all the fault of that ruddy carwash, it is." I proceeded to feign interest in what the apples were about. From my vantage point, they looked a bit on the well-done side.

"Gatehouse, old chap! One is not supposed to drive a classic motor vehicle through a carwash!" Ian winced and shrugged. "It ruins the coachwork, you see. And," he added, "if you do not mind me saying so, old boy. Not content with destroying my sole mode of conveyance, you've destroyed the bounty of my harvest."

"Aye?"

"You have burned the apples to buggery." Ian scooted to a cobwebby corner where he kept his stock of lager. Having copped hold of a can, he removed bits of flaky plasterwork with a good hard puff. Then, he scurried to the sink where he seized hold of a screwdriver. Next, with can of lager in the right hand, screwdriver in the left hand, Ian raised the left hand and he brought the pointed end of the screwdriver down hard onto the can. Immediately, there came the sound of the gushing of air but, prior to the gushing of liquid, Ian raised his right hand high, opened his mouth, and he gulped and gulped. After the ruptured can had given of its bounty, Ian discarded the thing as he would a woman, save and except that he tossed it in the sink and not out of bed. "There are damnable..." Ian broke off momentarily and gasped. Either the last of the bounty had taken his breath away or some of it had disappeared down the windpipe. Either way, Ian ought never to have fallen for the cheap hype of a timeshare salesman and accepted a free weekend in Spain. But, having gone anyway and having conned the salesman into purchasing the whole of August, in perpetuity, in Rosemary Cottage (home of the yuppies, from September to July, when they were naturally not in Provence), he very definitely ought not to have gotten roped into a porron pitching contest. "There are damnable warnings and rules plastered all about that carwash," spluttered Ian, on half recovering. "Where on earth would we be, old chap, if everyone went around ignoring the rules?"

"France?" I said, nonchalantly. Ian was about to let rip and have another crack at me over the aqueous lines of his beloved motor car, when we heard the springing of bed springs above our heads. The springing was followed by a sigh and then the feminine sounds of snoozing. "Before you ask," I said. "Yes. It's the flame-haired Nurse Stringer. And," I added, sternly, "she's not in the mood."

"Isn't she, by Jove?" Ian spoke with a wince, shrug, chuckle, accompanied (on this occasion) by a glint in the eye. Employing his peculiar backwards lean, Ian motored to the sitting room. He made straight for the stairs but stopped on coming to the shelf. "My God, Gatehouse! Look you here at this!"

"Look you here at what?" I spoke with disinterest. Uppermost in my mind was that whenever Ian had female company, I was obliged to take a five-minute stroll around the parish, sometimes an eight-minute stroll, if he paced himself.

"She's presenting herself!" Ian rubbed both hands together. "Maud is lying on her tummy across that collector's item! Straddled, she is!" Ian bolted up the stairs. In all of the fervour he tripped on the penultimate step and he very nearly came tumbling all the way down. I'd have sworn his hands were shaking with fear, anticipation, alcoholic poisoning, excitement, call it what you may. "My God!" spluttered Ian, as he tried to regain his step. "I knew these nurses were up for most things, but never in a month of Sundays did I think that she would be up for this!"

And, before Ian disappeared from sight, I casually enquired of him, "So, shall I be gone for fifteen minutes this time?"

And, as I closed the big oak door and made my way down the garden path, I heard the flame-haired Nurse Stringer shrieking. "Help! Police! Get off me, you pervert!"

CHAPTER FIVE

The following day, we were obliged to rely on public transport. However, three yards from the garden gate, I deserted Ian three times, no less, so that I could return to the kitchen and check that the hob of the gas oven was definitely and honestly and truly turned off.

"Gatehouse, old dear. Your propensity to check and double check everything is both wearisome and troubling." Ian shrugged and winced. He next produced the clay pipe from within his dark barrister-type jacket.

"Better safe than sorry," I said, and, "Whoops!" I added, popping off for a fourth trip to the cottage. "I've left my papers behind, I have. I won't be a minute, Ian."

It was naturally a lie that I had left my papers behind. But, hang about before you go condemning a chap because, when I'd triple checked that the lights were off, I could have sworn that the gas ring at the back of the hob was still lit. Anyway, I was equally certain that my bit of deception had fooled Ian. I was, after all, a barrister and so lying came, sort of, natural.

"You're lying," said Ian. "The damnable papers are stuffed under your damnable arm where even a blind man could detect them." He dove an arm deep into his trouser pocket and, after a bit of rummaging, he produced the little brass matchbox.

"Oh!" I said, feigning surprise that the papers were, indeed, lodged under my armpit and I reluctantly returned to the garden gate.

Ian placed the stem of the clay into his mouth and, between gritted teeth, he said, "Gatehouse. No longer content with avoiding crocodiles by dodging every damned crack in the paving slabs, you appear to have developed an uncontrollable urge to double check…" Ian flipped up the lid of the little brass box. "Indeed, Gatehouse," he expanded, after extracting a match with his free hand, "you are compelled to triple check, sometimes quadruple check that every household chore is attended to. And, I refer in particular to the wanton acts of turning off the oven, ensuring that the door that I purposefully keep unlocked is, in fact, locked and even…" The match, I should record hereabouts, was sweating profusely and, before it could be elevated to the height of Ian's pipe, the thing made a phishing sort of a sound and then it combusted. "Ouch, Gatehouse!" The clay fell from Ian's mouth and he threw both the lit match and the little brass box into a hawthorn hedge. There immediately came the sounds of squawking as a solitary magpie, sporting two-tone coachwork and doubtless a sore head fluttered skywards. Thereupon, Ian placed a palm to the forehead and, smartly, he saluted. "Good morning, Mr. Magpie. And, how is Mrs. Magpie today?"

"Crikey, Ian!" I said. "And you think I've lost me marbles? And," I added, as a second magpie arose from the self same hedge and joined its mate in madly sweeping the sky, "you've gone and saluted a solitary magpie that is not, in fact, solitary…"

"Meaning, old boy?"

"Meaning," I said, "that you've now brought bad luck on us both."

"That is superstitious nonsense, Gatehouse, old chap. And," he added, with a grin, "I am compelled to state, purely for the record, that coming as you do from the Black Country you already cart around bad luck in such abundance that mere Viking folk law ought to be of no concern."

I ceased tucking in my shirt. You see, as a result of all of the trotting too and forth, the item of apparel had escaped the waistband of my trousers. However, I wasn't about to render my hands totally redundant and, in barrister fashion, I employed 'em both by grasping the lapels of my jacket. "Plainly," I said in pompous barrister fashion, "you didn't notice that the thing had your matchbox in its beak."

Ian shrugged and he naturally winced. "Gatehouse, old dear, I know the precise whereabouts of the nest and I shall simply crawl up the old walnut tree later this evening for the purpose of recovering my property and..." He broke off momentarily and he winced some more but, in addition, he chuckled loudly. "I dare say that I shall also recover property that will be of interest to Billy, the pawnbroker. I refer in particular, old boy, to glittery items of personal adornment lifted from within the various open bedroom windows of the various cottages of this parish."

"Saving the tree for the benefit of the parish? You're nothing but a Fagin of the feathered friend world, you are."

"Oh, I'm being perfectly serious, Gatehouse, old chap. Indeed, the nest gave up a gold Swiss watch on the last occasion. It was in extreme bad taste being, as it was, encrusted with diamonds." Ian chuckled even louder than the first time. "Mind you, Billy paid me most handsome for that little beauty, he did."

"That's theft by finding, that is."

"Nonsense," said Ian, with a shrug, "I could not return the time piece because the owner had negligently failed to have the thing inscribed." The reprobate proceeded to tilt his head down; indeed, he lowered it so low that his chin became embedded deep into his chest. In that position, Ian finished off his defence to the accusation of theft by finding in a mumble that some might have said was, at common law, an actual admission, "I suppose, inscribed, or not inscribed, trash such as that could only have belonged to the yuppies recently moved from London and living in Rosemary Cottage."

Well, half an hour later found us at the Shipsford Railway Station. I'd have been quite happy to go the extra yard and hitch-hike all the way to Birmingham, but the snob had come out in Ian. "Gatehouse, old chap. We members of the Bar must not be observed clambering down from the passenger side of a six-wheeled juggernaut. As members of an historic and noble profession, it would be too undignified."

We occupied two spare seats next to a rather dainty-looking woman. She was too busy peering out of the mucky windows to notice that Ian had shoulder charged me out of the way thereby ensuring that it was he who was to sit right next to her. The woman looked to be right up Ian's street in terms of her being well beyond the first flush of youth and (judging from the absence of any ring) single and, all in all, potentially vulnerable. "Tell me, er…" He shrugged, winced (only a little) and then he jerked his head up a couple of times in manner to ensure not just that he had the woman's attention, but to encourage her to impart the name by which she was commonly known.

"Sally".

The stratagem had worked.

"What a beautiful name," said Ian, as quick as a flash. "Now, tell me er, Sally, can I interest you in having lunch with a barrister-at-law?"

"Why, thank you very much."

"What? Just like that?" Ian both sounded and looked astonished. He jabbed me the in ribs.

"Ouch! What did you do that for?"

"Gatehouse. I forgive you for the debacle of yesterday's date."

"Aye?"

"I have a dead certainty here, old boy." He winced, shrugged and, leaning in; he spoke in a chuckling sort of a whisper. "Gatehouse, instinct tells me that it would be altogether better were you to delay your homecoming this evening." He stopped and cranked his head towards the carriage ceiling. "Let me see now," he said in the manner of an all knowing, know bugger all, academic sort. "Just an hour or so should be sufficient, in my estimation, old dear."

"Judging from the last time, **old dear**, I'd have said that just five minutes or so should be sufficient. Although, tell a lie," I added, "I'd best make it fifteen minutes, so that you have time to shin up the walnut tree and recover your perishing match box. After all, **old dear**, I believe that, following the rigid exercise you've got in mind, it's traditional to sit up in bed and, over a smoke, discuss whether the other participant had had chance to enjoy the three hundred second dash."

"Mmmm. I see the point, Gatehouse, old chap." But, having thereby entirely missed the point, Ian turned his attentions on

Sally. He restarted his proposition thus. "On second thoughts, I have to prepare a closing speech at lunchtime for a trial in which the judge has expressed admiration of my expert cross examination..." Ian ceased jabbering for a mo', but only because he was momentarily distracted. You see, on overhearing that little ditty, I could not help but let out a cough. "We had better make it supper, Sally," said Ian on recovering his composure. "What say you, old girl? Good, then that's settled," so concluded Ian without Sally having any say in the matter touching on her virtue.

For much of the rest of the journey I nodded off and the only interruption was the occasional jab in the ribs launched from Ian whose sole motive for the sundry assaults was to obtain false testimony that his anecdotes were the God's honest truth. However, twenty minutes or so from our final destination, I was brought round by a jolt that was mightier than two, three, would you believe it, four of any jabs that the likes of Ian could muster.

"What the hell was that? Why have we stopped, Ian?"

Ian shrugged. He didn't do it by way of his normal involuntary nervous affliction. No. He shrugged for the intentional purpose of imparting to me that he had not the foggiest of notions why the seven fifteen out of Shipsford had decided to come to a juddering halt atop an embankment in the suburb of Solihull where the accent was as thick as treacle and as nerve shattering as cheap chalk on a dry board.

"It could be due to leaves on the line," said Ian, after a moment or two of silence.

Seconds later, there came a crackling from a speaker located somewhere or other. The announcement was, "We are sorry to announce that this train will be delayed while leaves are removed from the line."

"I must not be delayed," said Ian, anxiously, "I am before the magistrates at ten o'clock, charged with having run a red light."

"You stated that you were conducting a trial," stated Sally, accusingly. "Are you merely trying to impress me and, at the same time, get me intoxicated with cheap drink and then take me to your cottage on the pretext of showing me your prize winning pig, intending all along to take me to bed where you will show me something entirely different?"

It was impossible to tell whether Sally's sundry enquiries were borne of fear or hope.

Ian feigned hurt feelings. "Those are compound questions, those are." He did the feigning without hesitation. "Were I to answer with a simple yes or a straightforward no, there would be no way of telling which particular enquiry I was actually responding to. If you do not believe me then ask my colleague Gatehouse."

"Don't you go involving me, **old dear**!"

"As I was saying, Sally, before Gatehouse so rudely interrupted me. You have asked a number of questions at once and, save for the question touching my desire to impress you, all are scurrilous." Ian stood up and he took hold of the handle of the carriage door. "You have misjudged me, Sally, and now I must depart."

Sally lunged towards Ian. "No! No! Do not do it, er, whatever your name is! I beg you not to jump!"

"The name happens to be Ian."

"I am not worth it, Ian! I am so sorry!"

Ian winced and shrugged. "I shall meet you later, Sally, at The Case is Open. You know? It is the hostelry on the outskirts of Prestwick?" He turned the handle and pushed hard. "I simply cannot be late for Court." As Ian clambered out, he casually said, "Sally, just on the off chance that you arrive at the watering hole before me, mine will be a pint of beer and a large whisky chaser."

I leaned forward to observe as Ian made his way down the steep embankment. The grass was slippery with wet morning dew and, as a consequence, Ian's progress was initially slow. However, to the amusement of fellow passengers (some among their number even clapped and cheered) Ian slipped and came down hard on his rear. But, as undignified as the seating position was, the speed of Ian's decent was greatly enhanced.

At the bottom of the slope, Ian picked himself up, rubbed a few twigs and things from off of the knees and, seemingly oblivious to green grass stains and heaven knows what else all about the seat of his trousers, he gave a cheery wave and set off presumably in search of a gap in the hedge that might afford access to the highway.

At this juncture, I nudged Sally to one side and shouted through the window, "Ian! It's contrary to section 56 of the British Transport Commission Act, 1949 to go trespassing on railway property. You'll be fined or somutt, you will!"

"Nonsense, old chap!"

With a lurch, the train began to edge its way forwards. Ian tried in vain to clamber all the way back up the slope. It was no good. Each time that he clambered half way up, being neither up nor down (as The Grand Old Duke of York might have said) he fell and slid all the way back down again. Passengers stuck their heads out of the windows and clapped and cheered some more. Poor Ian. The last that I saw, as the train rounded a bend, was him running in the opposite direction with a British Railways police officer in hot pursuit.

"You are late," drawled Walter as I entered the reception of Globe Chambers.

"Yow am, yow am," concurred Damian, who, per normal, was seated atop the old plywood desk.

"Leaves on the line," I gabbled.

"My friend," said Walter, "one must always cater for unexpected eventualities. We have to depart at once for the purpose of a sentencing hearing. You will find, Izaak, that no judge will be interested in excuses for lateness, however reasonable the reasons might appear."

"But, Walter, I'll need to set out before six o'clock if I'm to have a cast iron guarantee that nothing will prevent me from being just a few minutes late."

"It woe do," said the learned clerk.

Walter snapped. "Do not be impertinent!"

"Sorry," I said, meekly.

"No, not you, you fool," and Walter pointed directly at Damian. "I mean that fool."

Damian looked astonished. "Who? Me?"

"Yes, I mean you, you fool." Walter performed a half turn. "Oh. And, another thing…"

"Yes, Mista Tweed?"

"For once and for all, I must instruct you to refrain from using the desktop as a seat."

Damian used both arms to hoist his bulky frame up and then down from off of the desktop. In the process, the seams from around the seat of his trousers gave up the ghost as was evident from a ripping sort of a noise.

"Bugger it! Oi must stop eatin' the babbies leftovers, we must!"

"Come, Izaak, my friend," said Walter, and he tutted as he did so. "We have a case to attend to."

"Before yow go," said Damian. "Oi have here robes for Mista Gatehouse to borrow." With that, Damian sauntered to the back of the desk and he produced a barrister's blue robes bag. "Here yow go," he said, thrusting the thing straight at me.

"I P!" I said, excitedly.

"Yow what?"

"You know? Look! The monogram! Igor Patterson's robes have turned up!"

My faith in fellow man was restored. Ian, who had stolen the robes from the room where I'd naively left them some weeks before, had obviously had a pang of conscience. Either that or he knew that he couldn't swan around in the robes of another knowing that the other was a member of the same set of chambers.

"Those aye Mista Patterson's robes them aye," said Damian, with authority. "Them am the robes of Ian Prospect, our new tenant." Damian plunged a chubby arm into the over-sized, school pump bag-type, bag and he produced a grey barrister's wig. "Yow can tell that Mista Prospect spends a lot of time in Court cos look…" he waved the wig under my nose. My faith in fellow man having been unrestored, I observed the wig. It was full of dust, cobwebs, and so forth where Ian had distressed the thing by use of a floor hoover turned on blow and not suck. "Now, doe yow let this lot get stolen like yow did in the case of Mista Patterson's robes. Yow have only got away with that by kind words from Mista Tweed, here, and by Mista Prospect generously permitting Mista Patterson to borrow his gowns from time to time…"

"Generous?" Walter's eyes opened wide. "Prospect has permitted Patterson the use of the robes only in return for a case of vintage port. Now, come along, Gatehouse. We simply cannot be late."

Well, we arrived in Court Two a few moments late. "What was that you were telling me earlier, Walter, about never being late?" I had every right to feel cocky considering the admonishment I'd received earlier. You see, per normal, everyone whom we encountered during the short walk from Globe Chambers to the Crown Court building were simply desperate to stop and enquire after the health and welfare of my pupil master. The road sweeper was at it, the newspaper vendor was at it. Why, even a young mum who'd gotten her pram stuck in the big swing doors was at it. "Why thank you very much. You're a gentleman, sir. And…" (*Here we go again*, I thought) "…I have to say that you're looking extremely well." The young mum peered down into her pram where a young'n, neither a suckling nor quite yet a nursling, was gurgling merrily away. "He's looking very well ain't he, Jason?"

"Werry, werry well," came a gurgling response.

Well, I thought, *would you Adam and Eve it?*

There was very little time to confer with our lay client, one Mr. Gino Fashceti. Walter simply explained that he intended to ask the judge to adopt the recommendation contained in a report. Mr. Fashceti didn't look at all nervous. Indeed, he was a cocky-looking kid, early twenties I'd have said, with a new romantic hairdo as big as his ego. Walter instructed me to explain the contents of the report to our client. Therefore, it was me, Yours Knowingly, who told Mr. Fashceti that, according to the report's author, probation was a far better alternative than prison in return for having taken a motorcar without the owner's consent and for having driven the said motorcar straight into the local canal.

Bewigged and gowned, Walter sat alongside reading the case papers. My reading matter consisted of *Dieu et mon droit* emblazoned in gold all across the back of the judge's chair, currently vacant. The only noise came from the tapping of Walter's fingers and the occasional sneeze coming from me as hair from Ian's bulldog (Dave, deceased) wafted down from the wig atop my head. The judge entered at last and he did so more or less immediately after an usher had shouted, "The judge is about to enter! Silence in Court! All rise!"

The judge (a proper, full time judge) came bounding in from a side door. Even before he'd had time to gather up his black and purple gown (not to mention the red sash), His Honour began to address the barristers present. "I must apologise for keeping the members of the Bar waiting. Would you believe that I started out from home at six o'clock?" His head shook despairingly right, then left and then right again. "Would you further believe," he said, upon his head coming to complete standstill, "that my train was delayed due to leaves on the line?"

Walter majestically got to his feet. He coughed. "Your Honour, if I may speak on behalf of the Bar, the delay is perfectly understandable; there is absolutely no need to apologise but it is nonetheless most gracious of Your Honour so to do."

Mr. Fashceti's case was called first, and so the person who took his place in the dock was, naturally enough, Mr. Fashceti himself. He strutted in a very arrogant fashion. You'd have thought that being, as he was, within a gnat's whisker of going to prison he'd have been a little more humble about the entire goings on. In fact, with a bouffant hairdo such as his, he plainly had no idea that, were he to be sent away, he'd be praying that the first gift item to be smuggled into Her Majesty's Prison was, not the standard file baked within a cake, but a bar of soap. Moreover, I do not refer to any old bar of soap but to one of those novelty soaps on a rope. Very handy, so went the rumour, for use in the communal showers where a chap wouldn't be wishing to go dropping things and then having to bend down to pick 'em up.

The Crown Prosecutor proceeded to tell the judge all about Mr.Fashceti's propensity to swipe motorcars from right outside the houses of the relevant owners at the dead of night, purely for the fun of it. He (the prosecutor that is) was like most eager prosecutors in that he looked and sounded as if he would be more at home within the ranks of the Hitler Youth. He had a jutting lower jaw and a fixed intense expression which made him look as if every single word that he espoused should be taken very seriously indeed. Why, even his, "Good Morning, Your Honour," to His Honour sounded, from his lips, as if he was imparting the fact that it was indeed morning but whether it was truly a good one was wholly dependent on His Honour handing down the very harshest of prison sentences within his remit and a good horse flogging to boot.

After he was done, Walter arose and, naturally enough, the arising was, once more, majestical. I'll tell you what though. You could have knocked me down with a feather when he told the judge, "I have an irksome sore throat and therefore, with Your Honour's permission, my pupil, Mr. Gatehouse, who sits beside me will submit why it would be appropriate to adopt the recommendation contained in the report."

Well, after my heart had performed a somersault, I looked firstly at Walter, who was grinning. Then, I glanced behind at our client. Having heard Walter's little revelation, he didn't look half as cocky. Indeed, I reckoned he was compiling his wish list and that soap on a rope was at the very top.

I stood up in an unmajestical fashion. Indeed, I sort of scrambled to my feet, knocking over a glass of water in the process. I could have sworn I saw His Honour wink at Walter.

"Well," I said, while simultaneously handling the wig atop my head (purely to make certain, you understand, that it remained in situ). "Well," I said again, "at least the defendant's choice of motor car means that there is one less Austin Allegro on the road for us to worry about."

I made the quip for the sole purpose of breaking the tension. I regret that I succeeded only in creating tension where, with the benefit of hindsight, there had been little or none to begin with.

"Would you care to explain that facetious remark?" said His Honour, while Walter (meanwhile) slapped his brow and sighed and Mr. Fashceti let forth a groaning, whimpering kind of a noise.

"Oh. Er, well, Your Honour," I stammered, wishing that the earth would swallow me up, "I actually meant to remark that, being as it was uninsured, the vehicle shouldn't have been where it could have been stolen in the first place."

I heard another slap coming from the direction of Walter's forehead.

As for His Honour. He, sort of, went all red in the face and he looked very much as if he was going to explode. He opened his mouth, with the presumed intent of letting rip, but His Honour was beaten to it by the prosecutor. "Not that it is at all relevant, Your Honour, but, as it happens, the vehicle was fully comprehensively insured."

"Aha!" I said. "Then at least, Your Honour, no one is a loser, then!"

"No one is the loser?" His Honour had spoken his words slowly and deliberately.

There came a deathly hush, broken (only for a split second, mind) by the sound of yet more flagellation of Walter's brow and, from the region of the dock, the name of The Good Lord being taken in vain.

"Well," I said, with my voice all of a tremor, "the insurance company will compensate the owner." The face on the judge was expressionless. "It will, won't it?"

His Honour came straight back. "You have omitted something."

"Oh! Ever so sorry, Your Honour! I meant to say, 'It will won't it, *Your Honour*? Your Honour!"

"No, no, no!" The judge looked in disbelief, firstly at me, then Walter, and then me, again. "Mr. Gatehouse," went His Honour, "who, at the end of the day, is out of pocket?"

"Why," I said, cheerfully, "the insurance company, of course." *And no bugger*, I thought, *has sympathy for them robbing pirates*.

"Mr. Gatehouse," went His Honour, all over again. "And, who is it that usually pays for increased premiums?"

I swallowed hard. "Er, the man of the household, Your Honour?"

"No!"

"The wife, if she's working and the husband isn't proud?"

"No, no, no! The puh..."

"Parents!" I said.

"No!"

"Well, surely not the prosecutor? I mean to say, look at him..."

"The public, Mr. Gatehouse! That's who!"

"Oh! Them!"

"Mr. Gatehouse!" His Honour sat back with such force that I feared he would go straight through *Dieu et mon droit,* the wall behind too and clean into the street; and being, as it was, a street situated within the boundary of the City of Birmingham I wouldn't have wished that on any man, not even a Circuit Judge. "Just forget the nonsense that this is a victimless crime and kindly proceed with points that are relevant!"

My hands scampered about the papers stretched before me. I was certain that something would leap out and save me further embarrassment. And I was spot on because a hand appeared from the side and, with a cough, its owner, namely Mr. Walter Tweed, barrister-at-law, lifted up the report on our client and he wafted the same under my nose.

I relieved the hand of its burden, and I cast my keen legal eye over the contents of the first page. It was regrettably necessary to have a second crack at that task because, after a moment or two, the realisation hit me that I was holding the thing upside down.

Walter put a hand to his mouth. "The conclusion," he mumbled, in a stylish kind of a drawl. "Refer to the recommendation at the end."

"I'm obliged," I said.

"What for?" said His Honour

"No, no," I said. "I'm obliged to Walter."

"Who?"

"You know? Mr. Tweed."

"Get on with it!"

"There's a report, Your Honour." I raised the thing for all to see. "The author, a Mr. Loom, makes a positive recommendation."

The judge leant forwards. He appeared to be rather confused. "Who did you say the author is?"

"Mr. Loom, Your Honour." I took another shufty. "Whoops! It's upside down, again. The author is, in fact, Mr. Wool!" His Honour said not a word but having successfully cleared up the point that was confusing him, I pressed on. "And," I laughed, "may I be permitted to state that Mr. Wool is not at all woolly in his recommendation?"

"No you may not! I have already warned you not to be facetious!"

"No, Your Honour. I mean to say, yes, Your Honour."

"Look," said His Honour, exasperated. "I am minded to follow the recommendation made in the report and order this defendant, if he is so willing, to serve a term of probation. Presumably you will not wish to persuade me to do otherwise?"

"Yes, Your Honour. Or should that be no, Your Honour?"

"What?"

Once again, my learned pupil master put hand to mouth and he mumbled. "If that is the course Your Honour proposes then I would not wish to persuade Your Honour otherwise."

"Your Honour!" I said, loud and clear. "If that is the course Your Honour proposes, then I'll have to persuade you otherwise, I will!"

"What?"

Walter was again obliged to converse through an outstretched hand. "On reflection, I would not wish to push against an open door."

"Phew, thanks," I whispered. "On reflection," I told His Honour, "I would not wish to push against an open door."

"Well," said the judge, shaking his head, "that is the only sensible thing you have said."

"Thank you, Your Honour. I'll sit down then, shall I?"

"Yes," whispered Walter.

"Yes!" barked His Honour.

"Please do," begged the prosecutor. I'd forgotten all about him.

"Thank God," sobbed the client.

So, out-gunned four to one, sort of thing, I sat down with a clatter. "Phew," I said, again. "I think that went rather well, don't you agree, Walter?"

CHAPTER SIX

Well, I'll tell you something for nothing, I will. You could have knocked me down with a feather when I arrived back in Prestwick. The usually sleepy parish was a hive of activity. As I strolled into the village, two police cars were departing, as was a fire engine, driven by one of the Shipsford volunteers who gesticulated at me with his left arm. And, permit me to add that, it was not a friendly gesticulation; indeed, the least said the better suffice to say that the bounder scurrilously alluded to what it was that I allegedly did for pleasure when all alone in the sanctity of my boudoir.

There had been dreadful thunderstorms for much of the afternoon. Indeed, before making a final dash to the village, I had been obliged to splish splash through muddy puddles and take shelter under the eaves of the electricity substation, down by Tyddemore Woods. Happily though, the final storm of the day was quick to pass. So, I deftly tore off a handy bit of rubber that someone had carelessly left attached to a wooden pole and I used the same to scrape mud from off my soles. It was therefore with pristine clean shoes, looking every inch a respectable professional, that I made the final dash.

A small crowd was gathered by the front gate of The Fly in the Ointment. As I came by and politely said, "Excuse me, please," two individuals within the congregation shook their heads despairingly. "And the same to you, mate," I said to another, who had chosen to interpret the fire fighter's hand signals. Fortunately for him, he had done the imparting from the relative safety of the back of the crowd.

There were pools of water everywhere. The pools were far too deep for mere rainwater. Furthermore, unless the radiator had gone and sprung a leak, the water could not have come from Ian's wreck of a motor car. You see, it was deposited just down the road where, according to the crowd, the fire engine had shunted the thing.

"Is there any one about?" So went my enquiry, as I went cautiously around to the rear of the cottage.

I strolled straight in. There was, in the event, no need to open the door because, where once the door had hung, there was a gap. And, purely for the record, where the kitchen had once been, there was a virtually empty room, blackened from floor to wall to ceiling. And, where the kitchen units had once been, there was a pile of sodden charcoal. The only item still standing was the receptacle used for washing vegetables and muddy boots. It was the lavatory, no longer used as such ever since the interior wall had given way. Oh! Nearly forgot! Ian was seated atop the lavatory. He looked to have a right cob on him. Indeed, his mood looked as dark as the barrister-type suit that he was still wearing.

"Where on earth is the door, Ian?"

Ian shrugged and winced, just a little. "Gatehouse! You locked the door that I repeatedly stated should be kept unlocked!"

"Meaning?"

"Meaning, old boy," said Ian, angrily, "that, for the purpose of gaining uninterrupted access, the volunteers from Shipsford fire depot took hold of a ram and went at the thing as would a horde of Vikings at the gates of an abbey."

"Couldn't they just knock like anybody else?"

Ian opted to ignore my perfectly reasonable enquiry and, typically, he changed the topic of conversation. "Gatehouse! You stated that you had checked that the oven was off."

"Well, I did try to tell you that I may have left one of the rings alight."

"You certainly did not, old boy!" Ian removed himself from the lavatory and he tootled over to the door of the sitting room. Other than for a char mark here and there, at least that portal gate was in good order. "It's too dirty in here." I craned my neck and realized that Ian was addressing The General, his prize winning Tamworth pig. "Stay in there with Colin." With an indignant hiss and meow from Colin, not to mention a squeal from The General, Ian booted the door closed. "Now then," he said, once more returning to the seated position on the disused jankhole. "You most definitely stated that it was your intention to return to the house for the purpose of collecting papers."

"Papers," I reminded Ian, "that were actually tucked under my arm at the time." I could tell that I had him thinking twice. "A point," I added, "that you were quick to remind me of."

"Meaning, Gatehouse, old chap?"

"Meaning," I said, "that, on your own admission, I wanted to re-enter the cottage on a pretext."

"Pretext?"

"Yes, Ian, a pretext." I put on my very best look of sincerity. I had practised the look for hours before a mirror because, as a barrister, it was essential to look sincere when lying. "You should have known that I simply wanted to double check things. You know? Just like them airline pilots do before whizzing off to the sun with a cargo full of hyperactive lager louts."

"Hyperactive lager louts?"

"Oh, alright then. Brummies."

"But, Gatehouse, old chap. You are always returning to check something or other..."

"And, I've been vindicated, ain't I, Ian!"

"I suppose that you have a point, old boy." Ian shrugged. "Mind you," he grumbled, in a rallying kind of a way and, I might add, in a manner far too cruel for my liking, "that is not to say I concede that crocodiles and tigers reside beneath the cracked pavement slabs."

I was about to protest and look sincere all over again but noticed that Ian was staring straight over my left shoulder.

I heard a cough and I turned and there, stood in the space formerly known as the back door, was an exceedingly officious looking man. I reckoned that he would have stood five foot nothing in his stocking feet, save and except that, in this instance, he wore a pair of black brogues that didn't go terribly well with the cavalry twill trousers. He had the look of a local government officer about him, and that's a fact. You know the sort? Never had to make an honest bob in his life and a stickler for enforcing every rule in the handbook no matter how nonsensical they happen to be. He wore a Fair Isle sweater beneath a greasy looking sports coat. Stuck in the breast pocket, a neat row of biros was standing to attention. Yes. He just had to be a local government official, all right.

"I'm from the Shipsford-upon-Avon Housing Department," he said, only going to prove that my powers of deduction were positively spot on. He uttered the introduction through teeth that were as neatly lined up as the biros save and except that the top row tended to jut out, even after closure of the mouth. If ever there had been a beauty contest for local council officials, this one would have walked away with a red rosette. "There is fire damage," said the man, following this briefest of introductions. As he brushed from his shoulders a concoction of dandruff and bits of asbestos, I was a-thinking, *your observational talents are wasted at the council, mate.*

"And, what business is it of yours, my man?" said Ian, dethroning himself and scooting to the gap where the before mentioned door had once been. On the way across, it was necessary for Ian to take the very shortest of diversions to avoid colliding with a light bulb that was dangling precariously from an electrical cable.

"Information has been forthcoming," said the man, whilst simultaneously spitting through his upper row of tombstones, "that this abode is uninhabitable."

"And, where, old chum, does this so called information originate?"

"As it happens, I have an appointment up at The Hall where I am to view converted barns..."

Ian interrupted. "Janie and her family are not informers."

"I am not at liberty to disclose my sources, but it is certainly not the inhabitants of The Hall."

"Aha!" so said Ian, with a shrug and, not one, but two winces. "It is quite obvious that my damnable landlord is once again seeking vacant possession free..."

"Yeh!" I chipped in. "Vacant possession free from all encumbrances, that's what he wants, mate."

"And, who, may I enquire, are you?"

"He is an encumbrance," said Ian.

"Whoever the informant might be (and I make no admissions, sir) the fact remains that this cottage is not fit for human habitation."

Ian shrugged and winced, but only the once. "The abode is perfectly habitable, my good man. What you witness here is a little smoke damage, nothing more, nothing less, and if you would care to accompany me to…"

Ian was interrupted, once again. Only the chipping in was not me, the encumbrance, but it was The General squealing to be let out.

"What in heaven's name is that?" spluttered the man from the council.

"What is what?" said Ian, with a shrug.

"Yeh," I said. "What's what?"

The General let forth a particularly ear piercing shriek. "My God!" said the man, and his eyes darted about the kitchen, or, to be exact, what was formerly the kitchen. "Those are the sounds of an Essex, and," he said, eyes coming to rest on the sitting room door, "the cries come from within!"

"That is nonsense, my good fellow! The noises emanating from within are those of The General, my prize winning Tamworth! Do you truly believe that such noble cries emanate from the likes of a Sally or a Trudy?"

"I simply must investigate," spluttered the man, and, without as much as an *excuse me, please* he side-stepped Ian, almost succeeded in side stepping the electrical cable, and said, "Ouch! Bloody hell, that's dangerous, that is!" He nonetheless made it to the door of the living room which he proceeded to open by means of the hand that did not look to be in urgent need of hospital treatment. "Good heavens, above!" That is what he hollered as The General barged past. "That, sir, is not a pure bred Tamworth! You have crossed a Duroc and a Tamworth! Amazing!"

"Well, actually, old chap, I crossed a Waddle with a Tamworth…"

"A Waddle? A Waddle?" Now, far be it for me to say, but he sounded exceedingly impressed. "I have heard of the recently imported Waddles, but never before have I encountered one."

Ian shrugged. Strangely, he didn't simultaneously wince. "You seem to be very well informed, my fellow."

"Well, Ian. I can be permitted to call you Ian, I hope?"

"Of course, old thing."

"Well, Ian. I was brought up on a farm and, indeed, I hope one day to return to life on a farm. My wife, you see, is a farmer's daughter." The bureaucrat within the man had vanished. Indeed, he addressed Ian with wide-eyed wonderment.

"It is like this, old thing," said Ian, placing his eccentric clay to the lips. "In the good old days, a bit of lard in the old Sunday joint was of no consequence because, come Monday, Freddy Farmworker would simply sweat the stuff off in the fields." Ian paused while he tapped both hands over his trouser pockets, presumably in search of his infernal brass matchbox. "Regrettably," continued Ian, after the tap tapping proved fruitless, "those times are forever gone and…" He paused again, only on that occasion to address the other party present. You know? Me, Yours Patiently. "Be a good chap and shimmy up the walnut tree and recover my chattel? I would do it myself but I have to attend upon our friend, here. Mr?"

"Oh! Please do call me Cecil."

"So, you see, Cecil, in keeping with the mood within the realm that animal fat tends to clog up the old arteries, I have crossed the sweet succulence of a Tamworth with the lean meat of a Waddle, recently introduced from the Americas."

"That is brilliant, Ian!"

"'Tis a shame the pig breeding association Johnnies do not have your foresight, Cecil, old thing." Ian clapped both hands. "Hence the necessity to pass off The General, here, as pure bred." Ian was plainly relishing the adoration. "Mind you, old sport, I did not reckon on winning best of breed at the County Show." Ian winced and chuckled. "I shall tell you what."

"What?"

"I will show you the litter, old dear heart. I have them in a rudimentary pen out back, if you would care to walk this way."

"Great! Thank you!"

"Mind the cable, old…"

"Ouch!"

"Too late."

"Blimey! I felt that meself!" Yes, I was still there but you would not have guessed it, what with all the aforementioned bonding of Ian and Cecil.

"Are you still here, Gatehouse, old dear?"

I stood smartly to attention as Ian came by. "I'll shimmy up the tree in just a minute, **old dear**, but, in the meantime, there is a favour that Cecil can do for me." I reached into my pocket and I produced the note, now crumpled, that I had prepared for Janie's eyes only. "Did you say that you have to go along to The Hall, Cecil?"

"Why, yes, I did."

I thrust forward the note and, by reason of reflex action or just plain stupidity, Cecil took hold of the same. "It's strictly for the attention of the addressee only," I said. "And, in view of its sensual, er…" I coughed. "In view of its legal nature, you had better make certain that the handing over of the note is done in secret, sort of thing."

Cecil raised both eyebrows. "Is this normal practice?"

Ian shrugged and winced. "I suspect, old boy, that there would be grave consequences was a note such as that flutter into the wrong hands. And, when I refer to a note," he added, "I do so loosely when one considers that it is the size of an average Dead Sea Scroll."

"Then, for you two gentlemen," said Cecil, boldly, "I shall ensure that the conveying of this communiqué is done efficiently and quickly. And," he added, after a brief pause which was presumably for dramatic effect, "I shall do so with utmost secrecy."

With that, I made my way across the road to the walnut tree. Ian made his way up the garden where the wall of the outside lavatory comprised one quarter of a makeshift pigsty and miscellaneous items of garden furniture borrowed from the various surrounding properties made up the remainder. He precariously steered Cecil by means of a right hand over Cecil's left shoulder. "Do you know what, Ian? I intend to ensure that the landlord is prohibited from illegally evicting you."

"Well, thank you very much, Cecil, old thing."

"The council will force him to carry out all necessary repairs."

"Well, thank you, Cecil, old chap. Much obliged to you. Now, mind that deep puddle, old thing."

"Agh!"

"Too late."

Meanwhile, I precariously ascended the walnut tree. You might know that the magpie nest was in the very highest of bows. Still, I made it up there, I did, and I did so by sustaining relatively few scratches and cuts. To afford free and uninterrupted access, I found it necessary to shimmy along a lower branch that tended to bend a bit under my weight. I recall fearing that, at any moment, the branch might snap and send me tumbling headlong into the paddock below.

I could hear Ian and Cecil jabberwocking. It was despite the fact that they were stood in the rear garden of The Fly in the Ointment. And, assuming that you've been paying attention, you will doubtless recall that The Fly in the Ointment was dead opposite the walnut tree and it was on the other side of the road. I'd seen the same, every noise shooting up from below, principle applied when I'd watched a programme on balloonists hurtling through the skies of Africa. Other than when the hot air thingy was letting out a blast, it was possible to hear a pin drop on the Serengeti.

"Take care that you do not go tumbling off the fence, Cecil, old dear heart."

"Oops!"

"Too late, Cecil, old chap. However, you will be gratified by the knowledge that pig muck is reputed to be good for the complexion, though I concede that jackets of the finest Harris Tweed tend to come off second best."

High in the canopy, I reached into the nest and I ferreted around a bit. The first item that I managed to cop hold of was the thieving *Pica Pica* herself who squawked, had a bash at pecking out my eyeballs, and then she hurtled off as would an Exocet missile. Next, came Ian's damnable matchbox. For the record, it looked a bit the worst for wear being, as it was, flattened. *Hmm,* I thought, *that's what happens when you go slinging objets d'art in the hedgerow, that is.* Then, I came across a set of car keys. They were attached to a leather fob, complete with a Porsche badge. I naturally assumed that the thing belonged to the local yuppies, recently moved from London. Porsches, you see, were very much in vogue with that sort and so I made a mental note to shove the keys through the fancy-looking letterbox of Rosemary Cottage when I was next passing. Last but not least, tangled up in nesting material (plus a gooey substance the source of which I never wish to know), I fished out a lady's ring. It was not any old plain ring but a glittery engagement-type ring. You simply would not have believed the size of the cluster. The thing was probably worth a small fortune to the likes of Billy the pawnbroker. Further and additionally, I reasoned, it wouldn't half impress Janie were I to sling that load of carats onto the appropriate finger of her left hand. *You little beauty,* I thought, and I promptly kissed the ring and secreted it in my pocket.

"Nesting is illegal!" The voice drifted up from below and, once again, I was reminded of balloonists in Africa. Only, I wasn't whizzing over the Serengeti and neither for that matter was the voice emanating from the lips of some tribal chief holding a bazooka. It was Police Constable Stringer and he had plainly decided to take a break from trying to solve the riddle of the disappearing garden furniture. In lieu thereof, he had obviously decided to apprehend me, Yours Forever Victimised, on suspicion of nicking wild bird eggs.

"I ain't contravened the Wildlife and Countryside Act, 1981!" I hastily made my way back to terra firma.

The officer placed both arms behind his back and, in the manner of a copper, he rode up and down on the balls of his feet a few times. There was an uncomfortable silence which at last was broken when the officer said, "If you're not stealing wild bird eggs, then tell me, jungle boy, why have you been up a tree with your thieving hands inserted in a nest belonging to wild birds?"

"Officer," I protested. "It's them ruddy wild birds who are the thieves; not me, mate, and that's the truth."

"So, we have ourselves a comedian, do we?" The officer reached into the pocket of his dark blue tunic and he produced a pair of handcuffs. "Follow me peacefully to the car, Mowgli, or otherwise I shall be forced to cuff you."

"Call a Mini Clubman a car? That's a good one, that is. And, what's more," I added, "I wouldn't go flashing those shiny handcuffs around if I were you."

"Why?" said the officer. "Will you accuse me of oppressive conduct, or something?"

"No. Not at all," I said. "It's just that the thieving birds will have them."

"Right! That's it! Let's have your wrists! I'm arresting you on suspicion of...!" The officer was interrupted by the frantic neighing of a horse. The neighing was immediately followed by shouting and yelps. We both cranked our heads in the direction of Tyddemore Woods and were just in time to spy a piebald horse rearing up and its rider sliding off the stern. "It's the Major!" shouted the police officer. "Major East has come off his horse!"

P.C. Stringer promptly dropped his handcuffs, ran to the edge of the paddock, whence he sprinted up the lane at a speed that would have done your average lion on the Serengeti proud. I placed cupped hands to my mouth. "I'd best try to phone for an ambulance!" It was necessary to shout so that I could be heard above a loud din as steel-capped boots worn by the officer clip clapped up the road. By the time that I reached the edge of the paddock (having naturally failed to act with the same degree of urgency), P.C. Stringer had very nearly reached the scene of the accident. The horse, meanwhile, galloped by with its hooves of iron going fifteen to the dozen on the unforgiving surface of the road.

Next, Ian emerged from the back of the cottage. He was quickly followed by the man from the council. Cecil, I am duty bound to report, was covered from head to toe in a foul smelling cocktail of pig muck and mud. "Gatehouse!" shouted Ian. "That was my damnable landlord's horse!"

"The Major's been thrown, Ian! It looks dead serious!"

"We can but hope, old boy!" The three of us; that's Ian, Cecil, and me, stood in line observing the servant of the people going about his duties.

"That's very odd," said Cecil. He was right, and all. For, what we observed was exceedingly odd. You see, upon P.C. Stringer arriving at the spot where Major East (otherwise referred to as the damnable landlord) was laying, there was no performance of the kiss of life or whatever other life saving techniques were traditional in such circumstances. Indeed, the officer did not bother to bend down. In lieu thereof, the officer of the law began jumping from one foot to the other and he whooped in pain, as would a High Court Judge who is handcuffed to the bed in a bordello.

We casually strolled up the road. "Ian," I said, "has he gone and joined the band of perverts that you're always hanging around with?"

"Not even the Shipsford Morris Men would accept the likes of him as a member, old chap."

"Sparks!" said Cecil, excitedly, whilst simultaneously spluttering through the tombstones. "There are sparks coming from beneath his boots!"

We broke into a trot and, as we neared the constable, I could see that Cecil was perfectly correct. Every time that the officer placed a boot on the ground, there came a crackle and a flash. And, as we drew near, I could hear the Major cussing. "Damnation, Stringer! Stop fooling around and help me to my feet!" The Major was still lying in the road, dead centre, to be exact. So, I went to assist him while Ian went to help the police officer and Cecil (in the nature of a local government official) stood frozen and did nothing. I grabbed the Major's arm and I tried to yank him to his feet. But, there were a pair of vicious spurs attached to his shiny brown riding boots. Just as soon as these came into contact with the surface of the road, sparks (just like those coming from P.C. Stringer) started flying. "Ouch! Good God, you idiot! Leave me alone!" And, with that, the

Major rolled onto his tummy and crawled towards the grassy verge. Meanwhile, Ian tugged the constable by his tunic and pulled him over to the opposite verge.

"What on earth has happened?" I said it whilst simultaneously helping the Major to his feet.

The Major hobbled around a bit, as if in pain. Firstly he rubbed his waist. Then, he rubbed the left side of his breeches. They were torn and were plainly destined for the rag and bone man. As would a spoilt child, the Major stomped both feet on the verge in quick succession. "I shall tell you what has happened," said the Major, after he was done with his display. "The dashed road surface is live with electricity. It is no wonder the bally horse has bolted."

P.C. Stringer, meanwhile, hastily removed his boots. "I certainly shall not be wearing steel toecaps and studs ever again," he said. "I shall have to call the emergency services and, in the meantime, have the road closed." He rubbed his head a few times. "It's a remarkable phenomenon. I've never come across anything like it before."

At this juncture, Cecil unfroze himself. "Dark and mysterious forces are afoot," he spluttered.

Ian winced, shrugged and (naturally) chuckled at that one. "Dark and mysterious forces? Total poppycock," he said. "Look you yonder at the telegraph pole."

We all looked yonder, sort of thing. "Where?"

"There," said Ian, with a nod. "Some damned fool has removed the rubber insulation from its base. That is why, good people, the road is live with electricity, what with all this damp weather an' all."

The officer of the law went as if to re-boot himself. He thought better of it, however, and in lieu thereof he rolled up the blue officer of the law type trousers. Then, with only a pair of socks between him, his person, and the road surface, the constable strode yonder towards the wooden telegraph pole. It was necessary for the officer to paddle through muddy puddles for the purpose of going about his duty. At journey's end, with his feet positively caked in mud, P.C. Stringer bent down and peered at the base of the pole. "You are quite correct, Mr.

Prospect. Someone has committed wanton criminal damage by tearing off the insulating hose. It's no wonder the road surface is charged with electricity." The officer looked in our direction. "For heaven's sake, remove any metal items from your respective personages."

"Stringer!" shouted the Major.

"Yes, Major East, sir?"

"I want you to apprehend whoever committed this crime and have the bounder horse whipped!"

"Oh, don't you worry, sir," said the officer, with determination. "My investigations will commence with immediate effect."

On the basis that attack is the best means of defence, I reasoned that it was appropriate to have my say. "I ain't in breach of section 1 of The Criminal Damage Act, 1971 and that's a fact! I weren't even here! And, even if I was here," I protested, "then I ain't done nothing, intentional or otherwise!"

I was about to follow through with notice of an alibi (naturally a false one, but all barristers are adept at promoting those ruddy things) when Major East waded in. "It's damned well obvious that the felon will have filthy muddy footwear. Look at the state of your feet, Stringer."

"Well," said the officer, "I can discount Mr. Gatehouse from my enquiries. Look at his shoes." All persons present, me included, took a long inquisitive look at my footwear. "Clean as a whistle," said the officer, as soon as the inspection was done with. "You, on the other hand…"

"Who?" Cecil pointed at his own chest. "Me?"

"Yes, you. Your feet are plastered in mud."

"As indeed is his entire person," added the Major, putting the metaphoric boot in.

"You have some explaining to do, sir," said the officer, sternly, fetching out a pocket notebook from a pocket. "Now then, you do not have to say anything if you do not wish to but anything you do say…"

The officer was interrupted by a feminine voice. "Gosh, Ian, I have heard about the fire. Are you all right?" The voice that interrupted the officer going about his duties belonged to none other than Sally. You know? Ian's conquest elect? Her from the train? You see, while the kafuffle was going on, Sally had strolled up the lane from Heaven-knows where.

"Sally, old girl!" Ian naturally said it with a wince and a chuckle.

"Sally?" spluttered Cecil. "I thought that you said you were intending to work late tonight?"

Sally blushed profusely. "I, er, it's sort of like this…"

Ian dived in. "What a small world we live in, Cecil, old chap. Sally, here, contacted me for the purpose of enquiring about the purchase of a wiener." He paused and turned to me, Yours Totally Baffled. "In other words, a piglet, Gatehouse." With that little jibe out of the way, Ian re-focused on Cecil. "I have the little fellow with the wattles on the face lined up for you, old chum…" I braced myself for another jibe. "Dangly bits to you, Gatehouse."

"That's Eric, that is! He ain't having Eric, Ian!"

I suppose that I had best explain that, of the eight piglets born of The General, Eric was my particular favourite. He trotted alongside wherever I went up the garden, especially when I was answering nature's calling in the outside lavatory. And, seeing as how my answering was usually done at gone midnight when ghosts, hobgoblins, rabbits, and heaven knows what else might be lurking, Eric's constant company came as welcome relief.

"Oh, Sally," sighed Cecil, with only the tiniest of splutters. "Here was me beginning to doubt you."

"I assume," said Ian, "that Sally is the wife of whom you spoke earlier?"

"She is, Ian."

"She adorns no wedding ring?"

"Adventist," said Cecil.

"Nonsense," I said. "It's months till Christmas."

"And, she, Cecil, old dear heart, is the one of farming stock?"

"Yes, Ian."

"Well, I'll be dashed."

"And, and," said Sally, having sufficiently recovered to do what comes natural to womenfolk, namely completely turn the tables, "I do not take kindly to you casting aspersions when I am here for the sole purpose of purchasing a suckling pig for roasting at your surprise birthday party!"

"I'm so sorry to have doubted you…"

Cecil was interrupted by the Major. "When you are quite done, my man, may I remind you that you are about to be incarcerated and horse whipped for causing criminal damage?" Major East turned towards me, Yours Devastated, at news of Eric's imminent demise. "Be a good fellow and pick-up my horse crop, would you?"

"A what?"

"My stick, you damned fool." The Major jabbed his forefinger in the direction of the middle of the road. "There it is. I cannot possibly go myself for fear of being roasted."

I nipped into the road and recovered a dark coloured stick made of leather.

"Thank you," said the Major, politely. "Now then!" he barked, with a change of tune and, at the same time, he thwacked the crop hard against the side of one of his riding boots. "Stringer! Arrest this man!"

Cecil, Ian, and Sally looked shocked at the Major's outburst. I simply made a mental note that there stood a walking talking example of the dangers of toffs marrying first cousins.

Police Constable Stringer returned the pocket notebook to his pocket and he reached for his belt. "Extend your wrists, please, sir."

"No point," I said.

"Keep out of this, jungle boy, or you'll be next."

"The handcuffs," I said. "You won't find 'em. Them thieving birds will have made off with them by now."

"While I am at the police station," spluttered Cecil, "I shall request that facilities are set aside so that I might ask questions of the Major under caution."

The offside of the Major's boot became the recipient of a further whacking. "Explain yourself, sir!"

"Yes," said Ian, with a shrug and a smug grin, "explain yourself, Cecil, old chum."

So, Cecil proceeded to explain himself. He explained that, by virtue of the Protection from Eviction Act, 1977, it was illegal of the Major to try to obtain possession of The Fly in the Ointment without due process of law.

"But, the dashed bounder pays me no rent!"

"It makes no difference," spluttered Cecil. "And, furthermore, the essential facilities within the property are in a state of disrepair."

"Meaning?"

"Meaning that, if you are to avoid prosecution, certain essential repairs must be carried out."

"But, it will cost a fortune."

P.C. Stringer grasped Cecil's arm. "Enough of this nonsense. I want you to accompany me to the police station."

"Now, now, Stringer," said the Major, having miraculously calmed down, "let us not be too hasty. Indeed, I think we should all adjourn to The Grange where Cynthia will make tea."

Cecil raised his eyebrows. "I'm rather confused. Who is Cynthia?"

"His first cousin," I said.

"Tea sounds a very sensible idea," said the constable.

"Oh no," said the Major. "My invitation does not extend to you. There is a horse on the loose, Stringer."

"Not any more there isn't." Would you believe that another female had crept up on us unnoticed? It was the flame-haired Nurse Stringer, wife of Police Officer Stringer, companion of Ian Prospect, and the Genghis Khan of men's surgical. "I have deposited the horse in a field, though not before I had to swerve to avoid hitting the thing and instead I hit a telegraph pole." We all stood open mouthed and, for her part, Nurse Stringer stood with arms folded, her long flaming red hair swishing about in the breeze. She eyed each one of us in turn, starting with me, Yours Victimised. "I might have known that you would somehow be involved." Sally was the last in the line-up. "And, **who** do we have here?"

"**I** am married to **him**," and Sally looked at Cecil. "But, I happen to be here because I have come to see **him**," and she looked at Ian. "Tell me, Nurse, er..."

"Stringer!" I volunteered, on behalf of the flame-haired one.

"Tell me, Nurse Stringer." It was Sally's turn, you see. "Why do you happen to be here?"

The red-haired harbinger went a bit flushed in the face. "**I** am here to see **him**," and, she also looked at Ian. From a square pocket in her stripy nurse-type dress, she fetched out her little dolly, Maud. Without uttering a solitary word, the nurse approached Sally, grabbed an arm and thrust Maud into an outstretched hand. "Ooops! Nearly forgot!" The harbinger retook the dolly and, slowly and purposely, she bent the legs so that Maud's tiny feet were actually wrapped around her tiny head. Duly contorted, the dolly was returned to Sally's palm.

Ian winced, not once, twice, not even thrice, but, four times. "Pervert," he said.

CHAPTER SEVEN

"Gatehouse!" Ian and I had returned to the cottage. "Eric is for the chop and there is nothing that you can do about it!" We were stood in the kitchen that resembled a disaster zone, but which Ian insisted had merely sustained a bit of smoke damage. "Furthermore, old chap, you will have to stay behind in the morning because, with Cecil's knowledge and consent, I have an engagement with Sally." He duly coughed.

"Yes, Ian?"

"The purpose, old dear, is to lay plans for the forthcoming pig roast." Ian winced, shrugged, chuckled (naturally), raised his eyebrows up and down five, six, seven times (in a knowing kind of a way), and then he added, "Gatehouse, old chap. The engagement with the Adventist, Sally is to be an adventurous one, if you get my drift?"

"Oh, I get the drift, alright. But, how come I have to stay behind especially when this..." It was my turn to cough. "When this adventurous engagement of yours is likely to take just ten minutes? Indeed, **old dear**, it ought to take only a couple of minutes taking account of the time necessary for disrobing and robing."

Oblivious to the jibe, as thick skinned as ever was the rind of a Tamworth crossed with a Waddle, Ian explained. "Your presence is required, old boy, for the purpose of handing over the sacrificial offering to the slaughterer."

"Slaughterer?" I said, aghast. "Slaughterer?" I said, again, with even more aghasting than the first time.

"Gatehouse!" said Ian. "It is time for Eric to depart this life and to take the starring role in the pig roast devoted to Cecil to which, I might add, you are cordially invited."

"But, Ian!" I cried. "I keep telling you that Eric's me favourite!"

"Gatehouse," said Ian, "it is a well-known fact that in that part of the world from which you hail. You know? Dudmore..."

"Dudsall," I corrected him, quickly.

"Wherever," said Ian, dismissively. "Anyway, it is a well-known fact that up in The Black Country, be it in Dudmore, Dudsall, even West Bromwich, for Pete's sake, the staple diet is *Sus scrofa domestica,* stuffed between entire loaves of white bread all of which have been liberally buttered."

"And, the point is?" I said scornfully.

"The point is," replied Ian, with a shrug and a wince, "do not be so dashed hypocritical."

Come midnight, I was to be found lurking in the back garden. Never mind the ghosts, hobgoblins, not to mention the fearsome rabbits; I had a mission to accomplish. The aim of my mission was to save *Sus scrofa domestica* from the chop. I would achieve accomplishment of my mission by removing and returning to its lawful owner a section of that part of the pigpen which comprised furniture stolen from the various gardens of the parish. *This here half-moon bench will do,* I reasoned. *Not even Ian will have the gall to demand the vicar to return his own half-moon bench.* Having duly afforded a theoretical route by which Eric could be assumed to have forever legged-it to the wilds (well, Breeve Hill if you want to go all technical on me), I would, in actual fact, plonk Eric in the compound of the electricity substation until the murderous slaughterer had come and gone. Why, I might even find time to nip down to the frozen food centre, purchase a few rounds of streaky Danish, and pass those off as prime Tamworth crossed with Waddle. *There ain't nothing*, I figured, *that can possibly go wrong.*

"Ouch! You little devil! You've bitten me, you have! Now, come back here before you get knocked down by a car or somutt!"

Eric took off as would a whippet chasing a poodle on Dudsall Common. By the time that I had reached the garden gate, the little porker had sprinted into the centre of the village. By the time that I had reached the centre of the village, he'd gone out the other side and was well on his way down the lane towards the river where all the posh houses were.

Heaven knows how (I was exhausted by the time that I'd reached the old village cross), but I managed a late sprint finish and was just in time to see Eric's curly tail disappear between a pair of wrought iron gates.

The gates squeaked a bit as I went through. *Could do with a bit of grease,* I thought. Then, just to my right, I saw Eric. He was standing stone still on a little grassy embankment. But, it was not possible to simply stroll over, pop the little fellow under an arm, and trot off, as would Tom, Tom the Piper's Son. The embankment, you see, was directly beneath a very large window of a very large house. Further and additionally, the light that emitted through the window shone like a beacon. So, I got down on all fours and crawled towards Eric.

"Got you, you little monkey. Now, stop struggling."

I heard the muffled tones of people talking from within the house. Naturally, I just had to pop my head up and have a peep through the window. And, who was in the room? Who was looking as lovely as ever? Yes, it was Janie! Let the Good Lord strike me down and commit me to eternal damnation if I'm telling you a lie. It was Janie, all right, and I had obviously wandered into the grounds of her abode, the mysterious Hall, of which everyone in the village spoke. And, moreover, that scurrilous rogue William Anker, you know, young Pinstripe? Well, he was there too. He and Janie were besides one another on a chaise longue. Pinstripe had plainly ingratiated himself because the bounder lay sprawled with both feet on the furniture. He hadn't even had the good grace to remove his shoes.

There were other parties present and I would have recognised them anywhere. They were Janie's so-called family and/or friends. They didn't hang around though because, after a bit of a chit chat and a few giggles, the said parties present went through a door of light oak and promptly became parties no longer present. By becoming parties no longer present, they had recklessly left their changeling in the clutches of the atrocious Pinstripe.

Just as soon as they were alone, young Pinstripe sidled over to a cabinet where, with one miserable hand, he seized a cut glass tumbler. With the other miserable hand, Pinstripe poured himself a whisky of gargantuan proportions. Next, he took hold of a pair of tongs and, from a pineapple-shape bucket he copped hold of a whole load of ice and slung it in the tumbler.

Clutching what greatly resembled a goodly portion of the Arctic shelf, the chancer returned to the chaise longue. He perched himself so close to Janie that you would have had a job inserting cigarette paper between the pair of them. Then, Pinstripe took a swig from the tumbler and he whispered something into Janie's ear. *My God!* That's what I thought. *He's going for second base!* Janie smiled. I daresay egged-on a bit, the scoundrel placed a before-mentioned miserable hand straight onto her thigh. Pinstripe had himself another gulp. It was a disgraceful sight to behold, it was. Anyone knows that no true gentleman would chuck ice cubes into a glass of single malt.

With his groping done, Pinstripe slithered off the chaise longue and he faced Janie on a bended knee.

"Ouch, you little sod! You've bitten me, again!" I dropped Eric and I instinctively shot to my feet.

"Izaak? Izaak? Is that you?" Janie's tones were muffled. She too shot to her feet and she hurried towards the window. "Izaak!" she went again, only her voice was clearer and somewhat louder. "I see that now you have turned to voyeurism in addition to everything else!" Janie looked positively angry (yet strangely attractive on account of it). But, it was a pity that she hadn't bothered to turn around and take a gander at Pinstripe's reaction instead of picking on me. Had she so done, Janie would have seen a face so contorted with anger that it would have put the frighteners on *La Cosa Nostra*. She wouldn't have relished waking-up next to that every morning, I can tell you. And, that's only assuming that, once he'd done with Janie and seized her assets, he would bother to come home from his previous night's whoring!

I heard a click and the whole of the front of the house became bathed in light. A large door opened and into the light stepped Janie's family and/or friends.

"Oh! Hi, there," I said, casually, "I'm chasing a pig that's on the loose, I am."

The beauty that was Janie's face appeared above their shoulders. One of their number, with gaping jaw, stepped aside so that she could come forward. "And, what pig is that then, Izaak?" Janie spoke coldly and calmly. It was very becoming, it was. She wore the usual trousers of dark linen only, this time, a cashmere jersey over her white shirt. Per normal, her ensemble was plain yet fetching and tasteful.

"It's Eric," I said. "He's escaped."

"And, where..." said Janie, still coldly and still calmly. "And, where is Eric?"

I looked downwards, southerly. "He's here somewhere, Janie, I promise he is." I performed a 360-degree anti clockwise turn. I raised both my arms, despairingly. "He's run off again, Janie. It's Ian, you see, he's... Oops!" I did all the degrees, again, only clockwise. Otherwise, the bogeyman might have got me. "He's out to murder him, dead, Janie, he is."

You might know that Pinstripe duly appeared and stuck his oar in. "Gatehouse, you maniac! This time you have gone too far!"

"It's you who's gone too far! I know your game, mate, and that's a fact!"

"You will be enjoined, Gatehouse!" Pinstripe stuck his sneering face to within inches of mine. I'd have sworn he was trying to goad me. "Miss Jetty will be applying to have you committed to prison for breach of your undertaking not to annoy her! In fact...!" He paused, only for a moment, mind, and then he pulled out of his trouser pocket one of the brand new mobile phone thingies that Damian, back at Chambers, was always playing around with. "I'm calling the law, Gatehouse!"

"What?" I said. "You'll make a call using that blooming house brick?" I had actually wondered what the bulge was in his pocket when I'd spied young Pinstripe trotting over to the drinks cabinet. I didn't like to report it to you at the time because you'd have only gone accusing me of smuttiness and inappropriate writings of the grand order. "And, here's me thinking, Anker, that you had gotten excited."

"Why, you...!" Pinstripe lunged, but I was too quick and he went headlong into the hydrangeas. "Dash it, Gatehouse, I've dropped my mobile!" I'd dodged tougher and quicker men than him in my time; in Dudsall on a Saturday night, to be exact, where the glam rockers at The George were likely to shove their Stratocasters where the sun don't shine if you so much as hinted that *Sus scrofa domestica* might fly before they would ever make it into the singles chart, let alone knock *T Rex* off the top slot.

"I should leave it for the magpies if I were you, Anker! Them ruddy toys ain't about to catch on!" Ignoring the prophecy, young Pinstripe determinedly groped about the shrubs in search of his mobile. I, meanwhile, made direct eye contact with my beloved Janie. *Oh, my dearest sweet love*, I thought, *can you not see that the rogue who is cussing in the shrubbery is without honour? Can you not see, Janie, that I wish only to love you and to devote myself to your everlasting happiness?*

"Listen, Janie," I said, "that tosser is just out to shag you rotten, rob you, and then cheat on you with a bunch of prostitutes!"

"Oh! Izaak! How can you say such things?"

"And, and, while I'm about it, listen to this Janie! Oh, yes! I'll shag you rigid, all right, but, but...!"

"Oh! Izaak!"

"But, at least it'll be my head on the pillow in the morning and not some horse's head, and, and...!"

"Oh! Izaak!"

"And, and, you can stuff the ruddy money cause I'd rather you be stony broke and, and, any case, I'll starve before I take money from you, I will!"

"Oh! Izaak!"

It was the turn of my hand to go plunging into a pocket. After a bit of ferreting, I located the glittery ring and I thrust it forth. In the spot lit setting, the encrusted ring sparkled and shone. I felt certain that any woman would be captivated by the beauty of the thing. As was traditional in such romantic circumstances, I took hold of Janie's left hand and I went down on bended knee.

"What say you, Janie?"

"What I say, Izaak, is what, in God's name, are you doing with my ring?"

"Aye?"

I inspected the ring. Then, I loosed hold of Janie's left hand and, by way of alternative, I took hold of her right hand. The mysterious glittery ring that always adorned the said right hand had mysteriously vanished.

Janie shook free the ring-less hand and she stepped back apace. Her huge and beautiful eyes were the most humongous I had ever seen them to be. "Izaak, I keep that most precious of rings on the shelf of my bedroom window!" She gasped. "Izaak! You have come only to steal from me!"

"Burglar! Thief!" It was naturally him, young Pinstripe, who was casting the aspersions. He had obviously given up searching for the house brick. Having crawled back from the shrubbery, Pinstripe was still on all fours and, as such, he once again managed to be right in my face.

I decided that it would be prudent to postpone my proposal of marriage until I'd gotten rid of a few judgement debts and was thereby eligible to order a diamante ring through a mail order catalogue. "Calm down, everyone," I said, and I nimbly leapt up. "Just you calm down and take a look at these." I reinserted my hand deep inside the pocket and fetched out the Porsche keys." There you go," I said, with confidence, "I keep telling everyone that the only thieves around here are them ruddy magpies."

As quick as a flash, Pinstripe also leapt up and, by so doing, he was in my face, again. "My God, Gatehouse!" He snatched the car keys from my hands. "You are trying to steal my Porsche!"

CHAPTER EIGHT

A few weeks passed. Matters on the breach of an undertaking point were ominously quiet; indeed, I was hoping that the whole thing might have died a natural death. I was not about to be wholly complacent, however, because it was common knowledge that the court service was at breaking point and cases were taking months to come before the courts. I therefore aired on the side of caution, kept my head down, and I used the potential false dawn as a window of opportunity to figure out whom I was, where I was going, and so forth.

The day of Cecil's celebration came and went without incident. Well, almost without incident. In fact, to tell the truth, it was a debacle. You see, the pig roast was the main feature of the party. Indeed, the shindig had been advertised as such. *A Pig Roast* went the written invitation, *In honour of my Beloved Husband, Cecil*. The word about the parish and surrounding countryside was that it was a pig roast not to be missed. It was intended that the centrepiece be the carcass of Eric, a succulent, pure-ish bred Tamworth, complete with a pleasing aesthetic touch in the form of an apple stuffed in his little cake hole.

"Gatehouse! You assured me that the slaughterer had come and gone and had taken Eric with him!"

"Technically," I said, "I simply omitted to tell you that the slaughterer had not, in fact, taken Eric."

"Gatehouse!" Ian plopped himself in the leather armchair next to mine. "He's rather cute, is he not, Gatehouse?" You see, having been told by Sally that I'd ruined the party; ruined her whole life, in fact, I had left the party early. I had returned to The Fly in the Ointment via the electricity substation where Eric had been holed-up. And, now Eric, you see, was contentedly snoozing at my feet. And, Ian, you see, was alluding to the fact that it was Eric who was rather cute.

"Look on the bright side, Ian. You still have Eric. Sally will have a job reclaiming the small fortune that she paid for a suckling pig."

Ian winced. "How do you make that one out, Gatehouse, old dear?"

"Well, **old dear**. It's like this. Sally wanted pork and, technically, pork is what she got."

"Damnation, Gatehouse!" Ian went over to the inglenook. "Whoops!" He tripped over Eric in the process. From a space where the bread oven had once been (but had not in actual fact been for many a long year), he seized hold of his ridiculously long clay pipe and he inserted the thing between gritted teeth. "I have a reputation as a breeder of fine pork and fine pure bred Tamworth pork..."

"A Tamworth surreptitiously crossed with a Waddle," I reminded him.

"Stop splitting hairs, Gatehouse!" Ian plucked a piece of flaming kindle wood from the fire and he lit the pipe. Between his customary puffs, Ian explained, "Listen to me, old boy! Pure bred, cross-bred with a Waddle, cross-bred with a donkey, even! What is for certain is that Sally was not expecting the centre piece of her feast to consist of the out of date stock of Shipford's frozen meat store!"

"I challenge any one of her guests to have known anything other than the fact they were scoffing prime home-grown pork!"

"Gatehouse! The half-ton of streaky bacon, the monosodium sulphate saturated spare ribs, not to mention the six pork chops, were impregnated with more words than the average stick of seaside rock. Furthermore..."

"I'll bet they didn't notice a thing."

"Gatehouse! The words were not *Welcome to Blackpool, the Las Vegas of the North of England* nor for that matter *I have been to Dudsall Illuminations*. Ian puffed at his clay and rode up and down on the balls of his feet in an authoritative kind of a way.

"Look, Ian," I said, losing a bit of patience. "Just cut to the chase."

"Cutting to the chase, old sunshine, is that prime home-grown pork from the shires of Old England does not ordinarily come impregnated from top to bottom, inside and out, with red dye proclaiming *GOOD BACON HAS DANISH WRITTEN ALL OVER IT* !"

I jumped up from the leather armchair. "I'm making tea," I said.

"No you are not, old chap."

"Why's that, then, Ian?"

"Because, Gatehouse, old chap, it has obviously missed your attention that we no longer have a kitchen."

I'd forgotten the bit of smoke damage so I returned to my seat, though not before pouring the two of us a large gin from the liquor still that we kept beneath the stairs.

"Any road," I said, after a swig, a sharp intake of breath, and a moment or two of contemplation, not to mention eye refocusing. "You're splitting hairs, you are."

"Splitting hairs, Gatehouse, old scout?" Ian stopped his rocking. "Cheers, old boy," and he raised his vessel (comprising an old jam jar) and finished the contents in one. Ian gasped and placed the jam jar down. "Cecil," he continued, looking somewhat flushed, "now finds his position as an officer of Shipsford Council compromised."

I looked at Ian in disbelief. "Nah!" I said. "You're just taking the Mickey, you are!"

"Gatehouse!" Ian started his rocking, all over again. "Of the sixteen attendees at Cecil's pig roast, eleven have been admitted into hospital suffering from salmonella poisoning and, of those eleven, five happen to be environmental health officers employed by the council."

"Well," I said, "if it was food poisoning, the whole lot would have gone down with it." I nodded my head, just the once, thereby communicating to Ian something along the lines of, *up yours, sunshine*.

"Gatehouse!"

Here we go, again, I thought.

"Gatehouse!" said Ian, but with only a wince and not a shrug. "Sally is vegetarian; I personally was far too upset to partake of provender having foolishly assumed that Eric was on the menu. As for you, Gatehouse, the persistent complaints that I was responsible for the cold-blooded killing of Eric had strangely ceased. And, at the first signs of food poisoning manifesting itself within the ranks of other persons present, you were heard to state, *sod this for a game of soldiers, I'm buggering off,* whereupon you did, in fact, bugger off. And that, Gatehouse, leaves just the guest of honour, Eric, who was not, as it transpires, there in the first place."

I counted down the list of casualties and survivors by use of my fingers and two thumbs. On arriving at the thumb of my right hand, I started all over again and finished off counting, for the second time of asking, the digits of my left hand. By my reckoning, I had therefore accounted for just fifteen, including Eric. "That leaves one more unaccounted for," I said. "There's still room for reasonable doubt, there is."

"Ah! You allude to the subject matter of the party, namely Cecil?"

"I do, Ian."

"Cecil was late for his own celebration," explained Ian. "He was late, Gatehouse, because he was falsely imprisoned by Janie."

"Imprisoned? By Janie? Falsely?" My lower jaw went vertical.

"Gatehouse!" Ian paused while he sucked on his pipe awhile. "Whilst attending to her zen garden, Janie discovered Cecil lurking within the grounds of The Hall."

"The zen, what, Ian?"

"Shut up, Gatehouse. It was the occasion of a further attempt by Cecil to deliver your blasted love letter. On being challenged, Cecil panicked and it did not occur to him that he ought simply to have intimated that, as an authorised local government official, he was inspecting the recently converted barns."

"He was supposed to have handed the note to Janie ages ago. No wonder I ain't heard a thing from her. Five times I've been up to the church at gone midnight, I have!"

"Gatehouse! Whatever made you think that a council employee was capable of carrying out a simple task such as delivering a love letter?" I opened my mouth and was about to protest. I intended to protest on my behalf, of course, and not Cecil's. "Say not a word, Gatehouse!" So, I buttoned my cakehole, and Ian ploughed on. "Initially, Cecil spent days at The Case is Open assuming that Janie would either call in (not that I have ever seen her in there alone) or stroll past. She did neither of those things. On the landlord concluding that Cecil had earned the right, by longevity of occupation, to become a member of the darts team, Cecil moved on. On one occasion, at the dead of night, he deliberately set off the burglar alarm assuming that Janie would pop out of The Hall to investigate."

"And, did she?"

"Of course not, Gatehouse. The bull mastiff popped out, as did Cecil's undergarments after the beast had ripped his suit of clothes to shreds."

"But, Ian," I protested. "Cecil was supposed to call in on council business and simply hand the note to Janie."

"Easier said than done, old chap, when the changeling is watched like a hawk. Hence the fact that Cecil was found wandering aimlessly within the grounds of The Hall."

"So, on being challenged, why didn't the idiot just hand the note to Janie?"

"Because the idiot who wrote the note didn't describe Janie's appearance."

"Yes, he did, I mean to say, and yes I did."

"Gatehouse! Phrases such as *she for whom I would lay down my life* and *eyes that dance and sparkle* is hardly the stuff of a Turnbull identification direction. And, that is not to mention *a chest that will not glow red with passion because that only happens when I am with her*. Shall I go on, Gatehouse?"

"You've made your point, Ian."

"Therefore," continued Ian, "Cecil did the only thing that he could."

"What was that, then?"

"He made representations that he was a computer repair man, of course."

"That's a new one on me, that is, Ian!"

I know that you may well mock but such folk, not to mention computers within a home, were relatively unheard of at the time.

"Is there a drop more gin, old boy?"

"Yes, of course, Ian," and I dutifully re-charged the glass jar.

Ian took the pipe from his mouth and knocked back in one the lethal concoction posing as finest Gordon's. He gasped, reinserted the pipe, and once again he addressed me through gritted teeth.

"As the trusting and unsuspecting person that she is, Janie took Cecil through to the computer which, I ought to mention, is plumbed into the family business. Thereupon, Cecil set about repairing the thing in the manner of a farrier shoeing a carthorse."

"What?"

"He smashed the thing, Gatehouse. Therefore Janie (some may say, reasonably) instructed him to either put things right or instruct his company to deliver a replacement."

"But, anyone can tell that Cecil is a local government official. For Pete's sake, Ian. He wears a sports jacket with leather patches on the sleeves and he carts around ballpoint pens in his breast pocket. Surely Janie was aware of that?"

"Apparently not, old chap." Ian chuckled and looked towards the ceiling. "For thirty minutes or so, Janie held the blighter prisoner until providence intervened or, rather, the telephone rang. Janie thereby found herself distracted. In its concussed state the computer, you see, had issued dismissal notices to all of the staff, and had simultaneously directed twenty pallets of produce intended for Tescos the supermarket to a sex shop in Soho…"

"But, Ian…"

"Do not interrupt, old boy, because it gets worse. Cecil seized the opportunity and made his escape, though not before bumping into a member of Janie's family whom Cecil thought may be Janie and he handed your note to her." Ian puffed some more at the pipe. "So, there you have the reason why Cecil was late for his own party."

"Ian," I said, "this explains everything! It's wonderful!"

"What?" And, with that, Ian very nearly bit through the stem of his pipe.

"Yes, Ian. You see, I'm not going mad! I assumed that one of the hounds of hell was on the loose up at the church. Now I see it all! Janie's family and/or friends had simply set the bull mastiff on me."

"In terms of Cecil's downfall, it does not stop there." Ian removed the clay pipe from his lips and he pointed the thing directly at me. "Gatehouse! Heaven only knows what possessed you to purchase a species that is entirely different than a pig for consumption at a roast that was advertised as a pig roast. Indeed," he added, with a wince and a shrug, "the species was not even warm blooded."

"The freezer centre had no more pork chops," I said, valiantly in my defence.

"Be that as it may, Gatehouse. The apparent consequences of marinating half defrosted raw shrimp in Sally's refrigerator together with her salad of mixed peppers are that Cecil, as you are seated here losing this argument, is confined to the intensive care unit of the county hospital."

"Intensive care?"

"Gatehouse!" Ian returned the pipe to his mouth for a quick puff. "I would hazard a guess that, by means of chemical interaction, you have inadvertently stumbled across the means by which to commit perfect murder." He removed the pipe, expelled tobacco smoke, winced, shrugged, and, with a chuckle, said, "I suppose that every cloud has a silver lining, old boy."

"Silver lining?"

"Yes, Gatehouse, a silver lining. Sally, you see, requires the comfort of a man whilst the life of her beloved Cecil dangles by a thread." He chuckled some more. "She is also desirous of paying for legal advice because of the imminent risk of prosecution by the chief environmental health officer, should he..." Ian coughed. "Should he survive the salmonella poisoning."

"Oh, of course," I said. "But," I added, "the council has no standing to prosecute because the blasted function was not commercial in nature."

"Ah, well, that is not entirely true. You see, old chap..." Ian plunged a hand into a pocket of his trousers and brought out a bit of crumpled paper. He handed the same to me.

"It's a piece of my note to Janie!"

"Damnation, it's the wrong note." Ian began ferreting around in the various pockets about his person. "Your note," he said, "was seized by the voluptuous Nurse Stringer from her husband's office. Next to it was a further note that read *this maniac should be locked away and it will not miss your keen eye that he is wholly illiterate.*"

Ian finished the search of his pockets and produced a further, equally crumpled, piece of paper. He handed that to me, and all.

I uncrumpled the paper. "Ian!" I said. "The pig roast..."

"Which, as it transpired, was not a pig roast..."

"Okay, okay," I said. "The pig roast that was not a pig roast..."

"Spit it out, Gatehouse, old scout."

"Ian? How did you think that you could get away with charging each one of Cecil's guests a twenty pounds admission fee?"

Well, back at Chambers the following week, Walter had a surprise in store.

"Izaak, my friend." As usual, my pupil master spoke his perfect Queen's English with a laid-back drawl. "It is time for you to expand your practical experience in civil law." My pupil master uncrossed his legs and rose from behind his desk. He went across to the window that afforded a panoramic view of the offices of The Regal Knight Insurance Company. From the filing away compartment, namely the windowsill, he seized hold of a pile of briefs that were all neatly tied-up with pink ribbon. "For the next few weeks, my friend, you will give written opinions and you will draft proceedings." Walter came across to where I was stood, namely that part of his office which afforded no views, panoramic or otherwise. "If the fruits of your labour are of a suitable standard, I shall pay to you the fee." He handed me the pile of papers in their entirety.

"Wow! I don't know what to say!"

"I suggest, my friend, that you say as little as possible."

"Why is that, Walter?"

"Izaak, my friend, the arrangement under discussion is, in my opinion, barely within the rules of the Bar." There was a moment's silence as Walter returned to his position behind his private desk. "Additionally, the arrangement," he carried on, after he was seated on his private chair, "may not meet with the approval of the tenants of Chambers. However, my learned pupil, it is a far better arrangement than the current one which my source informs me is collecting glasses in a public house. That, you see, is an occupation unbefitting of a member of the Bar."

"It's very generous of you," I said, whilst eyeing the paperwork that I held in outstretched arms.

"There is just one thing," said Walter. "I shall have to ensure that income tax at the basic rate is deducted from the fee because technically it will constitute income derived from me."

"I have no issue with that," I said cheerily, making my way to the door.

"Oh! Just one more thing, my friend?"

"Yes, Walter?"

"Informing a total stranger from behind the bar that the liquid in a litre sized coca cola bottle was, in fact, home distilled gin; that it was tax free, and that it was accordingly cheap at half the price, was not at all clever." My pupil master looked down, presumably to peruse some paperwork atop his desk. "Especially, my friend, when the stranger is none other than His Honour Judge Westmorland."

Do you know? No? Well, I shall just have to tell you. As I left his room, I could have sworn that Walter grinned, just a little.

It was mixed work; sometimes advising solicitors why their client had a good claim arising out of a road traffic accident, other times, telling the solicitors that it was proper to bring injunction proceedings for trespass, even where the trespass to land was inconsequential. You see, damages in lieu of an injunction were considered inadequate, the Court of Appeal having said so. Even land within the boundary of Birmingham was considered unique. Then, there was the time I had to give advice to an estranged husband who was accused of harassing his wife. *Very handy experience*, I mused, *should I be dragged before the courts to explain the ruckus in Janie's shrubbery.*

"Are you quite certain, my friend, that the client, Mr. Turbot, is adamant that he did not post to his estranged wife a live python?"

"Oh, absolutely, Walter. Here you go, take a butcher, er, I mean to say, take a look at his affidavit." I slid across the desk a document comprising six or seven, tell a lie, eight pages. "He says that it is ridiculous to suppose that he would have sent a ten-foot python by post."

From his customary seated position, Walter reached into a desk drawer and he produced a pair of spectacles. The lenses were small and round and, as such, the glasses greatly resembled those that had been commonly sported by the first of The Beatles to have become a posthumous inductee of rock music's Hall of Fame. Walter plainly sensed me staring because he suddenly looked up. "None of us are getting any younger," he drawled, and then he used both hands to loop both wire frames around both ears. My pupil master proceeded to peruse and consider my masterpiece. Prior to turning each page with his forefinger, Walter created lubricant (apparently necessary to plough through such heavy and meaty stuff) by dabbing the self same forefinger on his tongue.

The perusal and consideration was done in silence, broken only by the sounds of Damian muttering to himself on the other side of the door. Brummies, you see, never shut up as evidenced by the fact that you will never hear anyone from a silent order of monks talking in a Birmingham accent.

With each dabbing of the forefinger, I counted the pages in my head. *Six, seven, eight* "You'll see, Walter, that he's adamant…"

"Silence, please!"

Tell another lie, I'd clean forgotten about page nine which consisted of just the bit (I couldn't recall its name) where a client signs his name and swears by whichever deity he happens to believe in that he has told the God's honest truth.

"Izaak, my friend?"

"Yes, Walter?"

"The *jurat*..."

"That's the name I was looking for!"

"Do not interrupt."

"Sorry, Walter."

"The *jurat* is all alone," said Walter. "It should be on the same page as the last page of written evidence." My pupil master closed the eight, or rather nine pages, and he returned the document. "Instruct the solicitors to retype it. Other than that," and Walter removed his deceased Beatle-type glasses and he grinned, "the affidavit is suitable."

My opening of the door, on the way out, was met by an eerie hush. Damian, you see, had stopped muttering. However, the peace was short lived because the learned clerk of Chambers appeared in the doorway.

"They ain't gonna be at all happy, Mista Tweed." As usual, Damian wore his *the end of the world is nigh*, and even worse, *it's a Monday morning*, Birmingham-type, expression. "To cap it all, Mista Tweed, the trespass case has only gone in the list, an' all."

"I assume, my learned clerk, that you allude to the fact that the tenants of Chambers will not be happy at the news that a mere pupil is to conduct the injunction proceedings in this afternoon's court list?"

"Pupil?" I said, in a quivery, quavery voice. "Did you say pupil?"

"Ah! Yes, my friend," said Walter. "I omitted to state that, due to my commitments before His Honour Judge Westmorland in The Crown Court, you will conduct the civil court injunction proceedings before The County Court."

"But, Walter..."

"But, nothing," grinned Walter. "However, I confess that I did not have in mind that you would be conducting two sets of proceedings in the same afternoon. Still, never mind!" Walter snappily rose to his feet. "There is nothing quite like a baptism of fire."

My pupil master proceeded to grin, just a little.

CHAPTER NINE

The convention is that a barrister ought to arrive at Court in a calm, cool, and collected state of mind. Naturally, he should also be on time.

In breach of the convention, I was flustered and late. I was flustered because I had never before conducted one, let alone two, injunction proceedings. I was late because I was forced to go the long way to avoid some very nasty cracks in the paving slabs.

Just as soon as I walked into the County Court building, I was jumped on by an usher. He wore the customary black robe which, as was customary, did not fit. "You're lucky, Mr. Gatehouse, because Judge Hedges is a little late back from his lunch!" He held up high the customary clipboard. "You are first and second on the list, Mr. Gatehouse, sir."

Next, I was approached by a rather short, middle-aged, man. He had an exceedingly long, grey trench coat and a face to match. "Are you Mr. Gatehouse? I'm Mr. Turbot." He spoke with only the very mildest of Birmingham accents and, as such, I had no need to close my ears, no need to turn around, and no need to silently scream in anguish. I'll tell you something for nothing. It's a good job that all those Russian spies in all those James Bond movies use mere truth drugs, lasers, and so forth, and don't go pointing a jabberwocking Brummie in the face of our hero. Otherwise, 007 himself would plead for mercy and spill the beans!

Anyway, I digress. Mr. Turbot having introduced himself, I thought it right and proper to conduct a pre-hearing conference. It being a British court of law, the conference facilities naturally comprised the public corridor where anyone could listen in (and usually did).

"Now, Mr. Turbot," and I beckoned the client to come hither because half the corridor was listening in. "Have you familiarised yourself with the contents of the re-sworn affidavit?"

"I thought you barristers wore wigs and gowns?"

"Not for this sort of hearing we don't. Now, have you read the affidavit?"

"I'm not paying for a solicitor as well as a wig-less barrister. Where's the solicitor?"

"I ain't got a clue... I mean to say, I know not the whereabouts of the solicitor. I shall simply have to carry on without his assistance." I juggled around with my set of papers and, on finding a copy of Mr. Turbot's affidavit, I turned to page three. "Listen carefully," I said. "Did you post to your estranged wife a ten-foot python?"

Mr. Turbot promptly burst into tears. "No! I did not, Mr. Gatehouse, sir...!"

"Keep it to a whisper!" I shouted. "Now then," I whispered. "Why would she makeup such an allegation?"

"I shall tell you why, Mr. Gatehouse. Oh, yes. I shall tell you why, all right..."

"Then, for the love of...!" I checked my language and, while I was about it, the volume. "We do not have much time, Mr. Turbot."

"Mr. Gatehouse," said the client. He paused for a moment to wipe away tears. He used a piece of pink toilet tissue that he'd plucked from the inside of his trench coat. "Mr. Gatehouse," he said, when he was done with the wiping, "she is simply a compulsive liar. I mean to say, Mr. Gatehouse. How could anyone shove a ten-foot live python in the post?"

I was tempted to respectfully inform my client that the ladies who took part in the erotic dance shows at The Whippet Inn, Dudsall, on Sunday lunchtimes had propensities to shove live snakes in far tighter orifices than ever was the slit in the average Royal Mail post box. However, I was able to resist the temptation because someone from behind tapped me on the shoulder, and my conference with Mr. Turbot was thereby terminated.

"You are Gatehouse?"

"Are you asking me or telling me?"

"I am asking you, of course," said he who had prevented me from imparting to my client the finer points of management and coordination of objects that are part of a work process. Now, this individual looked a slick one, all right. He was about the same age as Mr. Turbot and he was about the same height too, perhaps even a little shorter on account of his pronounced stoop. However, whereas Mr. Turbot was thickset, this one was as thin and as slippery as ever an eel was. "I don't have all day, you know," he said, in a typical, officious, upper crust kind of a way. He simultaneously employed a hand to slick back his oily-looking hair of grey. Moreover, as if to advertise his toffishness, a gold ring adorned the little finger of the self-same hand.

"I **am** Izaak Gatehouse, as it happens." The little fellow stared at me intensely with beady, eel-like eyes.

"Jolly good. I represent the opposition, you see, and…" He broke off and turned his peculiar egg-shaped head to address another (barrister-looking) individual. "Good to see you, Henry, old chap," and he bowed to Henry, deliberately and slowly. "We must dine shortly, old thing." After Henry had gone on his way, with solicitors scampering about in his wake, the eel-like eyes were on me, again. "Henry's a delightful chap. He is one of the Rydeham-Smiths from Buckinghamshire, you know? Now then, as I was saying…" Now, would you believe it? The ovum-shaped head swizzled, again. "Why, hello, Giles, old thing! I have not seen you since the visit to the palace." Giles, whomsoever Giles was, simply brushed past without acknowledging anyone, let alone the little eel. "You simply must come around for supper, old chap!" The little eel was obliged to shout because Giles began to negotiate a staircase, two, three steps at a time, and he had already reached the summit by the time that the issuance of the invitation to supper was completed. "Giles is a simply wonderful chap." His voice trailed off, in a crestfallen kind of a way. "Giles is one of the Feltham-Jones' from Staffordshire, you know?"

"Now, listen here," I said. "When you say that you are the opposition, does that mean that you are against me in both cases?"

"Spot-on, old thing." His tiresome enthusiasm was back. "The name is Toidi. Jeremy Toidi. Do call me Jeremy, old chap. Now then, was it at the Old Etonians summer bash where we met?" The fellow despatched words as fast as a Gatling gun could despatch bullets at a tribe of natives brandishing sticks. "Of course, Izaak, old thing, you stand no chance of success in either case. Indeed, old fruit, why not offer undertakings in both cases?"

"Well," I said, and that's about as far as I got, because, as another entourage passed us by, Toidi, the eel, was at it, again.

"Stinky, old boy! It has simply been too long. I think it was the opera where we last met. We simply must..."

"Turbot against Turbot!" shouted the usher.

"You simply stand no chance," so the eel reminded me, as we all trooped into the judge's chambers.

The waft of garlic and cheap Merlot hit me just as soon as I entered the room.

"Good Afternoon," I said to the pallor-faced judge. He sat slumped behind an exceedingly large partners-type desk. These being proceedings convened within chambers, he too was without the usual finery of wig and gown. I could have sworn that the judge had been snoozing. You see, as I greeted him, he nearly jumped out of his skin. Judge Hedges was an unkempt and a generally grubby and seedy-looking specimen. Indeed, he looked as if he had been dragged through a field of hedges backwards. I knew his sort, and that's no word of a lie. After dinner at an Inn of Court there were more judges flocking around Lincoln's Inn Fields than ever there were pigeons. But, whereas both species were considered, in some quarters, to be a public nuisance, at least the pigeons didn't hanker after girls young enough to be their granddaughters and neither, for that matter, did they throw up in the trash baskets.

"How very nice to see you, again," said Toidi, as he slipped in. "Now then, Judge, forgive the impertinence but I was wondering if we could deal with the second case on your list first. My learned friend and I are in both cases. However, in the second case, I have a client who is simply desperate to get away for dinner at an embassy."

Dear God, I thought, *does he ever give it a rest?*

"What think you, Mr. Gatehouse?" slurred the judge.

"Does he ever give it a rest?" I said.

"What was that you said?"

"Do whatever is best," I said.

"Oh? Oh!" said the judge. "Very well." He looked straight through me, he did. "Usher!"

"Yes, Your Honour?"

"We shall be dealing with the trespass case first."

Another convention is that barristers ought really to convene their pre-case conferences, pre-case, sort of thing. It is considered proper, for example, to tell the client all about the chances of success or failure and, if the odds are in favour of failure, that far worse things happen at sea.

Well, in the matter of Tarquin Hogarth-Jones versus my client, Malcolm Black, the pre-case conference was convened post-case. In fact, it was convened while Mr. Black and the instructing solicitor were exiting the judge's chambers, with a "Tara a bit" from me and, from my client, "Are you certain you're on my side?"

Toidi, the eel, had started off in typical arrogant fashion. He had a few dirty tricks up his sleeve. "I trust Your Honour has seen the bundle that I have prepared?"

"Yes, thank you, Mr. Toidi." Judge Hedges extended the bottom of his judicial jaw; he took a sharp intake of breath and expelled garlic and liquor fumes upwards. The fringe of his mass of unkempt grey hair was thereby shifted from in front of his eyes. Having thereby succeeded in obtaining, albeit temporary, uninterrupted vision, the judge cast his keen legal eye over the bundle before him.

"I haven't been served with the bundle," I said. "Have you had it?" My enquiry was directed at the instructing solicitor whom, in common with the client, I'd not actually met. In common with most, if not all solicitors, he was pretty well nondescript and, as such, it would be a total waste of your time and mine were I to attempt to describe the indescribable.

The solicitor did not respond. I think he was still recovering from having been hoisted in ahead of the first case in the list. Never mind though. It was probably the most exciting thing to have happened to him that year.

The eel handed me a bundle. "My learned friend can have this, a further, copy," he said, thereby implying (without actually lying) that I had already received one copy; which I had not (honestly, I hadn't).

The judge looked in my direction. As a prelude to the judicial addressing, he sent a few more fumes skywards. The fringe, you see, had given up trying to defy Newton's Law. "Do you require more time?" I was about to suggest a month's adjournment but I held back my request to afford His Honour another attempt at shifting the donkey crop. It was a fatal mistake because, just as soon as the expelling of fumes was done with, the judge said, "No? Good. That is excellent. We shall proceed, then."

"I doubt if we shall be long," so proceeded the eel. "My client is the owner of Percy House. It is shown on the plan on page 9. It is a terribly grand property. Minor royals are frequent guests, you know? Rather large it is too. So much so that it was only relatively recently that my client (or should I say my client's gamekeeper) discovered that Mr Black, who is the defendant fellow, had begun to construct a garden wall that encroaches upon my client's land…"

"By how much?"

"About nine inches, Judge."

"Nine inches? Is that all?"

About the length of an eel, I thought.

"Yes, Judge," said the eel, "about nine inches."

"Very well." The fumes were once again expelled. On this occasion, they went horizontal because the judge sighed a heavy sigh. "Carry on, Mr. Toidi."

He carried on, all right. In between carrying on about all the dignitaries, all the celebrities ("I understand that he is an American fellow who has appeared in motion pictures and is rather well known among the masses."), he carried on about land being unique and that, in the nature of all things unique, mere money could not compensate for its loss and that an order removing Mr. Black's half completed wall was therefore the appropriate remedy.

"There should be no hearing convened to determine ownership," so went the eel's final argument. "You see, on page 30, there is an admission. It is a letter sent in 1939 by Mr. Black's father to my client's father, Sir William Hogarth-Jones. The letter, besides likening Sir William to a jack-booted, jumped-up fascist, states, and I quote, *the wall that I shall build to prevent me from having to gaze on your ugly face each morning will be constructed at my expense but on the land immediately adjacent to the old hangman's oak (where you should be hoisted) because the land on my side is too boggy.*" The eel looked as pleased as punch at that one. "Do you see the point? The defendant's predecessor in title made an admission by inference. He wrote **my side**, you see. That infers…"

"Yes, yes," said the judge, losing patience. "Of course, I see the point. I also see the time, Mr. Toidi, and I have a full list on which to adjudicate before I can return home."

Judging from the state of you, I pondered, *I adjudicate that your home is the local Merlot warehouse.*

The learned judge proceeded to direct his fumes in my direction. "The law seems clear, Mr. Gatehouse. The only remedy available against your client is an injunction."

The eel looked as pleased as if he had just managed to slither down a coalminer's trouser leg.

"Oak trees grow," I said. "And, we've had a few hot summers since the 1930's."

"Oak trees grow? A few hot summers?"

"Yes, Your Honour. The boundaries could well have changed."

"Well, how do you make that one out?"

"Easy," I said, to the monotonous whispers of *God, I don't think he's a proper barrister* emanating from the general direction of my client. "The girth of the tree must have broadened," I explained, "and I wouldn't mind betting that the bog has dried up a few times, and all."

"Oh, Judge, Judge, Judge," so went the eel, leaning eagerly forwards. "My learned friend cannot ask you to assume such things in the absence of a report from a recognised expert."

"What?" I said. "His Honour needs an expert to tell him that trees grow? I reckon that Your Honour can take judicial note of the fact that trees have propensities to grow without the need to call any treeologist, sort of a person, thingy." I opened my copy of the eel's own bundle. "Your Honour, do you see the old photograph on page 5?"

"Er, yes, Mr. Gatehouse."

"Now, look at the photograph on page 15. You'll see that there is a bird's nest on the bough to the right."

"Yes?"

It's probably a thieving magpie's nest, I thought. "It's bough," I said, "cannot be seen on the older photograph on page 5. Your Honour, that conclusively proves that…"

"That they are entirely different trees, Mr. Gatehouse."

"Aye? How do you make that one out, Your Honourable?"

"By the fact that I take judicial note that one tree is an oak and the other is an elm…"

"The latter was removed," said the eel, eagerly chipping in. "It was diseased, you see. Probably Dutch elm. You may recall, Judge, that young Ginger Snelsham, now a judge himself, had a rather large arboretum. I had lunch with him only last Thurs…"

"Yes, yes," said His Honour. The fumes, I record hereabouts, were back on me with a vengeance. "Is that it, then, Mr. Gatehouse?"

"Er, well…"

"I daresay, Mr. Gatehouse, that you may wish to submit that, in matters of equitable relief, the court always has discretion?"

"I daresay that I might, Your Honour."

"I daresay, Mr. Gatehouse, that you may also wish to submit that delay defeats equity?"

"Eh?"

"Mr. Gatehouse. Do you wish to submit that there has been delay in bringing these proceedings and that your client is thereby disadvantaged by reason of the plaintiff having sat back and done nothing while your client, Mr. Black, incurred the expense of constructing half of his wall?"

The eel almost choked on hearing that one. "Judge, I really must protest. Damages simply cannot compensate my client for the loss of a strip of land measuring only nine inches. Damages, as the courts of equity say, are inadequate."

"What say you, Mr. Gatehouse?"

"What I say, Your Honour, is that damages could be measured by the enhancement in value of my client's land, as opposed to the diminution in value of the plaintiff's property."

"Very novel, Mr. Gatehouse and, on that basis, I do not intend to grant summary, interlocutory relief and I will adjourn this case for a full hearing."

"But, Judge! He's playing with words," spluttered the eel. His beady little eyes darted hither and dither.

"Well, of course he is playing with words," sighed the judge. "He is a barrister, just like you. What do you expect him to play with? A game of monopoly?" His Honour, once again, looked straight through me. "Call on the next case, Usher!"

I watched from within the judge's chambers as the usher stepped outside. I swear that he was no more than nine inches from Mr. Turbot's face. "Turbot verses Turbot!"

The eel and I remained seated whilst Mr. Turbot and a woman, who was presumably Mrs. Turbot, came in. The judge, meanwhile, dropped his face and he appeared to be staring at the desktop.

The tussling spouses occupied chairs behind their respective counsel. So, Mr. Turbot (naturally) sat behind me.

There was a deathly quiet broken only, after a minute (which seemed more like an hour), when the eel coughed. The judge reacted, at last. However, the reaction was that of loud snoring.

"Ah! Hum!" went the eel.

"What, what, what!" said the judge, coming round and rattling his head. "Are you both still here?"

"Judge. You may recall that both Mr. Gatehouse and I are in the case that was first in Your Honour's list but is now second in the list."

"Very well, Mr. Toidi. Please proceed."

So, the eel proceeded. He proceeded by informing the judge that Mrs. Turbot was separated from Mr. Turbot. He told the judge that Mr. Turbot simply could not come to terms with the separation and that he had been troubling Mrs. Turbot something rotten.

"She's nothing but a liar, Mr. Gatehouse!"

"Instruct your client to be quiet, Mr. Gatehouse."

"Yes, Your Honour. Sorry, Your Honour."

The eel finished off his account with an account of Mrs. Turbot opening her birthday parcel whereby, in lieu of a tin of *Roses* chocolates tumbling out, a ten-foot python came slithering out.

"She's a liar, Mr. Gatehouse!"

"Mr. Gatehouse?"

"Sorry, Your Honour."

Next, the eel called his client to give evidence. Having asked her to swear to tell the truth the whole truth, and so on and so forth, the eel asked of her, "Is your affidavit true, madam?"

"Why, yes it is, sir."

"Thank you, madam. My learned friend may have some questions for you."

As it happens, I hadn't. Well, I mean to say. No one had been there to witness Mrs. Turbot unwrapping her birthday surprise. So, all I could do was take formal issue with what she had alleged, lest my cross-examination (or absence of it) be interpreted as an admission.

"Mrs. Turbot," I said. "I suggest that there was no ten-foot python and that the whole thing is a figment of your imagination."

"Well, you had better tell the folk at Dudsall Zoo that it's not a dangerous serpent that they recovered from my upstairs lavatory and that the thing now residing in their reptile house is, in fact, a figment."

"Thanks, Mrs. Turbot. That will be all." I make mention hereabouts that judicial note ought to have been taken that the judge was grinning from ear to ear. "I propose, Your Honour, to call Mr. Turbot!"

So, being a man of my word, that is precisely what I did. In common with his estranged wife, Mr. Turbot swore to tell the truth, as God was his witness.

"My friend may have some questions," I informed Mr. Turbot, after he had confirmed the accuracy of his sworn affidavit, and after the judge had admonished me over the fact that the *jurat* was not on the same page as the last bit of written testimony.

"Mr. Turbot," began the eel. "Why on earth should your wife make up stories?"

"Because, like I keep saying, she's a liar!"

"And, why would she say that you sent her a…" The eel coughed, for effect. "A gift in the form of a ten-foot snake?"

"Because, let the Good Lord strike me down if I'm telling a lie, she's a liar!"

"Then you deny, do you, that a ten-foot long python was recovered from the upstairs lavatory of your former matrimonial home?"

"Yes, I do! She's a liar, she is!"

"And, do you deny that a ten-foot long python now resides in the reptile house at Dudsall Zoo?"

"Yes, I do. She's a liar! That snake is no more than five feet in length."

"What?" The judge sounded astonished. "Do you mean to say that you admit posting to your wife a live snake?"

My client looked puzzled. "Why, yes. Of course I do," he said, calmly.

"Well, did you not inform Mr. Gatehouse of that fact?"

"He didn't ask me."

"What?"

"Mr. Gatehouse only asked whether I had sent a ten-foot snake, you see. It was never ten feet. It was only a five-foot snake." Then. "Ha!" He laughed aloud, so he did. "How could a snake of that length fit in a post box? You see, Your Honourable. Like I keep saying. She's a liar."

My fourth sense once again caught the full effect of the judge's lunch. "Mr. Gatehouse?"

"Yes, Your Honourable, I mean, Your Honour?"

"I take judicial note, without the need of a snakeologist, that a python, be it ten feet, five feet, or, five inches, is a dangerous animal,"

"Yes, Your Honour."

The injunction will be ordered in the terms sought by Mr. Toidi on behalf of his client."

"Yes, Your Honour."

"Which now leaves one more case on my list in which you are involved."

"Eh?"

"Jetty verses Gatehouse!" So shouted the usher.

"Another disaster, what say you, Mr. Gatehouse?"

"I can explain, Your Honour," I began to explain. I did so as the parties in the case of Turbot versus Turbot were led out.

The judge fixed me with a steely stare. "This simply will not do. First you come before me with an affidavit that has a defective *jurat,* and, and, now…"

"Yes, Your Honourable? Er, I mean to say, Your Honour?"

"You now present me with an affidavit which is defective by reason of your name appearing as that of the defendant. As if to compound matters, the defendant's name, one William Anker, appears in the space that is reserved for the name of your instructing solicitor. It simply will not do, Mr. Gatehouse."

I was saved by the usher entering. "There's no response from any other party, Your Honour. They must have gone off for a coffee assuming that the previous case, which was originally the first case and it became the second case, would take longer."

"Well, that is their fault," said the judge, leaning casually back in his chair. "I shall proceed in the defendant's absence."

"But, Your Honour…"

"But, nothing, Mr. Gatehouse. This fellow, Anker, is plainly a menace to Miss Janie Jetty."

"I wouldn't disagree with that, Your Honour." Indeed, it was the only sensible thing that the judge had said all afternoon.

"My word!" That's what the old soak said, as he thumbed through the papers. "The maniac even resorted to employing an individual named Cecil for the purpose of perpetrating his campaign of harassment! Mr Gatehouse?"

"Yes, Your Honour?"

"Fur! Rashes! Rabbits! Swan-like neck ablaze with passion!"

"Aye? I mean to say, I beg your pardon, Your Honour?"

"Computers do not have fur, but rabbits do!"

"Eh?"

"This sort of conduct, unless prohibited by injunction, always results in the death of pet rabbits! It is a good thing that Miss Jetty had the presence of mind to overcome this Cecil character! Otherwise, Mr. Gatehouse…"

"Eh?"

"It is as well that one does not dwell on what carnage may have resulted. It is customary, in these cases, for the wretches to be discovered in the cooking pot."

"Sorry?"

"Rabbits, Mr. Gatehouse! That is where maniacs such as Anker place the dead bunnies!"

"Yes, Your Honourable."

"I intend," said the judge, attempting to focus on the papers before him, "to grant you leave to amend the entire proceedings by deleting the name Izaak Gatehouse throughout and by inserting the name William Anker in its place."

"Your Honour, I think I need to do a bit of explaining."

"Well," said the judge. "Technically I suppose that you do, but…"

"Yes, Your Honour?"

"Killing rabbits? Voyeurism? Burglary? Threats of sexual molestation?"

"Yes, Your Honour?"

"Your careless drafting of the proceedings should not override the interests of Miss Jetty who must be protected from this maniac and his agents, especially Cecil. I shall immediately order William Anker to be arrested and brought before the Court to show cause why he should not be committed to prison for breach of his undertaking."

"Yes, Your Honour. Thank you, Your Honour."

"Will there be anything else, Mr. Gatehouse?"

"Yes," I said. "This maniac Pinstripe, I mean William Anker, should be ordered to pay costs."

CHAPTER TEN

No barrister in similar circumstances would have joined the California State Bar, intending to qualify as a US Attorney-at-Law.

Now, that's surprised you, hasn't it?

Well, with respect. I did serve notice earlier that, following my altercation with Eric, Janie, and Pinstripe, I had resolved to re-evaluate my life.

The re-evaluating had been a decision to disappear for a while and to let Janie stew in her own juice over the proper pickle that she had made of the proposal of marriage.

My departure from the shores of the United Kingdom was brought forward by reason of the issue of the warrant for young Pinstripe's arrest and a natural desire to be well clear of the Court's jurisdiction by the time that he had sweet-talked himself out of Her Majesty's Prison. Indeed, the ink was not yet dry on the warrant, and His Honour Judge Hedges would barely have had time to go sponsor the local wine bar, when I careened into the private office of Walter Tweed.

The face of my learned pupil master was a picture.

"Walter! Somutt urgent has come up!"

My learned pupil master casually leaned back in his chair. "You almost made me spill my tea," he drawled. "Pray, what is so urgent that it must come between man and afternoon tea?"

"I've had a premonition," I garbled.

"Premonition? Have you, by chance, been at Prospect's home-distilled gin; consumed a portion of his wild mushroom pâté, perhaps?"

"No, No," I said. "My premonition is that it would be prudent was I to take a break from Chambers."

"Pray, what does the premonition instruct you to do during this break?"

"I intend, Walter, to go west."

"Go west?" Walter looked puzzled. "You are surely not intending to practice law in Wales?"

"Further than that, Walter. I need to go to California."

"California? Well, thank God for that."

I pulled up one of the chairs normally reserved for clients. "The premonition, Walter, is that I take a short break and qualify at the California Bar."

Walter stood and went to the window that overlooked the Regal Knight Insurance Company. He always did his pondering while gazing out at the fine Georgian facade of the Regal Knight's offices. I imagined that it inspired him in moments of stress. Well, it was either that or he could not resist the urge to up-date himself on the daily goings-on between one of the second-floor managers and a particularly agile and imaginative secretary.

Walter eventually broke the brief moment of silence. "For how long, my learned pupil, have you been thinking about this surprise move?"

"On and off for a few weeks," I said. In truth I did not know the exact number of minutes, indeed, seconds that had passed since the debacle before His Honour Judge Hedges. You see, the mind plays funny tricks when it comes to traumatic goings-on.

"Well," said Walter, "I suppose that, from a long term viewpoint, the experience, and additional qualification, may bolster your credibility. I am minded to release you, my friend, and you may complete pupillage upon your return."

"Walter," I said, "I am so very grateful to you."

"It is my belief, Izaak, that you would be well advised to obtain health and travel insurance."

"Oh?"

"Come here, my friend." So, I went there, over to the window, that is. "Present my name to our esteemed clients yonder and I feel certain that they will offer you insurance at a favourable rate."

"I'll pop over straight away, Walter, and…"

"What is it, Gatehouse?"

"Dear God, Walter," I said. "Do you see her with him? I know someone who manipulates her little dolly into strange positions, just like that."

"Pervert," said Walter.

Well, by the next day, I had my cheap Freddie Laker ticket for New York. I also had full health and travel insurance. However, cover was subject to the condition that there were no underlying health issues. You see, in this regard, I discovered that there was recent paranoia in the insurance world over the issue of sexually transmitted deceases. Indeed, those of the male persuasion who were single were regarded as high risk. Accordingly, my health insurance was issued on the strict understanding that I attend a doctor's surgery the following morning (the actual day of my departure) for the purpose of a few tests. You see, the rationale was that insurance would be voided if I was subsequently showed to have failed the test.

The paranoia was such that the Regal Knight agreed to pay a doctor to carry out the tests. So, I was not in a position to object to their terms and, when all was said and done, I did not have a great deal to fear. I was, after all, single only on account of the dithering on the part of my intended, to wit, one Janie Jetty.

It was consequently most fitting that, as I was seated in the waiting room of Shipford's brand new medical centre, my dithering intended entered. Honestly and truly, she did.

My beloved looked as lovely and as stylish as ever in her customary dark linen trousers and white blouse. She appeared to have ridded herself of the damnable Pinstripe, though I concede that his absence had more to do with due process of law.

I watched in wide-eyed wonderment as Janie stood at the receptionist's little window. She delicately dabbed her nose with a white silken handkerchief. Though the waiting room was crowded with the sick and infirm, I had eyes only for Janie. The poor thing had obviously gone and gotten herself a chill although that was not surprising on the basis that she wore no cardigan, let alone a top coat. Upon duly checking in, Janie crossed the room towards the only vacant chair. You might know that it was dead opposite me, Yours Forever Smitten. It was only on sitting comfortably that Janie noticed me.

I gave a cheery wave and mouthed, "Hello". I was not one to bare a grudge, you see. However, she was having none of it. Indeed, Janie half raised herself and thereby conveyed the impression that she was about to make a bolt for the exit.

So, I half raised myself, and all. I ruminated on whether to go over and break it to my beloved that I was removing myself to the Americas thereby affording her a bit of breathing space prior to our inevitable nuptials. I also wondered whether I should go for broke and make out that, in another life, I had been a medical practitioner, and that if she wanted a thorough physical examination then I was her man.

As it happened, neither one of us had chance to fully rise to our feet because a familiar face popped out from the receptionist's little window.

"Well, as I live and breathe it is Mr. Gatehouse!" The face was elderly and it was the property of Jacob, the local pharmacist. I had last seen him prior to the ill-fated train journey. It was Jacob, you see, who had sold me two hundred out of date condoms for the purpose of protecting my aching appendage. It was those self same condoms that had come tumbling out of my busted suitcase and had showered themselves onto Janie.

"Jacob," I said, nervously and quietly. "What are you doing here?"

"I had to close the shop, Mr. G., and get a job, here, dispensing the medicines!" I had no idea why it was that Jacob felt obliged to shout. The little window was but a few feet away and, in keeping with the average doctor's waiting room, most other parties present were as quiet as church mice.

"I'm sorry to hear that, Jacob."

"I had been looking forward to retiring and purchasing a houseboat, Mr. Gatehouse!"

"It would be a very short retirement," I said, by way of consolation. "You'd have bronchial pneumonia within the week if you went to live on one of them ruddy things."

I spoke the truth because it was a well-known fact that it was the coughing and spluttering of the bargemen you could hear before ever their boats popped out of the Brewfin Tunnel down on the Dudsall Canal.

Jacob simply ignored my health and safety warning. "Damned local council, Mr. G.! They accused me of selling out of date stock!" Jacob extended his neck so far that it seemed almost as if he was about to clamber through the window and join us for a party in the waiting room. "Mr. Gatehouse! The autocrats are having a purge on the innocent traders. First, it was the frozen meat centre and now me! I am certain, Mr. G., that you had no complaints with the Screaming Thrusters and Spiked Sensations!"

A young mum along with her sickly child was seated immediately next to Janie. She appeared to mouth something. "Disgusting," I think, is what she said.

For her part, Janie mouthed, "Oh. Izaak."

"Anyway, Mr. Gatehouse!" It was Jacob, again. "I have some bad news for you!"

"What is it?" My enquiry was spoken in a precise, yet discreet, whisper.

"You will need to return later!"

Again, I responded in hushed tones. "Why is that then, Jacob?"

"I am afraid that your syphilis testing kit has not arrived!"

As miscellaneous patients made a mad dash for the exit, Janie stared in disbelief.

"That Jacob's a card, Janie!"

Janie too hurtled off. In the process, she raised the white handkerchief and I noted that she was dabbing, no longer her sweet nose, but, rather, her huge and beautiful eyes.

"Oh, Izaak," she said.

"Oh, Janie," I said.

I darted across the waiting area, intending to thwart Janie's escape. I would have intercepted her (at the water dispenser) had Jacob not distracted me, again.

"Doctor can still manage to inspect you for crabs, Mr. G.!"

"**Oh**, Izaak!" And, after fumbling with the door handle, Janie exited.

"Oh, Janie," I said and, after fumbling with the self same handle, I went in pursuit.

I caught Janie near a thick shrubbery. It had been planted around the surgery for purely aesthetic purposes.

Janie half turned as I approached. "Leave me alone, Izaak! I have a position to maintain in this community!" Tears from those huge and wonderful eyes cascaded down her cheeks.

"I'm sorting out some life insurance," I said. Little did Janie know that, in the event of my untimely demise, a small fortune would come tumbling her way. You see, I had appointed Janie as sole beneficiary. "Janie, just allow me five minutes to explain things."

Janie stopped on coming to a little wooden park bench. It was of the sort that had once been a common feature in the gardens of Prestwick. To my surprise, Janie sat down. Immediately on doing so, Janie crossed one leg over the other and the fabric rode up her ankle. As I stood over, I observed that it was a beautiful slender ankle; it was an ankle for which I could cheerfully have gone down on bended knees and kissed and embraced. "Sorry, Izaak," Janie laughed aloud through tears. "Have I stepped in mud?"

I reasoned that her banal question was born of embarrassment and that it was not in the nature of a genuine enquiry.

I initially remained silent because a mother with a toddler chose that moment to come by. I used the time usefully by trying to compose myself. "Janie," I said, after the intruders had, respectively, walked and skipped passed, "it is simply that I love you with all my heart and soul." Heavens knows why, heavens know how, I chose that moment to blurt forth my feelings. However, blurt forth my feelings I did. But, I wasn't about to stop there. I threw myself before Janie and began kissing the bare ankle. Honestly and truly, I did. And honest to God, even though we were in the open (on public display for all I knew or cared), Janie took no preventative action. She could easily have screamed, cussed, kicked me in the face, threatened to invoke the injunction, or done two or more of those things and she did nothing other than to cry some more.

"Oh, Izaak! Why did you never before say such things?"

"But, Janie, I did!"

"No, you did not!"

"Yes, I did!"

"Izaak! You have only expressed an intention, somewhat graphically, to use me for sex!"

"Ah, well I can explain that." I loosed Janie's ankle and stood up. It was as well I did because, no sooner had I done so, than an elderly man with a rolled up newspaper under his arm walked by. I said to him, "Good Morning," and, before heading off, he returned the compliment, and I carried on. "Janie," I said, "I have always thought the things that I just said, sort of a thing, but the other stuff, the sex things, just slipped out."

"Therefore, in your mind, Izaak, it was just sex that you wanted?"

I observed that a rash had begun to develop on Janie's swan-like neck. My eyes darted hither and dither in search of a domestic cat or indeed any variety of furry mammal that might account for the reddening. There was nothing, not even a grey squirrel, in sight. This represented conclusive evidence that the rash was a physical manifestation of the passion that lay within.

"Yes. I mean no. I mean you're playing with my mind now, Janie." Puffed-up pompousness was the barrister's last stand when he was losing an argument and I sounded adequately pompous. "What I mean to say, Janie, is that the sex thing was a means by which we could try for a family, let our bodies become one, failing that a bit of spanking (only mild though 'cause we don't want nothing perverted), get married, live in a cottage (and, I don't mean a cottage like Ian's hell-hole), not necessarily in that strict order, sort of a thing!" Janie brought her hands to her mouth and she sobbed loudly. "Okay, okay," I said, "forget the bit about the spanking, then!"With that, Janie sobbed louder.

"You idiot, Izaak!"

"Charming," I said, reverting to pompous mode. However, I noted with heart pounding joy that the rash had begun to spread to Janie's pure white chest and it made me glad.

"No, no," said Janie. "That is what I wanted."

"What?" I stepped back a pace, astonished. "You wanted a mild spanking?"

Janie rocketed to her feet. As soon as she was on the same level, her hands grasped my neck. In a pretend, playful sort of a way, Janie began throttling me. *Crikey*, I thought, *a mild spanking is one thing but this is out of my league, this is.* "You idiot, Izaak! You turn everything into a joke!" (*Who's joking,* I thought.) "You only had to talk to me and I would have been yours!"

Janie turned as if to hurry away. I was having none of that and, just as soon as I had re-charged my lungs, I reached out intending to grasp an arm. My simple and innocent intention was to thwart Janie's escape but, in my eagerness, I accidentally seized the neck of her blouse. The causative effect of Janie attempting to depart and of me attempting to prevent any such thing was a ripping of the blouse.

"Oh, Janie," I said, and, in the manner of someone French begging to surrender, I raised both arms high above my head. "I swear that that was an accident."

Instinctively, Janie placed both hands to her chest. She turned and faced me full on and I noted that the bare flesh around the cupped hands was positively ablaze with embarrassment.

"Here," I said, anxiously grappling to remove my jacket. "Put this on, Janie!"

Janie declined the offer to cover her modesty and, in lieu thereof, she knocked the jacket to one side. It followed that only one hand remained firmly cupped. Janie advanced. I stepped backwards and in the process my heel came against a curb and I began to teeter backwards into the shrubbery. I sensed spikes, brambles, and such-like whizzing past my face, the same having been bent back by my advance, only to be catapulted forwards. As I stumbled through the bush, brake, and brier, sort of a thing, I somehow managed to remain upright. My back came to rest against a small tree. For the record, it was a crab apple judging from the absence of fruit and the proximity of vomiting children within the local park.

Next, I was conscious of Janie standing before me. I noted that, before arriving at their final destination, the spikes, and brambles had struck Janie and that her swan-like neck and chest had sustained bloodied scratches.

"Izaak," said Janie, coldly, "I am injured as well as having been shamed before you." She raised a hand and I closed my eyes and I awaited forceful contact with the side of my face. However, though contact with force came, it was not from a damned good slapping. You see, Janie grasped my trembling hand and she place it gently on her flesh. The force, when it came, was the force with which Janie put her hungry mouth to mine.

CHAPER ELEVEN

"Oakland, please," I told the man in the yellow taxicab. "And," I laughed, "don't spare the horses."

The driver appeared a little standoffish. Indeed, his body language was all wrong. "Oakland? Is this some kind of a joke?" He spoke in a broad New York accent, just like in all the movies.

"No. I mean, yes. Oakland, please, cabbie." I made as if to enter the taxi and I very nearly placed my trusted suitcase across the rear seat. It was as well that I managed no such thing. The cab, you see, tore off and I was left standing forlornly in a cloud of exhaust fumes. "And the same to you!" I shouted. *Schmuck?* I thought. *What's a schmuck?*

I headed off for the centre of town. I had heard dreadful things about New York City and, most definitely, there were the sounds of sirens all around. I could see from the headlines on the newspaper stands, that there had been robberies, assaults, even the odd riot. *Not so dreadful*, I thought, *in fact, just like Dudsall on a Saturday night*. Even the steam that came ploughing out of the grids in the walkway did not bother me. It simply went to prove that my fear of fire-spewing dragons living under the footpaths was both rational and a worldwide phenomenon.

I eventually sauntered into the ticketing office of The Greyhound terminus. By that stage, I was beginning to suspect that California may be a long way from The Big Apple. There were, you see, no footpath signs to Oakland. Maybe it was even farther than the distance between Wolverhampton and West Bromwich?

I approached an exceedingly smart looking man at the desk and I placed my suitcase on the ground.

"How many miles is it to Oakland, please?"

"I reckon about two and a half, sir."

Phew, I thought, and "Phew," I said. "That's a relief, mate. When's the next bus, please?"

"It's not direct, sir. But, we'll be loading in an hour."

"An hour? I may as well walk."

The man looked at me intensely. "You're not from around here are you, sir?"

"Why do you ask?"

"I meant to say that the distance from here to Oakland is about two and a half thousand miles."

"How many?" I was astonished. I stepped back a pace and, in the process, I very nearly went tumbling over my case. "But, that's almost as far as I've already come."

" Where have you come from, sir?"

"I've just flown in from London, I have."

"Well, if you need to be on the west coast in just a few hours, sir, I'd take a plane to either Oakland or San Francisco airports."

"Take a plane?" I said. "California is in the same country, isn't it?"

The man looked pitiably at me. "It's a big country, sir."

"Ruddy hell, mate," I said. "I've come here to take the Bar exams. If I wanted to watch an old Gregory Peck movie I could have stopped at home and rented one of them new video machine, thingies!"

"Sir, I have a panic button. I will press it if you do not leave, straight away."

Touchdown at the city of Oakland, California was in the early hours and it was as well I'd slept on the plane. My slumber had been sound because I had dreamed sweet dreams of Janie. I had not expressly informed her of my departure. You see, on returning, in just a few weeks, I intended to surprise my love with the revelation that I had become a fully-fledged US Attorney-at-Law. It was dead romantic and was certain to lend credence to my credentials in the eyes of Janie's keepers.

Furthermore, I mused as the plane came in to land. *Pinstripe certainly can't compete with that.*

The only accommodation was at an exceedingly seedy hotel in downtown Oakland. The first of the exams would take place during the following morning and I was simply desperate for a few more hours of uninterrupted sleep. All through the night, however, I kept waking up with bells ringing in my ears. I also had reason to believe that trains were rattling through the bedroom. The experience put me in mind of my time in London when I had been forced to sleep rough on the concourse of various railway stations.

The upshot is that, next day, I was the last to arrive at the examination centre. Indeed, had I taken any more time, I fancy that I would have been refused entry altogether. You see, under no circumstances was lateness tolerated. Anyway, I went through a process of proving who I was, what I was about, and so on, and I was duly directed to take my place among a small group who were described as attorney-applicants.

Now, I shan't go boring you with a running commentary on every test paper and individual questions appertaining thereto; neither shall I bore you with the low-down on my fellow candidates. Not that they were at all boring. The majority of attorney-applicants, it seemed to me, were simply desirous of moving from their current state of residence to the state of California. Let's be honest, who could blame them? Sun, sea, sand, movie stars? For certain, contrast their English counterparts; the attorneys were not a bunch of sanctimonious, quasi-alcoholic toffs.

Well, come lunchtime of the final day, I was feeling relatively optimistic. Many of the questions had been based on the English Common Law. The man at the Greyhound terminus had said, "It's a big country, sir," and he was spot-on. The US system of government was a bit like how federalists wanted the European Community to work, save and except that the US system worked just fine. It was probably something to do with the fact that there were no French to get in the way. Anyway, each state had its own state law. As such, there was a definite rationale in testing everyone according to uniform, common law principles, even though many of the principles had, in practice, been overridden by state statute.

The chief examination invigilator was a larger than life character who put me in mind of the typical good guy's life-time buddy, with a beautiful daughter, who has turned sour and no one (other than the entire audience and the lady who sells ice-cream) suspected a thing till the eighty-fifth minute. You know perfectly well the sort of character I'm talking about. Indeed, I bet you can name at least a half a dozen movies in which he has featured. The invigilator was middle age and of medium height and rather overweight, especially around the midriff. Consequently, his stomach spilled out over the snake-buckled belt, which in turn was stretched to bursting point around a pair of tight denims. A bootlace tie adorned his neck and an exceedingly droopy moustache was fixed to the upper lip. The entire caboodle was topped off by a huge Stetson hat. There you go. I told you that you'd seen his character in half a dozen movies, at least.

All through the tests, the invigilator and his assistants prowled the avenues of desks. They were on the lookout for cheats, you see. At the beginning of each session the invigilator read out the rules which contained various threats and the consequences of being caught cheating. On one occasion, he challenged a bearded candidate to prove that his facial growth was, in fact, real. As it happened, the beard was false. You could have knocked me down with a feather when it came off and revealed that he was a she. Turned out, she was the wife of the real candidate and she was an eminent lawyer and would remain so for a couple more weeks pending disbarment.

Come lunchtime of the final day and the invigilator showed a human side by announcing that the entire dreadful experience was very nearly finished and he congratulated us all for having lasted the distance. I then bore witness to him, and his assistants, receiving a spontaneous round of applause. Then, when the last of the claps had clapped, I headed off for lunch. It was almost a party-type atmosphere.

I joined the throng of candidates making their way down a narrow staircase to street level. My mind, per usual, was all over the shop. *I wonder what Janie's doing at this very moment in time. I wonder if she is missing me. I wonder if I did the right thing by selecting option three for every single multiple-choice question. I wonder if I switched-off the gas oven before I left home. I wonder how the girl in front managed to squeeze into them trousers without splitting the seams.*

I was brought around from my day dreaming when the girl in front swung around and issued me with a mouthful of abuse.

"Can't you God damned look where you're treading, you mother…? There's plenty of room and you have to step on the back of my feet." Her face, freckly and rather pretty, was nonetheless contorted with anger.

"I'm-m-most-ter-ribly-sorry," I stammered. "I'm afraid that I wasn't looking where I was going."

The look of anger evaporated. "I can't quite make out what you're saying," she smiled sweetly, "but I can forgive anyone with such an adorable accent."

I was taken aback, I can tell you. Hailing from The Black Country and the recipient of a compliment on the accent simply had to be a world's first. "Why, thank you," I said. "And, once again, I do apologise."

"Here," said the girl, as we hit the fresh air, and she fetched out of her bag a pen and a scrap of paper. "Here's my number. Call me."

"Oh, right. Thanks," I said.

I waited to see which way the girl would go. She headed into town. So, I headed in the opposite direction towards the quay. It was a fine day and I was in good spirits especially after I had been the recipient of a compliment by a not wholly unattractive female. However, I opted to put temptation beyond reach by tossing the note into the nearest trashcan. Well, be fair, I was betrothed and my heart belonged to another.

Ever since my arrival, all that I had seen of the City of Oakland was the downtown area betwixt my hotel and the convention centre. I had not visited the famous quay where some intrepid explorer, come writer, had apparently set out on his travels. So, on the basis that I was already going in that direction, I decided that lunch on the quay would be civilised.

It was a grand quayside and there was much re-development going on. The work that was being done was sympathetic and very much in keeping with the era. Old warehouses had been refurbished and, why, there was even a pleasing aesthetic touch in terms of the old railway lines being preserved.

At the water's edge, I watched in child-like wonder as huge ships passed by. Each carried containers that were piled as high as ever seemed feasible. In high seas, I figured that it could not be totally uncommon for the odd container to work loose and set sail on its very own voyage.

I looked at my wristwatch and I made a mental note that according to the big hand, which actually comprised the left hand of Mickey Mouse, I had an hour before I needed to be back at my desk. It was then that a sign caught my attention. *Try Our English Beers*, that's what the sign above the entrance to the bar said. It truly did. I reckoned that my impending success in the California Bar examinations warranted a minor celebration. The fact that there were English beers on sale was truly a sign from above. *Besides*, I figured, *it would be rude to say no.*

So, I entered the place. "I'll have a glass from that one on the end, please."

I was immediately taken by the fact that the bar staff could actually understand what it was I was saying. "Gee, don't tell me. Liverpool, isn't it?"

"I ain't stolen any motor cars!"

I took my glass of the stuff from the one on the end across to a corner table. Between slurps, I looked around and took in numerous artefacts appertaining to the intrepid explorer, come writer, above-mentioned. Considering that the ale had travelled as far as the explorer, it wasn't a bad drink. But, at this juncture, I know what you're thinking. You think that I had another glass, maybe a third, and a fourth and that I missed my final test. I know that is precisely what's on your mind, so don't insult my intelligence by saying something entirely different.

If Mickey Mouse was to be believed, I had twenty-five minutes still to go. I politely returned a half-drunk glass to the bar and I soberly went on my way. So, you see, such are the dangers of relying on bad character evidence.

I began the short walk up the hill towards the convention centre but stopped on hearing the hollow, almost haunting, clanging of a bell. It was just like the clanging that I thought I had dreamt of in the loneliness of my hotel bedroom. Then, as if to suggest that I'd had a premonition all along, there came the distant clattering of a train. I clocked a locomotive coming into view and I realised that the disused tracks of aesthetic value were not disused at all and neither were they there just for their good looks.

Now, I am not, and have never been a train spotter. Indeed, I have never ever, in the whole of my life, owned an anorak. But, here was a sight that the likes of Izaak Gatehouse from the Black Country did not see every day. So, I naturally stopped to gaze as the monster trundled down the very middle of the road. Besides which, according to Mickey's left arm, I still had twenty minutes to go.

The locomotive passed by and it was enormous. Permit me to stress, once again, that, I, Izaak Gatehouse, am not and have never been a train spotter. Honest. However, the thing was amazing. Even more amazingly, as the locomotive went past, I realized that there was a second locomotive. It was as big and as huge as the first one. Well, actually, the two things were identical.

All traffic, pedestrian and motorised, was at a standstill as the huge locomotives rattled along. Even the beautiful retro-type trucks were dwarfed by the pair of monsters. Oh, and when I refer to American trucks as beautiful and retro, I do not expect any of you to request incontrovertible evidence that I am not and have never been the owner of an anorak. Well, okay, I once was the proud owner of a Parka with a *WHO* motif on the back but that had been nicked years before by a rocker riding a BSA Bantam. However, that, as they say, is a wholly different story, so keep your nose out of my private business.

After the monster-like locomotives had gone by, I saw what it was that they were pulling. If the engines were the biggest engines that I had ever seen, they were nothing compared to what came afterwards. I had never seen rolling stock quite like it. The sizes of each one of them, open wagons or closed cars, were such that the ground beneath my feet trembled.

I had another shufty at Mickey and, on that occasion, my heart missed a beat. There was no sign of the end of the train and I had only ten minutes before I would be locked out of the examination centre. On and on the rolling stock rumbled and all the while Mickey Mouse was reminding me that time waits for no rodent let alone a lawyer. Eventually, I concluded that there was no option but to go for it. I adjudged that there was adequate daylight between each one of the wagons and they were, when all was said and done, creeping along at a snail's pace.

In the manner of a Dudsall FC togga player attempting a penalty kick, I started with a run-up. However, on account of the fact that I did not consider myself a total, one-hundred per cent, idiot, I ran alongside the train and I spied a suitable gap through which I could nimbly dash. It would be necessary to ensure that I duck beneath the couplings. Otherwise, I was likely to end up in Alaska, where that intrepid explorer, come writer, had apparently gone.

The moment came, and I went for the gap. Seconds later, I emerged on the other side and I sprinted towards the convention centre. Regrettably, the sprint lasted no longer than three yards or so. You see, I sprinted into the front of a parked motor vehicle. Regrettably, it was no ordinary parked motor vehicle. Regrettably, it was a marked police car. And even more regrettably than all the other regrettables, it was an Oakland, California, marked police car.

As I lay spread-eagle on the bonnet of the vehicle, the doors opened and out sprang two burly-looking officers. "Spread yourself on the hood!" I don't know which one said it.

"I already am spread on the bonnet, hood, sort of thing!"

"Are you hurt, sir?" I think it was the driver who made the enquiry. I couldn't be certain. You see, all the cars drove on the wrong side of the road and consequently the steering wheels were on the wrong side too. It was very confusing, it was.

"No!" I said, "I'm perfectly okay, thank you, constable," and I made as if to slide off the vehicle's bonnet.

"Remain where you are, sir." It was him, again. You know? The one I reckoned was the driver.

Either way, whether it was the driver or not, the other officer then spoke. "Gee, I can't understand a word he's saying. He must be foreign."

"Or drunk," said the first officer.

"I ain't drunk!" I said. "I ain't foreign, either!"

"Stand up, slowly, and keep your arms where I can see them." So said the second officer. I wasn't about to argue with him, I can tell you. "Now, turn around, very slowly."

The first officer duly subjected me to a rubdown search. He and his partner were dressed in identical blue battle-type dress which made it even more difficult to differentiate between the pair of them. Both had side arms. Thankfully, they were not drawn. I'll tell you something for nothing, the officers were a mite more imposing than the average British policeman what with his pointed Toy Town-type hat and nought but a wooden stick for protection.

The second officer spoke. He did so, calmly. "That was a foolish thing to do, sir, and it was illegal."

"Yes, but you have to understand that…!"

"Do not shout at me, sir. Otherwise, I shall arrest you." He turned to his partner. "I can't understand a God-damned word, can you?"

"Pen and paper!" I shouted and, so that there could be no misunderstanding as to the nature of my request, I scribbled away with an imaginary pen in my right hand and I did the scribbling on an imaginary note pad situated on the flat of my left palm.

The first officer patted his various pockets and he eventually laid hands on a real pen and a real notebook and he handed the same to me.

This time, I scribbled away for real. *I am only shouting because of that noisy train and I only dodged beneath it because I am very late.*

When I had done with the writing, the officer snatched back his notebook. He read the contents with raised eyebrows and then he handed the thing to his partner.

"Firstly," said the first officer, "there is no need for you to shout because the train has gone."

"Secondly," said the second officer, "you dodged in front of the caboose."

"Eh?"

He understood that, all right, because he went on to explain, "In other words, sir, you dodged in front of the brake van."

"Eh?"

"The guard's van, sir. It's at the very end of the train."

"He's definitely been drinking," said the first officer to the second officer. "I can smell liquor on his breath."

I once more motioned with my hands that I required implements with which to write.

The communiqué that I duly composed went, *I shall take you to where I have been and the bartender will verify that I am **NOT** drunk.*

You'll never guess it, but even though I did the navigating, the officers nevertheless frog marched me to the pub. It was very embarrassing. As we briskly marched through the doors, the bartender stood with gaping jaw.

"Do you know this individual?" said the second officer.

"Well, officer, I don't kind of know him as such but he was in here just a few minutes ago. He's from Liverpool." The officers looked blank. "You know?" said the bartender. "Liverpool? It's the home of The Beatles…"

"What about the home of car crime?" I said.

"Oh, yes," said the bartender, "He denies having stolen a motor vehicle."

"Eh?"

"Aha!" said the first officer. "We have ourselves a case of grand theft auto."

"Look here, mate." It was the bartender to whom I spoke. "Remind them about the special relationship between Britain and the United States and ask them to let me go."

"What's he saying? What's he saying?" It was the second officer.

The bartender found himself momentarily distracted because the manager or someone called out from across the other side. He was enquiring whether assistance was required. "I can handle it! No worries, man!"

"What's the detainee saying?" asked the officer, once again. You had to give it to him; he was determined, all right.

"He simply wishes you to release him because of the special relationship that exists between his country and ours."

"Nah!" said the officer. "He's not French."

"Oh, for Pete's sake! Tell 'em," I told the bartender, "that I'll take them up to the convention centre where someone will confirm my identity."

The bartender addressed the officers. "He still denies that he's a car thief but wishes you to know that he has an alibi. He can prove everything by taking you to the convention centre."

"No, no! No! I didn't say…!" I shrugged my shoulders. "Oh, sod it! Come on then!"

"We'd best cuff him," said the first officer to the second.

"And Miranda him," said the second officer to the first.

"Sir, you do not have…"

"Yes, yes," I said, knowingly. "I've just sat through hours of exams on the subject of the Sixth Amendment."

"Fifth," said the bartender. "They are your Fifth Amendment rights."

So, cuffed and cautioned, I was manhandled towards the convention centre. As we approached the disused railway tracks, which had turned out not to be disused, a hollow-sounding bell once more began to toll.

"Shoot!" said the first officer to his colleague. "We'll be here all day. Shall we go for it?"

On approaching the convention centre, the first officer, while gasping for breath, said, "You will be entitled to one phone call, sir."

Well, that was typical, that was. The only phone number that I had was the one tossed nonchalantly into a trashcan. Having narrowly missed being run down by a mighty locomotive, we all needed a breather and the trashcan (conveniently situated near to the convention centre), was as good as place as any to stop.

"In there," I said to both officers, and I nodded my head towards the trashcan.

I was asked to turn around, whereupon, one of the officers un-cuffed me. I rubbed both wrists with vigour and, upon the circulation of blood being restored, I dove into the trashcan and rummaged about a bit.

"Here you go," I said to the officers, after I had done with the rummaging, and I handed to one of them the crumpled note.

We entered the convention centre.

"I'm sorry, but access is prohibited." It was the invigilator. You know? Him who looked just like the fellow from all those movies. "There is an examination in progress," he said.

"Don't I just know it," I muttered.

One of the officers (for the record, it was the second officer) told the invigilator that I was under arrest because there was probable cause that I had committed the offence of grand theft auto. "That's a felony," said the first officer.

"I know, because it came up on day one," I told him.

The second officer also advised the invigilator that my criminal activities had come to light as a result of having been nabbed for jay walking. "That's a misdemeanour," said the first officer.

"I know that too," I said. "It came up during the morning session."

"Now, see here," said the invigilator, and he flipped up the rim of his Stetson so that it casually rode high on the back of his head. "Is the detainee a Bar student?"

"Yes, he is," I said. "In fact, he's an attorney-applicant."

"Do you have any form of identification?"

"No," I said, "Everything is on my desk, but..." and I turned towards the two officers. "I have a note from another lawyer and she can confirm that I am, as I say I am, a candidate."

The officers looked at each other, raised their arms in despair, and shrugged.

The invigilator fiddled with the Stetson, some more. "He says that there is a note, officers."

One of the officers hastily produced the bounty of the trashcan.

"Says here," said the invigilator, "that he is Mary-Ellen Smith." He puffed out his cheeks and expelled air with force so sufficient that his moustache flapped in the breeze.

"What?" It was the first officer.

"What?" It was the second officer's turn. "Jeez, these French girls are hairy."

The invigilator nodded his head, knowingly. "I do believe that you two officer can leave the matter in the hands of The State Bar. You see, this is the second time that we have caught an imposter taking the place of a candidate. The first was a wife posing as her husband, and now…"

"My God," said the first officer, adding two and two and coming up with three by way of an answer. "How did this s.o.b. hope to fool anyone into thinking she was French?"

The invigilator glanced again at the scrap of paper. Then, he flipped the thing over. "Well, well, well," he said. "Not content with impersonating an examination candidate, this one has written down clues for most of the answers." He shook his head. "We have a zero tolerance policy."

"Eh?"

"Neither you, whoever you are, or Mary-Ellen Smith will ever be permitted to practice law in this State."

CHAPTER TWELVE

"Ian, the kitchen is fantastic!"

The kitchen, I will have you know was, indeed, fantastic. A complete refurbishment had taken place during my absence. Pristine white tiles, fitted units, a large Belfast sink (very handy for washing muddy boots and vegetables in place of the old toilet). Oh! On the subject of the toilet. The dividing wall had been reinstated and the old exposed toilet was now a new inside toilet. It was in its own little room with a bolt on the door.

"Never mind the kitchen, old boy!" Ian looked startled and he sounded startled. "What in heaven's name are you doing here at seven o'clock in the morning? I thought that you were in the colonies. You know? Jamaica or some such place?"

"No, no," I said. "It was the United States where I went."

"Exactly, old chap. The colonies."

"I'll tell you in a minute, Ian. In the meantime, is that a freshly boiled kettle?"

So, over tea, I told Ian all about my adventures in foreign parts. When I was done, Ian told me all about the fitting of the new kitchen and in particular how Cecil had cajoled the landlord into doing up the whole caboodle under threat of prosecution. "Cecil has made a miraculous recovery following your attempt on his life…"

"My attempt on his…?"

Ian slurped his jam jar of tea, chuckled, shrugged, and scooted into the sitting room. I followed but he got to the more comfortable of the two leather armchairs before me. "It is fortuitous, Gatehouse, old chap, that a locum doctor at the county hospital is both a stage door Johnny at the playhouse down on the river and a member of the Society of Toxicology."

"Playhouse? Toxicology?"

"You must have noticed, old chum, that the Elizabethan blank verse spouted by those overly-affected folk at the playhouse is just a front for regurgitating novel and sadistic ways to bump off characters and that generally the bumping-off is achieved by use of either sharp implements or by means of the victims ingesting noxious substances."

"Well, how do you know that?"

"I do happen, as you put it, to know that, because the thespians who portray the victims generally spend an hour spouting a dying declaration, also in blank verse, during the course of which there is made full disclosure of the name of the perpetrator and the means by which the imminent and long overdue demise has come about."

"Okay," I said, dumbfounded, "so dying declarations are an exception to the rule against admitting hearsay evidence, but so what?"

"But, so what, Gatehouse?" Ian sat eagerly forwards in his chair. "You may well ask, but so what."

"I just did."

"Gatehouse." Ian shook his head, despairingly. "Each one of the doctor's objects of his heart's desire has croaked it by some novel form in any number of Elizabethan romps..."

"Yes, yes. But, what's the point of all this? And where, pray, does the Society of Toxicology feature in the grand scheme of things?"

"Good heavens above, old chap. You really must learn to have a little patience." Again, Ian sat back and he casually crossed his legs. In doing so, there came a horrible whiff from the battered sandals. He insisted always on wearing the darned things whenever at home. "The point, Gatehouse, old chap, is that the doctor has become a bit of a conspiracy theorist. He suspects foul play whenever a patient presents himself at the Accident and Emergency Department complaining of anything from a nine-inch sabre wound to vomiting, hallucinations, not to mention the diarrhoea."

"Okay, Ian, but what has all this got to do with me?"

"It has everything to do with you, old boy." Ian winced, shrugged, and leaned forwards, once more. Indeed, he leaned so far forwards that he became perched on the very front of the chair and he appeared to me to be in imminent danger of falling onto the floor. From that position, Ian reached precariously into the rear pocket of his greasy corduroy trousers and he produced the infernal brass matchbox. "Phew, that's better. The thing was sticking straight into me, old chap. There are a few rough edges since you flattened my prized antiquity..."

"I flattened the...!"

Ian slid off the chair and he embarked on a journey towards the inglenook. As usual, various items of garden furniture, half-inched from the various gardens of the parish, were burning away very nicely. "Stop splitting hairs, Gatehouse. I was about to say, before you so rudely interrupted, that the matter was apparently drawn to the doctor's attention because Cecil ran through the occupational therapy unit screaming, *Gatehouse has broken the seals and he has set upon me the three horsemen of the apocalypse*, and..."

"Four," I said.

"I beg your pardon?"

"It's four horsemen."

"It was down to just the three after you electrocuted the Major's nag and shifted the blame onto Cecil. Now, as I was saying, after screaming that you had unleashed the horsemen of the apocalypse as aforesaid, Cecil was heard to allege, *it's my dearest Sally and not that Janie Jetty who he wants and he'll kill me just to get his mucky paws on my wife's voluptuous personage*. And there, dear chap, you have it."

"Well, Ian," I said, getting up and sitting straight back down again, only in the comfortable chair that Ian had vacated. I made it there just before Colin, the cat. "It's as clear as mud, it is."

"Gatehouse. Your ineptitude at thinking laterally, indeed thinking at all, is troublesome. Whilst restraining Cecil from making his escape via the nephrology unit, recently opened by Trudy the T.V. weather girl, the doctor deduced that lust is as good a motive for murder most foul as any motive is. Thus, he determinedly ascertained your whereabouts..."

"Well, how could he do that?"

"I told him, of course, that you had set sail for the new world. Thereupon, the good fellow deduced that your knowledge of marinating exotic peppers with raw *decapods crustacia* is as good a means of carrying out homicide as could be dreamed up in any one of the Elizabethan pantomimes that they put on down the road for the benefit of the impressionable and for the Americans."

"But, Ian, it's a load of rubbish!"

"Gatehouse, you attempted to execute a method of despatch known only to the Akawaio tribe and the head chef of the Waldorf. It being taken as read that you would not get past the lobby of the latter but taking it as read that you have recently frequented the continent where the likes of the Akawaio tribe are resident, the learned physician deduced that you possessed the requisite knowledge to accompany the motive."

"Hang about, Ian. The Aka what-not tribe are from South America. I went to California, and I went there after Cecil fell ill."

"Gatehouse, the distance between California and South America is just a few inches on the map."

"That's nonsense, that is." Be fair, it was indeed nonsense. Indeed, ask me now why I was bothering to engage with Ian and I could not begin to give you an answer. In fact, I was in danger of simply encouraging him.

"Gatehouse, old fruit." It was too late for I had already encouraged him. "It was not nonsense when you were apparently desirous of taking an afternoon's stroll between New York and Oakland. As for your journey taking place after the event, I assure you that upon *decapod crustacia* hitting the spot, the frequency and velocity of Cecil's exits to the lavatory were such that he very probably passed himself coming and going. Space and time had, in short, merged."

"Anyway, Ian. It's you who's after Sally and not me."

Ian flashed a look of mock surprise. He chuckled. "Not any more, old chap. It is Trudy the T.V. weather girl who has stolen my heart." He cautiously examined the ridiculous metal box, or more accurately, what was left of the box, and said, "Best not risk it." Next, he plucked the equally ridiculous clay pipe from its little residence, namely the space within the inglenook that had once been home to the bread oven. "It is fortunate for you that Cecil took my advice and, in the interests of Sally's reputation, agreed not to prefer charges. So, you see, old boy…" Ian paused while he put the pipe into the flames. After wiggling it about some, he withdrew the same but the bowl came clean off. Ian had obviously failed to take account that the vicar's rose arch was made of Victorian pine and, as such, the pipe was frazzled as is pig iron in a Bessemer converter. "Dash it, Gatehouse. Now you are responsible for the destruction of my best clay."

"Now listen here, Ian…"

"Now, now, old chap." Ian discarded the decapitated pipe by casually dropping the thing into the fiery cauldron. "The deception has enabled me to pursue Trudy the T.V. weather girl. Further and additionally, I have advised the good folk at The Hall that it is Sally who has your heart and no longer is Janie the custodian of the same. Brilliant, what?"

"No it damned well, isn't! My heart forever belongs to Janie!"

"Well, her heart, old sunshine, now belongs to young William Anker. Indeed, the engagement has been announced."

I instantly felt sick and my stomach performed a somersault. It was just like flying by Laker Airlines, all over again. "What? How? When?" I grabbed the nearest pillow and I adopted the crash landing position. "It's my worst nightmare, it is! Janie is nothing but a treacherous whore!"

"Steady on," said Ian. "That truly is a bit strong, old chap. I suggest that you take it like a man and wish the happy couple well." Ian coughed. "If you do not mind my saying so," he then added, "Should you insist on muttering directly into Colin's fur so, you will most likely contract the same allergy that so cruelly afflicts Janie."

I lifted up my head and, between spitting out bits of cat hair, I said, "Ian. My life is in tatters. How has all this come about?"

"It has come about, Gatehouse, because Janie was hauled before the County Court to state whether she has an issue with young Anker and, if not, whether the warrant for his arrest, which I might add was not backed with bail, should be discharged."

"Well, Ian, not that I'm bitter or anything, but, let's hope that when he was banged up his soap had no rope."

Ian approached and I swear that he almost placed a consoling arm about my shoulders. However, he thought better of it and it was as well he did, I can tell you, for where I came from you got hit in the face for going all Doris on a chap. Ian went on to explain that it was possibly the account of my imaginary infatuation with Sally that had sent my beloved running into the arms of young Pinstripe. "However, do not distress yourself, Gatehouse, old chap, because all is for the best." Ian placed both of his jittery arms firmly to his side where they belonged. "Janie and young Anker," he explained, "were so joyous that they withdrew the proceedings. It is akin to the granting of a pardon by the metaphoric White House turkey to the literal White House turkey." Ian looked ceiling-wards, as if to avoid eye contact. "That's not to say, I might hasten to add, that the injunction proceedings were going anywhere following the..." He coughed.

"Yes?"

"Following the untimely death of His Honour Judge Hedges."

"What?" I inadvertently dug my nails into Colin, who all the time had remained contentedly snoozing on my lap. With a growl and a hiss Colin leapt up and made off for somewhere or other. Frankly, though I loved the moggie dearly, it was sort of natural justice on him for all the times he'd dug his claws into me.

Ian dove both arms deep inside his trouser pockets and he began rocking back and forth on the balls of his feet. "The word is out, Gatehouse, old scout, that, nearing the end of his illustrious career, Judge Hedges' faculties were so muddled by Merlot that he knew not one end of a summons from the other."

"Why? What happened?"

"What happened, old chum, is that the judge collapsed on the floor of his chambers. Within his grasping hand there was discovered a document. Upon the bailiff prising open the hand and un-crumpling the document, it was found to consist of due process."

I was agog, I was. "Due process?"

"You heard, old boy. Due process." Ian stared in an accusing manner. "The due process, old dear heart, was an arrest warrant. And not wishing to countermand the old soak's final decree, the due process was duly processed."

"Duly processed?"

"Yes, duly processed." Ian stopped rocking, he bent slightly forwards, and he peered down in a very accusing manner. It was most intimidating, it was. "Turns out," said Ian, "that His Honour, deceased, but still warm, had ordered the arrest of the instructing solicitor in place of the defendant."

"Crikey," I said. "How do you think that happened?"

"How indeed, Gatehouse? How indeed?" Ian stopped peering and I instantly felt more relaxed. "The cremation, old chap, takes place later today. Every respected and respectable member of the legal establishment will be there. We shall be there too."

"Ian," I said, forcefully. "There is absolutely no way on this planet that I will show my face at the funeral."

"Ian," I said, with equal force, save and except that we were in the process of rounding a bend in the road on our journey to the chapel of rest. "The motorcar doesn't sound right!" It was necessary to shout, not only because of the roar of the engine and the wind noise and the sundry rattles but because each time that we rounded a bend the motorcar's hooter hooted. Moreover, the hooting was of the car's own volition. That, you see, is why I made my observation. No word of a lie, the motorcar just didn't sound right.

"The involuntary emitting of sound by the audible warning device has occurred ever since you half-drowned the old girl in the car wash!" Ian shouted his explanation so that he too could be heard above the noises, above mentioned.

So, that is how the journey progressed. Each time that Ian turned the steering wheel, the audible warning device gave an audible warning. Naturally enough, it was necessary to turn the steering wheel when we came to the turning-off for the crematorium.

"Duck, Ian! Everyone is staring at us!"

"Gatehouse! Of course everyone is staring! We are approaching a chapel of rest and not The Last Chance Saloon! Furthermore. No. I shall not, indeed, cannot, duck...!" Ian glanced to his port side where, for the avoidance of recognition, I had swiftly conveyed myself from the passenger seat to the foot well. "Whoops!" was a yell that he yelled whilst narrowly missing a couple of mourners. Moreover, to avert mowing-down another brace and to avert all of the consequential paperwork, Ian was obliged to juggle with the steering wheel with the result that the intermittent audible warning device sounded some more.

I popped myself back onto the seat and I did so just in time to observe that the hearse had already pulled up and a trolley to receive the dearly departed had been wheeled around. Many of the faces in the crowd were recognisable because I'd seen them in and around the law courts. They looked a sombre lot, all right (especially the ones in black crombies) but it was, after all, a funeral, so have a heart. Mind you, the sombre faces turned to faces of anger and despair when Ian turned the steering wheel so that we could park-up. You see, the hoot as we turned into the car park continued to hoot even after we had come to a standstill. In fact, now that I recall it, the noise was not a hoot at all. It was more of an ear-shattering blaring that just would not switch off. The intermittent sound of the audible warning device was, in short, no longer intermittent but it was as continuous as the blaring of the time to knock-off and go home hooter at Dudsall foundry.

Ian punched, slapped, pummelled, the button with the MG motif in the middle of the steering wheel but the audible warning device persisted in blasting out its audible warning. I looked over my right shoulder, hearse-wards. The heads on the mourners were slowly going east and west and then west and east and the expressions on the faces on the mourners were of disgust; save and except for the face of a handsome woman who was young enough to be the daughter of His Honour, now stone cold, about to be heated up to stone-melting point. Her expression was one of anguish. I reasoned that she was the old soak's widow, probably his first cousin, and all. One of the mourners placed a consoling arm about the woman's shoulder. You could have knocked me down with a feather when the face of the mourner turned towards me and revealed itself as the face of Walter Tweed. So, naturally, I slid back down to revisit the foot well.

Eventually, Ian gave up on flagellating the steering wheel and he leapt out of the vehicle. "It's no good, Gatehouse! I shall have to rip out some wires!" With miscellaneous mourners looking on, mouths gaping, Ian scooted around to the front of the wreck where, after a bit of fumbling, he lifted high the hood. I next bore witness to cables being torn out and flung into the air. However, the blaring of the audible warning device persisted. Indeed, if anything, the noise was even louder upon the miscellaneous workings of the wreck being uncovered by the lifting of the hood. Three times the hood clattered down and three times Ian was obliged to re-erect the thing. "Ouch, Gatehouse!" He said it three times. "I believe that I am concussed!"

A shadowy figure advanced. "Gatehouse, my learned pupil. I rather assumed that you were in the United States of America."

"Walter, I heard the news of the learned judge's death and I simply had to return to pay my respects!"

"I cannot hear a damned word," drawled my pupil master and he casually inserted a hand within the vehicles cockpit. He fumbled beneath the dashboard for a few ticks and then he yanked his arm. Praises, the audible warning device ceased emitting its audible warning. "Now then, my friend, what was that you were attempting to state?"

"Walter," I stated, "it all went wrong in California, sort of thing. Can I...?"

"Yes?"

"You know?"

"Yes?"

"Can I return to Chambers?" Walter placed a hand to his cheek, as if in contemplation. "Please, can I?"

"Gatehouse, my friend."

"Yes, Walter?"

"There is a totter that requires attention on Monday afternoon."

"Yes, Walter?"

"It is for hearing at the Persham Magistrates Court."

"Yes, Walter?"

Walter embarked on his return voyage towards the chapel of rest though, after just a couple of steps, he stopped. "Kindly attend Chambers during the course of Monday morning and collect the brief."

"Yes, Walter! Oh, and Walter?"

"Yes, my friend?"

"Thanks, Walter!"

CHAPTER THIRTEEN

Now then, in legal circles a totter is neither a falter, lurch, stagger, nor anything else that is associated with a propensity to walk unsteadily. The term, you see, is commonly used to describe a driving case in which the defendant has acquired so many penalty points on her (or his) driving license that he (or she) will automatically be banned from driving a motor car unless some very special reason can be presented to the Court.

It was not exactly the sort of mind-blowing case with which to relaunch my faltering career at the Bar, but at least it was a start. The result would naturally be pretty important to my client, Mr. James Henry Wildmore. You see, he was a travelling insurance salesman employed by the Regal Knight Insurance Company. As such, the loss of a driving licence would likely result in the loss of his job.

I spent much of the morning in the company of Damian Barker on whom, in the sanctity of Walter's private office, I attempted to practice the art of advocacy. He was not at all attentive which left me fretting that I might fail to captivate the justices of the peace who would be sitting at the Persham Magistrates Court later that very same day.

"Sorry, Mista Gatehouse. Oi car here yow and oi car even 'ear if the phone goes 'cause the window am open and them pigeons on the ledge am making a dreadful noise."

"Shoo! Shoo! Go away!" I shouted, and I banged an outstretched palm on the outside ledge. "Come back another day!" My actions, you understand, were designed to encourage *columbidae* to dramatically depart for the bright blue yonder or, in the case of Birmingham, the photochemical air pollution. Either way, I simply had to stop the interruption of my closing submission that, never mind the pesky pigeons, my client, Mr. Wildmore, had three hungry mouths to feed and that just this once he should be let off.

"Careful yow doe hurt yowself on them anti-pigeon spikes, Mista Gatehouse."

"Ouch! I'm maimed for life, I am!"

"Too late, we am afraid, Mista Gatehouse." I had never, ever before noticed that some damned fool had laid sharp needle-type things all over the ledge. The learned Clerk of Chambers tucked in his shirt and adjusted the waistband of his trousers. Next, he strolled in a lolloping manner to an ex-military-type filing cabinet of green metal. It had appeared out of nowhere during my grand tour of the Oakland police department. "Oil get yow a sticking plaster for them stab wounds we will. Oi warned Mista Tweed that sum stupid bugger would impale himself on them ruddy spikes, oi did." Damian tugged the door. "Them ruddy spikes doe work," he muttered, "just lyke this ruddy door doe work, either."

"Here, I'll give you a hand," and I joined forces with Damian by pulling, pushing, and, eventually, kicking the door.

"Doe yow go dripping blood all over we, Mista Gatehouse." To the accompaniment of a shrilly scrape of metal on metal, the door popped open and, from the top shelf, a baker's dozen (yes, thirteen, no more, no less) of brown paper bags revealed themselves and proceeded to adhere to Newton's Law. "Watch yerself, Mista Gatehouse, sir!" On impact with the lino floor, the bags bust open and out of the same cascaded piles and piles of corn kernels.

"Please don't tell me that you've been feeding the pigeons with this stuff!"

"Ar, as it 'appens, we have."

"Then, it's no wonder that the anti-pigeon things don't work! *Columbidae* must think that Christmas has come early!" I shook my left foot and stepped back. I shook my right foot and stepped back, some more. You see, there was more corn scattered on the floor than you'd find in the Nickelodeon on a Saturday night.

"Mista Tweed keeps collecting stuff from the auction rooms, Mista Gatehouse. He's lyke someone possessed, he is." Damian flapped his arms in an overly defensive Brummie kind of manner. I stepped back even further because I didn't want to succumb to Damian's fate by becoming stranded in a sea of yellow. "It's lyke this," explained Damian, with Brummie logic. "Mista Tweed needed to check whether them anti-pigeon spikes worked, but there were no pigeons, so…"

"So, Damian?" I tried reversing some more but was thwarted by a wall.

"So," said Damian, "I decided to use the corn that Mista Tweed purchased. He obtained it for experimental purposes. You see, he needed to encourage the pesky devils with corn just so he could tell whether the spikes discouraged 'em!"

As Damian spoke I could not help but notice that one of the pesky devils had cheekily perched himself on the ledge. Over his left shoulder, wing, or whatever you call it in ornithological circles, there were five or six of his mates and they had craftily thwarted the anti-pigeon thingamajigs by wedging their little undercarriages between each and every spike.

"Damian," I said, "I reckon that you ought to close the window."

"Why is that, sir?"

"Too late," I said, as the first-mentioned pesky devil entered the room. He was followed by the others, and more besides. Before I knew where I was, the room went dark as half the pigeon population of Birmingham entered.

"Oh, heck as lyke, Mista Gatehouse, sir! Christopher Columbus is doing things all over the papers! Mista Tweed will kill we, he will!" Damian outstretched both his arms. "Oi am making lyke we am a scarecrow!"

"Damian," I said, "you are making like you are Nelson's Column."

Rather predictably, some of the little chaps took a well-earned break from their flapping and dive-bombing and promptly settled on Damian. "Dear, dear me, Mista Gatehouse! Oi watched a film once and ever since we have had an aversion to things that flap!"

"*The Birds*," I said.

"Ar! That's the word we was looking for, Mista Gatehouse! Oi have an aversion to birds, we have!"

"No, no," I said. "The film is called *The Birds*."

"Yow barristers am too clever for the lykes of we, Mista Gatehouse!" A particularly cheeky little chappy took it on himself to settle on Damian's head and he began peck, pecking, away. "Dear me! Oi am being eaten alive, we am!" Initially, I assumed that the attraction was merely dandruff. However, I bore witness to *columbidae* popping out of Damian's thinning thatch and he had a kernel in his beak. Next, I noted that a quantity of corn had actually managed to settle on the front of Damian's trousers. "Whoo! The missus will be angry and frustrated and eyeing up the postman if they do damage down there!"

A squadron broke off from the main assault and, as the crow flies, came at a straight line at me. I waved both arms madly in an attempt to thwart a landing. Unfortunately, it is my duty to file a report that I succeeded but only to encourage the flight to engage in low-level tactical bombing. I fear that, within seconds, my head, dark suit, my shoes, even, for Pete's sake, were plastered in smelly grey pigeon droppings.

It was unfortunate, not to mention degrading, that Walter chose that very moment to casually stroll in.

"What in the name of...? Both of you step into reception, **now**!"

"Okay, Mista Tweed!"

"Okay, Walter!"

"Kindly ensure that you close the door behind you!"

Damian and I made a dash for the reception. We managed to beat the flock to it. Well, almost we did. You see, a brace managed to enter and they performed a swift circuit of the reception and fluttered down the corridor.

"Tracy!" came a shriek from the vicinity of the ladies' bathroom. "I swear that I'm being watched!"

"Rachael! Something has just done something disgusting on my new rah-rah skirt!"

"Shall oi goo to the rescue of the damsels in distress, Mista Tweed?"

"No, you damned well will do no such thing!" Walter's eyes were ablaze with fury and yet, remarkably, he still managed to sound casual and laid-back. "You will kindly provide an explanation for the debacle to which I have borne witness!"

"With respect, Mista Tweed, It's yow what's attracted them pesky birds by purchasing seeds for them to consume!"

"You disrespectful fool," said Walter. "You have flooded my office with the basic ingredients, indeed the sole ingredient, for popcorn at my daughter's forthcoming birthday party."

"Oh, Blimey Ol' Riley!" Damian slapped an outstretched palm onto his pink and perspiring brow. Aided and abetted by guano, the learned clerk thereby left an impression of his fingerprints and of a wedding ring on the forehead, centre right. "Oil gathers up the popcorn and it will be just fine for the party!"

"It will be just fine for infecting half the eight year olds in Sutton Coldfield with histoplasmosis! Telephone the Council's pest control..."

"Shall oi make tea first, Mista Tweed?"

"Telephone **now.** And **you**..."

"Yes, Mista Tweed?"

"No, not you, you fool. I mean **you**, Gatehouse."

"Yes, Walter?"

"You are late for Court."

Not for the first time in my fledgling career as a barrister, I found myself in flagrant breach of protocol. For starters, as I pelted pell-mell up the steps of the Persham Courthouse, I was not on time. For seconders, I was not calm. For thirders, sort of thing, I was not dressed in the manner of a toff at the in-laws. Indeed, I really rather looked as if someone had gathered up all of the pigeon droppings from Trafalgar Square, London, England, and had proceeded to dump the whole caboodle over my personage.

On reaching the summit of the two flights of steps, I pushed the brass handle that had a little notice next to it which read *pull*. It was an almost Birmingham-sort of a thing to do. Indeed, it was almost as Birmingham as playing soccer next to the sign that reads *no playing on the grass* or touching the big red door next to the *wet paint* sign.

Eventually, someone pushed the door open. The person, you see, was on the other side of the door which meant that they had to push and not pull. Regrettably, the person pushed the door straight into my face. "Ouch! Careful!" I promptly dropped my case papers.

"Terribly sorry, sir," said an elderly gentleman in a black gown. He was plainly the court usher. Only ushers, you see, wear gowns in a magistrate's court; unless it is the City of London Magistrates Court in which case every man and his dog wear, not just any old set of robes, but robes adorned with the fur of dead animals. Be that as it may, as I keep impressing upon you, this was the Persham Magistrates Court. It followed that, even though I personally looked as if I belonged in Trafalgar Square amongst the lions and the famous sailor fellow, the gentleman who stood before me was an usher because only the ushers wore gowns. It was, you see, most definitely Persham. Got it?

"I'm counsel for Mr. Wildmore," My announcement was said in a splutter and, at the same time, I went down on hands and knees and became gainfully employed in the pursuit of scooping up and piecing back together the case papers.

The usher examined a clipboard on which the list of cases was presumably clipped.

"There appears to be no case by that name on my list, sir." The usher bent forwards and he shoved the clipboard beneath my nose. "Do you see, sir? There is no Wildmore on the list for today, sir." Next, by way of an aside, he casually remarked, "There is a very strange and pungent smell, sir?"

"Well," I said, and I began pulling myself up to my full height. I let forth a short groan and rubbed my right knee. You see, the steps on which I had knelt were as cold as marble and as hard as marble. Indeed, that particular phenomenon was very probably brought about by reason of the fact that the steps were made of marble. "Well," I said, again, when I was done with the rubbing, "I happen to know that Mr. Wildmore's case is for hearing this afternoon." I juggled with my case papers a little. "Here," I said, thrusting forth a copy of the notice of hearing. "Two o'clock in this Court. That's what the notice says."

"Oh, no it does not, sir." The usher shook his head and he unclipped a pencil. It had been lurking beneath that part of the clipboard which consisted of the clip. He proceeded to jab the pencil at my notice of hearing. "The notice states, sir, that Mr. Wildmore's case is to be heard at the Persham Magistrates Court."

"Well, I am at the Persham Magistrates Court," I said, with authority. "I **am**, ain't I?"

"No, sir." With that, the usher jabbed the pencil, again. Only he did the jabbing in the direction of a road sign, some thirty or so yards down the street. "Do you see that, sir?"

"Er, yes."

"It says Persham 8 miles."

"Meaning?"

"Meaning," said the usher, "that this is Eveshore Magistrates Court and that Persham which, as the name implies, is the venue for the Persham Magistrates Court, is 8 miles away."

In breach of protocol to an extent that beggared belief, I pelted up the steps of the real Persham Magistrates Court, late, flustered, and still looking as if a joker had dropped on my head an entire bat cave full of guano.

"I'm here to represent Mr.Wildmore," I gasped, as I came through the polished oak door having done so, I make mention, at the first attempt. You see, I pulled when I was supposed to pull and I did not push.

I discovered that the only incumbents on plain view were members of the public. Some were stood silently still, their backs against a grimy wall. Others were deposited on a cluster of plastic bucket seats. The only noise came from a toddler who appeared to have broken loose from his parent and he was trotting around in circles. His parent, whomsoever she, or indeed he, happened to be, did not care a jot, for not one of the occupants of the seats bothered to glance up, let alone rise and quieten the little shaver.

Above an inner door there was a plaque and it read *Court Three*. From beyond the door came a gentleman in a black gown and he held a clip board. Purely for the record, I confirm that in terms of appearance he was not dissimilar to the gentleman down at the Eveshore Magistrates Court. Indeed, he was not dissimilar from most court ushers up and down the country.

The usher looked a bit stressed. Mind you, he was not the only one.

"Are you Mr. Gatehouse?" He sounded a bit stressed, and all.

"Yes, I most certainly am."

"You're very late."

"Yes, I most certainly am." He was quick off the mark, he was.

"Your client," spluttered the usher, "is seated in the conference room, but…"

"Thank you very much."

"But, as I was about to say, sir, he is much stressed and the magistrates have been waiting for you."

"A few minutes," I said, and, while I was saying it, I raised all the digits on my right hand. "Just tell the magistrates that I need just a few minutes. Okay?"

"Okay, sir. I shall ask for six minutes."

"Eh? No, no," I said. "I ain't from Cambridge. That one's a sticking plaster that's worked loose."

"Those are nasty cuts you have there, sir."

"Five minutes," I said, barging past.

The usher sniffed the air. "What a very strange and unpleasant smell, sir."

"Five minutes," I said, again, on reaching a door in which the joiner had cut a tiny porthole-type window. I pushed but on the realisation that I ought really be pulling, I pulled. "Five minutes," I said, for the purpose of conveying that, beyond all reasonable doubt, I required just three hundred seconds to confer with my client.

Beyond the threshold was a room. It was a tiny room. Indeed, so tiny was the room that it was as well that the door had required pulling and not pushing. The room was dominated by a plywood-topped table. Seated at the table was a business-suited gentleman whose face was dominated by a pair of dark, plastic-rimmed, spectacles. "Mr. Gatehouse? Thank goodness you are here." He was exceptionally well spoken with no detectable accent.

The gentleman looked me full on. I could not help but notice that the lenses of his spectacles were as thick as and as round as the bottoms of gold top milk bottles. "I'm so sorry for my late arrival, Mr. Wildmore."

"Will you be able to save my driving license, Mr. Gatehouse?"

"Well, I'll give it a damned good try."

My client sniffed the air. "Mr. Gatehouse?"

"Mr. Wildmore?"

"There's a most pungent and unpleasant smell, Mr. Gatehouse?"

The face of the usher appeared at the porthole. From the mouthing and tap tapping on the glass neither Mr.Wildmore nor I needed to be adept in the art of lip-reading to detect that our presence in Court was required as a matter of some urgency.

The usher feverishly darted towards Court Three. I feverishly followed.

The usher opened a swing door so that I could enter.

"Thank you very much," I said.

The usher looked anxiously about. "Where on earth has your client gone, sir?"

I stopped dead and turned ninety degrees intending to retrace my steps. Mr. Wildmore did not see that particular movement coming, as evidenced by the fact that he careened straight into the middle button of my grimy white shirt. You see, he was vertically challenged as well as visually impaired. In the event, my client had also feverishly followed and the usher hadn't noticed him.

Mr. Wildmore pivoted his head in an upwardly direction. I found myself staring down into eyes that were significantly magnified by the milk bottles. "What on earth is that strange smell, Mr. Gatehouse?"

"Don't know what you mean," I said. *Cheeky bugger, I thought, It's obviously the phenomenon of the heightening of one sense as a result of the decline of another, namely your eyesight, old chum.*

My client continued to stare. I was tempted to waft an outstretched hand in front of the milk bottles. The motive was to check the exact extent of his apparent visual impairment. However, before I had chance to raise an arm, let alone wave, Mr. Wildmore demonstrated that he had the eyesight of an average mole because he sort of barged straight into me and I was propelled backwards into the courtroom.

"The next case, Your Worships," said the usher, "is the matter against Mr.Wildmore. He," added the usher, with a certain degree of authority, "is represented by Mr. Gatehouse, of counsel."

I turned to face the court and, as I did so, I caught one of the justices, a lady magistrate, mouthing the word counsel. I reckoned she was probably in her thirties but dressed as she was in a thick tweed jacket and, her neck being adorned as it was by a double row of pearls, she looked twice that age. The magistrate had done the mouthing to the chairman of the bench. He was seated to her right. "Barrister," mouthed a gentleman magistrate. He was seated on the other side. Never mind his tweed jacket finished off with leather elbow pads, what with his grey moustache and hairless head, he was most definitely thirtyish times two. The mouthing by the lady and by the gentleman of, respectively, "counsel," and, "barrister," was because, for the most part, it was solicitors who appeared before the magistrates and consequently the appearance by a barrister was a rarity especially, so it appeared to be the case, in Persham.

I hurried to the front of Court and I occupied a chair immediately next to the prosecuting lawyer. He was just a solicitor and, as such, deserves no better introduction than just that; the solicitor. It was soon apparent that the magistrates were desperately anxious to go home because their clerk, whose job it was to advise the justices on points of law, was soon asking Mr.Wildmore to confirm that he had previously written to the court to confirm that he was guilty of speeding and further that the court had adjourned the case in his absence so that he might have an opportunity of attending in person and say why it was that he should not have his license to drive taken away. "I agree," said Mr. Wildmore, though on what basis he could agree the basis on which the matter had been put off was beyond my intellect bearing in mind the common consensus that Mr. Wildmore had not actually been in Court the time before.

Anyway, with that little formality done and dusted Mr. Wildmore was permitted, indeed ordered, to take a seat, and, up popped he who you simply must forgive me for referring to as just the solicitor.

"Your Worships," said the solicitor. *So far so good*, I thought and the solicitor ploughed on. "This defendant..."

"Which defendant," interrupted the clerk of the court. "You have not afforded me an opportunity to identify the defendant." The clerk, a thickset man in twenties, looked as pleased as punch at having undermined the solicitor. He proceeded to address my client. "Are you James Henry Wildmore?" He spoke officiously and without a modicum of respect. That's what justices' clerks do, you see. They are usually solicitors, barristers, sometimes, and they do not work in private practice. Clerks frequently have chips on their shoulders and the condition manifests itself in officiousness and bad manners.

"Er, yes, I am." Mr. Wildmore both looked and sounded a bit taken aback. "I just told you that I had previously written to the Court."

"Well, how am I expected to know that it was you?" The clerk asked my client to provide further details, namely his date of birth, address, and for confirmation that it was very definitely him, Mr. Wildmore, who had previously written to Court admitting that he had been caught tear-arsing around in his motor. All questions, in common with the first, were uttered disrespectfully.

"Good!" So said the clerk on being satisfied that Mr. Wildmore was very definitely who he said he was and that it was he who had very definitely driven the motor vehicle on the day in question, in the manner alleged. "Sit down then, Wildmore!"

"It's Mister," I said, politely.

The clerk went a bit pink in the jowls. He wore spectacles, and all; of the nondead Beatle variety, to be exact, and they were perched on the very end of his nose. He used the spectacles to look down his nose. "I beg your pardon?" In keeping with everything else he had said thus far, he said it in an aggressive and disrespectful fashion.

"My client," I said, rising, "is **Mr**. Wildmore."

"Well, that's what I said!"

"No you didn't." I looked towards the gods, namely the long table on a platform that the three magistrates occupied. "He said Wildmore," I said. "My client is, in fact, **Mr**. Wildmore," I went on to submit.

"Oh, I don't think we should have any unpleasantness," said the chairman, pleasantly. "Shall we simply proceed?"

So, while the prosecutor (you know, just the solicitor?) got to his feet, the clerk sniffed the air. "There's a damned funny smell coming from somewhere," he said.

"That is the case for the prosecution," said the solicitor, ignoring the clerk's observation.

"What do you mean, that is the case?" The enquiry emanated from the chairman.

"Well, your learned clerk has already provided a full outline," said the solicitor, snappily, and he promptly sat down.

Now it was my turn. As would a well-tuned athlete, I took a few sharp intakes of breath and I waited for the nod from on high. But, no nod was forthcoming from the chairman and, in lieu thereof, he went into a huddle and began conferring with the other two justices.

When the chairman was done, he at last nodded. However, the nod was not directed at me but at my client. "Stand up please, Mr. Wildmore." My client dutifully obeyed. "You will be disqualified from driving for a period of…"

"I hesitate to interrupt," I said, without hesitation while simultaneously clambering to my feet. "With respect," I said, without a shred of respect, "you have not considered any representations on Mr. Wildmore's behalf."

"Oh, sorry," said the chairman. It was his turn to turn a bit pink in the jowl department. "Counsel may proceed with his submission."

"No point," I said.

"What?" You have probably guessed. It was him, the clerk, sticking his oar in. The short interlude had done nothing to improve his manners.

"I do not suggest," I said, intending to impugn the integrity of the bench, "that the integrity of the bench is impugned. However…"

The lady magistrate took in on herself to usurp her chairman and it was she who interrupted my flow. "How dare you suggest that we are prejudiced?" Hailing as she did from the market town of Persham, with its predominantly white middle-class population, that was a bit rich, that was. Indeed, it would have been be all the more shocking had she been anything other than prejudiced.

"With respect," I said, and naturally I said it without a modicum of respect, "justice must not only be done but it must be seen to be done."

She began to ferret with her shiny white pearls. "Counsel should note that justice is to be done."

"But, it must be seen to be done." I coughed for effect and, from a decanter before me I began pouring water into a plastic beaker. I immediately regretted doing any such thing because my hands were shaking and I missed the beaker and I managed to pour half of the water over the table and, in the process, my papers. "Imagine this," I said, ignoring the bore gushing my way, "imagine that, despite submissions to the contrary, you decide to disqualify my client having given the distinct impression that your minds are already made up?"

"Well, we do intend to disqualify him," said the chairman. He didn't beat around the bush, I'd give him credit for that. The lady magistrate decided to call time on the ferreting and, by way of alternative pursuit, she gave her necklace a sharp yank. With that, the string bust. The causative effect was that a dozen or so pearls plopped down onto the table from whence they rolled forwards and cascaded upon the clerk who appeared to be daydreaming in his lowly place below. As the clerk leapt up, startled like a rabbit in headlights, and, as instinct took hold and he began brushing the pearls from his hair, the lady magistrate giggled nervously.

"I'm afraid that Mr. Gatehouse has a point," said the clerk, eventually. The lady magistrate did not bat an eyelid and neither did she convey concern that her pearls were now plopping off the clerk's desk and, one by one, were rolling down a grid cum drainage duct. It was incontrovertible evidence that the pearls were fake or worse, had come from Spain. The clerk seized hold of a large black Bakelite-type telephone. After a few crackles and pops, he mumbled into the thing. When he was done with the mumbling, the clerk announced, "Court Two is free, Your Worships. I shall immediately request one of the ushers to deliver the papers to Court Two."

The five minutes that it took for the prosecutor in Court Two (again, just a solicitor) to acquaint himself with the case gave me sufficient time to conduct a proper conference. As a travelling salesman it was naturally a condition of employment that my client travel. Furthermore, the three hungry mouths that required feeding belonged to boys who attended school some ten miles from his home. For the purpose of making ends meet, it was necessary for Mrs. Wildmore to work nights at a bottling plant, three times per week. Consequently, the duty to collect the boys and their hungry mouths fell on Mr. Wildmore from Monday to Wednesday inclusive, excluding bank holidays.

The bench of magistrates in Court Two comprised three males. The clerk of the court was female. Pleasing on the eyes she was and pleasing on the ears, and all. Just a kid, early twenties, I'd have said.

Anyway, no sooner had the clerk remarked, "There's a rather unpleasant smell in here," than the chairman of the bench conferred with his colleagues, stood up and proclaimed that he intended to stand down.

"I know this defendant," said the chairman. "I am a director of the Regal Knight Insurance Company."

The chairman shuffled along the bench, shuffled past the colleague to his left, trod on the colleague's feet, apologised profusely to the colleague and he occupied a chair at the very end, near the door of the magistrates' retiring room.

"We will proceed with a quorum of just two," said the clerk, pleasantly.

The proceedings began. They started with a brief outline from the prosecutor. You know? Just the solicitor? When he was done, I took my sharp intakes of breath, again, and clambered to my feet, again.

"Have you by any chance fallen?" enquired the clerk and, naturally, her enquiry was delivered very pleasantly, indeed.

Oh, I've fallen, mate, I thought, *I've fallen for Janie, big time*. "No," I said. "Why do you ask?"

"Oh, it's just that..." Though still sounding pleasant enough, the clerk seemed a bit flustered. "It is simply that you appear to be covered in a greenish grey muddy substance."

"I had to pull a pensioner from the wheels of an oncoming tractor laden with fertiliser." My increasing propensity to tell lies in common with all the other barristers was very troublesome.

"Good heavens above," said the magistrate. It was the one who'd had his feet crushed. "Shall we adjourn for a few moments to enable you to clean up?"

"Nah," I said bravely. "My client is most anxious to proceed." So, proceed I bravely did. To have any chance at all of saving my client's driving license it would be necessary for the magistrates to hear from him on oath. As such, there did not appear to be any point in hanging around so, without further ado, "I propose to call Mr. Wildmore," I told the magistrates.

Mr. Wilmore had not been expecting to be called quite so early in the proceedings. Indeed, come to think about it, I had clean forgotten to tell him that he would be required to take the stand. However, take the stand he did, but not before he had managed to stumble up the solitary step beneath the entrance of the witness box.

"Yes, I am," my client said, in response to my leading question that he was one, James Henry Wildmore.

"I think," said the clerk, "that we should permit Mr. Wildmore to take the oath before he gives sworn evidence." She still sounded, sort of, pleasant but I could have sworn that there was a smidgen of sarcasm.

I looked around for an usher. None were about. Therefore, I myself, me, Izaak Gatehouse, tootled over to the witness box and, on arrival at my port of destination, I told Mr. Wildmore to take the Good Book in his right hand. Next, I asked him to read the words on a card that I'd found lying on one side.

"I can't quite make out the words," said my client, peering through the milk bottles.

Therefore, I began to read the oath. However, at the half way mark I was interrupted.

"I'm an atheist," said Mr. Wildmore "I do not swear on the bible."

"Well, why didn't you tell me?"

"You didn't ask, Mr. Gatehouse."

"Don't you **ever** swear on the bible, then?"

"No."

"What? Not even just the once, like, to impress the magistrates?"

My client stood rigid and stretched himself to his full height. "No, Mr. Gatehouse. It would not be Christian and against my religion to do that."

There was writing on the back of the card, so I reversed it and held the thing before my client's eyes. He squinted, copped hold of the card, squinted some more and he held the card to within, I swear, half of an inch of his face.

"How about that as a form of oath, Mr. Wildmore?"

"No," said Mr. Wildmore, snappily. "Neither do I worship *Please Do Not Remove From The Courtroom*. It is the fresh air that we breathe and the water that flows and the rocks with which we build our humble homes that are my masters."

"Well," I said, sounding a bit flustered, "take a deep breath of that fresh air, and here…" I had spied the water decanter. So, I took hold of the thing and held it aloft. "How about swearing on this, then?"

"No."

"Hang about," I said. "The water in this decanter isn't blessed. In fact, I'll wager that it's come straight out of the tap."

The minx of a clerk smirked. I swear that she did. "I suggest," she said, "that the witness be affirmed."

"Nah," I said. "Do you have any rune stones laying around?"

Strangely, the clerk ducked beneath her desk and, sort of, disappeared from view. She reappeared seconds later with what appeared to be a white silken handkerchief. Stranger still, it was stuffed in her dainty mouth.

An usher entered Court and came galloping to the rescue. He was identical to the ushers with whom I'd hitherto come into contact, except that this usher was of the female persuasion. She asked my client whether he solemnly, sincerely, declared and affirmed, and so and so forth, that he intended to tell the God's honest truth even if he did not believe in God in the first place.

So, with the usual formalities done and dusted, my examination of Mr. Wildmore started.

My client confirmed that he was still, most definitely, James Henry Wildmore and that even though he was a heathen, the Regal Knight employed him as a travelling salesman of insurance products. The questions that I asked were designed to ensure that Mr. Wildmore put forward a sound case to show that he was a God-fearing fellow at heart and that there would be exceptional hardship were he to have his driving license taken away. You see, he would automatically lose his job and, as God was his witness, the bank would foreclose and take away every single rock that cumulatively comprised his humble abode.

It was going very nicely, thank you for asking. Why, even the clerk of the court had stopped laughing. So, I thought I'd ladle it on a bit thick by prompting my client to explain that his family and private life would suffer very badly were the magistrates to disqualify him from wreaking havoc on the highway.

"Where," I enquired, "does Mrs. Wildmore work?"

"My wife, Mr. Gatehouse, is employed at the Persham preserving factory down on... "

My client was interrupted by a loud cough coming from the direction of the substitute chairman. "This is most embarrassing," said the sub, "but I too must stand down."

The clerk leapt to her feet and turned her back on Court. There ensued a series of whispers. When the minx was done, she turned her back, again, only this time she turned her back on the magistrates.

"I am afraid," said the clerk, "that one of my justices is employed as a foreman at the Persham food preserving factory. He fears that he may be acquainted with Mrs.Wildmore."

There came a gasp from the region of the defendant's chair.

"Don't worry, Mr. Wildmore. We'll get around it."

"He's certainly got around my wife, Mr. Gatehouse."

"Eh?"

"Mr. Gatehouse. I always suspected that the gifts of pickled cabbage on Thursday nights were suspicious, I did."

"Shush, Mr. Wildmore. The bench can hear us."

"Not to mention the jars of pickled eggs that now stretch from the far end of the kitchen, through the hallway and halfway up the stairs to the bathroom."

"Shush!"

"And back again!"

The prosecutor, you know? Him, the solicitor rose to address Court. "I have no objection to the matter proceeding without the gentleman in question." Submission done and dusted, he returned to the chair that he'd vacated just seconds before.

The clerk indicated that she was even more afraid than the last time she had spoken. "I am very much afraid," she said, "that we cannot proceed with just one lay magistrate, but…" she made a dive for the court telephone and soon she was at the whispering, again. "Good," said the clerk after she was done, "I was just in time to prevent the stipendiary magistrate from leaving. This case will now be heard in Court One."

"Oh, good," I said, as the telephone was returned to its cradle with a clatter.

"Oh, God," I heard my client say.

Now, at this stage in my reporting on the case against Mr. James Henry Wildmore I had best explain that a stipendiary was a full time, legally qualified, magistrate. Nowadays, they are called District Judges. It is simply a ruse to make them feel more important than they actually are. The causative effect is that, dead chuffed at being called judges, they don't go asking for pay rises.

I entered Court One just in time to witness the stipendiary telling off the prosecutor (he was just another solicitor). It was something or other to do with the fact that the solicitor did not have a sufficiently good grasp of the facts of the miscellaneous cases that he was presenting to Court. He (the stipendiary, that is, and not the solicitor) was fairly softly spoken but there was an edge to his tongue and it was not at all pleasant.

"I shall expect you to be better prepared the next time that you appear before me."

"Yes, sir. Sorry, sir."

Having torn the solicitor off a strip, the stipendiary looked down his nose and through his half-moon spectacles at Mr. Wildmore and me. The more he looked down his nose the fatter his neck appeared to get. Indeed, by the time that the stipendiary had finished looking down his nose it seemed rather as if he had a good half a dozen or so pancakes under his chin.

"I assume that this is the addition to my list?"

"I believe that it is," I said, sitting down on the front row of benches.

"I take note," said the stipendiary, "that you do not have the courtesy to stand when you address me."

"Eh?"

" Neither do you have the courtesy to address me as sir."

"Eh?"

"Furthermore, there is a damned strange smell coming from somewhere."

"Oh," I said, with nonchalance. "That's me that is, sir."

"Eh?"

I shrugged. "A tractor towing farm waste was about to run down a babby, I mean to say, a baby in a pram and I went to the rescue."

The stipendiary leaned forwards and his eyes opened wide with astonishment. "I say, Mister...?"

"Gatehouse, sir."

"I say, Mr. Gatehouse, I apologise for having spoken to you sharply. You must be rather shaken. Do you require time to compose yourself and, perhaps, brush-up?"

The change in demeanour was startling. He was plainly as nutty as a fruitcake.

"Nah, I mean, no thank you, sir." I shrugged. "These things happen but the show, as they say, must go on."

"That's the spirit, Mr. Gatehouse." The stipendiary turned towards the prosecutor; him, the solicitor. "You see, Mr., er...? Counsel, Mr. Gatehouse, here, shows the spirit."

"Yes, sir. Thank you, sir," said the solicitor arising. "Perhaps, sir, I may be permitted to open the case?"

"Well, there is not much to open is there, Mr. er...?"

"I wouldn't say..."

"See you here," said the stipendiary. "The defendant already has nine penalty points on his driving license. He admits speeding. The imposition of at least three further penalty points for speeding is mandatory. It will take the defendant to twelve penalty points because three added to nine equals twelve. Twelve penalty points, as I am certain you are aware already, renders the defendant liable to be disqualified from driving unless exceptional hardship will result."

The solicitor returned to his seat. "Yes, sir. Thank you, sir."

"Now then, Mr. Gatehouse?"

You will gather that, by inference, it was my turn. "Yes, sir?"

"I note that your client was exceeding the speed limit at approximately 5.00pm."

"Yes?"

"On a Thursday

"Er. Yes?"

"Little Friday, Mr. Gatehouse. A day notorious for driving after having consumed alcohol at one of the many wine bars in and around this area."

"But, there's no evidence to suggest that my client had been drunk driving."

"Ha! Ha!" That's how the stipendiary went. The ha and the other ha demanded a great deal of facial distortion, so much so that the miscellaneous chins were sent a wobbling. "I have observed these salesman-types in the local bars, Mr. Gatehouse." The stipendiary leaned back in his chair and he buried the chins deep into his chest. Indeed, he put me in mind of a sumo wrestler. "I have observed these salesman-types in the local bars," so said the stipendiary, again. However, he expanded his making of a judicial note thus. "They ply young office girls with cheap alcohol and they get them tipsy and into bed. That is not to suppose," he supposed, "that I frequent such places."

"Of course not, sir."

"Even if I did, I certainly would not be attempting to get young girls tipsy on port and lemon…"

"No, sir."

"Nor, indeed on any other form of alcoholic beverage."

"Oh, absolutely not, sir."

"Then, Mr. Gatehouse, these salesmen-types tear off home to their wives and children and they are lucky if they are not caught for being drunk behind a wheel as well as speeding"

"No, sir."

"Eh?"

"I mean, yes, sir."

The stipendiary nodded, knowingly. "Lucky not to be caught with lipstick on the collar too, I'll wager."

"There is a statement, sir."

"Yes?"

"It is a statement of an officer who performed a road side breath test."

"Yes?"

" He confirms that there was no trace of alcohol."

"Meaning?"

"Meaning, that the defendant was cold stone sober."

"Then why was he speeding? Did he have lipstick on his collar? Good God! Was he so eager and so tight fisted that he departed without purchasing a drink for the poor girl?"

There was no doubting it that the stipendiary magistrate for the district of Persham was stark staring bonkers.

"Well," I said, trying not to roll my eyes. "He just was. Sober, that is."

"Oh? He just was, was he?"

"Er, yes?"

"Well, Mr. Gatehouse, the scoundrel had better come forward and take the Good Book and be sworn."

"No, he won't," I said. "Take the Good Book, that is."

"What?" The stipendiary leaned forwards and he stared firstly at me, then the scoundrel, and then at me, again.

"He's agnostic or sommut, I mean something, sir."

"A damned heathen what, Mr. Gatehouse?"

"Not at all, sir. He worships the air that we breathe and the water that flows, sort of..."

The stipendiary sighed. "Very well, Mr. Gatehouse. Your client had better come forward and be affirmed."

So, that is what my client did. And after he had, not for the first time that day, promised to be truthful, as God was his witness except he didn't believe in God in the first place, my client explained that he would lose his job if he was prohibited from terrifying the populace behind the wheel of his speeding motor car.

When Mr. Wildmore was done, I asked him to remain where he was just in case anyone else wanted to ask questions of him.

"Mr. Gatehouse," said the stipendiary.

"Yes, sir?"

"If I wanted to ask questions, I would say so."

"Yes, sir"

"Very well, your client may stand down."

"Thank you, sir." I turned to address my client. "Would you return to me please, Mr. Wildmore?"

"Oh, no he will not."

"Aye? What was that, sir?"

"**He**," said the stipendiary "should be seated in the dock."

"**He**," I said, "is not a criminal."

"But, he is, Mr. Gatehouse." The stipendiary leaned forwards once more. Indeed, the maniac leaned so far forwards that the pile of pancakes enveloped the whole of his collar and tie.

"Well, how do you make that out?" I was now in danger of sounding impertinent.

"Do not be impertinent," said the stipendiary. "It certainly is criminal, and if it is not then it damned well ought to be, to go plying young girls with alcohol." Next, he addressed my client. "Get in the dock, now!"

I held aloft an outstretched hand. "Stand right where you are for a mo'!"

Mr. Wildmore, hands in pockets, dilly-dallied betwixt witness box and dock.

"What? Have you taken leave of your senses, Mr. Gatehouse?" It was him, the stipendiary, again. "Furthermore, remove your hands from your pockets."

"Sorry, sir," I said.

"No, not you, Mr. Gatehouse. I meant your client. But, no!" The stipendiary lifted his chins which presumably afforded him an uninterrupted view of the advocate's bench. Simultaneously, the lunatic afforded an uninterrupted view of a collar splattered with red lipstick. "No! I mean, yes! You too, Mr. Gatehouse! Kindly remove your hands too!"

"Yes, sir." So, I duly obliged the mad man and I aligned both hands perfectly with my trouser seams where everyone could see them.

"I intend," said the stipendiary, "to disqualify your client from driving a motor vehicle for a period of a fortnight."

"I haven't given a closing submission, thingy yet!"

The maniac leapt from his chair.

"Your client," said the stipendiary, on his way out, "should recognise that a ban from driving for fourteen days is minimal punishment bearing in mind his propensity to ply young girls with port and lemon!"

As the fellow disappeared from view, I crossed the well of the court, intending to converse with my client. Mr. Wildmore failed to see me coming and I was obliged to tap his spectacles. "Good heavens! Is that you, Mr. Gatehouse? That is a truly splendid result, Mr. Gatehouse."

"But, I'm afraid that you've lost your license, Mr. Wildmore."

"It is the best possible result," said my client, eagerly. "I am due for a fortnight's vacation. And, and..." As you will gather, Mr. Wildmore was having problems getting his words out. "And, when my license is returned, Mr. Gatehouse, I shall have no endorsements!"

"Meaning, Mr. Wildmore?"

"Meaning, Mr. Gatehouse, that I can collect nine more penalty points for speeding without the risk of disqualification!"

"Just doing my job, Mr. Wildmore."

We strolled towards the exit. I permitted my client to go first. It was regrettable that I did so because Mr. Wildmore failed to notice that the door was closed; indeed, he failed to notice that there any door there at all.

"Here, Mr. Wildmore, permit me to assist you to your feet."

"Do not touch me, Mr. Gatehouse. I have no desire to come into contact with the foul smelling substance about your person, even though you are apparently a hero by having saved the life of a pensioner, or was it a baby in a pram?" Mr. Wildmore clambered up all of his own accord and, when he was once again vertical, I looked down only to be confronted by the magnified eyes looking straight up "If you will care to make yourself respectable, Mr. Gatehouse, I shall take you for a celebratory drink."

"No, thanks, Mr. Wildmore. I'd best head back home, I had."

My client tugged at the door on which a sign instructed the user to push. "Ouch! But, it is market day, Mr. Gatehouse."

"Meaning?"

"Could you help me to find my glasses Mr. Gatehouse? Only, though I know you will find it difficult to believe, I am rather short sighted without them."

"There you go, Mr. Wildmore, though I fear that one of us may have trodden on them."

"Not to worry, Mr. Gatehouse." He placed the broken spectacles across the bridge of his nose. "On market day, the young girls from the offices pile into the bar, they do." Mr.

Wildmore looked furtively about with the presumed intention of ensuring that no court users were within listening distance. "The girls," he said, on presumably being so satisfied, "are especially grateful if an older chap stands them a glass…"

"A glass, Mr. Wildmore?"

"A glass of fortified wine, of course, Mr. Gatehouse. It is just as Bill says, Mr. Gatehouse."

"Bill?"

"Yes, Mr. Gatehouse, Bill. You know? He is, of course, the stipendiary magistrate."

CHAPTER FOURTEEN

One bus journey, a couple of train journeys, and a hitchhike or four later, found me strolling down the lane towards the village of Prestwick.

Well, talk about *déjà vu*? The distant rumble of thunder over South Warwickshire had been audible all the way home. As I entered the village, wisps of mist swirled around my ankles because the sun was doing his very best to vaporise all of the surface water and send it back to the heavens where it belonged. Next, and as if to confirm that I had well and truly contracted a case of paramnesia, a big red fire engine (stuffed to the gunwales with jeering and waving volunteers) came hurtling past. And as if to prove that the sun was not doing a very good job, the front wheels of the fire engine hit a particularly large puddle and the contents came whooshing my way.

Sopping wet, I came to The Fly in the Ointment where, as before, a small crowd had gathered. For the purpose of affording free and uninterrupted access through the small gate and up the pathway, it was necessary to skirt around the crowd. As I did so, I felt compelled to shout at one of the fellows. "Same to you too, mate, with brass knobs on!"

I went around the back and entered the cottage and, just like the time previous, I did so through the kitchen door. Or, I mean to say, what was left of the kitchen door. "Gatehouse!" It was Ian, of course. The brand spanking new kitchen units had been frazzled and the once brilliant white ceiling was covered in scorch marks. "I was correct about you, all along!" Ian made his observation whilst sat upon the lavatory. You see, the brand spanking new dividing wall had gone. He sniffed the air and winced. "There's a damned strange smell in here," said Ian, by way of an aside. "And I do not refer to the stench of doused charcoal," he added as an aside to the aside, sort of thing.

"I ain't responsible for the gas explosion this time, I'm not, and that's the truth! Further and additionally," I added by way of traverse, because it's what lawyers do, "that's not to say that I formally admit doing it last time!"

"No, no," said Ian, dismissively, and, at the same time he wafted about his very latest clay pipe. The bowl was strangely shaped into the head of a Native American chief; Iroquois, I'd have said, judging from the startled look. "I am correct," said Ian, tapping the chieftain against the flush system, "that your propensity to check and double check everything is tiresome and wearisome."

I made for the kettle intending to make tea. I did so by way of diversionary tactic and not because I was gagging. But, the surface on which the kettle normally lived was no longer there. "How do you mean, Ian?" I said it with suspicion. "How do you mean, checking and double checking?"

"Gatehouse! I now know that on the occasion of the last incinerating of this abode you were not, against all odds, responsible."

"Aha! I knew it!" I gave up looking for the kettle on noticing that the tea caddy and contents really rather resembled an urn containing the ashes of a dead uncle. "Victimised I am, Ian, and that's the truth!"

"Gatehouse!" Ian crossed his legs, winced, and put Tadodaho's stem to his mouth. "I knew all along that your habit of returning to the cottage three times, four times, sometimes more, for Pete's sake, solely to check that the oven was switched off was without just cause because it turns out that the gas was actually turned off!"

"Well, how the hell did the fire start last time, then?"

"The same as this time, old chap."

I breathed a sigh. "Okay, Ian. Well, how the hell did the fire start this time. Oh, and, Ian...?"

"Yes, old dear heart?"

"Don't go telling me that it started like the last time."

"I would never dream of so doing, old chap." Ian, along with the chieftain, vacated the toilet and he scooted through to the sitting room. "Do you see the walnut tree, Gatehouse, old chap?" He spoke with both hands plunged in his pockets and with Tadodaho hanging on to his bottom lip for dear life.

I too tootled into the sitting room. The big inglenook was blazing away which I recall thinking was rather remarkable, possibly criminally negligent, bearing in mind that the fire fighters had so recently laid off dowsing down the kitchen.

"Ian," I said, "of course I can see the tree. The blasted thing gives me nightmares, it does."

Ian removed the pipe and he plucked from the inglenook a smouldering chunk of post and rail fence. Having thereby provided an explanation for the recent three-car pile-up, in which the vicar's wife was obliged to swerve her Ford Cortina to avoid hitting the pony belonging to young Toby Horobin-Smith which had weirdly galloped out of his paddock, Ian put the chieftain to the torch. "That blasted tree," said Ian, with a wince, "is a public nuisance and should have been removed years ago." He returned the pipe, intact but a little singed, to his lips and puffed a wee while in silence. After a brief interlude. "You may have noticed," said Ian, "that the parish church is directly in line with the tree."

As was customary, I deposited myself in the better of the two leather armchairs. "Listen up, Ian," I said, "you're talking in riddles, you are."

"Come you here and look out of the window," said Ian. He came over to where I was at and he tugged my shoulder. "Yuk," said Ian, rubbing together the forefinger and thumb of his left hand. "Pray, what substance is it that you have plastered all about your jacket? Furthermore, pray what is…?" He paused, only for a second, mind, as he raised the hand to nasal height "Pray, **what is** that abominable odour?"

I stood all of my own accord and, ignoring Ian's allusion to the fact that I was plastered in pigeon doings, I joined him for the purpose of gawping from the window. "Yes, Ian, the church is in direct alignment with the tree. The church," I added, "is a fair bit higher, and all." It was true. You see, whereas the tree was sufficiently low for the base of its trunk to be obscured from view, the church was stood proud on the highest ground in the whole of the parish. I knew that as a fact because it had been the devil's own job dragging one half of a lynch gate down the slope at two o'clock in the morning, in a roaring gale, just to keep the inglenook from going out.

"The church steeple," explained Ian, jabbing with Tadodaho, "is equipped with a lightning conductor."

"Well, of course it is," I said. "All churches have them things, except for the ones from in and around Dudsall."

"Eh?"

"The conductors," I explained, casually, "tend to be nabbed by the tatters, who clamber up to steal lead from off of the roofs, you see."

"Aye?"

"It's sort of like nabbing a trophy," I said, thereby referring Ian to the anthropology of the average Black Country native.

"Well, Gatehouse." Ian jabbed the pipe so furiously that the chieftain clonked his head against the windowpane. I felt it myself, I did, such was the force. "Churches in Dudmore…"

"Dudsall, Ian."

"Churches in Dudsall may very well burn to the ground as a result of lightning strikes. But, not so the Parish Church of Holy Trinity. No, by heavens!" Ian began rocking back and forth on the balls of his feet. "It would appear, Gatehouse, that *fulgur* unleashed from the hand of God has a propensity to strike the steeple from whence it is diverted towards that blasted tree. And, and…!" he was building up a real head of steam.

"Spit it out, Ian!"

"And, that blasted tree unleashes the sizzling sheets straight in our direction, namely, through this window and through to the kitchen where it incites all combustibles to combust!"

"That's fanciful, that is, Ian. Trees, not even blasted walnut trees, conduct electricity."

"Gatehouse! The damnable walnut tree has a propensity to cast down lighting at a rate greater than can ever be mustered by the characters who allegedly possess the force in that new *Star*

Wars movie flop. The nest in the highest bow, you see, is stuffed full of metal objects pilfered by your friends the magpies."

"Aha!" I exclaimed. "Those ruddy magpies, again! I might have known that they were behind it." With that, I made a dash for the front door.

"Where are you going, Gatehouse?"

I stopped, with the door half open, or, as a resident of Birmingham might say, half closed. "Why," I said, with wide-eye innocence, "I'm off to report these here events to Janie, of course."

"Gatehouse!" Ian scooted over and he slammed shut the half-closed door. "Do you not realise that today and tomorrow is the Shipsford Hobby Horse Festival?"

"But, but…!"

"Do you not realise, Gatehouse, that Janie judges the artwork of the local teenagers at the said festival?"

"But, but…!"

"No buts, Gatehouse! Should you go gate-crashing that little gathering there will be no let-off this time!"

CHAPTER FIFTEEN

I decided to resist the temptation of gate-crashing the Hobby Horse Festival. My credibility, you must understand, was sufficiently shot to pieces without compounding matters by presenting an appeal against Janie's conviction that I was a serial stalker, that I had shinned up to her bedroom window, that I had stolen a precious ring and that I had had the audacity to go down on bended knee and, by way of gift of betrothal, demand that she adorn the second from last digit of her left hand with her very own ring. I was certainly in no position to present fresh evidence. The Almighty, you see, had headed off an appeal on those grounds by ensuring that the most recent sheet of lighting projected from the parish church of Holy Trinity had well and truly wrecked the nest and, judging from the singed tail feathers, the inhabitants had been flash fried.

That night, I declined an invitation to drown my sorrows at The Case is Open. In lieu thereof, I spent an evening before the inglenook with just Colin, the cat, for company.

Come the midnight hour, I was thinking of retiring to bed. Bed, in my case, consisted of a pile of scatter cushions located beneath the stairs. Ian was not due to return for a couple of hours. You see, before departing he had served notice that the landlord of the pub intended to have a lock-in party to which anyone with money in their pocket was cordially invited.

I yawned and rose from the best of the leather armchairs and seized Colin. He had been sleeping in my lap. Colin was not at all happy at being awoken and he did his customary hisses and growls.

"Shush, shush," I told the mangy moggie, and I held him by the mane and sallied forth towards the front door.

I extended my spare hand, intending to open the big oak door and let go the cat so that he could pursue his nocturnal antics. Just you imagine the shock that I had when the doorknocker did what it had done for the whole of its life and knocked loudly.

"Izaak? Izaak?" The voice was feminine. "Are you there?" Now, I just know that you are assuming that the voice belonged to my beloved Janie. Well, such are the dangers of relying on circumstantial evidence. It was Nurse Stringer, you see, and not Janie who was calling my name.

"Yes, it's me." I duly opened the door. "You generally just stroll in," I told the nurse, grumpily.

"Izaak," said Nurse Stringer, softly, ignoring my observation. At that juncture, I must concede that I began to take more than a passing interest. Never before had I heard the police officer's wife talk in such feminine and hushed tones. "I know that Ian is indisposed and I am simply desperate for assistance." There was a full moon and the light shone directly onto the nurse's flame-red locks. Why, what with her stripy nurse-type uniform (low cut, and all), she looked really rather fetching.

I opened wide the door, thereby affording the nurse free and uninterrupted access. "So, what can I do for you, Nurse Stringer?"

"Please call me Fizz, Izaak."

Fizz, I thought. "What? Fizz?"

"It is short for Felicity," said Fizz.

"Well, do come in, Fizz," I said. "Oh! I see that you're already in."

"Izaak," said Fizz, and she deposited herself in the best armchair. She crossed one leg over the other and, in the process; she exhibited black nurse-type stocking tops. I gulped. "Izaak," she said again, because I fear that she may have assumed that I was distracted by something or other. "I know that we have had our differences, but..."

"Yes?" My interjection was untimely but born of acknowledgement that Janie and I were not, after all, intended to be as one. And to be fair, I, Izaak Gatehouse, was merely flesh and blood. And, when all was said and done, the voluptuous

Nurse Stringer (Fizz, apparently, to those in the know) was already possessed of intimate knowledge of my flesh and blood. It had been strictly in the line of duty, of course. But, *either way, I figured, if it's a bit of aftercare she's after then who am I to put up a fight?*

"Izaak?" Fizz uncrossed her legs.

"Yes?"

"Why are you staring at me in that weird way?"

"Smoke," I said, snappily. "It's smoke from that ruddy rose arbour."

"A rose what?"

"I mean, the ruddy firewood, thing, like."

"Look here, Izaak." With that, the flame-haired one stood up. She brushed the front of her nurse-type dress because the tricky fellow was clinging to her thigh, not that I took much notice, of course. "Ian, as I say, is indisposed and I simply must have male company for the purpose of venturing to the Whispering Knaves."

"Whispering Knaves?"

"The stone circle, of course."

"What?" I made a dive for the leather armchair (the best one, of course). "That spooky stone circle on the other side of Breeve Hill? You expect me to go up there at gone midnight?" I proceeded to demonstrate to the saucy nurse that she wasn't the only one who could cross legs and I did so, and all, except that I did so in the manner of a shrinking violet. "Strange things happen up there, they do, Fizz."

"Izaak!" To be fair, there was a certain something about the nurse when she sounded angry. "You are surely not frightened, are you?"

"Nah," I said, casually. *Too bloody right I'm frightened*, I thought. *Heaven knows what ghosts, hobgoblins, and hippies lurk around that place after dark.* "Me," I said. "Me? Frightened? Nah! Come on." I uncurled my legs and leaped up. "Let's go then, Fizz."

"That's the spirit, Izaak!"

I darted for the door. "After you, Nurse, er, after you, Fizz."

"Why, thank you, Izaak."

"Er, Fizz?"

"Yes, Izaak?"

"Why are we going to the stone circle?"

"Izaak," said Fizz. "If you will assist, I fancy that you will find that Maud is receptive, come sunrise."

"Fizz," I said, on settling into her car. "That doll of yours ain't sommut to do with voodoo, is it?"

"Jacob, the pharmacist," explained Fizz, as we drove through the village of Oakley Castle, "has been dismissed from his employment at the medical centre." Her striped, nurse-type dress rode high up her legs as she changed gears. Not that I was staring, I'll have you know. The flame-haired one quickly looked my way. Had I been staring at her thighs, I'd have had to look away, smartly, to avoid embarrassment. "There will be time for games later," said Fizz.

I swallowed hard. "I wasn't staring, like, I'll have you know." I said it in my best courtroom voice. It was guaranteed to sound believable.

"As I say," said the nurse dismissively, "we can play games later. In the meantime, Jacob is in urgent need of assistance."

We came to a sharp bend and, thankfully, Fizz returned both her eyes to the road ahead. She changed down a gear. I also returned my eyes to the road ahead. Well, I returned one of them, at any rate. "So, why on earth does Jacob require assistance at this time of night and up at the stone circle of all places?"

The sharp bend having been duly negotiated, the nurse looked my way, once more. "Out of sheer desperation, Jacob has been taking whatever employment comes his way."

"I know the feeling," I said, knowingly.

"Izaak, he is currently working for the Borgo family. He is selling ice creams in the car park that is adjacent to The Whispering Knaves."

Now then, all members of the local Borgo family looked and sounded Italian. Furthermore, they kept themselves to themselves. It was ample evidence for the locals to brand the entire crew gangsters. In truth, the family operated an ice cream business and I had it on good authority that they also owned a pizza franchise in the middle of nowhere (West Bromwich, to be exact).You see? I told you so. Such are the dangers of relying on circumstantial evidence.

"Well, Fizz," I said. "You've got me flummoxed, you have."

"Izaak." Thankfully, the nurse chose that moment to look at the road ahead. A tractor, you see, with headlamps on full beam, was coming from the opposite direction. "Izaak," she said, again, upon regaining control. "Jacob, as we speak, is selling ice creams from a mobile van."

"What? At this time of night?" I don't know about my eyes. I turned my entire self in the direction of the flame-haired one. "Has he gone totally mad, or somutt? Is that why we have to go there? Do we have to restrain him?"

"No, no, no," laughed Fizz, and she changed another gear. "There is a full moon tonight..."

"Exactly," I said, knowingly.

"I was about to say, Izaak, that there are plenty of potential customers at the stone circle whenever there is a full moon. It's just that..." She paused as the tail lights of various parked vehicles came into view. "You are aware, are you not, that my husband is the local police officer?"

I huffed. "Well, of course I am."

"Well, I am reliably informed that, sometime during the course of this evening, the police will be carrying out a raid. My husband, you see, has an informer who states that illicit alcohol is being sold."

"Aye?" That's all I managed to say because, without warning, the nurse yanked the steering wheel and we veered off into a field. Thereupon, she braked hard and the vehicle came to a juddering halt. I, sort of, was knocked off balance and my face went straight into Fizz's lap. It was a strange and wondrous experience.

The nurse grabbed my hair and she used it to hoist me up. "I have already told you, Izaak, that we shall have time for games later. In the meantime, we must warn Jacob." With that, she opened the driver's side door. "I see the ice cream van parked over by the hedge. Follow me, Izaak!"

The flame-haired one took off across the field with the velocity of your average whippet at Dudsall Racetrack. I remained firmly in the passenger seat. "There are strange and horrible things out there," I mumbled to myself. "I ain't about to get dragged kicking and screaming into Satan's nutting bag, I ain't."

There came a sudden knocking at the window. I nearly jumped out of my skin.

"Do you know this area, man? Are you wokal?" The enquiry naturally emanated from the other side of the glass. As such, it was uttered in tones that sounded, to me, a bit muffled. I duly withered and dithered, prodded and poked, and eventually I managed to locate a winder which I wound around and around and, eventually, I managed to wind down the window. A head covered in a dark hood popped in. "I just wanted to know if you are wokal, man?"

"Wokal?"

"Yeth, wokal, man"

"Oh!" I said. "You mean, am I local?"

"That's what I just said, man. Well?" The head popped back out. "You see, I'm looking for the wicker, man."

I hurriedly located the door lever. It was dangerously close to the widow winder and I was instantly reminded why a generation of travelling salesmen had perished on the roads of Britain after accidently bailing out of their Mk II Ford Cortinas at 70 mph on stinking hot days. "Help me!" I barged the door straight into the midriff of the hooded one and sent him reeling. "You ain't burning me to death in a wicker man!" I sprinted off up the field. "Felicity! For God's sake protect me!"

I skidded through cowpats and juddered to a halt next to the van that bore the livery *Borgo's Finest Ices. Stop Me and Buy One.*

"He's not here," said Fizz. "Jacob must have entered the stone circle. What's more," she added, "I must insist that you wipe your feet before getting back into my car."

"Listen up," I said. "There are strange noises coming from the other side of the hedge. Let's go park-up somewhere nice and quiet."

"Oh, Izaak." The nurse tutted and then she tugged my sleeve. "Come on. Let's go to the circle."

So, I bravely took the lead. Well, it was difficult not to take the lead bearing in mind that Fizz was pushing from behind.

"My God!" I said it on being pushed through a gap in the hedge. "The place is full of hooded devil worshippers!" I made as if to double back. "Let's go and play doctors and nurses!"

"You stay right here," hissed Fizz. In the light of the full moon her green eyes glowed. "Now," she said, "keep your eyes open for Jacob. We simply have to warn him."

With considerable reluctance, I terminated my attempts at doubling back and I tried to make out the identity of the hooded figures who were wailing their heads off in the centre of the ring of Whispering Knaves.

"Look, Fizz," I said, presently. "Can we go and play if I ask the important looking one if he's seen Jacob?"

"Which important looking one, Izaak?" The nurse leaned over my shoulder as she spoke and her long auburn hair wafted in front of my face. I could barely wait to be tussled up in those tresses, I can tell you. Indeed, had obsessive-compulsive disorder existed in those days, I'd have been cured on the spot. Playing games was uppermost on my mind and not counting the seventy-seven whispering knaves.

"There," I said, pointing and, at the same time, nestling in a bit, so much so that I could smell her sweet breath. "The one who's holding the big wooden stick with a skull for a knob? He must be the chief witch, druid, intergalactic storm trooper, kind of a thingy."

The flame-haired one shoved me forwards. The power of her thrust was very considerable. Her biceps had probably become overdeveloped by manhandling one too many National Health Service beds. "Yes. Go for it, Izaak," she said, in a loud whisper. "Tell him that Jacob is around here somewhere and that we simply must find him."

I tippy-toed towards the very centre of the moonlit circle of stone. "Oops! Sorry, mate," I said, interrupting the wailing of a witch-type person whose hush puppy I trod on. "And the same to you, mate," I also said, adding for good measure."You might be interested to know that that's a Viking word and Vikings weren't even invented when your lot were dodging Caesar."

I approached the hooded chief druid. He was stood with his back to me, right next to a puddle of water that, weirdly, appeared to be glistening. Now then, whereas, the assistant druidy-types had now begun chanting in a low monotone, the big cheese druid was caterwauling and he appeared to be reaching fever pitch. Indeed, he was building up such a head of steam that you'd have had a job distinguishing his voice from that of the popular music artist Barry White. As his warbling got louder (I'd have laid odds it was the crescendo), both arms popped up and, at the same time, the sun appeared over what would have been the horizon, had the local sewage plant not been in the way. Having elevated both arms so, the one belonging to the hand that held the long stick began wafting from left to right, or, possibly from right to left, depending I suppose on which dimension you were in at that particular moment in time. Well, either way, something strange was happening.

I looked towards the hedge with the intention of assuring myself that the flame-haired one was still there. She was, except that a pair of assistant druids appeared to have laid off the chants and were accusing her of being Boudicca, raised from the dead. "Go on," she mouthed, ignoring the pair of them. At the same time, she encouraged me to go on by making go on type gestures with both arms.

"We obey, mighty queen!"

"No, not you two idiots! I mean that idiot over there!"

"Excuse me, mate!" I grabbed hold of the arm of the chief druid. It was the one that was waving the stick. You see, I'm not a total idiot and I had the sense to reason that, if I restrained the arm with the stick, he couldn't turn around and wallop me with it.

"Eh? What?" The big cheese turned around. I loosed the arm and he raised the stick as if to strike.

"Jacob, the ice cream man, is here!" I had to shout to be heard above all of the chanting, you see, and not because I feared that he was about to strike.

The druid lowered the hand and then he lowered his hood. "What was that you said?" He did not much look like a druid, especially not a chief druid. Not, you understand that I knew what druids were supposed to look like in the first place. Never in my life, you see, did I imagine that a chief druid would be as bald as a badger, wear designer sunglasses at gone midnight, and have not a tooth in his head. Mind you, he did have a medallion around his neck and that, coming from one who was fast developing expert knowledge in the ways of druidry, was in keeping with what you'd expect a druid, especially a chief druid, to be wearing; save and except, that the medallion bore the image of a soccer ball and not a moon or a sun, and it was inscribed *Wembley, 1981. I was there.*

"I said!" I said. Then, I paused. Not for dramatic effect, you must understand. I paused purely for the purpose of waiting for the chanting from the assistants to die down a little bit more. "Jacob," I explained, on a suitable opportunity occurring, "is the ice cream man and he's around here somewhere. We must go to him."

"Oh, we must, we must," said the head honcho. The druid turned his back and up went the arms, stick, and all. "Oh, Mighty Prince of Darkness! I beseech thee to wait at the portal! I beg that you hang around a bit while I nip over the hedge and purchase a tootie-fruity ice cream!"

The chief faced me, once more, and thereby he turned his back on the Prince of Darkness. He handed me the stick. "Back in a jiffy," he said.

So, having been left holding the baby, come stick, I thought it best to face the sewage works. "He says he won't be long, Your Honour." My voice was quivery. "He's gone for an ice cream, if that's okay with you." I made as if to trot off back to the hedge but then I checked myself. You see, though I didn't believe in all the hocus pocus (anyone with half a brain knew that monsters preferred to live under paving slabs), I nevertheless had no desire to leave matters to chance. So, I raised the big stick. "In case you are offended, Your Honourable..." I sensed that my voice was nervously trailing-off. It was a bit like appearing before an appeal court. "I'm quite certain," I said, "that he'll get you an ice cream too, 'cause I'm equally certain it's a bit hot where you come from." I began to stroll casually away. However, I didn't want to leave things between the dark prince and me on a sour note, so. "In your case," I added, "he'll probably make certain that you have at least two scoops and a chocolate flake, I shouldn't wonder."

"What did he say, what did he say?" asked Fizz, anxiously, on my return. "Izaak," she added, "you look rather pale."

"Here," I said, and I handed the big stick to the nurse. "The chief druid has gone to find Jacob, so can we go now and play doctors and nurses?"

As we conversed, streams of assistant druids came by. They were chuntering something along the lines that the moment had come and passed, that the portal gates had slammed shut for another year, and that it was all the fault of some idiot who had strolled amidst the Whispering Knaves advocating that the Prince of Darkness ought to try a lick or two of Borgo's finest ice cream.

"Look," said Fizz, and she pointed towards the centre of the stone circle. "There is a shadowy figure kneeling. It may be Jacob. Come on, Izaak." Next, with her stripy nurse-type dress flapping in the breeze, she was off again.

In hot pursuit of Fizz, I bumped and bashed my way through the stream of assistant druids. Some were discarding their robes, presumably in disgust.

I got to the shadowy figure just ahead of the flame-haired one. "Is that you kneeling, Jacob?"

"Good grief, Gatehouse!" The shadowy figure leapt to his feet.

"Ian!" I said. "What are you doing here?" I then added. "Why are you dressed in a barrister's wig and gown?"

"Gatehouse!" Ian removed a lit cheroot from his mouth. "Before you ask," he said, because he had noticed me staring, "my very best clay pipe has disintegrated."

"Ian!" It was the flame-haired one. "What, in the name of heaven, are you doing here? Why in the name of hell are you dressed in that ridiculous costume?"

"I am the Prince of Darkness, of course. I have been waiting hours for those idiots to disappear so that I may accept the offerings."

"Offerings?" It was me who said it.

"Offerings?" Fizz said it, and all.

"Yes," said Ian. "Look you into the magic pool." Ian tutted. "Not in the sky, Gatehouse!" He pointed downwards. "I mean the thing that you're standing in!"

I stepped back apace and looked into the puddle. It glittered and sparkled. "Ian!"

"Gatehouse?"

"I knew it! Those ruddy magpies are possessed, they are!"

"No, no, Gatehouse!" Ian winced and shrugged. "It's not the magpies this time."

"Well, it surely ain't the ducks, Ian!"

"No," said Ian. "The treasures that you see in the sinkhole before you…"

"Do you mean the puddle, Ian?"

"Very well, Gatehouse. The treasures that you see in the puddle…"

"By treasures," said the nurse, "are you referring to the collection of Christmas baubles, a pair of franc coins, a Barbie doll who is weirdly dressed in a silver foil dress, and a fifty pence piece?"

"Now, see you here." Ian returned the cheroot to his lips and he took three or four drags in quick succession. "Times are hard," he said, wafting away smoke. "It is the fault of the current incumbent of Number 10 Downing Street that the worshippers have little else to offer their master."

"Worshippers?" It was Nurse Stringer.

"Do you mean the druid-type folk?" That was me, that was.

"Druids?" It was Ian. "If, by druids, you refer to the assistant manager of the co-operative grocery store, miscellaneous office clerks, a chorister, two or three pot-addled new age travellers, the vicar's wife, and the entire committee of the Shipford's Young Mothers' Association then, yes, it is the druids to whom I refer."

"We are here," said the flame-haired one, "to warn Jacob that the police are on their way."

"Police?" Ian shrugged and winced.

"Yes," I said, anxiously, "they suspect him of selling illicit alcohol, they do."

Ian casually tossed the cheroot into the sinkhole. "Alcohol?" He said it above the hisses, as the cheroot died a death by drowning. "Gatehouse. It is my understanding that the Licensing Act does not and has never restricted the sale, for public consumption or otherwise, of rum 'n' raisin ice cream."

"Now, see here, Ian," I said. "If we don't find Jacob, I don't get to play at doc…"

"I still can't find the wicker, man!" It was him. You know? The hooded Lord Summerisle.

I darted around the back of the nurse's dress, intending to hide behind all twenty-nine of the stripes. "Saints preserve me, Fizz, he's out to toast me, he is!"

"My dear fwiend," said the hooded one, coming over. "I'm wost, man. I can't find my way awound." He janked down the hood. Thereupon, I realised that it was merely an anorak that he was wearing. "Are your fwiends wokal? Perhaps they know the way to the wicker, man?"

"Look here," I said, "I'm really sorry, but I…"

I was about to tell the individual that I had not the foggiest of notions what it was he was attempting to convey when Ian butted in. Ian placed an arm about the stranger. "Come, my friend, I shall take you to the fountain where ale is both plentiful and cheap."

"But, but…"

"No buts, old chap. Just you come quietly with me."

"Aha! Caught red handed!" Now, it was P.C. Stringer's turn to come busting through the hedge. He was followed by two other uniformed police officers. "Got you at last, Prospect. You are under arrest for incitement to provide unlicensed liquor."

Ian shrugged and winced. "There is no such offence, my old adversary."

"Tell me why on earth are you dressed in a wig and gown? That has to be a criminal offence, surely?"

"No, old chap."

"Well, it's certainly a crime against nature, then."

"It's a crime against Igor Patterson," I muttered, "who will turn up at the Royal Courts of Justice tomorrow morning with now't but a side of bacon in his robes bag."

The officer gave the rest of us the once over. Having done so, his eyes settled on the saucy nurse. "I see that you are in Prospect's company, once again."

"Actually," replied Fizz, casually, and she linked her arm with mine. "I am with Izaak, here."

"Ha!" That's how the officer went. He was as dismissive as that. Then, he addressed the man in the anorak. "Okay, John, show me where Prospect keeps the liquor and you'll get paid."

"But, you said you'd pwotect my identity especially fwom the wocals, man!"

"Aha!" It was the flame-haired one. "So, this is your informer, is it?"

"Anyway," said the man in the anorak. "Who said anything about wicker?"

"You did, that's who." The officer sounded rather angry.

"No, no." The man shook his head. "That's what I meant." With that, he pointed towards the gap in the hedge.

We all looked. I swear that I almost fainted. There, coming through the gap was Janie. She was with a group of teenagers but I had only eyes for my beloved. The sun had risen over the sewage plant and its rays caught Janie's hair. It looked almost as if she had a halo. *Very fitting*, I thought. *An angel has come to protect me from the evil of this place.* But, you might have guessed that the abominable Pinstripe was in tow. Helping the teenagers, he was, to drag bits of art and craft into the stone circle.

The officer and his colleagues approached. "Er, I'm sorry about this, Miss Jetty. I have it on good authority that you have alcohol about your person."

"I beg your pardon?" The magnificent silken bloom of Janie's face drained. "William," she said, "I am feeling rather faint."

The atrocious Pinstripe placed a miserable hand around her waist.

"Officer," said Janie, upon being steadied. "We are here to set up the crafts display for The Hobby Horse Festival. The Chief Constable and I shall be judging, the display that is, later on today." Janie sounded magnificent when she was indignant.

One of Stringer's colleagues unwisely chose that moment to chip in. "Furthermore," he said, "none of your accomplices look old enough to drink."

"Except him." It was the second officer. As he made the observation, he pointed directly at Pinstripe.

"Oh, him," I said, choosing that moment to have my six penneth. "He's William Anker, he is. He's a tricky one, and that's no word of a lie."

Janie's humongous eyes opened wide. "Izaak! What in the name of the Devil are you doing here?"

Fizz strode forwards and, as luck would have it, a particularly strong bit of breeze caught the stripy nurse-type dress and lifted it stocking-top high. "He," said the mischievous nurse, flattening her five and two dozen stripes, "is simply worshipping The Prince of Darkness. Here," she said. "This is the staff with which he summons the dark forces." The nurse held aloft the chief druid's stick. "This," she added for good measure, "is the means by which presently my mood shall be known." Next, no word of a lie, the nurse plucked Maud straight out of the pocket of her stripy nurse-type dress.

"Oh! Izaak! Stone circles! Your obsession with magpies! Voodoo dolls! It all makes sense!"

"No, Janie! Don't listen to that temptress! Her's having you on, her is!"

I grabbed the stick and I made as if to approach Janie. Though I concede unconventional, I had it in mind to suggest a marriage ritual right there and then. I was certain that the chief druid would be about somewhere and, for the price of two scoops of ice cream; he could perform the appropriate ceremony.

"Now, look here." It was P.C. Stringer wrecking the magical moment and, as he spoke, he came between Janie and me. "I must insist on carrying out a full search for the contraband liquor."

"No! No!" The informer came forth. "I keep twying to say that it's wicker, not wicker!" He approached a startled-looking teenager and pointed furiously at a basket that she held. "Look! Are you bwind? It's made of wicker. These bounders have cut wicker fwom a pwotected willow twee!"

The face on the officer of the law went pink. "Why on earth didn't you say it was wicker and not liquor?"

"Who said anything about alcohol, man?"

P.C. Stringer raised his arms despairingly. "Miss Jetty, I am so, so sorry!"

"Janie, old thing!" It was Ian, of course. He grasped both sides of his gown in barrister-type fashion. "I advise you to report this debacle to the Chief Constable." With that, Ian spun around and, with his peculiar backwards lean, he scooted towards the gap in the hedge. "Ah! Jacob, old chap," I overheard him say. "You have returned. I shall have a pint of beer from the tap marked chocolate ice, if you will be so kind."

"Certainly, Ian. Will that be with a vodka or a whisky ice cream chaser?"

Meanwhile, on our side of the hedge, Janie and her party recommenced their journey. However, as Pinstripe came by, P.C. Stringer held his strong arm of the law aloft. "Halt!" He bent forwards and stuck his nose straight into Pinstripe's startled face. The officer sniffed, not once but twice. "Have you by chance been driving, sir?"

"Yes," said Pinstripe, with his usual arrogance. "As it happens, Miss Jetty and I arrived here in my Porsche."

"Well, I am sorry to say, sir, that you smell very strongly of alcohol. I must ask you to accompany us to the squad car where I shall require you to provide a sample of breath."

"But, but!"And as Pinstripe was led away, I heard him cry, "I swear that I've only had an ice cream!"

And I hollered, "Tell us if you need a good lawyer, Anker!"

And Janie said, "Oh! Izaak!"

CHAPTER SIXTEEN

Of Janie I heard not a thing until Ian announced that her wedding day had been brought forward. The devastating news came out in passing conversation.

"On the way into town, old boy, I shall need to stop off at the tailor's shop."

"Oh! Why is that, then?"

"I must collect the coat and tails, of course."

"Not another hunt ball? You told me that you have no time for that bunch of fanatical toffs."

"Gatehouse?" Ian winced and shrugged, per normal. "The members of the local hunt are not fanatical and neither are they, as you so succinctly put it, a bunch of toffs."

"Ian," I said, "hurtling around the English countryside dressed in red coats…"

"Pink , old chap. The word is pink."

"Okay, Ian, dressed in pink following a pack of dogs…"

"Hounds, old dear. The word is hounds."

"Okay, okay," I said, despairingly. "Red, dogs, pink, hounds. Either way, **old dear,** sitting atop an old nag hollering jallops and cripes and tally-ho and thundering around the before mentioned English countryside as if in pursuit of a man-eating beast could, in normal circles, be regarded as behaviour that is commonly associated with toffs…"

"But, Gatehouse…"

"Ian, we are not talking about Bengal tigers. The shenanigans that I describe relate to the pursuit of a mammal the size of a large domestic cat."

"Oh, very well, Gatehouse. They **are** a bunch of toffs but no, Gatehouse. It is not another hunt ball to which I am cordially gate crashing. I am, of course, attending a wedding, and look you here at this." Ian tootled to the far corner. He rummaged around a while and, when he was done, he turned to face me. I noted that Ian held aloft a terracotta pot, sort of a thing. "This," he said, proudly, and he dangled the object from a piece of string that was tied around its neck, "is a wedding gift."

"What on earth is that load of old tat, Ian?"

"This piece of tat, as you so succinctly put it, is my invention and very likely it will earn many thousands of pounds. I call it an inside out pot."

"A what?"

"Gatehouse! Someday, no home will be complete without one." Ian approached and he proffered the pot and I instinctively copped hold of the string. It followed that I thereby became the custodian of the dangling thing "Do you not see, Gatehouse?"

"No, I do not."

"Gatehouse! Any fool can see that it is an inside out, upside down, flowerpot."

"What?" I swizzled the string a bit and so sent the inside out pot spinning. "Is it meant for Australia, then?"

Ian snatched back his invention. "The idea, Gatehouse, is that plants, herbs, and such like are planted upside down but, in the fullness of time, they will gallantly rise towards the heavens in pursuit of light. Gatehouse!" Ian smiled, broadly. "Even a Luddite such as you must concede the brilliance of the invention."

"Ian," I said, "surely the average gardener requires a conventional pot that permits plants to grow straight up, vertical, as nature intended. That thing is far too inventive for the likes of your average little Englander."

Ian shrugged and winced and went quiet for a few seconds. However, the silence was short lived. "French, Gatehouse! By golly, that is the solution to the problem that you so accurately predict!"

"Aye?"

"Gatehouse! I shall simply dream up a French name for the thing and then every jack man pretentious toff in the county will want one," and, with that, Ian discarded his treasured invention by chucking it on an armchair.

"Any road," I said. "What's with this wedding? Who's the happy couple?"

Ian winced and shrugged. "Janie Jetty and Anker, of course, old chap. I must inform you that I shall not be gate crashing," he said proudly. "You see, I have been appointed usher, and..." Ian stopped on noticing my lower jaw going south. "You do know of the wedding do you not, old thing?"

"Ian," I said. "Will you phone Chambers and let them know that I have been stricken with a tummy bug?"

The day of the wedding arrived without further incident.

Pound to a penny, you are expecting me to recount how it was that I went careening into the church to speak up on the basis that I had no intention of holding my peace.

Further, or in the alternative, I'll wager that you anticipate me telling all about how it was that I turned up at the wrong church and at the wrong ceremony where I duly spoke up and ruined the lives of two total strangers.

Well, you'd be wrong. True, in the manner of the countless heroes in the countless movies, I did dally with the idea of bombing up to the parish church of Holy Trinity. However, such action would have been far too predictable. Besides which, I would have risked toasting the couple's happiness by the raising of a tin mug within the confines of Her Majesty's Prison. So, whilst treacherous Ian enjoyed the jollities in a marquee that was erected for the occasion, somewhere within the grounds of the mysterious Hall, I went for a stroll.

My stroll took me all the way to the town of Shipsford where I popped into the fish 'n' chip shop.

"You look a bit glum, Mr. G.." It was Jacob standing behind the counter. He held a strip of raw codfish in his hand and he dragged it through a tray of creamy-white batter. "As you have perhaps gathered," said Jacob, with a sigh, "my excursion into the frozen desert industry did not work out." He plopped the piece of fish into a huge fat fryer and then he wiped both hands down the front of his pharmaceutical white coat. Above the hissing and sizzling, as the codfish was frazzled, he said, "Mr.

Gatehouse. I have a huge piece of haddock, here, that simply will not sell. You may as well have it for free."

"Why, that's very kind of you, Jacob. Thank you, very much." *Fish 'n' chips for free,* I thought. *Suppose things could be worse.*

Jacob attempted to use a pair of tongs to remove the fillet from a greasy glass cabinet. It looked as if it had lain there, awaiting an unsuspecting customer for two weeks, at least. On being lifted, the fish broke clean in two. "Oops! I sincerely apologise, Mr. G.."

"Just use your hands, Jacob. I'm sure they're clean."

"Very well, Mr. Gatehouse." Jacob rubbed his nose with the palm of a hand. However, on noticing my looks of disdain, he reached behind for a tub of sanitizer and wiped both hands thoroughly. When he was done, Jacob used a hand to wipe his nostrils, once more. "I have to say, Mr. G., that never have I seen you looking quite as glum." He laid the two broken pieces onto a sheet of greaseproof paper and he instinctively went for the condiments. "Will you be requiring salt and vinegar?"

"Nah. Not for me, thanks… oh, too late, not to worry."

"Tell you what, Mr. Gatehouse. I'll shut up shop for half an hour and you can enjoy that haddock in the back room with a nice mug of hot tea."

So, while that lot up at The Hall enjoyed their lobster, pineapple chunks with cheese on sticks, even *Mateous* rosé, I shouldn't wonder, I attacked my bit of fish. I sat on an old Windsor chair and Jacob occupied an exceedingly large sack with *Potatoes Produced in England* printed all over it. I had not eaten for at least twenty-four hours; such was my sorrow at having loved and lost. It was as well that eating disorders had not been invented. Even so, I found myself attacking the fish with gusto.

"It's true," I said, crunching the batter. "I am feeling a little under the weather. Oh, and as an aside," I said by way of an aside, "have you by chance a couple of battered sausages? Stuffing myself makes me feel comfortable. You see, Jacob, this is the worst day of my whole life."

Jacob rose from the sack of potatoes. "It may very well be the last day of your life if you continue to gulp your food so, Mr.

G.." He tazzed off into the shop. "You're in luck," he said, loudly, "I have three sausages!"

I swallowed the last chunk of fish and washed it down with a swig of tea. Thereupon, Jacob returned bearing a gift in the form of a trio of battered sausages swaddled in crunched up greaseproof paper.

"If you do not mind me saying so, Mr. Gatehouse, you appear to have gone a little pink in the face."

In my eagerness to make way for the consumption of the sausages, the last bit of haddock had gone down without chewing. And a fishbone, or something, had gone and lodged itself in my throat.

I continued to sit upon the Windsor chair, except that in lieu of bemoaning my lot in life, I was gasping and generally fighting for my said life.

In the manner of someone who is choking to death, I was restricted from participating further in any conversation, lively or otherwise. So, hereinafter, all I can do is recount what it is that Jacob said. On the basis that I was drifting in and out of consciousness, the words that I attribute to Jacob are not strictly verbatim. The gist, however, is true to the best of my knowledge, information, and belief.

"Good Heavens! You appear to be choking, Mr. Gatehouse! Now, I did warn you about gulping your food. However, before I call an ambulance, would you consider it callous was I to ask you to sign the briefest of notes exonerating me of all or any blame in this most unfortunate of episodes?

What is that you are trying to say, Mr. G.? Tell you what, I will bend down and come a little closer, shall I?

Now, Mr. Gatehouse, that is a very unpleasant thing to tell me to do and, if you do not mind me saying so, it would not, in any event, fit especially not sideways. I sincerely hope, Mr. G., that you do not live to regret those harsh words. And when I say that I hope you do not live, I do not mean that I hope you are about to depart this life because that would, indeed, be callous.

Oh! Now you appear to be turning a little blue, Mr. Gatehouse. Ah! Here is my best fish knife. If you would care to gently lift your rapidly swelling face, Mr. G., I shall attempt a minor surgical procedure known as a tracheotomy. On second thoughts, I will telephone for an ambulance because you appear to be going into spasms. Gosh! Anyone would think that you are attempting to strangulate me. I know you are grateful, Mr. Gatehouse. However, if you could stop hugging and simultaneously let go of my throat, I will make my way to the invention of Alexander Graham Bell without further ado. Oh, Mr. Gatehouse. Stay with me because you appear to be drifting into a state of unconsciousness. Now, where did I drop that fish knife?"

I came to in an ambulance, flat on my back on a stretcher, with a medic seated next to me. He was poking and prodding in and around my mouth. The ambulance was rocking and swerving and I could hear the siren going like the clappers. I could also hear the driver cussing. "Get out of the way! You farmers in their tractors should be banned from the roads!"

"You beauty!" So said the medic, and, he held aloft a pair of forceps. "It's a piece of fish so overdone that it's as hard and as sharp as a razor blade! Now then, let's see what I can do about the puncture wounds to the throat." He wore a dark blue uniform and, from a badge on the breast pocket, I could tell that he was a volunteer and that, as such, he spent most of his spare time clutching a first aid kit, hoping and praying that fate would deal the likes of me a hardy blow.

"Get out of the way!" It was the ambulance driver, again. "You cyclists on your cycles should be banned from the roads!"

The medic leaned forwards and I heard a little clunk sort of a noise as, on opening the forceps, the piece of fish fell into a metal bowl. "Do you know?" He leaned right over and stuck his concerned-looking face directly into my own face. "It is my belief that you could sue whomsoever it was that fed you this health hazard."

"I have a written indemnity!" In my state of semi consciousness, I had hitherto failed to notice Jacob sitting at the end of the stretcher. "Look here," said Jacob, "I acknowledge that it is unconventional to find a disclaimer written in tomato ketchup on a sheet of greaseproof paper but, Mr. Gatehouse, here, is a lawyer and he will confirm that it is all perfectly lawful."

Jacob passed the bit of greaseproof to the medic. "Says here," said the medic, "that in anticipation of his unexpected exit from this life, Izaak Enoch Gatehouse, leaves all his worldly goods to the love of his life, namely Janie Anker, Jetty, as was!"

Jacob shook his head left to right, right to left and he did so slowly. "Mr. G.! How could you mislead me?" When his head came to a standstill, "Enoch?" he said, on presumably the penny dropping.

"Get out of the way!" Once again, it was the ambulance driver. However, on this occasion, his opinion on the nature of road user who should be banned from the highways of Warwickshire made me sit up and take notice. "You honeymooners in your fancy sports cars dangling pots from stupid bits of string should be banned from the roads! Oops a daisy!"

There came a sickening crunch of metal and a shattering of glass. I was thrown backwards and the last thing that I recall was an airborne metal bowl hurtling straight at me.

I awoke covered in a white shroud. I deduced that I had very probably died and gone to heaven. Indeed, as only a lawyer could, I began trotting off in my mind a spot of mitigation just on the off chance that St. Peter needed persuasion that I ought to be shown leniency and, just the once, be permitted entry through his pearly gates. Then, I heard the gasps and cries of a female and I realised that the shroud was, in fact, a billowing wedding dress. Its wearer was laid on a stretcher dead opposite to mine. *This is romantic*, I thought, *perhaps I have died and gone to heaven, after all?*

Janie's huge and beautiful eyes were terribly bruised and were fast closing. Blood flowed from her nose, so much so that the front of the dress was no longer creamy-white but it was crimson. She had a bump to the forehead the size of Mount St. Helens.

"Is she okay?" My enquiry was directed towards the medic. He was busily taking Janie's pulse. The medic took no notice. I therefore grasped both sides of the stretcher and I hoisted myself into a sitting position. "Less of that, mate," I had reason to say, as the medic began to loosen Janie's clothing. "I think she would prefer me to do that sort of thing."

Janie sighed and groaned.

"You look lovely, Janie."

The ambulance lurched forwards and, as a consequence, my head went back and struck the partition behind. "Ouch! This ruddy ambulance is a death-trap!"

"Izaak, Izaak. Is that you?" Janie spoke slowly and quietly.

"Yes, it's me, Janie."

"Oh, Izaak. Thank heavens that it is you. I have had the most awful of dreams that it is William whom I have married."

"Oh, Janie," I said, and I swung around, simultaneously lifting my legs, and I placed both feet firmly on the floor. "Hang on, Janie. Just as soon as this ruddy ambulance stops rocking, I'll come and lay with you."

Jacob coughed. "May I congratulate you on a remarkable recovery, Mr. Gatehouse?"

"You're a witness," I said. "Write down what she's just said on the back of the disclaimer."

"Disclaimer, Mr. G.? Do you refer to the last will and testament?"

Well, you might know that Pinstripe chirped up at this juncture. It was typical of him to ruin his own consummation of marriage by proxy. I hadn't seen him sitting on an oxygen tank. "Can you not see that my wife is dangerously delirious? Have you not done sufficient damage, Gatehouse, by wrecking my Porsche?"

"What's more important to you, Anker?"

"Why, you!" Pinstripe hoisted himself up from the oxygen tank. "You are long overdue for a damned good thrashing, Gatehouse! I intend to beat you to within an inch of..."

The ambulance came to an abrupt stop and, seconds later, the rear doors popped wide open.

Pinstripe was the first to exit. He edged past Jacob. "Just a moment. I know you, do I not?"

"I do not think so, sir."

"Yes, I do!" Pinstripe stopped. "You are the maniac who sells ice cream at gone midnight amidst Celtic stone circles!"

"Listen to me," I said. "Now is not the time to purchase an ice cream sundae, Anker. Janie requires medical assistance."

"Damnation, Gatehouse!"

A pair of burly porters duly dragged Pinstripe from the ambulance. After telling him to button his lip and keep out of the way, the porters clambered aboard. They each copped hold of an end of Janie's stretcher and slid her towards the exit. As Janie's battered, bruised, yet still beautiful face came by, our eyes met and she mouthed something or other. I bent my head and placed an ear against her lips. "Oh, Izaak," she whispered, "what have I done?"

I sat open mouthed as Janie's stretcher was lowered to the ground and then taken away.

Next, Pinstripe popped his head through the rear. "I want you," he told Jacob, "to sign a statement confirming that you administered an alcoholic substance without my knowledge and consent!"

"I have no writing paper, sir, other than that upon which is written a last will and testament."

"And," I said. "Even a solicitor like you should know that you don't go defacing them things, mate." I shuffled along to the rear. "Make way for the walking wounded!"

I was prevented from exiting the vehicle because Pinstripe blocked my path. "You have nothing to smirk about, Gatehouse. With sweet Janie Anker now in hospital, I am free to control the books of account. And, and..." He provocatively came close. Indeed, it was as if he was emulsion and I was a wall. "I trust that there are no internal injuries because, while the mare is laden with the growth I've put in her belly, I shall be keeping myself amused with the girls of the village." He leered a twisted leer. "Have you got the telephone number of that red-haired certainty, Gatehouse?"

"That's it, Anker...!"

"For pity's sake, somebody help me!" That's what Pinstripe screamed as he ran through the corridors of the Accident and

Emergency Department. Upon barging through a pair of rubber swing doors, he ran directly into a startled orderly. Pinstripe sunk slowly to his knees and he gripped the bottom of the orderly's coat. "There is a maniac on the loose," he whimpered. "He threatens to force feed me with his last will and testament and to insert a battered sausage where the sun don't shine."

CHAPTER SEVENTEEN

You might know that the abominable Pinstripe played a blinder. By day, he was the doting husband. He attended to Janie's every need. By night, he was out on the town or, rather, he was out and about the parish. Of that I was certain because I had insider knowledge in the form of Nurse Stringer (Fizz, to you and me). Between the times known to you and me as sunrise and dusk, he was fiddling Janie's accounts, doing insider deals, making dodgy investments, and so forth, or so I reckoned.

There was nothing that I could do. I resolved to plough on with my faltering career at The Bar of England and Wales. And it was while ploughing on as aforesaid that, some many weeks later, I was sat in the reception of Globe Chambers when an exceedingly dodgy-looking character strolled in and announced to Damian that he had arrived for the purpose of a conference.

The individual occupied one of the plastic bucket seats while he presumably waited for another party to arrive. It was bad form, you see, for any barrister to meet with a lay client unless or until the instructing solicitor presented himself.

"Oi'll get yow a cup of tea, we will," Damian informed the visitor, and the learned clerk and his empty kettle departed with the presumed intent of filling the same from the tap in the gent's lavatory and not, I hoped, from the fire bucket in the corridor.

"Excuse me," said the client, just as soon as Damian had departed. "I feel certain that I know you."

From his greasy slicked-back, jet black hair (straight out of a bottle), right down to his cheap shiny black shoes, here was an individual who looked, every inch, your typical confidence trickster.

"I can't say that I can recall, Mr...?"

"Madison," he said. "The name is Madison. Pleased to meet you," and he held forth his right arm.

There was insufficient time to accept the invitation because Walter chose that very moment to appear from his private office. The intervention was timely because I swear that I'd have felt compelled to check that every single finger and my thumb was still in situ had I placed my hand in his.

"Ah! Charles, my dear friend." Per normal, Walter said it in his laid-back drawl.

"Walter, dear chap!" The con merchant offered Walter the same arm that I had dodged by the narrowest of margins. Disappointingly, Walter had no qualms at reciprocating and his arm shot out, and all. "I have not seen you in ages, Walter!" *Next,* I thought, *you'll be telling him how well he looks.* "I have to say, Walter, (*here we go*) that you are looking exceedingly well!"

"I see that you have already met my learned pupil, Gatehouse. He is the one of whom I spoke."

"I most certainly have, Walter…"

"He has almost completed his twelve months and he is acquitting himself rather well in the courts."

That came as a surprise, I can tell you. Indeed, I was certain that there must be a catch because never, ever, had I heard Walter speak of me in terms quite as glowing as that.

"Izaak?"

"Yes, Walter?"

"You will be assisting with this matter." Told you there was a catch. "Come and join us, my friend."

I joined the pair in Walter's private office. Walter invited me to occupy his very own private swivel chair that lived behind his very own private desk. It was naturally an honour, though uppermost on my mind was that I had been saved the trauma of having to sit alongside the slimy-looking con merchant, Madison. That honour went to Walter.

The discussion started with a resumption of the small talk. However, whilst Walter and Madison whiled away the time, I took note of Madison's beady black eyes. They were everywhere other than on the person whom he was addressing, namely Walter. What, with his pencil line moustache and fingers and wrists laden with gold jewellery, it was difficult to imagine how Madison could get away with conning any one because, as previously intimated herein, here was a character whose very physical appearance advertised the fact that he was adept in the black art of the confidence trickster.

"Very well," said Walter, with the chitchat seemingly drying up, "let us make a start."

"Er, shouldn't we wait for the solicitor?" I knew it was impudent of me, a mere pupil, to say such a thing.

Madison laughed. "You told me that Gatehouse, here, had a keen sense of humour!"

Walter shuffled a bit. "Er, yes, Charles. My learned pupil knows perfectly well that you are, of course, the instructing solicitor." Walter glared and he prompted by means of a nod of the head that I should respond.

So, respond I did. "Of course," I laughed. "I know that Madison, here... er, I mean to say that I know that Charles, here, is the solicitor. In fact, he thinks he knows me. You do, don't you, Charles?"

"Also," said Madison. "I have recalled where I know you from."

I coughed and gulped. "From where is that, then?"

Madison stretched out his legs and crossed one over the other. He slunk low in his seat and, casually, he positioned both arms at the back of his head. "I've seen you out and about in the village of Prestwick. In particular, Mr. Gatehouse..."

"Do call me Izaak..."

"In particular, Izaak, I have seen you at a public house of notorious repute..."

"The Case, The Case is Open..."

"In the company of another barrister of notorious repute..."

"Prospect," said Walter. "Ian Prospect."

"That's the fellow," said Madison. "Well, I happen to live in the adjoining village..."

"Oakley," I said. Oakley Castle...?"

"No," said Madison. It was only a matter of time before the guessing game faltered. "I happen to reside in Brakes Norton."

He uncrossed the legs and sat bolt upright. Simultaneously, both arms were removed from the back of the head and, in an altogether more professional manner they were placed on the desk before him. "Our client happens to reside in..."

"Oakley Castle?"

"No."

"Blimey. Surely not Solihull?"

"No. He is from Prestwick. And our client," said Madison, "is accused of defrauding a local business of hundreds of thousands of pounds."

On Prestwick and local business being said in the same breath, it was my turn to sit bolt upright. I also shuffled to the very edge of the chair.

Walter chose that very same moment to have a say. "Susan Blesham..."

"Who?"

Walter tutted. "Susan Blesham is a tenant of these Chambers, Gatehouse. You would be aware of that fact was it not the case that, in the manner of your dodging cracked or broken paving slabs, you dodge each and every opportunity of forging a relationship with your brethren."

Madison smiled. "I admire a chap who keeps himself to himself."

"Well, be that as it may," said Walter. "Susan Blesham was instructed to conduct the trial in just two days' time but on nearing completion of her last trial..."

Damian, fully laden with a tray of tea, chose that moment to bluster in. "Her last trial being her first trial and as things 'ave transpired Mista Madison, sir, her last trial will, indeed, be her last trial..."

"Get out of here, you impudent fellow!"

"Sorry, Mista Tweed, like. Oi was just tryin' to assist, sort of thing and it woe 'appen again."

Damian departed and he took with him the tray, with its cargo still intact."

"I was about to explain," explained Walter, "that, nearing completion of the trial, Susan Blesham rose to present her closing speech to the jury whereupon she sustained a fractured skull."

I edged as close to the edge of the chair as it was possible to go without slipping off. "A fractured skull, Walter? Never on my life! How could that have happened?"

Walter tutted, once more. His irrefutable presumption that, as a matter of law, those whom he encountered could read his mind was oft' troublesome.

"Gatehouse, my friend. A fractured skull was the causative effect of getting to one's feet to address the jury, breaking into a cold sweat, screeching, *Oh, my God, I knew I should have been a solicitor*, and collapsing. Indeed, the sickening thud of her head ricocheting off the bench and onto the stone floor was audible in the adjoining court." I opened wide my mouth to interrupt but there was no stopping Walter. "She went down, as you might say, Gatehouse, as would heavy metal in a Dudsall foundry."

"Walter," I said. "That's terrible, that is. How is she, sort of thing?"

"Fortunately, my learned pupil, a member of the jury intervened and prevented the sustaining of further injury."

"Further injury?"

My not altogether unreasonable enquiry was again met with tutting. "His Honour Judge Outman leapt from the bench in the manner of that wretched fellow who regularly dresses in black rubber..."

"Batman," I said, knowingly.

"No," said Walter, dismissively. "Mr. Justice Thresher."

"Oh! Him."

"Yes, Gatehouse. Him. And whereas one of the jurors was content to passively observe sundry attempts at resuscitation including, but not limited to, the loosening of garments (including under garments), chest rubs, and mouth-to-mouth, he considered the implementation of the Heimlich manoeuvre wholly inappropriate. Thereupon, the juror announced that he was a medical practitioner; he forcibly removed the learned judge from Susan Blesham's person, and he demanded that the Court Service telephone an ambulance."

Madison sat forwards at this juncture and he completed the anecdote. "In the ambulance, Miss Blesham vowed to retire from practice at the Bar because she could never ever go through that sort of trauma again."

"I'm not surprised," I said, shaking my head and simultaneously excelling air from the mouth. "I imagine that conducting a jury trial is too stressful for some."

"Gatehouse, my friend." Walter was at it, tutting, again. "A bit of stage fright during one's first trial is to be expected. The trauma resulting in Blesham's sudden and unexpected retirement from the Bar was as a result of stress induced by molestation at the hands of His Honour Judge Outman."

"In a sense," said Madison. "His Honour's over active libido, not to mention over active imagination, has done you a favour…"

"Me?" Then, as if to underline that I was referring to me, Izaak Gatehouse, I pointed at me, myself. "Why has that done me a favour?"

"Because, my friend." It was Walter, now having a say. "You will be conducting the trial of Charles's client."

I resisted the temptation of leaping up, punching the air, performing a few victory laps around the office, screaming that I had maybe died and gone up to heaven. In lieu thereof, I casually said, "I'm obliged to you both."

Madison said that he would explain the facts of the case. "The injured party," he began, "is a family company and one of the owners is a Mrs. Janie Anker. The story goes that, whilst recuperating from injuries sustained in a road traffic accident, Mrs Anker and her co-directors entrusted my client to make certain investments on their behalf. He offered fantastic returns on shares that were worthless, non-existent, even."

My heart sank. "I know this woman. I can't possibly act against her interests; especially not carry out a cross examination."

"Well," said Madison, and he resumed the casual pose of outstretched legs (crossed), and hands at the back of the head. "Mrs. Anker's evidence is agreed and, as such, can be read to the Court. It is our client's defence that he was duped by the so called expertise of a hot shot commercial lawyer by the name of..."

"Pinstripe," I said, knowingly. "It's young Pinstripe."

"No?" Madison's expression was one of dumbfoundedness. "His name is also Anker. He is the brand new husband of Janie Anker."

Walter, as you can tell for yourself (if you're paying attention), had remained relatively passive for a tick. However, at that moment, he reached behind and, from a small side table he copped hold of a large bundle of papers that were tied up with green ribbon. It was very curious because, traditionally, all briefs (save and except treasury briefs) were tied with ribbon that was of the colour pink.

"Aha," I said, "green ribbon. It's obviously indicative of sommut."

"Yes," said Madison. "It is indicative of the fact that my office ran out of pink ribbon."

Walter slid the papers over the desktop. "The trial, my learned pupil, will be won or lost on your ability to question this atrocious fellow Anker. Your cross examination must be performed effectively and aggressively and you may even reveal to the Court that it is he who is the villain." As I eagerly grabbed the papers, Walter grinned, just a little.

CHAPTER EIGHTEEN

After the conference, Madison offered to drive me all the way home to Prestwick. Well, as he had already explained, the village where Madison resided was close by and, as such, it was no skin off his nose to drop me off.

As you have possibly surmised, it was an exceedingly and unseasonably wet summer. True to form, it was raining cats and dogs on the return journey to South Warwickshire.

In keeping with his loud suit, slicked back hair, dodgy moustache, and chunky jewellery, Madison drove a large Ford Zephyr saloon. As such, it was even odds that he would skew off the road before reaching Prestwick. That, of course, was only supposing that, in the interim, the exhaust pipe wouldn't go dropping off and the rear nearside door could resist the temptation of flying open all of its own accord.

"Don't worry, Izaak!" Madison yanked the steering wheel hard right and, by so doing, he was just in time to prevent the front end from disappearing down a ditch. "I have a sack of coal in the trunk! It's always guaranteed to keep these tin lizzies on the road!"

He had no need to tell me of that. It was a known fact from where I came from that, come the first sign of bad weather, piles of coal in the outhouses of Dudsall habitations had tendencies to shrink at the exact same time that the travelling salesmen fetched out their Fords.

"The cottage is just around the next bend, Charles." I tapped the brief atop my lap. "I shall ensure that I read the papers tonight, Charles. Perhaps we can meet the client tomorrow morning, in Chambers, for a conference?"

"Nah," said Charles, and he pulled up behind Ian's wreck of a motorcar that, per normal, was parked directly outside The Fly in the Ointment. "We all live in this area and so we may as well have the conference at my home. Perhaps the pub?"

"Oh, I can't permit that, Charles. We have to meet in Chambers. It's the rule, you see."

The rule of which I spoke was that barristers must parley with their instructing solicitors at no place other than in Chambers.

"Listen, Izaak." Charles leaned across my lap and he opened the passenger's side door. Both my arms, you see, were weighed down with the voluminous brief. "I'll meet you at The Case is Open at lunch time tomorrow."

One of the chunky bracelets dangling from Charles's wrist caught the brief's backing sheet and ripped it. The tear went from the edge and ended in the middle, directly where the green ribbon was tied in a tight bow. I had hitherto thought of everything imaginable that pertained to the trial, save and except the identity of my client. Upon taking a shufty at the backing sheet I noted, for the very first time, the name of my client, the accused. My eyes, I swear, nearly popped out when I read that Regina's opponent before the Crown Court some thirty-six hours hence was none other than Jacob or, to be exact, Jacob Hamish Gaylord Henderson.

Well, as I clambered out, Madison simply winked and, with a grinding of gears and a backfire or two, he was gone.

At the rear of the cottage, I came across a very strange sight. Ian, you see, was seated at a picnic table. For the purpose of fending off the heavy rain, he was holding aloft a black umbrella. Next to Ian was a woman, heavily made up, and becoming increasingly wet because the rain from the brolly was being diverted directly onto her bleached blonde head of hair. Strangely (especially considering the atrocious weather), the woman was dressed in a skimpy summer dress.

"Ah! Gatehouse! Permit me to introduce you to Trudy."

"Who? Her who presents the weather forecast on the local TV?"

"It is she, old chap!"

At being overlooked, Trudy looked indignant. "I **am** here, you know." Trudy sounded indignant, and all. When she spoke, her eyes rolled about. Indeed, the eye rolling was the sort of affliction that I associated with the lot who hammed it up down at the local theatre on the river.

"Well, you ain't much of a weather girl," I said, snappily. To be fair, my observation was entirely rational bearing in mind that Trudy was supposedly an expert at forecasting what the heavens had on offer on a day-to-day basis. Yet, there she was, dressed in a skimpy summer dress (not a shawl, hat, cagoule in sight) with the equivalent of a whole months' worth of precipitation cascading on her collapsed bouffant.

Trudy got up but, in the process, she poked an eyebrow on a spike of Ian's umbrella. "Oh, my word, Ian!" The rolling stopped at a point where only the whites were showing because her eyes had strangely come to a halt in a position whereby she appeared to be looking upwards, vertical, namely in the direction of clouds that had apparently snook up on her. "Ian," she said. "The producer will be most annoyed if I have scratched my face!" I duly noted that Trudy's skimpy dress was so sodden that nothing much underneath was left to the imagination, if you get my drift. Indeed, was she intending to appear on screen before the nine o'clock watershed, I reckoned it was highly likely that Trudy would be responsible for the shutdown of the entire TV station. "I shall go inside, Ian, and await the arrival of the crew." Trudy came by. "What are you staring at, er…?"

"Izaak," I said. "I'm the lodger, I am."

Trudy stopped momentarily. "So, what are you staring at, Izaak, the lodger?"

"Everything," I said, running my eyes down, up, and then down, again, where they duly settled.

Trudy looked south and she let forth a squeak, cupped one hand across her chest, cupped the other one somewhere else, and, with a good hard wallop across the bottom (courtesy of Ian, I'll have you know and honestly not me), she tippy-toed over to what was left of the kitchen door and went in out of the rain.

Ian duly took to his feet. By use of the thumb of his right hand, he depressed a little button that was situated near the top of the umbrella and, no word of a lie, the said umbrella snapped shut all of its own accord. Was it not for the fact that I'd seen John Steed in *The Avengers* perform the very same stunt I would have been exceedingly impressed. "I shall keep Trudy company, old chap, whilst we await the crew." Ian winced and then he winked in a knowing kind of a way.

"Well," I said, "Let's hope they take only a matter of a couple of minutes to get here, Ian, because you'll otherwise have very little with which to occupy the time." I said it, of course, out of envy, resentfulness, call it what you may. "Oh. Another thing," I also said. "What the hell is this crew? You're surely not expecting a lifeboat to come floating down the road, are you?"

"Film crew," said Ian. "Trudy refers to a film crew. During her award winning weather slot on this evening's local TV news, Trudy and I will be showing the viewing public my prize winning pigs." With his peculiar backwards lean, Ian too scurried towards the kitchen and, with a wince, a chuckle, and a "Now come you here to me, you dashed fine filly," he was gone from view.

No sooner had Ian gone from view, when a peculiar little man popped his head around the corner of the cottage. "Good evening," he said. He said it in a nasally, high-pitched kind of a way and, though very unpleasant on the ear, the pitch of the voice somehow seemed to be in keeping with how you'd imagine a character such as him to talk. "I'm here to take away the wood for the pianos."

The little man toddled over, managing to miss a puddle of rainwater as he did so. He was sixty, at least, and he was no taller than a garden gnome was (okay, I exaggerate a mite. He was five feet four-ish... no more, mind) and he was as thin and as wiry as a ferret in mid-winter.

"Wood?" I said it in a surprised, indignant, lofty kind of a way. That, you see, is how barristers were meant to sound. "Pianos?" I added that for the sake of completeness because tying up the loose ends and so forth was what barristers were meant to be about.

"My name in Raymes," said the little chap. He rubbed what little the sixty or so years had left by way of hair atop his pointy scalp. Then, he wiped his sopping wet hands down the side of a pair of tweedy-type trousers. I refer, of course, to his trousers and not mine. "You will have heard of me," said Raymes. I had not, honest to God, heard of him ever before in the whole of my life. "My family made pianos in Poland. When they, my family that is, came to England, they began making pianos here too." He puffed up his little chest.

"Well," I said, "the only wood around here is firewood and, until such time as we can find time to nip over the vicarage hedge, there's not a lot of that about." I duly puffed up my chest reasoning that two could play at that game.

The little chap seemed crestfallen, that is, until Ian poked his head around the remnants of the kitchen door. "Alan, old chap!" Ian appeared to be stuffing the tails of his tunic barrister-type shirt into the tops of his smelly green corduroys. You had to hand it to him; Ian had completed what he was about in double quick time beating his own very best personal record. The visitor's expression immediately lightened. "Follow me, Alan, and I shall show you the merchandise." Ian scooted outside and into the rain and, as he disappeared around the corner, the shirttails were still in the process of being tucked out of sight.

Alan took off in hot pursuit. I naturally followed, though not before overhearing a moaning and a groaning from within the cottage. "Ian? Where are you, Ian? Is that it then, Ian?"

By the time that I rounded the corner, Ian was through the front gate, over the lane, and over the fence of the paddock. He trotted to the middle of the paddock and beyond without even having to skirt around the former residence of the thieving magpies, now dead, burned to a crisp. The tree, you see, had gone!

At the far end of the paddock, Ian came to a deep drainage ditch and he stopped. In my eagerness to ascertain what was what, I had overtaken Alan and, by a process of elimination, you will deduce that I was next arriving. In the very bottom of the ditch lay a large piece of tarpaulin. "Lend a hand," said Ian, eagerly, and, without as much as a by your leave, he grabbed my sleeve, jumped into the ditch, and, in the process, he dragged me down with him. Ian grabbed hold of one corner of the tarpaulin and he instructed me to cop hold of the far end. "Lift, Gatehouse!"

Beneath the tarpaulin lay a tree trunk. It was, naturally, the trunk of the walnut tree. The evidence was incontrovertible because the tree was easily identifiable by scuffmarks left by Ian where he had spent many a long, not to mention fruitful, night shinning up for the purpose of relieving the magpie's nest of its wondrous bounty.

Alan's muddy brown brogue shoes juddered to a halt on the very edge of the ditch. Indeed, so close to the edge was his footwear that he managed to shunt a sod of earth, with grass attached, straight into my face. "Excellent," said Alan, ignoring my regurgitation of cud. "You are a wonder, Ian. I shall be in a position to manufacture a dozen pianos, at least, from this little lot." Alan stuffed a hand into his back pocket and he produced a wad of pound notes the thickness of which I had never ever, in the whole of my life, clapped eyes on before. "This should cover it, Ian, and, as a gesture of good faith, I shall arrange collection."

"Well," I said, casually. "I'm no expert when it comes to musical instruments, sort of thing, but anyone can see you'd get one piano if you were lucky out of this pile of firewood."

"Veneer, Gatehouse. Wood veneer." Ian dropped his end of the tarpaulin as he spoke. "It is the marble facade of the middle classes."

"Aye?" I dropped my end, and all.

"Gatehouse. He who turns a sinner from the error of his ways will save his soul from death and will cover a multitude of sins." Ian nodded, just the once. "That's James, that is. Five, paragraph twenty."

"Ian," I said. "He who harvests timber illegally will become a sinner and liable to a term of imprisonment not exceeding seven years, a fine, or both. That's the Theft Act, that is. Section seven."

Alan, at that juncture, clambered down into the ditch. He thrust the bundle of green backs into Ian's eager outstretched hand and then he turned to me. "Ian is alluding to the fact that, in my line of business, it is traditional to glue thin layers of walnut onto the panels of the piano which are actually made from any old wood."

"That is precisely what I just said." Ian uttered his words in an almost astonished kind of a way. Simultaneously, the notes of the realm were finding themselves secreted in a back pocket. "Do you see, old chap? The walnut covers a multitude of sins."

I was thwarted from responding by a hollering coming from the direction of what was left of the kitchen. The hollering was feminine and emanated from the lips of Trudy. "Ian! The film crew has arrived!"

I glanced over the crown of the ditch. Remarkably, Trudy was now dressed in keeping with the weather. But, talk about going from the sublime to the ridiculous? *Oh dear, oh dear, oh dear*, I mused. On her head, was a so'wester of bright yellow and, more remarkable than that, she was kitted out in a green waxen jacket. I had seen Janie let herself down badly by dressing up in the same sort of clobber. I had previously thought it and, I thought it again, *Tat like that ain't about to catch on.* Trudy had even gotten herself a pair of wellington boots. However, whereas wellington boots were usually black, hers were green. On my life, they were actually of the colour green!

Ian placed cupped hands to his mouth, one to the right, the other (naturally) to his left. "I shall be with you presently, old girl!" Upon returning the makeshift megaphone to his sides, Ian addressed me. "When I've done with her…" He chuckled at that juncture. "I shall take you for a celebratory noggin at The Case."

Meanwhile, and presumably not to be outdone, Trudy was performing acrobatics with her very own hands. She had them clasped together and her arms were in a sort of a loop and were swinging from side to side. She obviously figured that it was a coy thing to be doing. When she next spoke, her voice went all coy-like, and all. Then, in a manner that she plainly thought was also coy, she lolloped her head. "Huwwy, Ian! The sooner we are finished with the filming, the sooner we can cawwy on!" Heaven only knows why Trudy had suddenly developed a speech impediment. I figured that, in keeping with everything else, she thought it was coy. To be honest, it was actually annoying especially since, in all matters pertaining to life, like has a tendency to attract like.

"That twee was pwotected!" I simply know that you have guessed it. Yes, it was he who'd frit me half to death up at the stone circle. He had popped up from behind the far hedge where he had presumably been carrying out observations. "It is a twagic end to a pwotected twee!"

Once again, Ian placed cupped hands to his mouth. "It was only protected by virtue of the fact that it is I who obtained the ruddy protection order!"

"Then you should wuddy know better!"

Alan raised an arm and he used it to tap Ian on the shoulder. "Er. Is there a problem? Should I be asking for my money to be returned?"

I raised both my arms. I did not do so with the intention of simulating a loud haler. I did so with the intention of hoisting myself out of the ditch and, after a bit of scrabbling, that is precisely what I did.

"Gatehouse!" Ian shrugged and, of course, he winced as he spoke. "Come and lend a hand while I attend to the film crew!"

"Not likely, mate," and, as I spoke, the tree preservation individual advanced. He was dressed in the same jacket as before but, on this occasion, the hood was down.

"I intend to weport this outwage," he said, as he came by.

"It was nothing but a robber's hideout," I said, referring to the fact that the walnut tree had provided refuge for the thieving magpies. I noted that Trudy and two strangers (both male) had ascended the hedge and that they too were hotfooting it across the paddock. One had a rather large camera. It appeared to be perched, somewhat precariously, on his shoulder. His mate clasped a long stick at the end of which was a fluffy object. It was a microphone. I knew that as a fact because, when not head down dodging cracks in the pavement slabs, I had seen similar devices held aloft whilst strolling by the Royal Courts of Justice, Strand, London, England. "You'll catch a cold," I informed Trudy, as she strolled by because I noted that, beneath the strange waxen jacket, she wore very little else. I proceeded to address the man with the microphone. "Watch where you poke that thing, mate."

I returned to the cottage and I was thereby afforded respite from the pounding rain. From the front room, I observed miscellaneous goings-on in the paddock. Trudy appeared to be in conversation with the tree preservationist. The man with the camera had his shoulder pointed directly at them. This was evidence that he was filming the pair of them. It was equally evident that there were technical difficulties because the soundman was winging his stick up, down, right and left. Eventually, the stick came to rest dead centre and it was most unfortunate for the tree preservation man whose head came into contact with the same. As a direct consequence of the contact, the man appeared to open his mouth wide (it was presumably for the purpose of letting forth a scream or a yelp) and he staggered backwards and fell into the ditch. As he fell, Trudy placed both hands to her mouth and she too mouthed something or other.

Now then, when I state that the tree preservationist fell into the ditch I tell the truth, the whole truth, and so on and so forth. However, he did not fall directly into the ditch. You see, he fell onto Alan and then he landed in the ditch. Got it?

Well, Alan staggered about a bit and he grasped Ian, presumably for support. Ian, on being tugged by Alan, reached out and grabbed Trudy. On the basis that Ian was already occupying the ditch and, on the basis that Trudy was not, it followed that Ian grabbed Trudy by her ankles or, rather, he nabbed hold of her green wellington boots. Consequently, Trudy fell backwards and she joined Ian, Alan and the tree preservationist in the ditch. However, Trudy did not go down without putting up a fight because, before going down, she grabbed hold of the man with the stick. The man opened his mouth as wide as it was ever possible to open a mouth and I imagined that his yelps, screams (call them what you will) were as loud as loud could be because Trudy grabbed him in the worst of all places, if you get the point. It was much to the amusement of the cameraman. He began to roll around laughing. He stopped laughing, however, when the microphone stick hit him in the same region. Well, at that, both men began to tussle and, on nearing the edge of the ditch; one of them put a foot wrong. For the sake of historic correctness, I think it was the cameraman but I wouldn't swear to it in a court of law. Either way, not a lot turns on the issue because all you need to know is that the pair proceeded to slip into the ditch, camera, microphone, and all.

With a wry smile, I turned and, in the process, I narrowly missed tripping clean over Colin. As ever, the lazy cat had slunk up unnoticed and he was curled beneath my feet. I went through to what was left of the kitchen and I stopped dead, my jaw gaping. Standing at what was left of the kitchen door, wet through and through, was Janie. I tell you the truth. It was Janie Anker, Janie Jetty, as was! No word of a lie, Janie held a crib!

I avoided eye contact by staring at a hock of ham dangling from a hook on a beam. "Janie! I simply cannot discuss the case!" I ensured that I sounded suitably dismissive. "You are a witness for the Crown!"

Janie let forth a quiet whimper but I feigned disinterest. She glanced momentarily in the direction of mine own eye line (in other words, the hock of ham) and, when her eyes returned to me, I swear that she was just in time to catch me staring at the content of the crib. I nimbly returned my gaze to the hock of ham, I can tell you.

"Izaak, does my child and I disgust you so much that you cannot stand to look at us?"

I called time on checking-out the hock and I faced Janie. Her humongous eyes, though still beautiful, no longer danced and sparkled.

"Look, Janie," I said, coldly, "I am representing Jacob and, although I'm told that your evidence is agreed and can be read, you are nevertheless a Crown witness."

"I wish only, Izaak..." Janie stopped and the floodgates opened. Though sodden with rain, the tears that flowed were clearly visible as they settled on her top coat; such were their size and so profuse were they in number.

"Here," I said, advancing forwards, "let me hold this thing while you slip off your coat."

She handed me the crib. A bit of gurgling came from within. Cute, some may have said but I was damned if I was about to acknowledge the fruit of Pinstripe's damnable loins. I placed the crib on the ground and Janie began the act of slipping off her sopping wet cashmere coat. Even that simple act was, at Janie's hands, living art, a piece of theatre. Beneath the coat, she wore her customary white linen top and black linen trousers.

"Let's go through to the sitting room, Janie." She nodded her assent that we should, indeed that we would, go through to the sitting room. So, Janie collected up her abomination and the three of us went through. It was necessary for Janie to bend her swan-like neck, ever so slightly, as she came through the doorway.

I made as if to embrace Janie and, Crown witness or not, I found myself within a hair's breadth of placing loving arms about her pale, freckled shoulders. At the same time, I was about to reaffirm my everlasting love and devotion. However, I checked myself and I cleared a frog from my throat. "It's awful weather for the time of year," I said, gruffly. Even as I was saying it, I was wishing that I'd left well alone and let the frog have his say.

Janie seated herself in the very best of the two armchairs and she place the crib beside her.

"Come on then," I said, harshly. "What is it that you want to say?"

Janie began to explain. She did so between sobs and she did so between profuse apologies for an undignified outburst (as she saw it) and for her squalid appearance. On neither count did she owe any apologies or excuses. Janie was a proud, private person and I considered her outburst (as she had put it) intimate and, as for the dishevelment, it was an honour that only I was privy to the runny mascara and pale blotchy skin. I already had prior knowledge that there was rather more to her cool exterior than met the eye. I had never, not once, wanted Janie to harbour thoughts that my feelings towards her were anything other than of love and total commitment. I refrained from saying anything that might give away my feelings. However, there was no reciprocation on Janie's part because, between telling me that her business interests were on the brink and that it was all the fault of the abominable Pinstripe, Janie told me that she had known since the day we had first met that it should have been her and me as one and not she and Pinstripe as two and then three, sort of thing.

I told it to Janie, straight. "You were damned quick off the mark in marrying the blighter!"

Tears bigger than I ever imagined possible cascaded onto the white blouse. "Izaak, you left me without saying a word. What was I to think?"

"Ha!" That's how I responded. "Ha!" I did it, again. "I was gone for just a few weeks, Janie." I stood over her in what must have been an intimidating fashion. "I return to find you marrying him. For God's sake, Janie, why him of all people?" I then added, in a manner most cruel, that even to this day shames me. "You even let him get you pregnant with that thing!"

"Izaak!" Janie shot to her feet, her eyes ablaze with fury. "Never, ever, address my child in those tones!"

"Okay, okay," I said, and, I backed off, in the direction of the inglenook, to be exact. "That was out of order, Janie, and I apologize."

"I can understand that you are upset, Izaak." Though matter-of-fact in her address, Janie appeared to accept my apology because she instantly became calmer. "The fact remains, Izaak, that I was led to understand that you had emigrated to the United States of America."

"Ha!" That's how I went, again. I was fast in danger of adopting it as a habit. It was a habit that I needed to break because it caused a little cry to come from within the crib. "Who on earth told you that rubbish, Janie?"

"Why, it was William, of course. He stated that, in view of miscellaneous indiscretions, you would never be permitted to practice at the Bar of England and Wales and that to frustrate due process of law you had fled the jurisdiction." Janie returned to her seat and, as soon as she had done so, she dangled a slender arm into the crib. "There, there, my precious," she said, softly.

I averted my eyes from the sickening spectacle. "You were damned quick up the aisle, Janie." I steadied myself and I took a good hard look at her delicate hand. It was attempting to comfort the thing in the crib. "Perhaps, Janie, I should say that you were damned well quick to go to his bed and then up the aisle?"

Janie sobbed aloud. To my everlasting shame, I simply tutted and told her to get on with what it was she wanted to impart.

Accordingly, between her crying, Janie informed me that Pinstripe had coerced her and her family and/or friends to invest in a financial scheme that was guaranteed to pay an incredible amount of interest within a period as short as the blink of an eye. She told me that Pinstripe had recruited hard-up locals, Jacob included, to market the scheme.

Janie imparted everything despite strange noises coming from outside the cottage. The strange noises were in the form of a heated debate between Trudy and Ian. From what I could tell, Trudy was telling Ian that he was no gentleman. Now, do not go blaming me if the following report is not wholly accurate because I was more interested in the teardrops glinting, as would diamonds, on Janie's pure pale skin. However, I had pride and I was not about to admit to the cheap hussy that I still loved and adored her. Anyway, as I was saying, Trudy was telling Ian that he was no gentleman. She was explaining, in a rather excitable manner, that no true gentleman (especially when there was a camera rolling) would clamber over the wooden enclosure of his pig pen without waiting for her; that no true gentleman would stroll off, casually enquire (without turning around) whether she was okay, especially when anyone hearing her blood curdling screams would know that she was very definitely not okay. Further and additionally, no true gentleman would castigate her for causing harm to his chattel, namely the fence, especially when she was lying on her back in pig muck with one leg wrapped around the top rail, while the other one was being chewed by a piglet and a tosser in an anorak was telling her, "That fence wail you've bwoken is made fwom a pwotected twee."

Anyway, when Janie was done I suggested (though I said it in an appropriate manner) that she and the abomination in the crib should depart.

Janie's response was surprising, not to say electrifying. You could have knocked me down with a feather when, with crib in hand, Janie came at me and crashed her lips straight into mine.

I swear that our mouths would have remained locked together all night had we not heard more commotion at the back door, or, what was left of it. Janie broke loose and straightened her top. It had weirdly worked loose, but I refuse to go into that one. "I am emotionally and financially ruined, Izaak," so said Janie. "I am a broken woman."

I was about to tell her that, as far as I was concerned, her money had been an obstacle to our enjoining and that her sudden impecuniosities was a blessing. I might have added that we could still be happy because there were boarding schools and such like where the thing in the crib could be sent. I said not a word, however, because Ian and Trudy chose that very moment to barge in. Janie and I took a backwards pace apiece.

"Ian," said Trudy. "You have treated me as one would the lowest of whores from the back of Henry's."

"Where, old girl?"

"It's a department store," I volunteered, as the weather girl's mouthpiece. "Bad taste and frequented by them with more money than sense."

"And what is more," said Trudy, without as much as a thank you for my *résumé* on the retailing guide to Birmingham, "When the crew have stopped laughing, they intend to forward the film of my misfortune, that debacle, to *Candid Camera*! As a prospective presenter of serious documentaries, I am ruined!"

No doubt sensing that her presence did not suit, Janie announced that she would depart.

"Sorry, old thing," said Ian. "I did not notice you and the sprog."

Trudy immediately mellowed. "Oh, my word," she gushed. "What a sweet baby." Trudy looked my way. "Do you see, Isaiah…?"

"The name is Izaak," I snapped.

"Do you see, Izaak? He is the most adorable baby ever!"

I responded with cold sarcasm. "Is it **really**?"

Janie sobbed. "Oh, Izaak."

CHAPTER NINETEEN

The period between seeing off Janie and gearing-up in the Crown Court dress of a barrister was fairly hectic. Having, as I say, seen off Janie, I spent the entire night reproaching myself for having acted abominably towards the one person who truly mattered. The following day (besides a continuance of the reproaching as aforesaid), I firstly got to grips with the case papers and I secondly conducted a case conference at one of the cribbage tables down at The Case is Open.

I now shift attention to the Crown Court, some twenty-two hours later.

I was due to meet with Madison and Jacob at ten *ante meridiem* British Summertime. My client, Jacob, had navigated his way through sixty-odd years without any brush with the authorities, other than for selling out of date stock to unsuspecting members of the public, of which I was one. The manufacture and sale of alcohol without a license did not count because Jacob had not been apprehended for that minor indiscretion.

At the end of his long walk through the gothic arches, and on arrival at the big wooden doorway that belonged to Court One, Jacob offered me his right hand.

"You look very grand in the wig and gown, Mr. G.. I am humbled that you are devoting your time to correcting these wrongs."

I informed Jacob that it was I who was humbled and inwardly I reproached myself some more. You see, uppermost in my mind was exacting revenge for the wrongs that had been done by the abominable Pinstripe. *Jacob's acquittal*, I reasoned, *will naturally follow*. That is the extent to which my judgment as trial counsel was clouded. I see it now, but I did not see it then. When it came to fooling with the lives of others, I was no better than Pinstripe.

We, that is Madison, Jacob, and I took our designated places in Court. To be exact, Madison sat immediately behind. Poor Jacob found himself seated behind Madison. He was in the dock, you see. Flanked between a pair of burly-looking prison officers, Jacob nervously fingered his tie of bright green.

Nervously, I fingered my stiff starched collar of grungy white and, as I did so, I took in the surroundings. It was an old-fashioned courtroom, no windows other than for skylights, and dark wooden panels just about everywhere. To my side, there was a wooden box and it contained a pair of benches (one behind the other). The benches looked as if they could accommodate six persons apiece. On a wall, high above the wooden box, was a clock. Its face was saying ten twenty-five o'clock. It was another way of imparting the fact that it was high time prosecuting counsel turned up. Otherwise, the judge who I predicted was only moments away from strolling in would be none too pleased were he to find himself presiding over a trial short of a barrister. Just then, I heard one of the swing doors open and I also heard an enquiry as to the health and welfare of whomsoever it was that had opened the door. The sounds of footsteps approached and, on the basis that enquiries as to health and welfare appeared to be following their owner, I reasoned that the footsteps were vested in Walter Tweed.

Madison confirmed that my deduction was spot-on. "Good morning to you, Mr. Tweed," he said. "I was hoping that you may be ill but, I naturally say that in jest because if you do not mind me saying so '(*Here we go*, I thought)' you look exceedingly well."

"Walter," I said, "please don't tell me that you are prosecuting?"

"It is nothing personal, Gatehouse." Walter grinned, just a little. "My case has settled and Igor Patterson..." The learned Head of Chambers observed my puzzled look and he paused. "You did know that Patterson was prosecuting?"

"No, I didn't, Walter."

"That incompetent clerk of mine was instructed to inform you. Also, and I say this by way of aside, the gown that you wear appears to be covered in mud and grass stains." Walter gathered up his own black gown and he started to squeeze by. "Permit me to pass, my friend." Walter duly squeezed by and he deposited himself alongside. He placed a large brief on the table. "Patterson," said Walter, "was in London and the damned fool has missed his train."

"London? What was he doing there?"

"He had intended to collect a new set of robes." Walter looked me up and down. He looked a mite puzzled. "You do know, do you not?" I looked blankly and Walter looked puzzled, all over again. "It was essential for Patterson to replace the robes that Prospect had apparently mislaid on somewhere or something known as Breeve Hill."

Further conversation was thwarted because an usher started hollering. "Be silent in Court! All rise!" So, all of us did just that and, as I had predicted, the judge arrived.

"Good morning," said the judge, pleasantly (and that came as a pleasant surprise), and he, except that he was in actual fact a she, came down on her chair of red leather with a loud plop. Immediately on becoming settled, the judge addressed Walter. "Are we ready to proceed?" Walter opened his mouth as if to have his say but the judge was having none of that sort of thing. "Good," she said. "We will start the trial without further ado." The judge's hairdo seemed not at all practical because it was coiffed in a kind of 1950's beehive of the type common amongst teenagers of that era and, if the jowls had anything to go by, she had definitely been a teen of that era. Anyway, the inevitable consequences of a hairdo such as that was that the judge's wig rode a good six inches, perhaps as many as nine, above her head. "Before the jurors in waiting enter Court," she said, and both Walter and I scrambled to our feet, "I am anxious to ensure that the usual reasons for being excused jury service, pre-booked holidays, medical appointments, and so forth, are not communicated to one another." Next, Her Honour demonstrated that she was one in the majority of judges who held the public, and jurors in particular, in contempt because, "Otherwise," she said, "they will all know how to avoid jury service."

"Your Honour is most perceptive," said Walter. He said it in his customary drawl and by saying it he acquiesced in the empanelling process taking rather longer than normal because a questionnaire was handed to each and every member of the jury panel.

Therefore, it was getting on towards lunchtime before we had a duly constituted jury and it consisted of eight men and four women, true.

Her Honour looked at the big clock. "It is twenty-five minutes to one," she said, which at least proved that here was a judge who could tell the time. "It is Monday," she added, only going to prove that at least one member of the judiciary actually knew which day of the week it was. "We may as well adjourn early for lunch," she said, only going to prove that her priorities were in the same sort of order as any other judge. "We will reconvene at two fifteen," she added, only going to prove what o'clock it was when the wine stopped flowing in the judge's dining room.

After the judge and the jury had gone, I turned to Walter. "Walter," I said, "shall we go for a sandwich or somutt, I mean, something?"

"I, my friend, intend to attend to Chambers business." Walter exposed his pearl black head by removal of the horsehair wig. He casually tossed the same onto the table. "I suggest, Izaak, that you miss luncheon and attend the police office just down the corridor."

"Police office?" I was confused.

Walter's initial response was to ask that I breathe in a bit as he squeezed by. After coming by, he stopped. "My friend," he said. "There is unused material that may or may not assist your client. I suggest that you use the next..." he looked at his watch. "I suggest that you use the next one hour and thirty-five minutes wisely. The material is available for inspection pursuant to the guidelines set out by the Attorney General."

So, down at the police office, bewigged and gowned, I asked if I could have a word with the exhibits officer in the case of the Queen versus Jacob Hamish Gaylord Henderson.

"It is I," said a short bespectacled man. He had answered my knock at the door. "Mr. Tweed informed me that you would be calling in. I have to say that Mr. Tweed is looking exceedingly w…"

"Yes, yes," I snapped, and I removed my wig or, rather, I removed Patterson's horsehair wig. "I know that he's looking well. In fact, he's looking so bostin' that he'll be playing centre forward for Birmingham City Football Club next season, I shouldn't wonder."

The man scrunched his eyebrows, looking every inch as if he was baffled. "Er, I was about to say, sir, that Mr. Tweed is looking exceedingly worried. It is my belief that he is concerned that the trial may overrun. Mind you," he added, with a grin. "Now that you come to mention it, he is, indeed, looking extremely well."

I was shown to a desk and the man handed me a large folder.

"What's the provenance of these documents, Mr. er…?"

"Knight, sir. Detective Constable Knight." The officer scrunched his eyebrows, all over again. "And, how do you mean, sir?"

I leaned back in my chair. I had nabbed the thing without invitation. I thereby found myself addressing the officer's left nostril. "I mean to say, Detective Constable, where was it that these documents were discovered?"

"Ah," said the officer, and he reached for the far corner of the desk and he copped hold of a bundle of papers. "I refer you to my statement at page ten, sir," and the officer thumbed through the papers and he stopped at what I imagined was the tenth page. "It is my statement, sir, and you will observe that it is I who seized all papers from the home of the defendant."

"In which case, officer," I said, politely, "we had better not engage in further conversation."

"Why is that, then?" His response was not particularly polite. Indeed, there was a certain kind of an edge.

"I'm going to ask you to give evidence, you see."

"Well," said the officer, with a shrug. "It's up to you but, you'll appreciate that it is normal practice to agree the sort of continuity evidence that I give." The officer dragged up a vacant chair. He hitched his cavalry twill trousers and sat himself down. The officer's proximity was such that my personal space was well and truly invaded. He was oblivious. Though, thinking back, it was probably a ploy designed to throw me off my stride. "I am obliged to supervise the inspection process, sir. It is to ensure that nothing..." He coughed. "Goes missing, if you get my drift?"

I nudged my chair up, just a bit. It served no usual purpose because the officer simply nudged up a bit, and all. "You can search me on the way out, if you prefer," I said.

The officer slowly and deliberately shook his head. "I don't think that that is allowed, sir." He eyed me, just as if I was a participant in a cattle show. "Tell me, sir," he said, after a moment's silence. "Have you conducted many fraud cases?" The officer waited for an answer but none was forthcoming. He changed tack. "Indeed, sir, have you conducted many cases at all?"

In the manner of a High Court Judge confronted by his (or, her) spouse with an accusation of inappropriate behaviour with a member of the opposite (or, indeed, same) sex, I decided that I would not dignify the officer's enquiry with an answer. I therefore told him just that. "I will not dignify your question with an answer." I might just as well have told him that, in the case of the Queen versus Jacob Hamish Gaylord Henderson, I was appearing for the very first time before judge and jury of twelve men true, unless you want to get all technical on me, by which I mean that there were actual eight men and four women, true.

I observed that, in the far left corner of the room, there was an exhibits bag. I could tell that it was an exhibits bag because its neck was sealed with a strip of lead.

"Officer," I said, officiously. "What's in the sealed bag?"

"Nothing of any interest, sir."

"Then, why is it sealed, sort of thing?"

"In order to keep my sandwiches fresh, sort of thing, sir."

"Oh," I said, sheepishly. "Just checking, like."

"You are too smart for the likes of me," said the officer, in a manner which suggested that his thought processes were just the opposite. He vacated his seat and went over to the other far corner. He picked up a supermarket-type shopping bag. "This bag contains the only other material seized from your client's house." The officer plonked the bag before me. "It contains rubbish and has no relevance, whatsoever."

While the officer stood over, I fished around inside the bag and pulled out various scraps.

Now, for the benefit of the uninitiated I had better tell you about the Attorney General's guidelines. For those who are actually initiated, you may as well jump a paragraph or two. The Attorney General is the government's main legal adviser. The Attorney General, you must understand, was a bit worried because convictions were being overturned quicker than the paddleboats on the pond at Dudsall Arboretum. It was happening because the police were suppressing material. Not just any old material, you must understand. The material could indicate whether a person was, in fact, not guilty. It was a matter of particular concern that innocent defendants had been sent to prison. Well, to tell the truth, it was a matter of particular concern that the Attorney General's head might roll.

To save his skin, the Attorney General introduced guidelines that there must be disclosure of any material that may have a bearing on the charge and the surrounding circumstances. So, that was the basis on which I was going through a supermarket-type bag.

Later on, the guidelines were changed so that defence lawyers could have access to any material that tended to assist or could be said to undermine the prosecution case. However, solicitors began to rack up costs by pretending to spend hours trawling through material when they had done no such thing. Therefore, the rules were changed, again. It is now the rule that the prosecutor, who is hauled over the coals if there is an acquittal, has the job of selecting any material that suggests a defendant may be innocent.

So, you see. Things have gone full circle. The police can, once again, suppress material. Innocent people can, once again, be sent to jail. Most importantly, the Attorney General's head will not roll. It follows that, with the possible exception of the innocent who have been sent to jail, everyone is a winner.

When I was done with the rummaging, I handed to the officer a scrap of paper.

"Officer," I said, "please ensure that you take this into Court."

The officer took the bit of paper and he considered its content. After a couple of seconds, he raised his eyebrows and tutted. "You really haven't done many of these cases, have you, sir?"

It was almost time for Court to reconvene. Therefore, after finishing with the inspection process, I hurried back through the gothic arches. Half way through my journey, I called time on dodging the cracks between the stone slabs because I was obliged to negotiate a T-junction. It was a junction at which the Victorian architect had taken it into his head to have courtrooms going left, courtrooms going right, and a law library going straight ahead.

I turned to the left and, immediately on turning the corner, I noticed Janie. I swear I did! The love of my life was seated on a stone bench. It was set back into a little alcove. Janie was dressed in her customary white linen blouse and dark trousers. There was a child's pram parked directly in front of Janie. I assumed that its cargo was fast asleep because Janie was not flapping around. Indeed, her head was bowed as if in deep contemplation.

"I'll give you a penny for your thoughts," I said, as I approached, trying to sound cheerful whereas, in truth, I could not have been more miserable.

Janie immediately looked up, somewhat startled. I noted that the sparkle within her humongous eyes was still noticeable by its absence.

"I have been a fool, Izaak." That's what she said. "Now I must pay the price for having been a fool."

I swished my gown (or, rather, Patterson's gown) to the front of my personage and I lifted it up, just a little. In the fashion mentioned, sitting down was made easier. And that is what I did. I sat down, immediately next to Janie. "You can leave him, Janie. You know that you can."

The beautiful eyes swelled. "Izaak. I have entered into a contract of marriage and now I must pay for what I have done."

I tutted. "Janie," I said. "This contract, as you call it, surely did not entitle him to rob you blind?"

"Izaak." The tone of her voice gave away raw emotion and it set my heart a fluttering. "I know that you attempted, in your somewhat unorthodox manner, to warn me. I consider that what has befallen me is punishment. Izaak…?"

Janie stopped and tears flowed. They were perhaps the biggest teardrops that I had ever before witnessed. Indeed, they were so big that, in no time at all, the front of Janie's pure white blouse was sodden.

"Janie, Janie," I said, lovingly and I placed my hand, and consequently Patterson's horsehair wig, around her shoulder. "Whether or not you thought that I had gone for good, the speed with which you agreed to marry him is beyond belief. Janie, you know perfectly well…"

"Yes, Izaak?" Janie interrupted because it was the turn of mine own eyes to swell. She nestled her mousey locks into my chest.

"It should've been me," I said, quoting Memphis Curtis. I kissed Janie gently atop her silken hair.

Janie sniffed a bit because her nose had started to run. From anyone else it might have been off-putting but not so in the case of Janie Anker, Jetty, as was. Indeed, I considered it rather endearing. "Love stories do not always have a happy ending, Izaak."

"No," I said, coldly, and I snappily removed my hand and consequently Patterson's horsehair wig, and all. "Love stories certainly don't come true if you go looking for problems instead of simply taking the plunge."

Janie effectively ignored my inference that she was the creator of a self-fulfilling prophesy. "At first," she said,

"William was so kind. He represented stability, Izaak. Now it is as if he detests the two of us." At that juncture, Janie focused her attentions on the contents of the parked perambulator. Through tears, she smiled, a little. "William stated that he did not care whether the child was a boy or a girl as long as he, or she, was healthy and had ten toes (*or eleven*, I thought, on the basis that the abominable Pinstripe was from Cambridge). Are you listening, Izaak?"

The child decided that it was his turn to turn on the waterworks. I reckoned that it was the hollering of his birth mother that had set him off.

"I'd best go to Court, I said, in an offish manner. "Also, I think that you'd best quieten that thing."

"Oh, Izaak!" Janie sobbed uncontrollably. "Detest me, Izaak, but pray do not detest my innocent child! You cannot bear to address him by name, even!"

Inwardly, I wanted to scoop up Janie in my loving arms. In the event, I stood up, unswishing my gown in the process so that I set it off flowing freely, once more. "What is its name then, Janie?"

Janie's beautiful face collapsed into her hands and she said something or other. I couldn't make out what it was because her voice was muffled. I casually shrugged and, at that, Janie lowered her hands. "**It**," she said, slowly and clearly, with anger in her tone, "is named after **its** father."

"Ha!" That's all I could manage to say. Beggar Janie's anger, for I had never felt as angry in the whole of my life.

Janie half rose. "Oh, Izaak!"

"Just, just get on with playing nursemaid, Janie!" With that, I plonked the wig atop my head where it should have belonged, was it not Patterson's in the first place. I strode off and, as I did so, I was thinking, *Good grief! That's just what the world needs, that is. Two William Ankers; William Anker, the younger and William Anker, the elder!*

CHAPTER TWENTY

Back in Court, I was still seething. However, I hid it rather well as Walter went through his opening speech to the jury.

Walter's delivery was crisp and concise and he held the attention of the eight men and four women, true. Indeed, he somehow managed to hold everyone's attention, the ushers, the stenographer, even the judge. He explained how Jacob had become an employee of Janie's business and how he had professed personal knowledge of an investment scheme that was guaranteed to make a huge return within a very short period.

"He abused," said Walter, "the trust placed in him by a family lawyer and business adviser, one, Mr. William Anker." On uttering the name of that atrocious individual, I could have sworn that there was a twinkle in Walter's eye. "The defendant stated that the huge returns would come about as a result of something called leverage. And this," so went Walter, and he held aloft a piece of paper, "is the document that was offered to Mr. Anker by way of guarantee. It is, ladies and gentlemen, a government bond for one million dollars." At that juncture, a few of the men true gasped and excelled air. A woman turned to the woman true next to her and raised an eyebrow. "Mr. Anker," drawled Walter, "could be forgiven for assuming that, with one million dollars by way of security, his wife, Mrs. Janie Anker, could not possibly be taking a risk by advancing to the defendant five hundred thousand pounds of her hard earned money by way of an advanced fee. The only problem was..." and Walter paused for dramatic effect. "The name of the country on the bond is nonexistent, and..." he paused, again, "the investment scheme did not exist, either."

Well, when he was done, Walter informed the judge that, with her permission he intended to call the exhibits officer. "My learned friend," said Walter, "wishes to have the exhibits officer give evidence," and, with that, Her Honour raised an eyebrow. "If the officer goes first, Your Honour, he can remain for the purpose of assisting the Court and me with the paperwork."

"An excellent idea, Mr. Tweed." So went Her Honour, and the whole of the inhabitants of the Court nodded their approval.

"Yeh, bostin'." So went me, except that it was under my breath.

With that, Walter told the judge that, again, only if she permitted it, he would turn his back on her. And on a permit being granted to do just that, Walter turned his back on the Court. "Call Detective Constable Knight!"

In a blind panic, an usher went scurrying off to find Detective Constable Knight. No court would be a court without an usher who was in a blind panic. It is a common trait in ushers that they move about by scurrying. The tendency to panic probably derives from the fact that ushers get the blame for everything. If the courtroom is too hot in summer (it invariably is), the usher will get the blame. If the courtroom is too cold in winter (it always is), then the usher had better watch out. I have even known ushers to carry the can for the fact that a witness has told a bare-faced lie ("he was plainly distracted by that panicky-looking usher, Your Honour"). I would add, purely for the record, that the tendency to scurry is derived from the fact that ushers are either retired police officers and, as such, they have the onset of arthritis or they are (in the case of Birmingham ushers, at any rate) from the ropey-looking housing estate next to the Cadbury factory and, naturally, were born with rickets.

Anyway, as the usher in the particular instance scurried through the swing doors, a voice was heard from a little wooden box. It was a box situated next to the dock and it was generally reserved for members of the press and probation officers. "I'm D.C. Knight, Your Honour. Shall I go and ask the usher to return?"

"No, thank you," said Walter, gallantly, for and on behalf of Her Honour. "Kindly approach the witness box."

Next, the officer pointed the Good Book towards the heavens and, to the sounds of the panicky usher drifting in going, "D.C. Knight! D.C. Knight, please!" D.C. Knight was actually swearing that the account he intended to give to the Court was nothing but truthful, as God was his witness.

When the officer was done, he replaced the Good Book into a little wooden pocket where it apparently lived alongside the Bhagavad Gita for use by Hindu witnesses, the Pentateuch for those witnesses who were of the Jewish persuasion and a wooden stick (bleached white by the ocean) with miscellaneous items dangling from it including a crow's feather, a bit of ribbon, an unemployed benefits book, some moss and a condom filled with water. That was probably for those witnesses who were of the Hippy persuasion, that was.

Well, just as soon as the Good Book came to rest as previously mentioned, D.C. Knight explained to the Court who he was and what rank he held. However, as if to cast doubt on the officer's veracity and as if to generally undermine his credibility as a witness, the usher burst in and hollered, "Detective Constable Knight is not here!"

"Yes, he is," said the officer.

"Oh, no, he's not!" So said the usher.

Her Honour sat bolt upright. "Who is this imposter? Remove him from Court and have him questioned!"

The officer rose both of his arms and, in the manner of a pair of aeroplane wings, he held them horizontal, thumbs up. "But, Your Honour, I'm supposed to be questioned in the Court! Otherwise, the jury will not be able to hear me!"

Walter coughed and he thereby gained the Court's undivided attention. "Your Honour," he casually said, "it is my belief that the person who stands before you is, indeed, Detective Constable Knight."

The judge spun her head around in the direction of the witness box and she did it so quickly that it was a wonder that her wig kept up and did not, for example, remain facing the front or even topple off the bouffant. "Well," she said, "are you Detective Constable Knight?"

"Who, me, Your Honour?"

Her Honour sat back and gasped. "Yes, I mean you. The person who is stood before me in the manner of a Tiger Moth that is about to take to the skies!"

The officer snappily lowered his wings and he stood to attention. "Very sorry, I'm sure, Your Honour!"

Walter coughed and, once again, he commanded unrivalled attention. "Did you, officer, carry out a search of the defendant's property?"

"I did, sir."

"And, did you seize certain items of property?"

"I did, sir."

"And, do you produce a list of those items?"

"I did, sir. I mean to say, I do, sir."

Walter casually returned to his seat although, on the way down, he casually told the witness to remain where he was.

It was my turn.

"Officer," I said, "I represent the defendant."

"I know," said D.C. Knight.

Her Honour pounced. She was no different from most judges in that she could not resist the temptation of diving in when a witness may be on the ropes. "Officer!" The jumpy usher almost dropped his clipboard. "How can you possibly know?"

"Because," said the officer, "Mr. Gatehouse is the only other barrister in Court. Therefore, by a process of elimination, I deduce that he acts for the defendant."

The judge leaned eagerly forwards. "Do you hear, ladies and gentlemen of the jury? That is police training for you in modern Britain and we should all be proud."

"Also," said the officer, who was plainly on a high, "Mr. Gatehouse introduced himself to me over the luncheon adjournment."

"What?" The judge's head spun towards the witness, then me, then Walter, and to me, again. "Mr. Gatehouse?"

"Yes, Your Honour?"

"Is it correct that you have conversed with a Crown witness?"

Walter majestically rose. "It was with my knowledge and consent, Your Honour."

A look of relief flowed all over the judge's face. "Well, that is all right then." She next refocused her attentions on me. "Well, why didn't you say so?"

I was tempted to tell the truth and put it to the daft bat that it may have occurred to her razor-sharp legal brain that she had not actually asked.

"Well," went the judge, "I am waiting?"

She plainly was not about to let me off the hook. To the melodious noise of a clipboard dropping on the stone flags and bouncing a few times, "The usher," I said. "The court usher distracted me."

"Ah ha!" The judge's tone mellowed. "I offer my apologies on behalf of the Court, Mr. Gatehouse, and I will ensure that I have appropriate words with the chief administrator. We cannot have panicky ushers distracting members of the Bar."

"Yes, Your Honour. I mean to say, no, Your Honour. Thank you, Your Honour." I focused on the witness. "Item thirty," I said. "Will you produce it, please?"

The witness duly handed me, via a panic-stricken usher, item thirty.

"That's the one," I said, and, I thrust forth an arm intending that item thirty be returned to the witness. "Oh," I said, looking this way and that. "The usher's gone." I gathered up my gown (I did not wish to go tipping over water decanters or any other items on the table, you see) and I strolled across the well of the courtroom and I thereby transported exhibit thirty to the witness.

I began cross-examination of the officer before even I had returned to my place. "It is a note that appears to have been made by the defendant, is it not?"

"Well," said the officer, shrugging, "it is certainly a note, sir, but as to its author...?"

"You ascertained that the note was in the defendant's hand, did you not?"

"Er, I can't rightly remember but the style does greatly resemble that of the defendant's..."

"Thank you," I said, cutting in, again. "In that case," I said, (and, it should be noted that I was addressing Her Honour). "In that case," I said, again, for dramatic effect.

"Get on with it."

"Yes, Your Honour. Thank you, Your Honour. Perhaps the document can be exhibited?"

"Perhaps," said the judge, "I may see it first?"

"Okay," I said. "I mean to say, very well, Your Honourable. I mean to say, Her Honour. No, no! I mean, Your Honour."

The judge sighed. "Just pass it here, will you? No, not you, Mr. Gatehouse. And, not you, either, Officer. Where is that usher?"

Following a bit more clattering, as another clipboard hit the deck, the document was passed to the judge.

"Mr. Gatehouse?"

"Yes, Your Honour?"

"This is just a piece of scrap paper with doodles all over it. It is rubbish."

"Yes, Your Honour. I mean to say, no, Your Honour." At that juncture, my throat started to seize. I therefore poured a glass of water from a decanter or, rather, a glass milk bottle. Unfortunately, I was prohibited from putting vessel to lips because my hands were shaking too much. "The note, Your Honour, is probative as to the defendant's state of mind. He did not, you see, envisage that any third party would read it."

"Well, how can you possibly know that?"

"Because its provenance is a locked drawer in which the defendant also kept reading matter for his own, personal consumption. If you get my drift, like"

"Describe this material, please," and, with that, Her Honour leaned eagerly forwards, as did every single one of the twelve persons true.

"Very well," I said. But, I got no farther than that because, from behind, there came a clattering.

"Mr. Gatehouse?"

"Your Honour?"

"Is it that usher, again?"

"No, Your Honour. It's the defendant."

"Then, kindly request your instructing solicitor to tell him to be quiet and then, kindly proceed."

"The reading material, Your Honour, was *Houseboat Keeping Quarterly*, *Scandinavian Girls Must Be Punished*, and *Model Aeroplane Construction for Beginners*."

"What? That is disgusting."

"No, no, Your Honour," and I shook my head. "The model aeroplane magazine had never been opened. It was still in its cellophane wrapping, you see."

There came another clattering. Walter half rose. "My apologies, Your Honour. I appear to have dropped my spectacle case."

"Anyway," I said, "the note shows an investment scheme…"

"With wholly unrealistic projections," said the judge, interrupting.

"That may very well be so, Your Honour. However, you will see that the defendant has drawn a little arrow showing his projected percentage and, at the end of the little arrow, is the drawing of a houseboat."

"I still do not get the point, Mr. Gatehouse."

"The point, Your Honour, is that the jury may very well infer that, whether or not the projected returns were ridiculous, the defendant himself believed them to be true. How else, you see, was he hoping to earn sufficient to purchase a houseboat?"

"Ah!" That's how Her Honour went. "A point well made, Mr. Gatehouse. Have you anything to say, Mr Tweed?"

"No, thank you, Your Honour," said Walter, getting to his feet. "Like," he added, with a grin.

"Very well," said the judge. "The note will henceforth be known as exhibit D1." She did a bit of scribbling and handed the duly baptised note to the usher, now frit to death. "Well, Mr. Gatehouse? Have you any further questions?"

"No, thank you, Your Honour."

" Do you wish to re-examine, Mr. Tweed?"

"No, thank you, Your Honour."

The judge looked a bit puzzled. But, she soon snapped out of it. "Then, call your next witness, Mr. Tweed."

"Call William Anker!"

As the cries of "Mr. Anker!" from the petrified usher drifted in, I sat forwards in eager anticipation.

As the atrocious Pinstripe made his way towards the front of Court and up into the witness box, I couldn't help but notice that he looked a deathly shade of grey.

The usher asked the abominable individual to take the oath.

"Put that stick down, usher, and hand to the witness the New Testament!"

"I'm very sorry, Your Honour."

Pinstripe jabbed the book heaven-wards. He thereby perjured himself from the off because he promised that he was going to be truthful (as if that was at all possible coming, as it did, from the lips of a solicitor and a City solicitor at that).

Just as soon as Pinstripe had re-inserted the Good Book inside the little wooden pocket, I was on my feet.

"I suggest to you that it is all lies!"

"Might I suggest," said Walter, casually rising, "that it is traditional that I proceed firstly with the examination in chief?"

The judge looked fit to bust. "I entirely agree, Mr. Tweed! Mr. Gatehouse?"

"Yes, Your Honour?"

"Who is your pupil master? She, or he, has plainly neglected to teach you the basics."

"Just a slip-up, Your Honour. It won't happen again, like."

"I should think not! Anyone who has watched just five minutes of *Petrocelli* knows that the cross-examination has to follow the examination! Otherwise, poor Mr. Tweed will not know what to ask!"

"Eh?"

"Mr. Gatehouse! By reference to the answers offered by the witness, Mr. Tweed will have to guess his own questions!" The judge lowered her head and began scribbling. At the same time, she started with her lecturing, again, save and except that her voice began trailing-off. "Like," is what she said, only to rally and exclaim. "It will be impossible for Mr. Tweed to guess his own questions were the answers to the questions that had not been asked prove to be a pack of lies in the first place!"

"Exactly, Your Honourable!" *By George,* I thought, *she's got it.*

In the fashion above-mentioned, the judge's ruling was that Walter should have an opportunity of asking his questions of the witness.

"Mr. Anker," said Walter, "Are you…?"

He was cut short by Pinstripe. "I know what you're going to ask me!"

Walter stepped back, astonished. "Do you?"

"Yes, I jolly well do. You intend to suggest that, as a commercial lawyer, I was reckless in the choice of investments for and on behalf of my spouse."

"Was I?" Walter tried to step back a little more but he was thwarted by the oak panels that separated us from the solicitors. "I think that you may very well find, Mr. Anker, that it is my learned friend, here," and Walter pointed at me, "who will pursue such issues."

With that, Walter set off again. He elicited from Pinstripe that Jacob had gone to the food plant looking for work and that work had been duly offered because Jacob, as a qualified pharmacist, had knowledge of mixing potions and so forth. Such knowledge, so reasoned Pinstripe (on Janie's behalf), was not far removed from mixing food ingredients.

"He abused my trust," so said Pinstripe, sounding suitably pompous. "He was given five hundred thousand pounds and, in return, he offered a bond by way of security."

Walter waved a piece of paper about. "Do you recognise this?"

"Yes."

"Well, go on, then."

"That," said Pinstripe, "is the bond. You will see that it has a face value of one million dollars. **That man**," and Pinstripe jabbed an accusing forefinger dock-wards. "That man stated that, for howsoever long I held onto the bond as security, he would triple my money, I mean, my wife's money, every single day *ad infinitum.*"

With that, Walter began to close a bundle of papers before him. "And, how much money did this investment produce?"

"Absolutely nothing."

"Thank you, Mr. Anker. Kindly remain where you are because my learned friend has some questions."

With that, the judge looked at the big clock. "Not tonight he doesn't. We will adjourn until tomorrow morning at ten thirty."

Outside Court, I agreed with Walter to meet him in the privacy of the barristers' robing room. It looks bad, you see, for barristers on the opposing teams to be seen together on a chummy basis.

I walked through the gothic arches in the company of Jacob. Janie was still seated on the stone bench. On one side of her was the pram and on the other side of her was Pinstripe. The content of the pram appeared to be kicking up a ruckus and Pinstripe was addressing it and Janie in hostile terms. Regrettably, I could not intervene because the atrocious individual had not concluded his evidence and any conversation under those circumstances would be highly improper and might even jeopardise the trial.

I caught Janie's eye as I passed. It was plain that she had been crying and it was equally plain that, unless he desisted, Pinstripe's behaviour would reduce her to more tears.

"Can you not keep the brat quiet, woman? I knew the thing would be trouble the very minute it was wrenched from your disgusting body!"

Janie un-hooked her gaze and she addressed her husband, and she did so calmly. "William," she said, "I fear that he cries only when you are near."

Protocol or no protocol, I was sorely tempted to seize the wretch by the scruff of his neck. However, I resisted the temptation and walked on by but, as I did so, I was thinking, *when this case is over, Janie, I shall have to take you away from this and it will be my honour to be left holding his baby.*

Jacob must have noticed that my mind was in a faraway place because he found it necessary to gift me a nudge in the ribs. "If you do not mind my saying so, Mr. G., you appear to be deep in thought. I am privileged that you are so devoted to my welfare that you have time to think of little else."

"Eh, what? Sorry, Jacob."

"You know, Mr.G.?" With that, Jacob stopped dead in his tracks. His actions took me by surprise and I automatically carried on a few paces before coming to a stop myself, whereupon I engaged reverse gear.

"What is it, Jacob?"

"It must be very dreadful for you to contemplate cross-examining Mr. Anker when he and his good wife have extended to you an incredible compliment."

I shuffled about a bit, and looked the way of Janie and Pinstripe and the perambulator. "What on earth are you talking about, Jacob?"

"The baby, of course," said Jacob. "It is an incredible compliment that the baby has been named Izaak."

CHAPTER TWENTY-ONE

"Gatehouse!" It's the word that I recall hearing next. "At least Susan Blesham had the common sense, not to mention common decency, to wait until her address to the jury before clattering to the floor, as would an usher's clipboard!" Those are the harsh words that followed, those are.

"My head hurts somutt rotten, Ian!"

"That is simply on account of your head hitting the ground, old chap. It will soon pass."

I opened both my eyes. "Oh my God, I'm blind!"

"That is simply on account of you hitting the home made gin, old chap. It will soon pass."

I squeezed and scrunched my eyelids and, as light returned, I discovered that I was lying in state in the outhouse of The Fly in the Ointment. The object upon which I was laying in state was a credence table that had been dragged down the hill. Of that I was certain because my head was nestled on a somewhat uncomfortable brass plaque proclaiming *property of the diocese.* Ian was bent forwards. I observed that he was dressed in his customary white tunic shirt. I figured, pound to a penny, that his leg wear consisted of the grubby corduroy trousers.

I sat up and, as I did so, Ian had cause to say, "Mind yourself, old boy," and, thereupon, my head came into contact with an object that was hanging by string from the ceiling. By way of reflex action, I recoiled only to go clunking into a similar item. "I suggest that you sit perfectly still, Gatehouse, old chap!"

I did as had been commanded and I noted that the entire outhouse was festooned with inside out pots. The majority were empty but a few contained plants that, naturally, were growing out of the bottom and, as Ian had so accurately predicted, they were in the process of bending in an endeavour to clamber towards the heavens, or, in the immediate instance, the hole in the slate roof which was the causative effect of Ian's negligent action in failing to chop up the village hall's trestle table by way of prelude to its inevitable combustion. Three or four pots contained what appeared to be herbs. One of the things, I swear, had a cactus poking out its side.

"Ian," I said, groggily, "how did I get here? What's happened to me? And," I added. "Why have you put me in the perishing wood shed and not on a comfortable bed?"

Ian reached forth and nabbed hold of the pot on which I had clonked my head. It was still swinging, you see, and therefore in danger of setting off some sort of bing, bang, boing effect with its fellow pots. "Gatehouse," he said, and he wiped both hands down the side of his corduroys. "Starting in reverse order…"

"A bit like your ruddy pots, then?"

Ian shrugged. "You are here, in this makeshift infirmary, because it is courteous that my visitor from Gaul and I occupy the bedroom."

"Aye?"

"As for the remainder of your enquiries, I brought us here, to my country seat, after you had hit your head on the floor in the main corridor of the Crown Court."

"What? The floor?"

"Gatehouse. I understand that the expression in Dudmore…"

"For Pete's sake, Ian, it's Dudsall…"

"Either way, old chap, you went down as would heavy metal in the foundry."

I gingerly placed both feet on the ground, dodging inside out pots as I did so.

"How did this come about then, Ian?"

"Gatehouse! I should not be at all surprised was it to have occurred as a consequence of your realisation that you had trodden on a crack between the flagged stones of the gothic corridor and thereby assumed that you were in mortal peril of being eaten alive by trolls, or, more likely snakes, on the basis that the incident occurred outside the solicitors' assembly room.

The other, more popular, view is that you ended up horizontal on the realization that a much-anticipated Little Gatehouse is on the parish register having entered this world without your knowledge.

"I cannot figure it out, Ian."

"I should jolly well hope that you do!"

"No, not that, Ian." I stood up and began rubbing my sore head. It was difficult to know whether to start with the bit where I had hit the deck or the bit that had come into contact with the terracotta pot. "Ian," I said, after I had rubbed both areas (but I forget which came first so don't ask). "I simply cannot understand why Janie conceived our child and then went and married Pinstripe!"

"Gatehouse! However it was that you and Janie became one…"

"It was after I'd been to the doctors," I garbled. "You know? It was the day I left for America."

"Well, well," said Ian, and he shrugged, not once, but twice. "Now, it all makes sense."

"Eh?"

"Gatehouse! You make love and you immediately leave the country. Janie must have been at her wits' end!"

"But, Ian," I protested, "I was intending to come back, I was!"

"Well, Gatehouse. How was Janie to know of your intentions when you left without saying a word?"

"But, Ian, it was meant to be a surprise!"

"Oh, it was a surprise alright, especially when Janie discovered that you had made her pregnant. As if to compound matters, young William Anker informed Janie that you were gone for good."

I felt my blood beginning to boil. "Now look here, Ian! She's deceived me and, and…!"

"Spit it out, old chap!"

"She, she has even deceived Pinstripe!" I returned to the seated position namely on the credence table and, in the process, I managed to dodge the festoon of pots. "Blimey, Ian! I almost feel sorry for the blighter!"

"Well," said Ian, calmly, "I should not, if I was you, feel sorry for young Anker. You see, old chap, Anker believes that he has discharged his family duty by siring a son and heir even though, I might add, mystery abounds the Anker clan as to Janie's insistence that the child be named Izaak."

"But, Ian!" I was still far from calm; indeed, I felt just as if I was in very choppy waters. "Ian," I said, again, "Janie doesn't love him and she's gone and ruined our lives, she has!"

"Look you here, Gatehouse. Janie was alone, pregnant and vulnerable. By her deception, she gained respectability. However, by manipulating her vulnerability, Anker got his slithery hands on the assets. It is now common knowledge that he sought to make incredibly poor, if not illegal, investments and he has shifted the blame Jacob's way."

I collapsed my aching head into my arms. "This is a total mess, this is!"

"Which I, Gatehouse, have had to clear up."

Before I could pursue the matter further, there came the sweet sound of a woman yawning and a pitter-pattering of feet upon the path. "*Alluh?*" It was a voice, with a sweet-sounding accent.

"Ah! Our visitor has recovered from her exertions and has awoken, old chap." Ian winced and chuckled. "I am in here, old girl!" He said it sufficiently loud to ensure that his voice could be heard by anyone stepping out of what was left of the kitchen and venturing forth up the garden path.

Next, the door of the outhouse opened. Then a face appeared in the gap. "*Ah! Alluh.*"

She was dark, slightly built, with an olive complexion and she wore a long cheesecloth-type dress that was popular at the time (could still be, for all I know and care) with Northern Europeans, Druids, and transvestites. The top three buttons were indecently undone and, on noticing me, the woman began furiously doing-up the things.

"Gatehouse," said Ian. "This is Agathe."

"Agathe?" She simply nodded. "This is Gatehouse."

For the second time of asking, I alighted from the credence table. In my state of confusion, I forgot all about the festoon of pots and, at the exact time my feet landed on *terra firma*, my forehead landed on terra cotta. "Ouch! Bugger!" I extended my right arm but Agathe's right arm remained where the left arm was at, namely at the top of her dress where the buttons were having none of it.

"Agathe is French, old boy. She will not understand such expressions and, moreover, you had better talk slowly and clearly."

"Hallo," I said. "I trust that you are well?"

Agathe bent forwards and she looked intensely into my eyes. "*Eh?*" That was the sum total of her riposte. "*Eh?*" No more, no less.

Ian winced, shrugged, and chuckled. "Gatehouse, here, is from foreign parts too, old girl. That was his attempt at greeting you and, simultaneously, old thing, he was seeking to convey a general enquiry as to your health and wellbeing."

"*Ah! Oui!*"

Ian squeezed by Agathe and, on his way, I swear that he must have pinched her bottom or something because she squeaked. He approached the door, dodging hanging pots as he did so. "If you are feeling sufficiently recovered, old chap, I suggest that we adjourn to the house."

We duly adjourned as Ian had suggested, and it was in the front room where I occupied the armchair that was not as comfortable as the armchair in which Agathe decided to sit.

Ian stood by casually. He overlooked the inglenook. No doubt the reprobate was assessing whether it was time to satisfy the inferno's appetite with a wooden fingerpost *pick your own strawberries 3 miles ahead.* Having fed the flames and, in the process, having provided perfectly legitimate and admissible circumstantial evidence as to why the farm up the lane was chucking out unsold rotting fruit and that hordes of day-trippers were stripping bare the allotments of the parish, Ian told me that Agathe was visiting Warwickshire for the hunting. "Agathe was riding past the cottage, old chap, and she made enquiries as to my inside out pots."

"I imagine that they were frightening the horse," I said, while simultaneously thinking *and I reckon that I know where you told her the best samples were stored.*

"Anyway," said Ian, "Agathe duly inspected the better samples which, naturally, I store upstairs for safe keeping and *voila*! Her company intends to pay me most handsome for a license to produce the product!"

"That's great news, Ian." I duly addressed Agathe. "It is good news !"

"*Eh?*"

Ian tutted. "Look in my direction, old girl." He said that because Agathe was staring at me, with her nose (freckled and browned by thirty or so summers of Provence) all scrunched up. "What Gatehouse is attempting to impart, old thing, is that the news of the contractual undertaking entered into by your business and me is music to his ears."

"*Ah! Oui!*"

Next, Agathe rose from the comfortable armchair. I rose too, as would any gentleman when a lady gets to her feet. However, as I did so, she cast a suspicious look and then she swished her dark hair. Agathe set out on a journey intending to reach Ian. She did it by navigating past the window and she approached her berth via the side of the inglenook where the bread oven had once been. The route was not as would the crow fly. Indeed, it was the longest way around but it resulted in Agathe not having to go anywhere near me.

On arrival at her port of destination, Agathe whispered into Ian's left ear.

"Ah!" So went Ian. "That sounds a jolly good idea, old girl!"

I ought to have told the pair that it was very rude to whisper. But, I did no such thing. Instead, I eagerly asked Ian to reveal the nature of the good news.

"Agathe," said Ian, and Agathe looked longingly into his eyes, "has simply suggested that we pop down to The Case for a noggin with which to celebrate the entering into of the agreement."

I made one and a half steps towards Agathe, no more than that, mind. With that, Agathe huddled up to Ian. Upon that, Ian pulled Agathe close and he chuckled. I decided to speak. "Drink at pub sound good!" I said it so loud and clear that a foundry man with a dozen percussive hand-guided tools hammering in his ears would have heard.

"Ce que tente cette maniac à dire?"

Again, Ian tutted. He did so with disdain. He really did! "Gatehouse is simply trying to communicate to you, old dear heart, the fact that he endorses with relish, indeed, with gusto the suggestion that we adjourn to the local hostelry for the purpose of partaking of a celebratory beverage."

"Ah! Oui!"

"Oh, and, Gatehouse?"

"Yes, Ian?"

"You had better invite your client, Jacob, to accompany us."

"What on earth for?"

Ian let Agathe loose, but she squeaked as he did so leaving me in no doubt that he was at it again. You know? Behind my metaphoric back and her literal back.

"By a stroke of good fortune, old chap, Jacob, the erstwhile pharmacist, ignored Anker's instructions to squander Janie's money in his hair-brained investment scheme." Ian rat-tat tapped Agethe's bottom and she squeaked and fled for the door and Ian followed on, rat-tat tatting some more.

"Hang about! Hang about!" That's what I said and Ian stopped momentarily.

"Yes, old chap?"

"What do you mean that he ignored Pinstripe's instructions?"

"Good heavens above, Gatehouse! Must I spell out everything? Jacob," said Ian, and he chuckled, "preferred my financial advice and he invested in a high yield investment scheme of my making, namely the inside out pots." Without as much as a by your leave, Ian fled and, as he did so, he was calling, "Come you to me, my little French fancy!"

I retraced my steps, backwards, one and a half times, and fell backwards into the armchair. "Blimey," I said. *"Sacre bleu!"*

TWENTY-TWO

It was the second day of Her Majesty's attempt to bang-up Jacob Hamish Gaylord Henderson on fraud charges. I anticipated that the abominable Pinstripe would be finished with his evidence shortly after tea and biscuits.

As I sauntered through the gothic arches, I spied Janie seated on the very same stone bench as before. She looked just as sullen as before. As before, the perambulator was parked by her side.

On account of my bitterness as hereinbefore described, I was yet to view the pram's content. Therefore, as I travelled by, I craned my neck intending to have a sneak preview of Little Gatehouse. All that I observed was a wee wisp of hair peeping out of the top of a white blanket. Janie did not acknowledge me. Initially, I figured that it might have been because I was wearing the robes of a barrister, the barrister being Igor Patterson, of course. As such, I probably looked identical to any other barrister. All looking alike in fancy dress is, of course, a deliberate ploy to mask ineptitude from public scrutiny. It also affords the high and mighty an opportunity to dress up and intimidate his brother man. Anyway, just when I was a-thinking that Janie was thinking that I was not looking, I caught (out of the corner of my eye) Janie looking at me through the corner of her eye.

I was naturally tempted to impart to my love that, by virtue of Agathe's investment in Ian's pots, her finances were saved. Naturally, I said no such thing. Indeed, I said nothing because it would have been regarded as highly improper so to do.

Before entering Court, I turned and, with weird and yet heart pounding joy (verging on the perverse), I noted that Janie's warm, humongous eyes were bulging with tears.

I spun around and returned to the stone bench. Rules or no rules, I simply had to parley with Janie.

"This is ridiculous," I said. It was not the most romantic of greetings I'll grant you but at least it was succinct. "I know you feel the same way, Janie. Otherwise, you would not have named your baby or, rather, our baby after me."

I reached out a hand intending to hoist the white blanket.

Janie pushed my hand away. "Do not touch!"

Her voice was devoid of emotion. It was very confusing especially because tears had begun to flow. I had always assumed that emotion and tears were bedfellows.

"Don't I have any right to see Izaak?"

Janie proceeded to address me and she did so with ice-cold indifference. What Janie said appeared to be, from where I was standing, well-rehearsed. Indeed, it was as if she had been practising, as would a barrister, before a full-length mirror. "The child," so began Janie, as I say, as cold as ice, "is named after his father. The father, you may recall, would not address him other than as 'it'."

"Janie, I can explain all that. You see…"

"Be quiet while I am talking."

"Yes, Janie. Sorry, Janie."

"I have named my child after the father in an endeavour to preserve, to some degree, his true identity. Izaak, you must promise…"

"Yes? Anything at all, Janie."

"You must promise never, ever to see my child…"

"I won't do that!" I swear that that's what I said **and** *Meatloaf*, the rock star, was not even invented!

"I will make no alimony claims," said Janie, as if I cared one iota. Indeed, Janie's comment could not have been more insulting had she tried.

I hoisted up Igor Patterson's gown by the front and I sat next to Janie. "I know that you feel the same," I said, quietly.

Thereupon, Little Gatehouse began whimpering. Possibly, Igor Patterson's wig had done it or perhaps it was just my voice. Either way, Janie laughed aloud. It was entirely inappropriate coming as it did midway through a conversation that touched upon the happiness and well-being of the two and one half persons present.

I very nearly stormed off in a huff. However, as I studied the face of my only true love, I realised that, hidden within the guffawing, Janie was actually sobbing.

With that, I placed an arm about Janie's shoulders. She brushed it away.

I decided to address Janie with a little speech of my own.

"Janie," I said. "Look me in the eyes and say that you wish never to see me again. Do that now and I'll walk away, never to return."

Janie fixed me with her beautiful and tear washed eyes. "Izaak," she said. "I never wish to see you again."

Bugger, I thought, *that weren't supposed to happen.*

"I'll put it another way, Janie." I returned my arm to her shoulders and, on that occasion, Janie chose not to brush it away. "Janie," I said, "have you ever loved me?"

"Yes, I have."

"Janie?"

"Yes, Izaak?"

"Do you love me now?"

Janie said not a word at first. The tension was dreadful and, when the response finally arrived, it was as if it had blown in on an Arctic wind.

"I am not prepared to answer that or any more questions, Izaak."

I opened my jaw intending to state the case, but I was prevented from so doing because a nervous-looking usher shouted out what o'clock it was at that particular moment in time and he thereby conveyed to me that it was high time that I state the case of another.

My first question of Pinstripe was whether it was true that he was a solicitor who professed to have intimate knowledge of all matters commercial.

He naturally answered in the affirmative.

"Well," I said, "you were aware that Jacob Henderson was, by profession, a pharmacist?"

"Yes. However..."

"And, you did not think to check for yourself whether the bond, the guarantee for your wife's investment, was real?"

"Well, everything looked perfectly in order."

I asked the witness to look closely at the government bond.

"Did you not think to check whether the Kingdom of Bharus exists?"

"No. It sounds Middle Eastern."

I was tempted to suggest that Scheherazade sounded Middle Eastern and that she was fictitious, and all. In lieu thereof, I decided to play it safe. "You are a commercial lawyer are you not? And, my client," I said, ploughing in with compound questions, "is a pharmacist, turned factory worker, sometime ice cream sales person? And, I suggest that he is your scapegoat?"

"And, you are a quasi-alcoholic itinerant, turned barrister, sometime stalker of respectable women. And, I suggest that a magpie is your scapegoat."

That comment appeared to wake up Her Honour. "Mr. Anker!" She sounded dead angry. It was a shame for Pinstripe because it was the only sensible thing he had said all morning. "Do not be impertinent to learned counsel," said Her Honour. "You are here to answer questions. I shall be the judge of whether those questions are appropriate."

As I steadied myself for the next onslaught, Her Honour drifted back into her coma, muttering. "Magpie? The fellow is having a mental breakdown. I shall report Mr. Anker's conduct to his professional body."

"Pinstripe! I mean to say, Mr. Anker," I said, "you informed my client that there exist special bankers who will invest funds on behalf of special clients in high yield schemes?"

"Well," said Pinstripe, puffing himself up to all five foot eleven of his full height. "Anyone such as me who operates in the square mile of the City of London is aware of that fact."

"And, you told him that the schemes were so secretive that the special bankers cannot be contacted otherwise than through special persons such as you?"

"I, er, well." Pinstripe nervously fingered the four-in-hand knot of his tie.

"So, in truth, my special client was relying on you?"

"I, er, well." His arrogant face turned pink.

"And, as a commercial lawyer, you must have calculated that, had the scheme truly existed, the yield offered to investors would have amounted to the equivalent of the economy of the whole of California?"

"I, er, well."

"You are a solicitor, Mr..."

The judge came to from her coma. "I think that the jury may very well have grasped the point, Mr. Gatehouse. There is no need to labour the issue. Moreover, I am quite certain that the ladies and gentlemen are simply dying for a cup of tea."

The ladies and gentlemen true nodded as one thereby communicating to Her Honour that a cup of tea would be just the ticket. "Court will adjourn for fifteen minutes," said Her Honour.

The judge rose to her feet and, naturally, everyone else imitated her. I reckon she would have left the room there and then had the clerk of the court not spoken up.

"There is a note from the jury, Your Honour!"

The judge returned to her swivel chair and the clerk handed up a crumpled note. The addressor was one of the male jurors. He was middle aged, smartly dressed. Worryingly, he had given the impression throughout that he was following and understanding the proceedings.

The judge uncrumpled the note and considered its contents. "The Bar should note," said the judge referring to Walter and me (so we both stood up), "that the message from the jury is not relevant."

On the judge's say so, I simply nodded acquiescence and sat down. Walter remained on his feet.

"Your Honour," drawled my pupil master, "I am naturally obliged. However..." Walter paused and I supposed that, in common with most barristers, even he was supposed to treat members of the British judiciary with reverence.

"However, what, Mr. Tweed?" Her Honour looked not best pleased that her decision was possibly the subject of questioning.

"Your Honour," began Walter, all over again. "It is appropriate that we members of the Bar have an opportunity of knowing the contents of the note so that we may satisfy our respective clients that it does not have a potential impact on the proceedings."

The judge sighed. "Very well." She wafted the note before the clerk of the court's bifocals.

The clerk removed the note from Her Honour's hand, said, "Thank you, Your Honour," and the note was handed down to Walter.

"Thank you," said Walter to the clerk and he opened the note. Thereupon, "Oh," said Walter.

"Yes. Oh," said the judge. "Well, I suppose that Mr. Gatehouse had better see it as well?"

"Thank you," I said, as Walter handed over the note. "Oh," I said, on reading the note's contents as follows:

Dear Your Worshipful,

Does the tea come with biscuits? Chocolate digestives would be just what the doctor ordered. The darker the chocolate the better, of course, providing that the provenance is not from the rat infested factory up the road, because (though our blood sugar levels are rapidly decreasing and, in the case of the Rastafarian gentleman seated next to me, is precariously rock bottom) it would not be in the interests of justice were one of our number to succumb to a Leptospirosis induced coma gifted from that sanctimonious bunch of tossers at Bourneville.

Yours,

Juror number 10. Or is it 9?

I rose to address the Court. "As Your Honour intimated," I said, smugly. "The note is not relevant."

"Thank you, Mr. Gatehouse." With that, Her Honour, stared daggers at Walter.

As the judge departed, juror number ten turned to juror number nine and mouthed, "No chocolate biscuits, then. Will a packet of salted peanuts circumvent hyperglycaemia?"

During the short adjournment, I informed Jacob that the trial was motoring along far faster than the court had anticipated.

"You are very kind to keep me informed, Mr. G.. I am also very much obliged to the jury for paying close attention to the scurrilous case that has been brought against me." Jacob beckoned that I ought to come closer and, on doing just that, he whispered in my ear. "It is also scurrilous, Mr. Gatehouse, that my peers..."

"Who?"

"You know? The jury, Mr. G.. It is a scandal that they are deprived of biscuits, especially when they have given up their valuable time to ensure that justice is done. Perhaps, Mr. Gatehouse, I may be permitted to reward them? Perhaps an assortment box containing both plain and milk chocolate varieties?"

"That wouldn't be a good idea, Jacob."

"But, Mr. G. I will ensure that the manufacturers originate from the City of York and that they are not the people from up the road in whom the gentleman juror has little, if any, confidence."

"Nah."

"Very well, Mr. G.. How about a few stock market tips, by way of alternative?"

I pondered a wee while. "Nah, Jacob," I said, after I'd weighed up the pros and cons.

I was sorely tempted to provide Jacob with advice and assistance on the Contempt of Court Act, 1981 and other law relating to jury nobbling. However, I did no such thing because there were matters to attend to such as Mother Nature's calling, and so forth.

Presently, I sauntered into Court. As I did so, a nervous looking usher shouted, "All rise!"

The judge breezed back in and she performed the customary bow. We did the customary bow straight back at her and she ordered that eleven members of the jury be shown in and that the one in the colourful hat be assisted in.

Walter leaned in. "I sincerely hope," he whispered, "that the learned judge has the good sense to remove the crumbs and chocolate stains from around her mouth."

After the twelve persons true had taken their places, Her Honour addressed Walter and Walter, naturally, got to his feet.

"I have no wish to hurry things, Mr. Tweed, but could you give an indication to the Court as to how long the Crown's case is likely to last?"

Walter removed a fob watch from his breast pocket. "I can inform Your Honour that the Crown's case will take a further..." He paused and studied the watch face. Next, he took a gander at the clock face sitting above the heads of the persons true. On presumably being satisfied that both faces corroborated each other, "I estimate a further ten seconds," he announced.

"What?"

"Yes," said Walter. "That is simply the time that I require to inform the Court that I do not wish to re-examine the witness, Mr Anker, and that I have completed the Crown's case."

"In that case," I said, popping up, cockily, "I call the defendant, Mr. Henderson."

I heard a phishing kind of a noise coming from the region of the dock. I naturally turned around. Jacob, still flanked by a pair of prison officers, was pointing inwards, towards his very own chest. "Who? Me?"

"Yes. **You.**"

The two officers stood and they instructed Jacob to follow their example. One opened the door of the dock and the other one said, "Thank you," and he (not the other one) said, "Not at all, Jim. No problem, mate, and, as an aside, I swear that, though she moaned and groaned, squealed, scratched, and begged for more, more, more, it was just sex, mate, and it's you who she loves (as would a sister love a brother)," and he (the other one) departed the dock (got it?). Then, he who had had cause to express his gratitude (and be comforted as aforesaid), tearfully handcuffed Jacob and he told Jacob to follow his lead and, on Jacob agreeing to comply (saying, by way of aside, "They are all harlots, mate. Do not distress yourself and, by the way, if this goes badly, meaning that Mr. G. is having an off day, help yourself to the packet of chocolate digestive biscuits which you will find secreted next to my copy of *The Financial Times*"), the pair of them walked to the front of the court. On arrival, the handcuffs were unclicked and Jacob was invited to enter the witness box. Jacob duly accepted the invitation. The prison officer (Jim, to Jacob), remained standing guard, lest Jacob leap the barricade and make a break for freedom. The precautions were despite the fact that, during each and every adjournment (short and long), Jacob had been on bail, such was the trust placed in him that there was no real danger of him fleeing and thereby depriving Her Majesty of her bit of a lark.

"Ladies and gentlemen," said Her Honour. "You will treat Mr Henderson as you would any other witness." Next, she addressed the prison officer (you know? Jim). "If you suspect him of attempting to run for it, let me know and we will instruct Mr. Tweed to apply to have him cuffed. What is more," she added, curtly, "for heaven's sake shape up, man! There are plenty more fish in the sea!"

Jacob duly gave his solemn assurances to The Almighty that he would tell the truth and he thereby implied that Pinstripe should be committed to eternal damnation for having said that he would do the same and for having done the exact opposite. You see, one of them had to lying.

I took my witness through the usual formalities and arrived at the bit about the investment scheme. In essence, Jacob told the Court that Pinstripe had indeed done the opposite to what he had sworn to do. "It was Mr. Anker who advised me that I could earn a healthy commission was I to take the funds and invest the same with his City contacts."

"And, did you ever meet the City contacts?"

"No, Mr G., I mean no, Mr. Gatehouse. I was instructed that the scheme was so secretive that even I could not be privy to the identity of those who organised it."

"And, did you earn the commission?"

"I certainly did, Mr. G.."

At that, the judge snapped out of her daydream. Walter who was fiddling with his spectacles dropped the same and eleven of the twelve persons true leaned eagerly forwards.

There followed a brief moment's silence. After a few seconds that seemed more like a few decades, her Honour spoke. "I suppose," she said, haughtily, "that the so called commission came from Mrs. Anker's own money?" The judge looked jury-wards. "Some sort of advance fee was it, Mr. Henderson?"

"Oh, no, Your Ladyship. That would have been dishonest in the extreme." It was Jacob's turn to look jury-wards. "Any idiot could tell that Mr. Anker's investment scheme was fanciful. Accordingly, good people (who are riveted to my cause, save for the poor gentleman in the large woollen and colourful hat who does not look at all well), I ignored his instructions and I invested in an entirely different scheme."

Her Honour decided to come in on hearing that one. "Mr. Henderson!"

"Yes, Your Reverence?"

"The term is Your Honour."

"Cannot I hold you in reverence, then?"

Her head twizzled up, vertical, with so much force that it forever remains a mystery how her precariously balanced wig remained in situ.

"You are charged with having placed the funds in a scheme that was dishonest. You cannot now stand there and say that you did no such thing."

"But, why not, Your Honourable one?"

Her Honour tutted. "Because it doesn't work like that! You have to have put the money in a scheme that was dishonest because, because..."

"Yes, Your Reverend Ladyship?"

"You cannot come here not having done the thing that you are accused of doing. Otherwise, it will spoil things!"

"I am so very sorry, Your Honourable Ladyship, and I promise that it will not happen again."

Her Honour squinted, as if deep in thought. "What will not happen again?"

"You know?" Jacob looked towards the judge with child-like innocence. "I will not, not do what you have told me I must do and I will therefore avoid spoiling things for both you and the gentleman who prosecutes who, I have to say, looks remarkably well, unlike the gentleman of the jury who, though of the same creed, looks somewhat unwell from where I am standing."

I grasped both collars of my dark jacket, as barristers do, and I looked at the other court users in a knowing sort of a way. "Tell me, Mr. Henderson," I said, and I proceeded to lead the witness something rotten. "Did you invest in some inside out pots?"

"What?" the judge said it.

"Gatehouse?" that was Walter.

"You know?" I said, leading the witness some more. "Pots that hang from bits of string?"

"Ah!" Jacob gaped as the proverbial penny dropped. "I presume, Mr. Gatehouse, that you refer to the French company with which The Prince of Darkness has been doing business?"

"Yes, I do," I answered my witness.

"Hold on," said the judge. "Just who is supposed to be asking the questions? And," she added, after a moment or two of contemplation. "Who or what is The Prince of Darkness when he is at home?"

Walter coughed politely and majestically rose. "If I may assist, Your Honour, the gentleman to whom the witness refers is Mr. Ian Prospect. He is a member of the Bar. According to sources close to me, he has recently invested heavily in a French company..."

"French?" So said the judge and she jerked her torso, bolt upright. "Dark forces indeed, Mr. Tweed."

"Quite so, Your Honour," said Walter, nonchalantly. "As I was saying, the company is apparently known as *Crazy Dans Des Pots* and, according to today's *Financial Times,* the company is bankrupt." Walter returned to his seat and, on his way down, he grinned, just a little. "I am afraid, Gatehouse," he said, quietly, "that your client's goose is cooked."

"Aha!" said the judge. "Now we are getting somewhere!" She began scribbling feverishly in her judge's note pad. "Let me get this straight," she said, after a while. She said it whilst looking at the ceiling and it was therefore difficult to deduce whom it was she was addressing. "The defendant has retracted his denial that he invested in the fraudulent investment scheme and his retraction is false because he did not invest in that fraudulent scheme but another, equally fraudulent, scheme."

The twelve persons true looked this way and that and at one another. Juror number five quite forgot where he was, he put what appeared to be a chocolate biscuit to his mouth, and he took a goodly bite from the same.

I looked Jacob-ward, and then I looked at the munching juror, and I looked at Jacob, once again and, Jacob winked. "Assortment box," I swear he mouthed. "From the shop next door, Mr. G.."

"I released my collar from the barrister-type grip. I coughed, in a barrister-type way. "No further questions," I said, meekly, and I returned to my seat. Once settled in, I placed an elbow on the desk and rested my head on an outstretched palm.

It was Walter's turn and he wasted no time with formalities. "You are a crooked financial adviser and you have frittered away Mrs. Anker's assets by investing in an insolvent company! And, not just any old insolvent company but a **French** insolvent company!"

Jacob stepped back as if blown that way by the icy blast. "No, I have not," he said.

"Yes, you have!"

I heard the back of Jacob's heal hit the rear of the witness box. You see, he had tried to step back some more but he had run out of space. He, sort of, had no other place to run. "I do not intend to spoil any person's fun, not least the fun of someone as noble and as healthy-looking as you, sir, but I must insist that I did no such thing."

Walter grinned, just as I imagine a Bengal tiger might grin when going for the kill. "My fellow," he said, "you have already admitted investing in a bankrupt company."

Walter glanced at the twelve persons true. Juror number five barely managed to pop the remainder of his biscuit in the post.

"I said no such thing, sir."

Walter laughed aloud. "Who pray did say it, then?"

"She did," and, Jacob pointed directly at Her Honour.

The judge dropped her pen. "Mr. Tweed," she said, "is this man in the throes of a mental breakdown?"

"I can easily explain, Your Venerable One."

"Then you had better explain," said Her Honour. "And…!"

"Yes, Your Majesty?"

"I am a Your Honour!"

"Everyone, including you, Your Honourable One, is labouring under the misapprehension that, in lieu of her husband's crackpot scheme, I invested Mrs. Anker's fortune in the equally crackpot, pot, scheme of The Prince of Darkness."

"Well," drawled Walter, casually, "you did, did you not?"

"I did not, sir. I invested in my very own rubber horseshoe scheme and I have to say that the inspiration for that is my learned counsel, Mr. Gatehouse, who modestly and rather casually sits next to you!"

My head came up with force so sufficient that my elbow was nudged clean off the edge of the desk. The consequence was that my head plummeted and struck that part of the desk vacated by the elbow. On recovering a bit of composure, I noted that all eyes within the room were focused on me. Even the juror with the colourful hat had snapped out of his coma. You see, he had used the distraction to craftily swipe a chocolate biscuit from under the very nose of juror number five.

Her Honour beckoned that I must arise and be addressed.

"Mr, Gatehouse?" That is how the undressing started. "Can you explain?"

I coughed. There was no tickle in my throat, or anything. I coughed purely for the purpose of affording myself the luxury of a bit of thinking time. It's a barrister-type ploy, you see. "Your Honour." I said, and I coughed, again. The second cough was no ploy. It was a manifestation of summary disbarment. "Other than to suggest that my client is, indeed, in the throes of a mental breakdown, I have no explanation."

"Mr G.! Mr.G.!" I noticed that Jacob was waving wildly, southerly, in my direction. "Your inspirational genius, Mr. G., hit me like a bolt of lightning!"

"Ah!" Relief came swishing in and, simultaneously, a light bulb over my head switched itself on and all thoughts of the Bar's disciplinary tribunal wafted away. "Mr. Henderson," I said. "Is it true that you have invented rubber horseshoes for the purpose of preventing horses from receiving electric shocks?"

A deafly silence fell upon all of Court. The impact was on a par with the racket made by heavy metal crashing to the ground in the Dudsall foundry. My client addressed the judge. "I fear, Your Noblest One, that learned counsel is in the throes of a mental breakdown. May I suggest the very briefest of adjournments for tea? You and the twelve persons who are my peers and who are about to acquit me will be delighted to learn that I happen to have on my person a quantity of tantalising chocolate biscuits of assorted varieties."

"I respectfully agree," said the judge. "But, just a moment," she added, "No! No! No! It is I who am the judge, I think, and I do not agree!"

"Is Your Eminence perhaps in the throes of a mental breakdown herself? I say that, as the barristers say, with the utmost of respect, except, contrast the said barristers (and the occasional solicitor), Your Holiness, I happen to say it with sincerity."

I decided to resume my questioning. "Well," I said. "If, as you say, the rubber horseshoes are not intended to protect horses from electric shocks, what are they for? And tell me," I added, which I immediately regretted, "where does inspiration from me fit into the scheme of things?"

Jacob opened his mouth to answer, but Her Honour got there before him. "Protect horses from electric shocks? Are you seeking to conduct a defence based on insanity?"

"Ah!" I said, with misplaced authority on the subject of *equus* and all things appertaining thereto. "You see, it happens in wet weather if telegraph poles are not properly earthed. It shocks them something rotten, it does. You see, metal conducts electricity..."

Her Honour started to address the ceiling, all over again. "For pity's sake, I know that metal conducts elect…"

Jacob interrupted her. "Perhaps, Oh Mighty One, I may be permitted to explain that it is Mr. Gatehouse's intimate knowledge of condoms that was the source of my inspiration." There was another deadening hush and thoughts of the Bar's disciplinary tribunal came whooshing back in as if on a spring tide. "The idea came to me after Mr. Gatehouse returned a large assortment of Screaming Thrusters and Spiked Sensations that were no longer required for the purpose of protecting his aching appendage. So, you see, I put them to good use on the Major's stallion."

Walter rocketed to his feet. "That is disgraceful, sir! I suggest that you beg Her Reverence for forgiveness!"

"No, no," said Jacob, casually. "You have it all wrong. Plainly, condoms are not manufactured in those sorts of length. I mean to say, sir, originating as you do from…?"

"Birmingham…"

"Well, I think you know what I mean when I say that, in common with the Major's stallion, it is more likely than not that you are hugely endowed."

Walter addressed me. He did so in hushed tones through the side of his mouth. "Your client is rather perceptive, Gatehouse."

Jacob ploughed on with his defence. "The stress on horses' hooves caused by clip-clopping around in unforgiving shoes of steel is very considerable, sir. Jacob began riding up and down on his heels, as would a police officer. "Upon placing over the stallion's hooves the out of date condoms that Mr G. returned to me with, I might add, very unkind comments and allegations that I had ruined his life, and so forth, I noted that the beast had a spring in his step. Therefore, after we had taken the gardener to hospital…"

The three of us, Her Honour, Walter and I interrupted on hearing that one. "Gardener? Hospital?"

Jacob shrugged. "In the absence of heavy metal nailed to his feet, the stallion took off as would greased lightning. And in the absence of the clattering of steel indeed, in the absence of any form of audible warning, the gardener (who was bending over the sweet peas at the time) found himself trampled beneath the pounding hooves." Jacob shook his head, despairingly. "It is a design fault," he said, "on which the manufacturers and I are currently working."

"That's dreadful," I said.

"It could have been worse," said Jacob, cheerfully. "The gardener is fortunate that twenty-four layers of out of date condoms cushioned the ferocious blows."

Her Honour dived in before either Walter or I could get there. "Twenty-four layers?"

Jacob peered at the judge in a manner to suggest that she was somehow slow on the uptake. "It is simple arithmetic, Your Honourable." For the purpose of adding a visual presentation, Jacob hoisted up his eight fingers and two thumbs. "Twenty-four divided by four hooves equals six condoms per hoof, you see?"

Her Honour gaped. "Ah! Now, I see it. Pray, do continue."

Jacob answered her prayer, thus. "Having established that our equine friends much prefer rubber horseshoes I deduced that, though original, the concept of rolling condoms over their hooves was unlikely to catch-on particularly in local pony club circles. Again, Mr. G.'s novel use of birth control paraphernalia was the source of my inspiration."

I spluttered and gasped and the vision of the Bar's disciplinary tribunal floated in, again."Aye? What?"

"A coil, Mr. G.. It is the female answer to the condom…"

"Yes, yes! I know that, but what is the relevance?"

"I have simply designed strips of rubber that are produced in coil form. In lieu of hammering away endlessly at bits of metal, the farrier need only cut a segment from the coil and bingo!"

"Bingo?"

"Yes, Mr. G.. Bingo! The segment of coil simply curls around the shape of the hoof."

Walter felt compelled to come in. "I respectfully remind the Court that I am cross-examining. With Your Honour's permission?" With a nod of her head, the green light was given for Walter to return to the attack. "My good fellow, do you not think it criminal to have frittered away a woman's fortune on this hare-brained scheme?"

"It is no hare-brained scheme, sir. Look here at this." Jacob reached into an inside pocket and he produced a document. "This," he said, "is a contract between a well know rubber company of the one part and Mrs. Janie Anker, Jetty as was, of the other part. It entitles the said Mrs. Anker to one pound sterling for every horseshoe that is sold."

Walter shook his head and he asked his next question whilst looking at the twelve persons true. It's an old ploy that is guaranteed to ensure maximum dramatic impact. "How many horseshoes do you suppose that the manufacturer will sell? A dozen? Perhaps one hundred in a good year, with no pun intended?"

Jacob took over Her Honour's role of staring up at the ceiling. "Mmmm," he went. "I would say, sir, that based on a world population of horses in the region of fifty million and, based on a requirement to shoe a horse on a regular basis, I estimate, on a very, very conservative basis, that we will service a minimum of three million horses."

The judge nearly fell off her swivel chair. "But, that represents a profit of three million pounds per annum!"

"With sincere due respect, Your Venerable Ladyship is incorrect."

"No, I am not!"

For the second time of asking, Jacob hoisted his hands. "Horses have four feet, you see." He began the finger count. "Three million multiplied by four equals twelve million pounds multiplied by two (being the minimum times that a horse will be shod in one year) comes to twenty-four million pounds less, say, ten pounds."

"Less ten pounds?"

"Yes, Your Eminence. I have taken into account the three legged race horse upon which Mr G. and The Prince of Darkness insist on betting their hard earned brief fees."

Her Honour addressed Walter. "Mr. Tweed?"

"Your Honour?"

"This man is a financial genius."

Walter stammered a little which was a most unusual reaction coming as it did from a man who was generally chilled out. "I, er, beg Your Honour's indulgence?"

"Very well."

"My good fellow?"

"Yes, sir?"

"When are the horseshoes expected to go into production?"

"In approximately two years' time, sir."

"Aha! Not such a short term, high yield scheme?"

"Which is why, sir, in order to tide the good lady over, I was inspired, once again, by Mr. G.'s brilliant misuse of birth control items."

I pretended not to hear though inwardly I was listening to the words of the chairman of the disciplinary tribunal.

"While waiting for the paramedics to take the Major's gardener to hospital I observed the Major's wife bending over for the purpose of painting her rustic show jumping polls. I could not help but be drawn to her because of the very tight jodhpurs that she wore."

"Get to the point, my good fellow."

"Condoms, as Mr G. will verify come in all colours."

"Eh?"

"Condoms stretch and can therefore fit incredibly wide girths, a fact, sir, that you will verify, having originated not from around these parts."

Walter looked down. "Gatehouse. This fellow's knowledge of cross cultural anthropology is outstanding."

"Anyway," said Jacob. "Inspired by Mr. G.'s ability to adapt contraceptive devices for uses other than for their intended purpose, I simply devised a sheath-type item that slips over rustic show jumping poles. The Major's wife now has no need to bend over in her tight jodhpurs."

"The return on these items is what? A few pounds sterling?"

"Oh, no, sir. Mrs. Anker, the former Miss Jetty, will be receiving, on a conservative estimate, a few hundred thousand pounds per annum. I regret, of course, the short delay she will experience in receiving funds from the multinational rubber company. However, I am as certain that the design fault will be ironed out as I am equally certain that the gardener will make a full recovery."

"That will be all, thank you." Walter collapsed in his seat. On landing, he turned to face. "The judge is correct, my friend. This man is a financial genius."

The judge instructed Jacob to return to the dock. "I do not think that we shall be requiring the handcuffs," she told Jim. "Mr. Tweed?"

Up went Walter. "Yes, Your Honour?"

"I shall be instructing the jury to formally acquit this man."

"That is an eminently sensible suggestion, Your Honour."

"Also, I wish you to advise Mr. Anker that I shall not be reporting him for professional misconduct. Indeed, the gentleman is to be congratulated on his extraordinary skill in appointing a financial adviser of genius. His wife should be proud and grateful."

I jumped to my feet. "No! No! This cannot be so!"

"Mr. Gatehouse?"

"Yes, Your Honour?"

"Whether you like it or not, I intend to acquit your client of all charges. Furthermore, you have Mr Anker to thank for that!"

TWENTY-THREE

I exited Court and I observed that Janie was seated on the same stone bench. Her legs were crossed and her hands were to'ing and fro'ing because hers was the hand that rocked the cradle, or rather the pram, sort of thing. However, adjacent to the pram was the abominable Pinstripe. He was addressing Janie loudly. He appeared to be doing so, solely for effect.

"The judge has offered me her congratulations," he said. "She has informed all of Court that you are lucky to be my wife."

"William," said Janie, without bothering to honour him with her eyes. "I care not for riches. Do with the money whatever you wish. You may spend it on your whores for all that I care."

I dillydallied for a while and, upon Pinstripe storming off, I made my move.

"Janie," I said, and I sat next to Janie. My intention was to resume our conference of earlier. I removed Igor Patterson's horsehair wig.

"Congratulations on your success," said Janie, and with further heart pounding joy, not to mention weird pleasure, I noted that, in addition to her eyes bulging with tears, Janie's chest and swan-like neck were blazing red with passion.

"Your husband is vindicated too," I said, and a fishbone stuck in the throat could not have caused more discomfort than the utterance of that word, *husband*.

"William has no idea that his contempt for me is with good cause because it is I who have deceived him." Tears cascaded from Janie's huge and beautiful eyes. "It was necessary that I lay with him just the once, and, Izaak…?"

"Yes, Janie?"

"Only by imagining that it was you could I go through with my deception!" With that, Janie laughed nervously.

"There, there, my love," and I kissed her gently atop the head.

"Izaak?" She softly spoke my name again and it made me feel ecstatic. "I am thankful that William satisfies his urges elsewhere."

There was a brief moment's silence and I put the interlude to good use by hugging and comforting my love. "Izaak?" she said, again. "That day…"

"Yes, Janie?"

"You were gentle, Izaak. William was not. Izaak?"

"Yes, Janie?"

"As soon as you had done with me I knew that I was with child."

I know, I thought, *I reckon it was that young Toby Horobin-Smith who was spying on us.* "I know," I said. "It was plainly intended that we two should become three."

Janie pulled away and by so doing she broke my grip. "Oh, Izaak, why did you leave without saying a word?" At that juncture, stirring came from within the pram and, like mother, Little Gatehouse began to blubber. I assumed that Janie would attend to our child but she did no such thing. In lieu thereof, Janie rose and she gently brushed creases from the front of her dark linen trousers. "I am riddled with guilt. I permitted that man to defile me and, in the process, he unwittingly defiled our unborn child." Janie bent forwards and she reached into the pram. After a bit of rummaging, she hoisted up a precious packet. "Here," said Janie, "take your child, Izaak," and, she passed the parcel. All done up in a white blanket, it was.

My eyes filled with tears as I spied, for the very first time, Little Gatehouse. I rocked him back and forth and the crying subsided into a whimpering. I looked at Janie, my face beaming with pride. "I seem to have a natural gift," I smiled.

Suddenly, and unexpectedly, Janie exploded. "I am an unfit mother!"

A nervous looking usher chose that somewhat inopportune moment to saunter past. He looked a heck of a lot more than merely nervous after he had gone by, I can tell you.

"Calm yourself, Janie," I said, softly.

"Ha!" It was not a happy laugh that emanated from Janie's lips. "This is a total mess! Take care of our child, Izaak!"

Can you believe it? Janie departed. Without as much as a by your leave, the mother of my child turned on her heels and headed off in the direction of the world beyond the court building.

For a few moments, I sat dumbstruck. I looked down at Little Gatehouse. *My God*, I thought, as the full ramifications struck home, *how will I ever explain to you that your mother has deserted us?*

My concentration was broken by a familiar sounding voice.

"I am disturbed to note, Mr. G., that on this most joyous of occasions you appear to be somewhat upset."

"Jacob," I said. "She's left me, mate. Janie has left me and she has left me holding the baby."

Quick-witted action was called for. Though devastated at the loss of my beloved Janie, I simply had to put the interests of our child ahead of mine own. In terms of fatherhood, I was nought but an amateur. However, whenever barristers require assistance on a subject calling for specialist knowledge, they rely on an appropriately qualified witness.

I knew just the witness on whom I could rely. "Jacob," I said, "I don't wish to be rude but I have to go somewhere."

With Little Gatehouse in my loving arms, I left Jacob standing open-mouthed within the proximity of the perambulator.

"Damian," I said, careening through the door of Globe Chambers. "Something remarkable has happened."

The learned clerk was seated atop the plywood reception desk. "It is indeed remarkable, Mista Gatehouse, that them ruddy robes belonging to Mista Patterson 'ave turned up in the very same week that he has purchased a replacement set."

"Never mind the ruddy robes," I said, and I passed Little Gatehouse to the learned clerk of Chambers. "Here", I said, "cop hold of the bab for a moment while I remove the precious robes!"

"Now, there ain't no call for unpleasantness, Mista Gatehouse, especially on a day when oi should be congratulating yow."

I placed upon the desk the gown that had formerly belonged to Igor Patterson. "Yes," I said, beaming at Little Gatehouse. "I suppose that congratulations are in order."

"Yow do know that we am referring to the case that yow 'ave just won?"

"Damian," I said, and I held out my arms and gestured that my son should, indeed must, be returned. "Permit me to introduce you to Izaak Gatehouse, junior."

There came no indication of shock, surprise. Indeed, no form of emotion emanated from Damian's direction. "Yow am a dark horse, yow am," he said. He vacated the desktop and he proffered Little Gatehouse. However, on doing so, "Phew, Mista Gatehouse!" he said. "This babby am in urgent need of a change of diapers!"

"A change of what?"

"Yow know? Nappies, Mista Gatehouse. He needs to be changed."

"But, I won't do that!"

"It is remarkable, Mista Gatehouse!"

Yes, it was the second time in two days that I managed to quote the lyrics of *Meatloaf* before *Meatloaf* had even been invented! It was, indeed, rather remarkable.

"Never before, Mista Gatehouse, 'ave babbies of my own consumed solid food at this tender age. It is, as oi say, rather remarkable."

"Damian," I said, "I must bond with my son and take time out to make plans for our future."

"Blimey, Mista Gatehouse!" Damian tucked in his shirttails. Per normal, they had been flapping around the waist of his bulging trousers. "Yow ain't in court for a fortnight so we can let yow go away for a short time."

"That is fantastic, Damian. I shall take Little Gatehouse to Venice, or somewhere!"

"Am it wise going there, Mista Gatehouse, bearing in mind the very nasty injury that yow sustained to your parts last time yow was in them parts? Furthermore, sir, I would be very cautious if I was yow of taking a babby on a plane. Them things can 'ave accidents yow know?"

"It is the safest form of travel," I said, adding, after a moment's thought, "unless you go by Laker Airways, that is."

"No, no, sir. Yow misunderstand. Oi mean that the babby might 'ave an accident in his nappies, lyke."

"Listen up, Damian. I know what I am doing. Now, I simply require your expert opinion on how to feed him, and..."

I stopped dead, deep in thought.

"Yes, Mista Gatehouse, sir?"

"I also require your expert opinion on the diaper, nappy things and then there will be no aeroplane accidents, will there?"

"Yow am in luck, Mista Gatehouse." The learned clerk waddled towards the metal cabinet. "Only today, oi took a journey to the Birmingham Bullring Shopping Centre where the babby shop am selling three packets of diaper come nappy things for the price of one."

Damian turned the handle of the cabinet door and, with a nerve-shattering screech; the door flew open and out tumbled a dozen or more parcels.

"Crikey, Damian! Do I need that many?"

My self-appointed expert stood with hands on hips. From the vertical movements of his miscellaneous chins, I deduced that the learned clerk was performing mental arithmetic.

"Yow will need at least that number, Mista Gatehouse." The chins stopped going up and down. "Oi 'ave that old busted suitcase of yours in the next room, Mista Gatehouse. Oil fetch it now and yow can use it to carry all them diapers!"

"Damian," I said. "One day, I shall be reunited with the mother of this child. In the meantime, I intend to bring him up by my good example and there is nothing that can possibly go wrong."

"The people surrounding you, sir, are security officers and they will shoot to kill unless you hand the child to me and then lie on your stomach with hands and legs apart."

"I will do anything," I said, "but, I won't do that!"

The gentleman behind the check-in desk ducked beneath his check-in desk. "Okay, chaps! Let him have it!"

"Oh, very well," I said, above the melody of safety catches becoming positively unsafe. I reached down and undid the string that was tied around my red suitcase. The lid immediately popped open and dozens of diaper things cascaded onto the concourse.

The wretched check-in gentleman popped up from beneath his check-in desk. "But, there's no baby in there, sir?"

I made as if to grasp the fellow by his lapels and I did so with every intention of dragging the individual over the desk. However, I was distracted from the task in hand by a load more clicking.

"For heaven's sake read my lips," I said. "I keep telling you that you were supposed to check-in this red suitcase. It contains diapers for my child. You were not supposed to check-in the holdall that has just gone up the ramp and through those rubber flaps because that is the bag in which I was carrying my child."

I paced the small security office as would a caged tiger. I had been dragged there kicking and screaming while simultaneously begging that I might be permitted to pop off and lay my body down at the end of the runway and thereby thwart the taking-off of all flights, domestic and international.

Two plain clothed officers from special branch, or something, were seated behind a desk. For the past hour, they had been playing good cop, bad cop.

"Try not to blame yourself, mate." He was the good cop. "You were not to know that baggage handlers, especially Heathrow baggage handlers, will lose everything including their heads if they are loose."

"Yes, but the baggage handlers are not responsible for the fact that you have kidnapped a child and that you attempted to smuggle him out of the country in a plastic holdall bag bearing the logo *Dudsall Football Club*." That was the bad cop, that was.

"To be fair." It was him, the good'n, again. "No one could have imagined that the plane bound for Buenos Aires would park directly in front of the flight to Venice."

The bad cop sighed. "I have to admit that the chances of Argentina having invaded the Falkland Islands shortly after take-off and the British Government having consequently declared war on Argentina are so remote that I almost feel sorry for this idiot. Indeed, I am minded to put in a written request that, henceforth, I be permitted to assume the role of good cop."

The bad cop leaned back in his chair and, casually, he placed both legs atop the desk. He proceeded to cross the legs and, at the same time, he deposited both hands at the back of his head.

A buzzer sounded and the bad cop turned good cop almost jumped out of his skin. He snappily removed the two legs and he removed the two hands from the back of his solitary head. "That is the telephone," he said. "I shall put it on loudspeaker."

The good cop, who was formerly the bad cop, leaned forward towards a long wooden box-type object. He flicked a switch and there came all manner of electrical-type noises. However, after the crackles and pops, and such like, had died down, I heard a familiar voice.

"Yow am through to Globe Chambers, can we assist yow?"

Both officers looked the way of each other and both shrugged.

The good cop who, throughout, had been the good cop was the first to recover.

"Good Afternoon," he said, "I am talking to you from Heathrow Airport. Over."

"Oh my good God, it am all over! Oi knew there would be an accident! Dow tell we there has been an accident!"

The bad cop, turned good cop, pushed a button and the phone went mute. "This idiot, Gatehouse, is simply playing the idiot. He is obviously a saboteur. Fetch out the rubber hose."

"Just a minute," I said. "What's happened to the good cop, then?"

"Terminated."

"My learned clerk," I said, "is simply fearful that the baby has wet his nappies, or worse, sort of thing. The clerk, you see is a native of Birmingham and, as such, he is rather emotive and he is prone to panic."

"Ah,' said the good cop, relieved. "That explains it." He turned to his colleague. "He's just a Brummie."

Meanwhile, the bad cop appeared to have released the mute button and he was busily searching a cabinet. It appeared to contain all manner of the vilest of gizmos.

"Gatehouse!" It was a brand new voice on the phone. "Are you there, old chap?"

"Yes, it's me, Ian. Over!"

"Gatehouse! What on earth are you playing at? Over!"

"Ian! Janie has rejected us. She told me that she was a bad mother, that everything was a mess, and that I must take Little Gatehouse. She has said that everything between us is over. Over!"

"You idiot, Gatehouse! Janie was talking hypothetically because young Izaak had had an accident and she had run out of diapers. Janie simply intended that you mind the child for a few moments to enable her to make a dash to the shop. On her return, you were gone, the baby was gone, and Jacob was removing the wheels from the perambulator muttering something along the lines that he had discovered the secret of perpetual motion and that the days of pollution brought about by the burning of fossil fuels is over. Over!"

"Ian! Janie must know that I am a responsible person? There was no need for her to panic. Over!"

"Gatehouse! It is entirely rational for Janie to have panicked. You disappeared once before having firstly and irresponsibly ensured that she was well and truly pregnant. Over!"

"Ian." It was the sweet sound of Janie's voice. "Please do not be so crude."

"Janie! You have returned. Does this mean, my love, that things between us are not over? Over!"

"Izaak! I simply went to the shop. Where is Izaak, junior? Over!"

"Are you sitting down, Janie? Over!"

"Yes, Izaak! I am seated. Over!"

"Janie! As you are seated there and as I am standing here about to be led away in irons, Little Gatehouse, together with the whole of the population of the Falklands, is a prisoner of war. Over!"

"Izaak! If this is true, our relationship is finally over. Over!"

"Janie! I know that our politicians are morons but even they won't risk lives over some place that no bugger has ever heard of. Everything will be resolved over tea and biscuits and the war will soon be over. Over!"

"Oh, Izaak!"

"Oh, Janie! Please don't tell me it's over. Over!"

"Oh, Izaak! Over and out!"